WITH
HONOR
—IN—
HAND

Nicky,
Keep doing your thing,
brother!

Almy!

WITH HONOR IN HAND

TERRON SIMS II

TATE PUBLISHING
AND ENTERPRISES, LLC

Published by Tate Publishing & Enterprises, LLC
127 E. Trade Center Terrace | Mustang, Oklahoma 73064 USA
1.888.361.9473 | www.tatepublishing.com

Tate Publishing is committed to excellence in the publishing industry. The company reflects the philosophy established by the founders, based on Psalm 68:11,
"The Lord gave the word and great was the company of those who published it."

Published in the United States of America

ISBN: 978-1-62510-829-6
1. Fiction / Thrillers / Military
2. Fiction / War & Military
13.06.12

Dedicated to the memory of Thomas "TK" Kennedy, Kevin "KJ" Smith, Leif Knott, Todd Bryant, and all those of the Long Grey Line who sacrificed their lives defending our nation's freedoms.

26 MAY 1999

0400 Hours: Somewhere in Northern Sudan

"How many friendlies?"

"Fifteen."

"Enemy?"

"Thirty-six."

"Good. This shouldn't take us any longer than half an hour."

"Good deal. I'll need a cold beer after this. I'm already starting to sweat."

"I'm with you on that, brother."

"Watch for the friendlies. We're not here to kill human shields."

"Roger."

"All right. Let's move."

The two camouflaged men creep stealthily across the harsh, rocky terrain. Their mission is to destroy a secret gold-mining outpost that is home to a Sudanese paramilitary group that also serves as a major financial source for Al Qaeda.

It takes seven minutes for Mac to scale the cliff, while Killer slides down and to the left of a hill in three minutes. Taking the rear of the outpost, like a shadowy ninja, Killer sneaks behind a guard, and takes him out with little effort. Killer then gives Mac the all clear sign. Seeing Killer's sign, Mac moves into the mining outpost and sets up the C-4 explosives on its three main buildings.

Killer moves one hundred fifty meters to the right of the motor pool, which is to the far-west side of the outpost, and picks off five men with his automatic rifle. The men hit the ground dead without the slightest chance of being able to react. Mac continues his route with barely having to pause. He springs over to a supply shed for cover then chucks two grenades into the mine.

Unexpected to the paramilitary fighters, the gold mine erupts with a thunderous explosion. Scattered and running around like chickens, twenty men rush toward the gold mine to investigate the brazenly overt attack on their outpost. Before they can even get to the mine, the fighters discover several of their compatriots lying dead on the ground. Though the fighters are shocked and disturbed by the unwanted surprise of their compatriots' deaths, their main concern is the status of the gold mine: their main revenue source. The chaotic situation causes the fighters to begin yelling and arguing among themselves. There is a lot of finger-pointing occurring among the group.

Seeing the paramilitary fighters argue among themselves causes a small smile to grow across Killer's face. Still in his earlier position, Killer, still smiling, picks off nine of the paramilitary fighters. Mac finishes off the rest then rolls left and shoots the front passenger-side tire of an old Chevy Tahoe that is parked in the motor pool. Spotting the Tahoe fall over onto its side signals Killer to setup the clamor mine and fire it into the motor pool. After firing the clamor, Mac ignites the C-4. The size and force of the explosion is so intense that it obliterates the outpost.

From the corner of his eye, Mac spies four scraggily men scurry toward the cliffs; he shouts at them, "Hey! Stop!" while firing over their heads.

Mac does not shoot the scraggily looking men because they do not have the same appearance or demeanor as that of the paramilitary fighters. As Mac believes, it is always better to ask questions first then shoot later.

The four men immediately freeze in their tracks. They are frightened beyond belief. The attack on the mining outpost has their minds racing at a million miles per hour. When the world seemed to be exploding around them and the ominous booming sound crashed the sky, only one thought came to these men: *Run!* And run they did. Now they find themselves in yet another unwelcomed predicament—a large man with an assault rifle who obviously knows how to use it.

Mac strides to where the scraggly looking men stand frozen in place while at the same time motions them to slowly move toward him and lay flat on their faces. The men obediently concur and lay with their faces in the dirt in front of Mac. After quickly, yet thoroughly, searching the men, Mac comes to an unexpected though not surprising discovery. The four men are merely slaves attempting to monopolize on he and Killer's attack on the outpost and using it as a diversion for their escape.

"All right. You men can get up now," Mac says to the four men in his best Arabic.

As the scraggly looking men pick themselves up from off of the ground, Mac asks them, "How long have you men been here?"

"Nearly five years, sir," one of the enslaved men quickly and politely answers.

Mac continues, saying to the man, "Well, since you spoke up first, I'm placing you in charge of this gaggle. I want you and your friends to round up whoever is left. I then want you to find the keys to that truck over there." Mac points in the direction of the motorcade, where there is a sole truck surrounded by carnage. "Next, get all of the supplies that you may need and whatever gold you want and leave this place. Do not, I repeat, do not tell anyone what has happened here. You tell whoever asks that the Sudanese army destroyed this outpost and that you narrowly escaped with your lives. Do you understand?"

"Yes, sir," responds the appointed leader.

"Good, now repeat my orders," Mac commands.

The selected leader repeats Mac's orders verbatim. Mac is somewhat impressed.

Once the appointed leader finishes repeating the order, Mac commands, "All right then. Go out and make it happen."

The four newly freed men race back to the outpost to follow through with Mac's orders, which they follow to the letter. Once the men are out of view, Killer walks over to Mac's position.

"Mac," Killer states, "I've got everything we need plus a couple of personal souvenirs."

Killer opens a small sack full of gold nuggets and shows them to Mac.

"Good," Mac coolly responds. "Let's get out of here before someone comes checking this place out."

Mac and Killer silently exit the scene as unnoticed as they had arrived, while leaving behind no trace that they were ever in the area.

0700 Hours: Eleven Miles from the Serbian-Croatian Border

"Sir, I have just received the mission statement from higher," Colonel Drasneb's executive officer informs.

"Hand it here." Colonel Drasneb glances over the document. Increasingly, his smile grows as he continues reading the mission statement. "Good, good. I have been waiting for such an order since this war started!" Colonel Drasneb shouts as he leaps from his chair and slams the mission statement on the table. "Tell the battalion commanders that I will brief them here in one hour."

"Yes, sir," the executive officer responds, who then quickly exits Colonel Drasneb's tent to execute his commander's orders.

While waiting for his battalion commanders and his executive officer to report, Colonel Drasneb writes his OPORD (Operations Order). Writing out the battle plan, Colonel Drasneb delights in the opportunity that has just presented itself. He has waited for so many years for the green light to spearhead the second assault into Croatia and restart the unification of a divided Yugoslavia. Serbia and Croatia have been at war for just over three years. The Serbs have been unsuccessful in penetrating the Croatian front lines due, most in part, to the aide of NATO and, most notably, the United States.

Colonel Drasneb is the commander of the Serbian Thirty-fifth Mechanized Infantry Brigade. His orders state that his brigade, along with a combat engineer platoon attachment, is to breach the Croatian border, a width of six hundred to eight hundred meters.

While pondering upon the mission, Colonel Drasneb rises from his chair and paces the small area within his tent. He smiles like the Cheshire Cat because now he has been given the opportunity to prove to his country that he is a great soldier and leader and prove to the world that the Serbian army is a force to be seriously dealt with.

Colonel Drasneb has proudly served his country for nearly thirty ysears since the days of Tito when Yugoslavia was the envy of all of communist Europe. The years have been kind to Colonel Drasneb. Though he is in his late fifties, other than a few wrinkles and his gray-haired crew cut, Colonel Drasneb looks rather good for his age. He stands five and a half feet tall, yet his hands appear to belong to a man much larger than his size. Because of his short stature, Colonel Drasneb built up a Napoleon complex over the years—his way of ensuring that people know that he is not to be missed with.

Enthralled in joyful thought, Colonel Drasneb's three battalion commanders enter his tent. The highest alphabetically ranking battalion commander walks two paces in front of Colonel Drasneb, comes to the position of attention, salutes, and reports. "Sir, lieutenant colonels Androff, Krien, and Spachev report as ordered."

"Pull up a chair," Colonel Drasneb responds. "I have something here that will make you men very happy. We have finally received the mission that we have waited for since we deployed last year. Before I begin though, let me say that if executed properly, our success will come from our momentum, the driving force that our great country needs to finally regain our rightful lands." Saying thus, Colonel Drasneb fully briefs his battalion commanders on their upcoming mission. Little does Colonel Drasneb realize the extent to which his mission is going to affect and refocus his outlook on life and the world around him.

1000 Hours: United States Military Academy (USMA) at West Point, New York

There is one thing that all cadets live for, and that is sleep. After a long night of heavy drinking with friends the previous night, Cadet Milton Johnson only wishes for one thing, and that is endless, undisturbed sleep. He does not want to be bothered. All he wants is to sleep until dinner or at least until he can no longer feel his head. Much to his dismay, he hears two soft knocks from the other side of his bedroom door.

Knowing that two knocks means that either an officer or a noncommissioned officer (NCO) is at the door, Cadet Johnson quickly gets out of bed and replies, "Enter sir or ma'am."

The door opens, and his company tactical officer (TAC), Capt. Christopher Weiss, enters the room.

"Major, can you come down to my office for a bit?" he asks. "I need to discuss something with you"

"Sir," Major responds, "is it all right if I wear gym A?"

"Sure. No problem."

"Roger, sir. I'll be down in a minute."

Cadet Johnson, already wearing the bottom half of his cadet athletic uniform and a white T-shirt, removes the T-shirt and replaces it with a gym-A shirt that is hanging on the back of his chair. He then puts on his white athletic socks and slips into his running shoes.

Hearing the commotion of Major getting dressed, his roommate, Calvin, rolls over and asks, "What's going on, man?"

"I'm not sure, dawg," Cadet Johnson responds. "I'll let you know what's up when I get back. Thank God I don't get into any trouble, or I'd really be sweating right now. Go back to sleep, man."

Saying that, Calvin rolls over, throws the covers back over his head, and continues sleeping as though the conversation with his roommate had just been a dream.

Cadet Johnson lives on the fourth floor of the thirty-seventh division of Grant Barracks. Originally known as Old South Barracks, Grant Barracks was constructed in 1931. It has battlements and rough-cut stone to blend the structure with those adjoining it. Grant Barracks' east wing contains Grant Hall—the cadet reception hall and a cadet restaurant.

Cadet Johnson runs down the four flights of stairs and out onto the stoops. He then leaps onto the asphalt, that is Grant Area, runs across it, jumps back onto the other side of the stoops, then strides into the twenty-sixth division. Walking inside, Cadet Johnson faces the first door to his right, which is his TAC's office.

After knocking on the door three times, Captain Weiss responds with, "Enter."

Cadet Johnson enters the room and proceeds to report. "Sir, Cad—"

Captain Weiss stops Major in midsentence. "Take a seat, Major. Relax." He motions Cadet Johnson to sit on the couch across from him.

After taking a seat, Major's tactical noncommissioned officer (TACNCO), Sergeant First Class Handson bursts into the room and bellows, "How're you doing, Major?"

"Not bad, Sergeant. A little tired, though. I had a long night," Cadet Johnson replies.

Captain Weiss and Sergeant First Class Handson look at one another, and laugh. While laughing, Sergeant First Class Handson says, "I hear yuh. I've been there myself a few times. How about you, sir?" He then takes a seat next to Cadet Johnson on the couch.

Captain Weiss slaps Cadet Johnson on the shoulder and replies, "More times than I can count."

With a spark of seriousness, Captain Weiss states, "Now let's get down to why we called you down here. Major, we want you to be the Ducks commander next semester. Between me, you, and Sergeant First Class Handson, you're the only guy we seriously considered for the job."

"Is that why you asked me what semester I wanted last week?" Cadet Johnson asks.

"Roger," Captain Weiss responds. "Just so you know, this is not official yet. Higher still has to bless it, but we figured that we would let you know first."

"Thank you, sir. In all honesty, to be a CO was the only job I really wanted next year. Everything else is a far second."

"Well, it's good to see that we both are getting what we want. I know you're going to do a great job. We have every confidence in you. You're very motivated and you stick to your guns," Captain Weiss tells Cadet Johnson. "I'm going to let you choose your lower level chain of command, all except for your XO and your TO."

"Roger, sir."

"Sara's going to be your XO, and Joe's going to be your TO," Captain Weiss explains.

"That's great, sir," Cadet Johnson exclaims. "Sara and I work well together. She's one of my squad leaders right now. I would have made Joe the TO even if you would have allowed me to fill that slot."

"Well, good," replies Captain Weiss. "I'm glad to see that we're already starting next semester off in the right direction. That's all I have for you. Do you have any questions for us?"

"No, sir," Cadet Johnson answers.

"All right then. I guess I'll see you around later on in the day."

"Roger, sir," Cadet Johnson replies as he rises from the couch. He shakes Captain Weiss's and Sergeant First Class Handson's hands then leaves Captain Weiss's office. *I cannot believe this*, Cadet Johnson thinks to himself. *I knew that I was up for the job, and God knows that I've earned it, but I didn't think that I'd actually get it. God! West Point has finally come through!*

Cadet Johnson jubilantly runs back to his room but is careful not to awaken Calvin. He sits down at his desk and picks up his telephone receiver to call his little brother, Will. While the telephone rings, Cadet Johnson kicks his shoes off and leaves them under his desk. After ringing three times, someone on the other end answers.

"Hello?"

"'Sup, Will?" Cadet Johnson replies. "I'm going to be company commander next semester."

"That's cool," Will dryly responds

"Yeah, it is. You know what that means, right?"

"Naw. What's it mean?"

"It means that no one would dare mess with you when you get up here next year. Even if I weren't a CO, they still wouldn't mess with you being that you're my little brother and all and that you're going to be on the football team, but now that I am a CO, you're safer than a dude in the witness-protection program,"

"Word?" Will exuberantly responds. "That's money, dawg."

"Sure is. Well, I've got to go. I just figured I'd give you a call and let you know what the word is. I'm tired as hell, so I'm going back to bed. Tell Mom and Dad what's up. Peace."

"Peace," Will echoes as he hangs up the telephone. His big brother does the same then immediately jumps back into bed. Fortunately, his headache is gone, making it easier for him to fall back to sleep.

2210 Hours: Serbian-Croatian Border

Though it is early summer, the Balkans provide little warmth for those who must stay outdoors for an extended period of time. The high elevation gives the impression of a late autumn night, instead of a nice summer day as it ought to be. Aside from the weather, the terrain does not do well for one's legs and lower back. Having been raised in and knowing only this terrain, the men of the Serbian Thirty-fifth (Mechanized) Infantry Brigade are not uncomfortable in any way. They are a bit cold, but the hopes of success in their upcoming mission keeps them warm. Their thoughts are not on their discomforts. Instead, they stay focused on the mission at hand.

Colonel Drasneb proudly rides in his BMP-1, a Soviet era mechanized infantry vehicle. With First Battalion to his front and Third and Fourth Battalions to his rear, Colonel Drasneb is able to move efficiently throughout his brigade formation. Each of his battalions is in a wedge formation, down to and including the platoons. As the Thirty-fifth moves within ten miles of the Croatian border, Colonel Drasneb receives a message over the radio. "Sir, this is Lieutenant Colonel Krien. First Battalion has reached checkpoint Alpha. We are all up and are now ready to initialize the next phase of the operation."

"Very good. Continue on with your progress." Colonel Drasneb then gets on an open channel and commands, "Androff, Spachev, commence with the next phase."

Simultaneously, Androff and Spachev respond, "Yes, sir."

Having received Colonel Drasneb's orders, Third Battalion gets on line and to the right of First Battalion, approximately fifteen meters away. Second Battalion stays in the middle rear of First and Third battalions. Colonel Drasneb and the engineer platoon attachment move in between First and Third Battalions.

2245 Hours: LP/OP on the Croatian Side of the Serbo-Croatian Border

On a hilltop overlooking a valley in Serbia, a US soldier of the Twelfth Battalion Third Brigade First (Mechanized) Infantry Division, uses the natural terrain to hide his presence. The soldier's task is to report to his battalion commander any suspicious activity that he may observe. What he must constantly watch for is the Serbian army moving within ten miles of the border.

Fortunately, a soldier who was on duty one day, unbeknown to anyone except his commander, took it upon himself to secretly measure and mark the distance. The marker is a single bush with violet blossoms planted in the middle of the rocky terrain.

The battalion commander runs two twelve-hour shifts a day for the listening post/observation post. The soldier who is currently on duty has been at his position for approximately nine hours. He has two hours and fifteen minutes until his relief comes.

Looking down into the valley with his NVGs (night-vision goggles), the soldier notices a large element pushing toward the border. He is unsure of the element's size, but he does know that it is bigger than a battalion, either a regiment or a brigade. The soldier also notices that part of the element has passed the marker. He puts his NVGs in one hand and picks up his radio with the other.

"Renegade 6, Renegade 6, This is OP1. Over," the soldier says into his hand mic.

"OP1, this is Renegade 6. What do you have for me? Over," a voice on the other end replies.

"Renegade 6, there's some activity near the border. The element's larger than a battalion. I'm guessing it's a brigade. They've passed the marker by about ten meters. Over."

"That's some good intel, OP1. I'll be right over to check it out. Renegade 6, out."

2249 Hours: Ten miles from the Croatian Border

As the Thirty-fifth continues with the next phase of their operation, Lieutenant Colonel Krien surveys the terrain. He looks to his front left and notices a lone bush with beautiful purple flowers.

Lieutenant Colonel Krien thinks to himself, *That's odd. With all of the fighting that's been going on around here, how could one lone bush remain unscathed? Oh, well. It's nice to know that some beauty still thrives through all of this ugliness.*

As Lieutenant Colonel Krien passes the bush, he smiles and thinks nothing more of it.

2300 Hours: LP/OP on the Croatian Side of the Border

The commander for Twelfth battalion, Lt. Col. Al Turner, and his battalion Operations Officer (S-3), move to the soldier's position at OP1. Looking at the soldier, Lieutenant Colonel Turner sees that his name is Corporal Kersey.

"So, Kerse, what you got for me?" Lieutenant Colonel Turner asks.

Kerse hands the night-vision goggles to Lieutenant Colonel Turner and states, "Here, sir. Take a look for yourself. I think you'll be pretty interested in what you see."

Lieutenant Colonel Turner crawls next to Kerse, takes the NVGs, then looks down toward the border. Having not been at this position before, it takes him a couple of seconds to orient himself onto the terrain below.

"You see down there, sir? About two thousand meters out? It's too far to be 100 percent sure, but it looks like there's a Serb brigade-size mechanized-infantry element moving our way in a split wedge formation. They've pushed forward about five hundred meters in the past fifteen minutes. From the way it looks, sir, they're hungry for a fight."

Lieutenant Colonel Turner hands the NVGs over to his S-3 and replies, "Kerse, I think you may be right. I don't like the formation that they're in now—too hostile. What do you think, Jim?"

Jim, the battalion S-3, answers, "I think we may have a battle on our hands, sir."

Lieutenant Colonel Turner picks up his radio and speaks to his XO. "Steve, this is Lieutenant Colonel Turner. We may have to put our training to use today. Get the men up and ready to go in ten mikes. Throw a quicksand table together, as well."

"Which plan are we going with, sir?" Steve asks.

"Let's go with Illegal Alien."

"Good choice, sir."

"Turner out." He hands the radio back to Kerse, rolls out of the prone and onto his back, then sits himself up on his butt and says, "Kerse, I want you to stay here. You are my eyes in the sky. I want you to find the commander of that makeshift Serbian unit. When you do, keep your eyes on him. Once we begin our assault, let me know where he is so we can isolate him and hopefully capture him."

"Yes, sir. Consider him found," Kerse exuberantly responds.

Lieutenant Colonel Turner and his S-3 roll back into the prone, slide down the hill, then leap up and run back to their base camp.

Standing at the edge of the base camp is Lieutenant Colonel Turner's sergeant major, Command Sergeant Major Tyler.

"Sir," Sergeant Major Tyler states, "everything's ready to go. The XO's waiting for you at your hooch."

"Good work," Lieutenant Colonel Turner replies. He, Jim, and Sergeant Major Tyler quickly walk over to the hooch where the XO and the three company commanders are waiting. "I'm glad to see that you all were able to make it," Lieutenant Colonel Turner jokingly states. His men laugh. They enjoy, and are used to, Lieutenant Colonel Turner's light heartedness and sense of humor.

After a few seconds of laughter among his men, Lieutenant Colonel Turner opens with, "All right. Let's get down to business. Corporal Kersey has informed Jim and me that the Serbs are heading this way. They should be about seven miles from the border by now. We are dealing with what appears to be a brigade-sized element. Two of their 'battalions' are on line. Another is in the rear. There also appears to be a small attachment in the middle. As I have already told Jim, we are going to go with Illegal Alien. This should neutralize them while maximizing our survival rate. I know you all already know it, but I'm going to run through it real quick, anyway."

Lieutenant Colonel Turner quickly explains to the XO and his company commanders how they are to implement Illegal Alien. After the quick brief, Lieutenant Colonel Turner asks his men, "So are there any questions?"

"No, sir," all four men simultaneously respond.

"Very well then. The next time I will hear from you all is over the net. Keep a clear head out there. I want as many of us to come back as possible," Lieutenant Colonel Turner states as he dismisses his XO and his three company commanders.

As the XO and the company commanders exit the hooch, Lieutenant Colonel Turner thinks to himself, *Well, Al, you knew this day would come. I guess it's time to prove whether American tax dollars were put to good use or not. You know your men are ready. I just hope to God that these Serbs pull back before anyone has to die.* Lieutenant Colonel Turner pulls a cigar out form his desk drawer and lights it then stares out into the star-filled sky.

2310 Hours: Six Miles from the Croatian Border

Colonel Drasneb feels very confident. He has no fear. It does not exist. Only one thing is on his mind, and that is victory. Anything less is not worth attaining. Colonel Drasneb would rather die than face defeat. He stands in the hatch of his BMP and surveys the terrain. The rocky hills remind him of his childhood home. He smiles. Colonel Drasneb does not detect any artillery pieces hidden in the hills. He does notice that he and his men are in somewhat of a valley, but that does not concern him since the border is three miles behind the hills and NATO forces are not permitted to cross the border without informing the Serbian government of their intentions.

Colonel Drasneb gets on the radio and asks, "Krien, how is everything up front?"

"Sir, all is well. Visibility is down due to the terrain and the time of day, but we had already calculated that into the mission."

"Very well. Continue on with the mission. Inform me if anything happens." Colonel Drasneb turns his radio off and sits back down.

27 MAY 1999

0045 Hours

The first phase of Illegal Alien is complete. Alpha Company, led by Capt. Roderick Eldridge, is in their pre-dug defensive positions, approximately eight hundred meters north of the border. Charlie and Bravo companies, led by captains Franklin Cedric and Daniel Adisa respectively, are in position one mile to the north of Alpha Company. They sit and wait for Lieutenant Colonel Turner's signal to move.

Lieutenant Colonel Turner gets on the radio to speak to his key leaders and says, "Men, make sure your watches are synchronized to 0045 hours on my mark." All of the men listening on the other end of their radios synchronize their watches on the command. "Remember," Lieutenant Colonel Turner continues, "our success depends on our timing, so ensure that you don't lose track of the time. Hoo-ah?"

All of the men reply with a loud and thunderous, "Hoo-ah!"

0100 Hours

Not enjoying the bumpy ride very much and wishing that he were back home with his wife and three young daughters, Lieutenant Colonel Krien pulls out his map and compass. He studies them then refocuses back out onto the terrain. He puts his compass and map away then picks up his radio.

"Sir," Lieutenant Colonel Krien says to Colonel Drasneb, "we have crossed the border."

"Very good, Krien. Continue on. We shouldn't see any action for at least another half hour."

"Yes, sir." Krien places the radio to his side and thinks to himself, *Well, at least I have thirty more minutes of peace. God, I hope I live through this hell so I can get home and see my wife and my babies.*

As Lieutenant Colonel Krien daydreams, his battalion is surprisingly attacked from its left flank. "My God!" he yells. "Where did they come from?" He picks up his radio to inform Colonel Drasneb. "Sir! We are under attack! Going into evasive maneuvers!"

"You should have spotted them before they attacked!" Colonel Drasneb angrily responds. "You better not cause us to fail our mission!"

"Yes, sir," Krien responds, his hands quivering from anxiety and fear. He turns his radio to another frequency to speak to Third Battalion's commander, Lieutenant Colonel Androff. "Andy, we're under attack over here. Most of the fight is over on my left flank. We're going to push back. Get a defensive line ready for us."

"I've got you covered," Lieutenant Colonel Androff affirms.

━━━━━━━━━━━■━━━━━━━━━━━

Charlie and Bravo companies come rolling down the eastern edge of the mountain range. They begin the initial stages of Illegal Alien by attacking the Serbian battalion that is in their southeast direction. Bravo and Charlie meet very little resistance.

Captain Adisa gets on the radio and informs Lieutenant Colonel Turner of their progress. "Sir, we've met very little resistance so far. I don't think they saw us coming. We're going to push through another five hundred meters before we begin phase 2."

"Sounds good," Lieutenant Colonel Turner states. "Make sure you stay on the watch."

"Roger that, sir. I think we can make it."

"All right then. Radio back to me at the two-minute mark of phase 2. Turner out."

Adisa turns the radio to another channel and says, "Ced, did you get all that?"

"Roger that."

Charlie and Bravo continue to push through the Serbian battalion. Because the Serbian forces are not causing them any trouble, Captains Adisa and Cedric do not have their men dismount from their Bradley

Fighting Vehicles that they are riding in during the battle. It is unnecessary. The Bradleys alone, with their fifty-caliber automatic machine gun and twenty-five millimeter cannon, are crushing the Serbs and are pushing them back in the direction that Lieutenant Colonel Turner had anticipated. After attacking the Serb battalion for five minutes of complete carnage, phase 1 of Illegal Alien is complete.

Charlie and Bravo pull back roughly four hundred meters then loop around to the south and attack another Serb battalion from the rear.

0105 Hours: LP/OP on the Croatian Side of the Border

Overlooking the battlefield, Corporal Kersey observes everything that is unfolding on the ground below. As he watches the first phase of Illegal Alien, he notices a small Serb attachment of some type separating itself from the brigade and moving to the southeast. He continues to monitor the attachment's movements.

Kerse thinks to himself, *I think I've got it. That has to be the commander there. Why else would that bunch reposition itself as it just did?* Kerse reaches for his radio with his free hand. "Sir, this is Corporal Kersey. I believe I've found the commander."

"Where is he?" Turner asks.

"Sir, he's moving in the southeast direction in between the other two Serb battalions."

"Good deal. Anything else for me?"

"Not at the moment, sir. Phase 1 is looking good from up here though."

"Yes it is," Lieutenant Colonel Turner proudly responds. "Keep me informed of anything out of the ordinary. Turner out." Lieutenant Colonel Turner hangs his receiver back up while thinking to himself, *Man, that Kerse is a smart kid. I've got to do something about getting him to the prep school once we get back to the rear.*

0107 Hours

Lieutenant Colonel Krien is racing for his life. His battalion is nearly destroyed. Only one thing is on his mind and that is survival—not for his men, but for himself. His gunner is standing in the hatch, firing its gun at the Americans. Krien knows that it is the Americans because he recognizes the vehicle that they are using to defeat him. Quivering in the backseat, he thinks to himself, *I hope to God that I make it out of here. I didn't ask for this. The Americans are picking us apart as if we were children. There is nothing we can do to stop them.*

Krien picks up his radio. "Androff, I and the remainder of my men are coming through. Be ready. The Americans are annihilating us. They're coming directly from the west. Their attack has let up some, but who knows what tricks they have planned. Keep your eyes open."

"Stop your babbling. My men are ready for those American pigs. We can handle them."

Krien turns to another frequency and orders his remaining company commanders and platoon leaders to move to the southern end of Third Battalion's position. They acknowledge the order and push in a southeasterly direction.

0110 Hours

"Sir, it appears as if the Serbian commander has isolated himself somewhat from the rest of his unit," Corporal Kersey informs Lieutenant Colonel Turner, while gazing over the battlefield.

"Where is he exactly?"

"Well, sir, if I'm right, the commander is to the west of his men, about three hundred meters from Alpha company's position."

"Good, good," Lieutenant Colonel Turner responds thoughtfully. "Get back with me in five minutes, unless anything overtly drastic happens between now and then. Turner out."

Lieutenant Colonel Turner changes frequencies to speak to his commanders. "This is Renegade 6, break. The Serbs are about three hundred meters to the west of Alpha's position. Eldridge, I want you to send out a decoy and lure them to your northwest. Ced, Adisa, I want you guys to continue engaging them from the south. The plan is to get them caught in a pocket. Once that's done, continue on with the rest of Illegal Alien. Any questions?"

"Sir, what is our time window?" Captain Cedric asks.

"No more than ten minutes."

"Roger, sir."

"Is that all?"

"Yes, sir?" the three commanders unanimously reply.

"Eldridge, when this phase of the op is complete, contact me. Turner out."

The three company commanders turn to their respective company frequencies and pass the word on to their platoon leaders.

0113 Hours

"Sir, the Americans have continued their attack from the south. We're doing all we can to hold them back," Lieutenant Colonel Spachev informs Colonel Drasneb.

"Fight at an angle in the southeasterly direction. This will force them to have to flank you from one of your sides. Krien and Androff will then be able to attack them while they are vulnerable."

"No disrespect, sir," Lieutenant Colonel Spachev begins, "but I do not believe that that is possible. The Americans appear to be staying on line. They've stuck to that strategy the entire time without much deviation. If I were to implement your strategy, sir, they would not wheel around our position. They'd wait or strengthen the side that was getting more heat."

Hearing Spachev's response, Colonel Drasneb boils with anger. He cannot understand how or why his commanders have become such cowards—that they can actually believe that the Americans are as powerful as everyone perceives. Colonel Drasneb suddenly begins to sweat profusely and his left hand begins to shake. Angrily, he changes his radio frequency to speak to his commanders.

"Listen! I am sick and tired of hearing excuses from you three and the Americans running through us like we weren't even here. Spachev, you will do as you were ordered. Is that understood?"

"Yes, sir."

"Androff, Krien, be ready for the Americans to flank Second Battalion. When they do, hit them hard, take no prisoners. It is time that the Americans understand who they are up against. Spachev, I'm going to send you the engineer platoon for further support. We must be successful here. There is no turning back. Failure is not an option." Colonel Drasneb again changes radio frequencies and informs the engineer platoon leader the changes to the plan. The platoon leader dutifully leads his men toward Second Battalion's position.

———————————————————————

Two squads from Alpha Company are engaging the Serbs from the east. To draw them out, one squad engages the Serbs by breaking through their lines about one hundred meters then quickly pulling back. In retaliation, the Serbs pursue the squad, but are attacked by the other Alpha squad, from the southeast.

From atop his position, Corporal Kersey continues to watch the battle unfold. While watching the game that the two squads are playing with the Serbs, he notices that Charlie and Bravo are within four hundred meters of their position. "Lieutenant Colonel Turner, sir, Bravo and Charlie are within four hundred meters form the two Alpha Company squads' position."

"Thank you, Kerse."

As Lieutenant Colonel Turner responds to Kerse's report, Kerse notices something unusual on the battlefield. "Sir, the Serb commander is moving to the southwest. If you have Charlie and Bravo push further north, the two squads can swing around to the east and capture him."

"Are you sure of this, Kerse?"

"Have I been wrong yet, sir?"

"Good point. Renegade 6 out."

Excited, Lieutenant Colonel Turner switches to his company net to speak to his commanders. "All right, boys, it's time for us to end this. Ced, Adisa, keep pushing north then swing around behind Alpha's defensive line and get in position to their south. Eldridge, have your two squads attack to the east. We're on the hunt for their commander. Make every effort not to kill him."

"Roger, sir," the three commanders reply.

0118 Hours

Charlie and Bravo Companies stay on line while pushing northward. Charlie is to the left of Bravo. They are met head-on with an overwhelming Serb element. The Serbs aggressively attack in a southeasterly direction. Charlie takes the brunt of the Serb attack but continues to slowly push forward. The Serbs are trying to force the Americans to flank them from either side. The Americans do not act as Colonel Drasneb had anticipated.

Captain Adisa gets on the net with his third platoon leader, Second Lieutenant Clay. "Clay."

"Yes, sir."

"I need you to wrap around us and Charlie and support their left flank. The Serbs are hitting them hard."

"Roger, sir."

"Adisa out."

Clay gets off of the net and relays the message to his platoon. Third Platoon halts their advance and wheels around Bravo and Charlie companies and strengthens Charlie's left flank.

■————————————————■

One of Lieutenant Colonel Krien's company commanders informs him that the Americans are not pushing back and are not flanking them as they had assumed. Krien picks up his radio to speak to Lieutenant Colonel Androff. "Androff, Drasneb's plan is not working, we need to push back and swing around to the south. I think the Americans are trying to trap us. Where, I do not know. All I know is that if we continue with our current plan, we will not survive."

"Are you saying that we disobey a direct order from our commander?" Androff asks. "Because if you are, then I cannot comply. Colonel Drasneb is a military genius. We cannot fail."

"Fool!" Krien frustratingly responds. "If we continue, we will die. We will not be able to see our families ever again."

"You sniveling coward. Take your men and leave if you want. I am going to stay and fight. Me and my men can push through without you."

"I will tell your family that you died valiantly." Lieutenant Colonel Krien switches to his battalion frequency to speak to his company commanders. "Men, we are pulling back. If we continue on our present course of action, we will all die. I cannot allow that to happen. We are going to move north, cut east, and swing around Third Battalion to the south. Follow me in a battalion V formation. Do not engage the Americans. They will not attack if we do not attack them first. We need to be ready to move in five minutes."

Lieutenant Colonel Krien turns his radio off, bows his head, and prays.

———————————————————————

The two squads from Alpha Company move across the terrain toward the southeast. They meet very little resistance. As they move, the lead Bradley spots a small unit to the south, coming from the northeast. The Bradley commander, Sergeant Coleman, radios in to his squad leader about the situation. "Ken, I think we may've run into that Serbian commander that the CO was talking about."

"Good. Change our direction and engage them. Be careful, though. We don't want to kill the guy, just capture him."

"Roger that."

S.Sgt. Ken Dell radios in to the other squad leader to inform him of the present situation. The two squads then change their direction and engage the Serb commander's element.

———————————————————————

"Damn it!" Colonel Drasneb yells as he peers through his binoculars from the hatch in his BMP. "The Americans are on us. How could this have happened? My plan was infallible! I can't turn back now!"

Drasneb gets on his radio to speak to the men that are with him. "We have to turn around. The Americans are behind us and are closing in fast. Now we will prove to them how deadly the Serbian army truly is."

Colonel Drasneb and his element turn around and engage the Americans.

0123 Hours

Lieutenant Colonel Krien and the remainder of his battalion retreat south, avoiding contact as they move expeditiously to return to safety. As he scans the terrain ahead, Lieutenant Colonel Krien spots a small battle occurring to the east, approximately four hundred meters away. As he passes the skirmish, he realizes that it is Colonel Drasneb who is in the battle, and even worst, the battle is not going in his favor.

Krien gets on his battalion net with his commanders and says, "Men, I know that I said that we would avoid any altercations with the Americans, but our commander is in need of support, and it is our duty to help him. I only want you to spearhead in and then quickly move out. Understood?"

"Yes, sir."

Krien changes his radio frequency to Colonel Drasneb's. "Sir, Krien speaking. I am coming in to help you out."

"Krien, you coward! Get over here now! We need relief immediately!"

"Yes, sir." Krien places his radio beside him and has his driver turn them due east.

The retreating Serb battalion races across the hilly terrain toward the battle. Lieutenant Colonel Krien has his men wheel around to the north side of the American forces in a horseshoe-like formation. Once in position, the men at the top of the position push forward, while the men to the left and right flanks close the gap, thus slowly enveloping the Americans.

———————————————————

S.Sgt. Dell gets on the net to speak with the other squad leader, S.Sgt John Austin. "John, we need to get the hell out of here before these Serb bastards over run us."

"Hear you. Which way you want to go?"

"Let's move southeast for about two hundred meters then cut east. We'll end up on the south side of our defensive positions."

"Sounds like a plan."

"Good. Let's get the hell out of here. Dell out."

The two squad leaders speak with their respective Bradley commanders to implement their pullback plan.

0134 Hours

One of Lieutenant Colonel Krien's commanders gets on the net to speak to him. "Sir, the Americans are retreating south. Do you want us to pursue them?"

Krien changes the net so that all of his commanders can hear. "Men, so you are aware as to what is going on, Captain Lyzg asked if we should pursue the Americans. The answer to his question is no. We are going to continue pushing forward until we get on line. From there, we will pick up our wounded and dead. Any questions?"

"No, sir."

Krien's battalion ceases their envelopment. The men to the north move south and get on line with the remainder of the battalion. As they move, Lieutenant Colonel Krien grimaces at the carnage that the Americans had left in their wake. He thinks to himself, *My God! How can such a small number create such destruction?*

The battalion continues its movement southward, stopping to pick up their fallen comrades and tend to the wounded. Lieutenant Colonel Krien has his driver stop his vehicle. He, his driver, and the three other men in his crew get out to trace the battlefield. As Lieutenant Colonel Krien slowly paces, his aide taps him on the shoulder to get his attention, points to the left of where they are standing, and says, "Sir, I think that's Colonel Drasneb's vehicle over there."

Krien looks over in the pointing aide's direction and, through the thick cloud of smoke and dirt, is able to recognize Colonel Drasneb's BMP, which is flipped over on its back, flames emerging from its belly. Realizing the severity of the situation, Lieutenant Colonel Krien and his aide run to the BMP to investigate. "Go see to the driver's condition," Lieutenant Colonel Krien orders.

Lieutenant Colonel Krien motions to his BMP crew to come to his location. When they arrive, he says to them, "Come over here and help me get these men out." The four men force the BMP door open and begin pulling the men out.

As Lieutenant Colonel Krien's crew works, one of them shouts, "Sir, Colonel Drasneb's badly hurt! His leg is broken, and his head is bleeding."

The crewman carefully lifts Colonel Drasneb into his arms and fastidiously carries him away from the wreckage. He lies Colonel Drasneb down beside a large rock about fifteen meters away from the decimated BMP. The crewman straightens Colonel Drasneb's leg out as much as he can then runs back to his crew members and continues helping them in their task. They all place Colonel Drasneb's fallen crew beside him.

Krien's aide sprints over to investigate Colonel Drasneb's driver's condition. He quickly returns and reports, "Sir, the driver is dead. His head is bashed in. From the way it looks, the driver hit his head on the control panel then on the right-side wall."

"Radio the medics and tell them to get over here." Lieutenant Colonel Krien's aide does as he is ordered.

Lieutenant Colonel Krien runs over to where his crewman had laid Colonel Drasneb. Approaching the site, Lieutenant Colonel Krien suddenly halts in his tracks. Gawking at Colonel Drasneb's leg, Lieutenant Colonel Krien gasps and thinks to himself, *My God! He may never walk again!*

Colonel Drasneb's right leg is a gnarly mess. If it were not for the fact that Colonel Drasneb is wearing a pair of pants and boots, Lieutenant Colonel Krien would not be able to tell that Colonel Drasneb had a leg to begin with. Colonel Drasneb's leg is smashed to such a point that it is only about two inches thick.

Some would say that Colonel Drasneb may never walk again. They should inform Colonel Drasneb first.

A few moments after Lieutenant Colonel Krien's crew finishes evacuating Colonel Drasneb and his fallen crew, the medics arrive on the scene. They place Colonel Drasneb and his crew, who are now conscious but very groggy, into the back of their ambulance-converted BMPs, throw Colonel Drasneb's driver into a body bag, and briskly take off to return them to the MASH station.

Krien turns to his aide and says, "Get the company commanders on the net and tell them to meet me here now."

0141 Hours

"Renegade 6, I believe the battle's over."

"I know, Kerse, but thanks for the update anyway."

"Did we get the commander?"

"No, we didn't. The two Alpha squads were attacked from the rear from a retreating Serb battalion. Probably, the smartest thing the Serbs did during all of this mess was run away."

Corporal Kersey takes another look through his binoculars and reports to Lieutenant Colonel Turner, "Sir, that battalion you just mentioned is pulling out now."

"I figured as much. We're going to let them go. They're not going to try this little stunt again for a while."

"Roger that, sir."

"Once we all get back to the rear, you can get relieved and return to base camp."

"Roger, sir."

"Renegade 6, out."

29 MAY 1999

1230 Hours: Serbian Military Hospital

With the second Serbo-Croatian War quickly reaching its apex, the majority of the Serb hospitals have exceeded their capacity. The hospitals are so full that many soldiers do not have rooms. They have no choice but to lie in their beds in the hallways. There are only two means in which a soldier can attain a room: a life-threatening injury or high rank. Fortunately for Colonel Drasneb, he has rank on his side. Much to his dismay though, he does not have a room to himself. In fact, he has twenty-three roommates. Colonel Drasneb's hospital room is not a room at all, but a makeshift corridor that was converted into a room a few months back to meet patient capacity demands. The hospital staffs throughout Serbia did not expect soldier casualties to reach the high numbers that they did.

One event that many injured soldiers look forward to is when their commanders come to pay them a visit. It shows that the commander cares for their welfare and appreciates the sacrifice that the injured soldier made for his fellow soldiers, his unit, and his country. Visiting the hospital today is Maj. Gen. Prynotstily Bruscev, Colonel Drasneb's division commander.

"Room! Attention!" a soldier on guard at the hospital ward entrance sounds off.

"Carry on. Carry on," Major General Bruscev firmly responds. He confidently struts over to a nurse and asks, "Where is Colonel Drasneb?"

"Sir, Colonel Drasneb is lying in the last bed on the right of this corridor, bed number 24."

"Thank you," he replies with a big smile.

Major General Bruscev strides down the corridor toward Colonel Drasneb's bed. Along the corridor, Major General Bruscev stops, smiling and shaking the hands of the other soldiers who have fallen victim to the war. Major General Bruscev's entourage shuffles behind him, trying, with little success, to keep their commander focused on the task at hand.

After an uncountable number of handshakes and praises to and from the soldiers, Major General Bruscev finally makes it to Colonel Drasneb's bed and says, "Colonel, how are you doing today?"

"Not good, sir," Colonel Drasneb pouts.

"Well, I've got something that should cheer you up."

Major General Bruscev's aide reaches into his brief case and pulls out two small boxes and a large manila envelope.

"Colonel, I have for you two medals, one for your gallantry on the battlefield and one for your wound. Post the orders."

Major General Bruscev's aide reads the two sets of orders for the awards. As the aide begins, everyone who is able jumps to their feet and stands at the position of attention.

The aide finishes reading the orders. Major General Bruscev then extends his hand to Colonel Drasneb and states, "Colonel, thank you for your unending service to our great country. It is great men such as yourself who make Serbia as great as it is." Colonel Drasneb reaches for Major General Bruscev's hand and firmly grasps it.

Major General Bruscev releases Colonel Drasneb's hand and waves his entourage away, thus enabling him to speak with Colonel Drasneb privately.

"You know, it's a good thing Krien found you when he did. Your leg could be a lot worse than it presently is, or worst, you could be dead."

"Krien! That coward. He may have saved my life, sir, but he did so in the process of retreating from the battle."

"That may be so, but he lived to see another day. He is the only one of your battalion commanders to live through that carnage of a battle. If he had stayed to fight, no one would have lived, including you," Major General Bruscev firmly states.

"No disrespect, sir, but I would choose death over my present condition."

"I knew that would be your attitude," Major General Bruscev replies, shaking his head. "I think I may have something that will spark some life and purpose back into your spirit. I have a job for you, Colonel."

Curious as to the content of Major General Bruscev's potential offer, Colonel Drasneb struggles to sit up in his bed then inquisitively asks, "What is it, sir?"

"Our army needs a new chief interrogator."

"Sir, I'll do anything that our country needs in order for us to win this abominable war."

"I knew that's what you would say. I spoke with your doctor already. He said that you could be out of here in two months if your therapy goes right. When that time comes, I want you to report to headquarters."

"Thank you, sir. It is reassuring to know that our country still finds me useful."

"Well, hopefully, through your interrogations, you will be able to attain valuable information to aid the war effort."

"There is no doubt that I will, sir."

"As always, Colonel Drasneb, I expect nothing but the highest quality of performance from you." Major General Bruscev leans forward and shakes Colonel Drasneb's hand again. "Well, you take care of yourself, colonel. I will visit periodically to check on your progress."

Major General Bruscev motions to his entourage that he is prepared to depart the hospital. They immediately scurry over to Major General Bruscev and swarm around him. As Major General Bruscev moves, the small swarm keeps in step with him, keeping the front clear, thus allowing their commander to see where he is going.

17 AUGUST 1999

0100 Hours: US Camp Near the Serbo-Croatian border

"All right guys, here's your mission packet." Major Rockney hands 1st Lt. Christopher Perez a folder containing his mission order, maps, and schematics. "It's pretty routine. You fly in over a Serb outpost, take a few pictures, catch some video, then fly back. You ought to make it back before first call."

"Roger that, sir. That's definitely the plan." Perez rises from his seat, looks at his crew chief, and laughingly states, "Let's get out of here and get ready. I want to be first in the chow line for breakfast."

"I hear you on that, sir," 1st Lt. Perez's crew chief acknowledges as they exit Major Rockney's tent.

0200 Hours

Standing outside on the flight deck, First Lieutenant Perez looks up at the night sky and counts the stars. Before every mission, he finds some time to count the stars. He does not know why, but it soothes his mind and helps him relax before a mission. It is a full moon out tonight, which gives him mixed feelings about the forthcoming mission. A full moon is good because he does not have to worry about visibility, but on the other hand, neither does the enemy.

Perez takes a deep breath and says to himself, *Lord, let this be another routine mission.*

As Perez meditates, his crew chief, Chief Warrant Officer 4 Anderson, silently walks beside him and states, "Sir, we're ready to rock and roll. Beauty's prepped and ready to go."

"All right chief. Let's get this mission underway so we can get back before daylight." The two men jog over and jump into their Black Hawk helicopter, which Chief Anderson christened "Black Beauty."

Waiting for them in Black Beauty is Sergeant Burns, the gunner/medic. "Another quick one, sir?" he asks.

"Yep. Flyin' low and taking some video."

"I hear that, sir. The shorter the better."

Chief Warrant Officer 4 Anderson fires Black Beauty up as they all buckle up. "Here we go," Anderson yells into his headset, as they take off.

0230 Hours: Fifty-six Miles across the Serbian Border

"Burnsy, keep your eyes open. We don't need any surprises this early in the morning," First Lieutenant Perez states.

"My eyes're open like a 7-Eleven, sir."

Sergeant Burns aims his .50 caliber toward the ground and scans the terrain as they fly low. First Lieutenant Perez takes Beauty so low that Burns's feet nearly touch the top of the trees.

"Sir, we should be approaching the site in about ten minutes," Chief Warrant Officer 4 Anderson states.

Flying fast and low, the crew prepares for the climax of their mission. Chief Warrant Officer 4 Anderson checks the instruments connected to the video equipment. First Lieutenant Perez ensures that Beauty does not crash into any trees. Sergeant Burns keeps his eyes peered to the ground, continuously scanning the terrain for any enemy activity.

0236 Hours: A Trail near a Serbian Patrol Base

A Serb squad patrols an area ten miles in radius around their patrol base. The squad consists of seven men and a squad leader. Each man walks ten meters apart from one another in order to prevent the entire squad from succumbing to an exploding grenade. The squad leader positions himself in the middle of his squad.

As they move along a trail, the point man quickly throws up his right fist, signaling to the squad to halt. He then points to the sky. The squad immediately looks up and sights a helicopter flying low over their position.

The squad leader briskly moves to the point man's position, places his hand on his shoulder, and says, "Get off of the trail and follow that helicopter."

After instructing his point man, the squad leader returns to his previous position in the middle of his squad. The point man changes his direction of movement and leads the squad off of the trail and into the wood line, following the helicopter's path. As the squad briskly moves through the thick terrain, the point man and the squad leader both notice the helicopter turn around and realize that it is circling their patrol base.

The squad leader, understanding the situation that is unfolding before them, runs to the front of his squad and signals them to get back onto the trail. The squad forms up and aims their weapons high and inward of the helicopter's circular path. The squad leader points to the sky then points to himself, signaling his men not to fire until he gives the order. The helicopter comes around for another turn. As it flies over the squad's position, the squad leader points to the sky. On command, the squad fires unmercifully upon the helicopter.

0251 Hours

Flying in a circular path over a Serb outpost, First Lieutenant Perez maintains his course and continues to map the earth by flying fast and low over the hostile terrain. Chief Warrant Officer 4 Anderson focuses on the video and photography equipment, ensuring that their mission is not awash. The worse thing the flight crew can do is return to base without any pictures or videotape.

Sergeant Burns remains glued to his .50 caliber, his eyes peered to the ground below. He does not spot any activity that appears threatening. The only discomfort that Sergeant Burns has is the fact that there are numerous trails around the patrol base. Anyone could be hiding within the bordering wood line.

Suddenly from out of nowhere, Sergeant Burns is forced to duck for cover. "Sir, we're receiving fire!" Burns yells. "I can't see where it's coming from!"

Damn it! This was supposed to be routine! First Lieutenant Perez inwardly shouts. He then orders, "Spray the area! Chief, get us the hell out of here!"

Chief Anderson pulls up and hard to the right on his stick in hopes to avoid anymore fire from the ground. Sergeant Burns's .50 caliber is nearly perpendicular to the ground. He is still unable to see who is firing at them, but he has a pretty good idea of where they are.

■————————————————————■

"Alpha Team, fire at the propeller! Bravo, fire at the gunner. We need to get that helicopter out of the air!" the Serb squad leader commands.

Upon his command, the squad shifts fires onto their respective parts of the helicopter. After a few seconds, the squad notices something fall out of the helicopter. As soon as the squad spots the object fall from the helicopter, the fire from the air ceases.

"Sergeant, we got the gunner!" the Bravo team leader shouts to the squad leader.

"Send a man out to check on the body. The rest, knock that bird out of the sky!"

■————————————————————■

"We're going down hard and fast, sir!" Chief Warrant Officer 4 Anderson shouts.

Beauty falls out of the sky like a meteor from heaven. The two men say a silent prayer as their lives flash before their eyes. Perez pulls up on the stick with all of his strength. He is able to slow Beauty down somewhat, but not enough to stop them from crashing or have a controlled landing. Unfortunately, his efforts are to no avail. Beauty falls fast, hitting every tree in its path.

"Brace yourself for impact, Chief!"

Beauty hits the ground hard. Still strapped to his seat, Chief Warrant Officer 4 Anderson flies through the windshield head first. His body is thrown up against a tree and ricochets off—his lifeless body falling limp to the ground like a rag doll.

The same grim fate does not befall First Lieutenant Perez. His seat remains safely secured in the helicopter. Instead, he hits his head on the instrument panel and passes out.

The Serb squad views the helicopter crash and quickens its pace toward its final resting place. They reach the site and spread out in a defensive position around the helicopter. The squad leader and his two team leaders move to the helicopter to inspect the wreck. They start from the rear and slowly pace around the right side to the front. Upon inspecting the front of the helicopter, they realize that the copilot and his seat are no longer where they should be. They look to the front of the helicopter and spot the copilot's body sprawled out on the ground.

"Go check on the condition of that body," the squad leader orders his Bravo team leader.

The Bravo team leader jogs over to the body and investigates the scene. Through the course of his inspection, he discovers that the head is destroyed in such a manner that the copilot's face is unrecognizable. The team leader rummages through all of the copilot's pockets and secures everything that his hands touch.

While the Bravo team leader inspects the fallen copilot, the squad leader and his Alpha team leader check on the pilot's condition. The squad leader touches the pilot's chest and realizes that he is still alive. He turns to the Alpha team leader and says, "Call the medics. We've got a live one."

1030 Hours: West Point

There are many eventful moments that cadets experience during their years at West Point. One such reoccurring moment is Reorganization Week. The first day of Reorganization Week, which is referred to as R-Day, always falls on a Wednesday. R-Day is the day when the new cadets march back from Lake Frederick to join their academic-year companies. The new cadets are entitled as such because they have not yet been accepted into the Corps of Cadets. That moment will come upon completion of the Acceptance Day parade, which is held on the upcoming Friday. Once the new cadets have marched in the Acceptance Day parade, they are no longer referred to as new cadets, but are now truly cadets. Of course, they are plebes, so their lives really do not improve significantly.

Sitting in his room, Cdt. Milton Aynes Johnson, known to everyone as "Major," due to the spelling of his initials, is speaking with his first sergeant, XO, and TO.

"With the kids coming in tomorrow morning, I want to do something big that's going to shock the hell out of them yet at the same time set the tone early and let them know that we're all about business. I was thinking about playing Darth Vader's theme song while they march into the company area."

"We can't do that, sir," Cdt. 1st Sgt. Dustin Bradford interjects. "Second Battalion's using that song. They have dibs on it since they are the empire."

"Understood," Major agrees.

"How about this?" Sara adds. "Let's play our theme song as the plebes march to the company area?"

The D-1 theme song is George Thurogood's "Bad to the Bone." The Ducks embraced the song back in 1986. No one is really sure why "Bad to the Bone" is the Ducks' theme song since it has nothing to do with ducks. Being that the song is such an oxymoron to how most would define a duck, "Bad to the Bone" has stuck with the company ever since.

"I think we should play our song," Major agrees, "but that doesn't strike fear into anyone's heart. Check out my idea. I want to have all of the team leaders standing in a line on the stoops where most of our company is. As the first sergeant marches the plebes over to the company area, I want some loud, angry classical song playing. I'll find one. First Sergeant"— Major turns and faces Dusty—"I want you to march the kids to the middle steps, halt them two feet in front of the steps, then have them form up into two even ranks. Once the plebes are properly formed up, I want one team leader at a time to walk to the front of the step and call his plebe's name out. That plebe will then fall out of the formation and go with his team leader. Once the last plebe has been taken, we'll play our song. How's that sound?"

"I like it, sir," Dustin agrees.

Sara shakes her head in approval.

Joe, on the other hand, states, "That's good and all, Major, but have you looked at the training schedule?"

"What do you mean?" Major curiously asks.

Joe gets up from his seat on the couch and walks over to his desk. He grabs his training schedule from off of his desk and hands it to Major.

Major glimpses over the training schedule quickly then suddenly blurts, "Are you kidding me!? When was this added?"

"It was a change that I got this morning after breakfast," Joe explains. "All of the training officers had a meeting with the brigade training officer."

"I swear to God! I am already sick of this, and the school year hasn't even started yet!" Major gruffly states.

"I'm sorry, Major. I thought that since I had the info, then you had it, too."

"Don't worry about it. From now on, we have to ensure that we are passing info on to one another, regularly. Shoot! That's why I made us roommates anyway." Major faces Sara's direction and asks, "Did you get any word of this change?"

"Kind of. Ann told me about it last night before we went to bed. She told me so nonchalantly that I assumed that you already knew. If I'd have known that you didn't know about the change, I would've told you at formation this morning."

"I know you would have," Major sympathizes. "Well, guys, I guess we all learned a valuable lesson here. We have to make sure that we keep each other informed on every issue that pops up, whether we think one of us knows about it or not. We don't need anymore surprises like this," Major emphasizes as he waves the training schedule in the air.

The change to the training schedule that the four cadets are referring to is in reference to the third class cadets. They have an information brief on the proper installation of their plebe's computer at 1155 hours, the same time that the fourth class cadets march back from Lake Frederick and join their academic-year companies.

"Sir, what are we going to do about the yucks and their brief?" Dustin asks. "They are the key element to the entire operation, and personally I feel that the team leader is the first person in the plebes' chain of command that they should meet."

"I agree, Dust," Major replies. "I'm going to talk to the BAT and REG coms and see what's up. Hopefully, we can get this thing resolved and have the yucks where they need to be. If you guys don't have anything else to add or tell me, then y'all can get out of here if you want."

"I have to go run, so I'll see you when I get back," Joe states as he darts out of the room.

Dustin and Sara stay with Major to help him formulate how he is going to approach the battalion and regimental commanders on tomorrow's yearling situation.

"The way I see it," Major opens, "the yearlings' place of duty is with their plebes, not at some stupid briefing. Most of them know more about their plebe's computers than the people who are giving the brief."

"I agree, sir," Dustin adds, "but you might get in trouble if you keep the yucks out of the brief. Technically, that's their place of duty."

"He's right, Major. If you keep them from their briefing, you could get busted," Sara agrees.

"You guys are right, but I'll take the hit on this one. We all agree that the yucks need to be in the company area, not down in South Aud. If Captain Weiss or anyone else says anything, I've got it. It's a hard decision, but it's the right one," Major affirms. "Are we all on the same page on this issue?"

Sara and Dustin both nod their heads in agreement.

"Good," Major happily responds. "Dustin, I want you to put it out to the platoon sergeants. Stress to them the importance of the yucks knowing that they must stay in the company area, and not go down to South Aud for the brief tomorrow."

"Roger, sir," Dustin dutifully answers. "Anything else?"

"Naw. Other than the remainder of the checklist, that's about it. Let everyone know that they're doing a great job. We're ahead of all of the other companies in the regiment."

"Roger that, CO," Dustin blurts. He springs from his seat and exits his room to take care of his first-sergeant duties.

"So you're really going to tell Donaldson and Putter that our yucks aren't going to the brief tomorrow, huh?" Sara asks.

Cdt. Capt. Michael Donaldson is First Battalion, First Regiment's Commander, and Cdt. Capt. Albert Putter is the First Regiment Commander.

"You're darn right, I am!" Major boldly states.

Major gets up from the seat behind his desk, moves over to his couch, and stretches his legs out on the coffee table. As Major moves, he continues, "If they disagree with my command decision, then I'll take the hit. Like I said earlier, the yucks' number 1 priority this week are their plebes, not some dumb computer brief that 99 percent of them are already near experts in."

"I agree with you fully. I thought it was somewhat weird when I heard about the schedule change last night. I can't remember a time when the yearlings weren't around for the plebes' initial introduction to their new companies. If you need me to back you up on this one, you know I'm here," Sara states.

"I appreciate that, XO," Major replies with a smile. He reaches out across the table and gives Sara a five. "I appreciate you having my back, but I've got this one," Major continues. "If I need you, I'll yell for you." Major throws his feet off of the table then sluggishly raises himself from off of the couch. "Well, I guess I had better go up and see Donaldson first, don't want to break the chain of command. I'll let you know how it goes."

"Knock 'em dead," Sara states as Major heads for the door.

Sara rises from her seat on Joe's bed and walks out of the room behind Major. They hang a left at the staircase and walk upstairs. At the top of the stairs, they reach Sara's room, where she enters. Major continues down the small hallway and turns left to face Donaldson's room.

Instead of knocking on the door, Major simply walks in. "Hey, Mike!" Major blurts as he enters Donaldson's room.

"Hey, Johnson. What's up?" Donaldson answers.

"I need to talk to you about something."

"Sure. Take a seat." Donaldson motions for Major to take a seat in his roommate's chair.

Major takes a seat in the cushioned swivel chair. As he sits, he begins his explanation. "I don't know if you saw the change to the training schedule, but did you notice that the yucks have to go to a computer brief the same time we're receiving the new cadets?"

"No, I didn't. Who did you find this out from?"

"My training officer and my XO. Ann told Sara last night, and Joe had some training officer meeting after breakfast where he was briefed on it."

"That's weird 'cause Jones and Anne didn't tell me about it," Donaldson remarks, rubbing his chin. Cadet Jones is the Battalion Adjutant (S-1).

Donaldson gets up from his seat and walks over to Jones's desk. "Excuse me, Johnson," Donaldson says to Major as he reaches for the top desk drawer.

Major rolls himself out of the way and waits for Donaldson to finish rummaging through the drawer.

"Here we go," Donaldson says, lifting his head up. "Let's take a look here," he says, scanning Jones's copy of the training schedule. "Here's the change right here, Johnson."

Major gets up from his seat and goes over to Jones's desk, where Donaldson is standing with the updated training schedule. "So what are we going to do?" Major asks.

"I'm not sure yet. I'm going to have to go talk to Putter about this," Donaldson answers.

"Yeah, I figured as much. Just so you know though, my yucks have already been ordered not to attend the brief. I want them in the company area when the new cadets get here tomorrow," Major informs Donaldson.

"Dully noted, but be prepared to augment your decision. I don't really know what Putter's guidance is going to be on this."

"Got you," Major answers, raising his eyebrows quickly. "I'm going to bounce now, you have anything for me before I go?"

"No. I'll get in contact with you as soon as I can."

"All right then. I'll see you, dawg," Major states as he leaves Donaldson's room.

On his way back to his room, Major says to himself, *I hope Putter sides with me on this, but either way, my kids are going to be at my formation and not at that stupid brief.*

18 AUGUST 1999

0900 Hours: Red Bank, New Jersey

The New Jersey suburb, just an hour south of New York City, minus traffic, of course, is home to Amos Man Killer Stewart, loving husband and father. Most people refer to him as "Killer." There are many places where Killer goes that warms his heart, but nothing beats home. Home is where his family is. When Killer is home, he does not have to stress about someone trying to kill him or vice versa. He can lift, run, work in the yard, and, more importantly, play with his kids. That is what Killer loves most of all—playing with his kids: Doug, seven, Pete, five, and Angela, three. His kids mean more to him than anything. Sometimes, he wonders how his continuously being away from home for such extended periods of time affects his kids. Killer knows that they are happy. He can see it in their faces every time he returns home and hears it in their voices when he speaks to them on the telephone before he boards a plane for an upcoming assignment. Killer just feels that he is missing out on his kids growing up. He feels more like a regular visitor than permanent party. He knows that something is going to have to be done to remedy the situation because he cannot continue living this lie. Killer is going to have to talk to Mac and J about it.

Killer lies in bed. Since he is not on assignment, he can sleep as late as he likes. There is nothing he hates more than wasted time, so instead of just lying in bed all day, Killer decides to get up and do some work in the yard. Killer rolls over to the left side of the bed, which is Sharon's side, and notices a note on the nightstand, leaning up against her reading lamp. Killer reaches for the note and opens it. The note reads:

Hey Babe,

If it's like any other day when you're home, then you're probably reading this note at about nine o'clock or so. Just so you know, the boys are at school and already know to come straight home afterward. They have football practice over at Payton Park at five. Make sure they get there. Angie's at Susan's. I told her that you were home and that you would probably pick Angie up early. I shouldn't be any later than seven, can't wait to see what you throw together for dinner. I'm thinking of you...

Your Love,
Sharon

Killer smiles after reading his wife's note and thinks to himself, *Yet another reason to get out of the business.*

Killer folds the note up while getting out of bed. He then walks to his dresser and places the note in his top drawer among all of the other notes and letters that Sharon and his children have written him over the years.

Killer looks over at the clock that is on the bottom of the television and notices that it is 9:05 AM. "God, she's good," Killer whispers, shaking his head in reference to Sharon's ability of knowing what time he was going to wake up. Killer has never been able to comprehend how his wife is able to peg him so easily.

I guess that's why we're married, Killer laughingly thinks as he walks to his closet.

He retrieves his running shoes, shorts, and a white T-shirt. Killer sits on the edge of the bed and quickly gets dressed. Dressed, he dashes down the stairs and immediately starts off on a four-mile run. Most people would stretch first, but not Killer. He likes to just get the run knocked out. He knows his body well enough and relies on it so often that he knows whether he has a strained muscle or not. In any case, straining or pulling a muscle is the furthest thing from Killer's mind and, as far as he is concerned, is as likely to occur as a cow jumping over the moon.

Finishing his run in just under half an hour, Killer jogs to the backyard and begins his hour-long routine of Yoga and Thai Chi. Killer performs both exercises for the relaxing effect they have on his body. Moreover, it is always good to stay flexible. In Killer's line of work, he never knows when his life is going to rely on full body mobility and control.

West Point

Major sits at his desk, checking his e-mail and shuffling through some company paperwork. All that is on his mind is how smooth everything is going to go once the new cadets march in from Lake Frederick. Major has been waiting for this day for a long time, and now it is finally here.

Today's the big day! Major happily thinks to himself, pumping his right fist in the air.

As Major engulfs himself in personal joy, he hears three knocks at his door. "Enter!" Major loudly calls.

Quickly, the door swings open and his first sergeant enters. "Hey, sir, I rehearsed the ceremony with the team leaders and briefed the platoon sergeants on how everything's going to work today. I had to change a few things, but I know you'll like it."

"No problem with the changes. Whatever it is, I know they're good," Major replies. "Donaldson e-mailed me last night and said that we're cleared to have our yucks not attend the computer briefing today. We just need to ensure that our information systems officer and NCO are present. I don't see any problem with that, so as far as I'm concerned, we're good to go. I already told Sara. She's going to make sure that the IS team's at the brief."

"That's great to hear, sir. It's good to see the upper chain of command listen to reason."

"I hear you on that, First Sergeant," Major replies as he spins in his chair. "Do you have anything else for me?"

"Yes, I do. I got an e-mail this morning stating that we need to volunteer three people for the Lake Frederick baggage detail."

Major stands up then shakes his head. "I want my entire chain of command present today, so get three staff NCOs to do it. Tell them they can get two days of PMI (post meridian inspection) for it."

West Point has three types of inspections: SAMIs, AMI, and PMI. SAMI, or Saturday AM Inspections, are when the cadets' rooms have to be in total compliance with the regulations. Cadets loathe SAMIs because they are the most stringent of all inspections. There are moments when it takes an entire evening for cadets to clean their rooms in preparation. SAMI generally occur on the Saturdays of home football games, but the chain of command can hold a SAMI whenever it feels.

AMI inspections are not nearly as stringent as SAMIs. AMI generally occurs every school day from the moment the cadet wakes in the morning until lunch formation. During AMI, the wardrobe doors must remain open and the hanging clothes must be within regulation. The only technical difference between a SAMI and AMI is that during AMI, the dresser drawers are closed, thus allowing the cadets to place miscellaneous items in them.

PMI is the less stringent on inspections. The wardrobe doors are closed; therefore, only the room itself is open for inspection. Because the drawers and the wardrobe are closed, the cadets do not have to do much cleaning in the morning. They simply throw whatever items they want into the drawers and wardrobe and go about their business. The room is only inspected for cleanliness. Also during PMI, cadets are allowed to sleep in their beds. There is nothing a cadet loves more than sleeping during the day.

"Yes, sir," Dusty responds. "Do you have anything else?"

"Naw. That's about it. I'll be walking around the area, if you need me. If you can't find me, find the XO. She'll be around as well. I may be in and out of meetings until the plebes get here. Hopefully, the meetings won't take too long."

Major grabs the back of Dusty's neck and squeezes it as they walk out of the room and down the hallway. Major releases his grip as they step onto the stoops. Dusty leaves the area and enters another division to take care of his first-sergeant duties.

The South Bronx, New York City, New York

Though Douglas "Big Mac" Pollard lives in the South Bronx, he by no means lives in poverty. Many years ago, he decided to live in the Dominican section of the South Bronx to keep his wits up and maintain some of his edge while he was not on assignment. Mac bought the building that he lives in eight years ago. His self-appointed landlord, Miguel, keeps the apartment building in very good shape. Because Mac is away so often, it is not possible for him to properly run his building, so he gave Miguel the freedom to make important decisions such as evicting tenants. Mac has some of the lowest apartment rates in the city. Though his rates are low, he does not allow just anyone to move in. Mac is very particular of who resides in his building. All of his tenants hold a respectable job of some sort and pay their rent on time. They neither sell nor use drugs, or at least they are discreet about their illegal activities. Mac's apartment is on the top floor. He had the entire floor converted into a penthouse. Mac has his space and his privacy, which he likes very much.

Last night was a very long night for Mac—a long night of drinking and partying with hip-hop celebrities and ghetto superstars. Mac is a close friend of a very renowned hip-hop artist who was one of his squad mates in the Marine Corps when they were first stationed at Camp Pendleton, California. Whenever Mac goes home between assignments, he contacts his friend and hangs out with him. Heavy partying is Mac's way of letting off the continuous steam and frustration that the business builds up inside of him.

Mac's friend, who is known to the world as X, is aware that Mac is rarely ever in the South Bronx for an extended period of time because X grew up in the South Bronx and still maintains many of his childhood and adolescent contacts. Though Mac and X are extremely close friends, like the rest of the world, X is totally in the dark as to how Mac earns a living. X does, though, continuously ask Mac to take over as his head of security.

Whenever X asks him this question, Mac simply laughs and says, "Naw, dawg. I want to roll with you, not work for you."

Well, last night was a good night/morning for Big Mac. He started partying at ten o'clock at night and did not return home until six in the morning. Partying, as Mac does, is hard on the body, but great for the soul. Although he stayed out all night, Mac does not like to stay in bed all day. He makes it a point to wake up at ten o'clock every morning. This way, his body will not become accustomed to too much rest. When Mac is on an assignment, he is unable to sleep for extended periods of time, so he makes every attempt to keep his sleep cycle as regular as possible.

As Mac comfortably sleeps, his alarm clock goes off, alerting him that it is time for him to start a new day or, in the case of last night, complete the remainder of the day. Mac rolls over to his clock radio and shuts off Cool DJ Red Alert in midsentence.

Mac slowly sits up and says to himself, "What am I going to do today?"

Mac does not have too many hobbies. The one thing that he likes to do that calms his nerves even more than partying is drawing. Mac has been drawing since kindergarten, mostly superheroes and beautiful women. Many of his friends and teachers thought that Mac was very talented. Mac wanted to stress fine arts in his high school curriculum, but his father told him that, "Real men don't take art classes," so instead, Mac took auto shop. His father's disapproval caused Mac to cease drawing until he enlisted in the United States Marine Corps.

Mac jumps out of bed and immediately into the shower. After his quick shower, Mac throws on a pair of shorts and goes into the kitchen to get himself half of a honeydew melon and a bowl of Sugar Smacks. With his breakfast in hand, Mac walks to his TV room to watch a videotape of GI Joe cartoons while he eats.

Having eaten, Mac leaves his dishes on the floor in the den and goes to his personal study. He sits behind an architecture desk and begins drawing a series of his personally created superheroes performing various actions and body movements.

After about half an hour or so of drawing, Mac thinks to himself, *Let me give the Killer a call and see what he and the family are up to.* Mac picks up his portable phone and quickly dials Killer's home phone number.

1130 Hours: West Point

Standing out on the stoops, Major soaks up the atmosphere, the warm sun beaming down on his face. Below him in Grant Area, cadets sporadically move to and fro in preparation of the new cadets' arrival. Major is not worried at all. He knows that everything is going to go as planned. His yearlings do not have to attend the computer brief and the first sergeant has rehearsed his little ceremony with them. If a knot does surprisingly occur in the plan, Major knows that he is prepared to handle it.

As Major stands and basks in the joy of his own little world, Sara sneaks up behind him and slaps him on the back. Major quickly turns around and faces Sara as she asks with a big grin on her face, "So, CO, you ready?"

"Hell yes!" Major boastfully acknowledges. "I've been waiting for this day for a long time now. You know?"

"Well, between you and me, I know you're going to do a great job. As far as I'm concerned, you're the only person I thought of who would make the right company commander, especially during the first semester. You're the right guy to set the standard for the plebes. Some people have it, and others don't. You, Major, definitely have it."

"Thanks, Sara. That really means a lot coming from you."

Sara winks at Major and taps him on his stomach. As CO and XO stand and converse with one another, Dusty crashes through the division door that is directly behind Sara and Major and pounces onto the stoops.

Seeing Major and Sara, the first sergeant stops in his tracks and says, "Hey, CO! I'm off to get the new cadets now."

"All right then, First Sergeant. I'll meet you over in Central Area."

"Roger, sir," Dusty replies as he continues in the direction in whence he was heading. Dusty is off to the apron where the new cadets' cadet basic training chain of command will release them and turn them over to their academic year chain-of-command.

As the first sergeant dashes off toward the apron, Major looks over at Sara, rubs his hands together, and says, "Let the games begin."

1145 Hours

"It's time to rock and roll, Sara," Major says as he glances at his watch.

Major, who is wearing his sword, takes it out of its scabbard and twirls it between his thumb and index finger twice. Major then pats Sara on the back as they step off of the stoops and head for Central Area.

Walking to Central Area, being what day it is, is not an easy task. Cadets move frantically from one place to another in preparation of the new cadets' arrival. There is a lot of loud noise mixed in the air, blaring in all directions from the barracks, much of the noise being loud music mostly from the works of Beethoven, Tschovstzky, Guns and Roses, and Metallica.

Sara and Major enter Central Area and join the other company commanders and executive officers in their battalion waiting for their battalion commander, Cadet Donaldson.

"'Sup, fellas? You all hype?" Major shouts to his fellow commanders, grabbing hold of Cadet Jon O'Hara in the process.

"Sure. Why not?" Cadet Charles snides.

"Aren't we excited?" Cadet Peterson snides. "With the way you sound, Brian, you would think that you don't like plebes."

"You're a smart dude, Rick," Cadet Charles retorts. "As far as I'm concerned, plebes suck."

"I guess we all know who the slug commander's going to be this semester," Jon sarcastically remarks. "Don't worry though. I'll make sure that Brian here doesn't get too crazy on us. We do have a reputation to uphold."

"You make sure you do that," Cadet Peterson adds. "Remember, Brian, plebes may suck, but they sure beat the hell out of yucks any day of the week."

All of the commanders and executive officers nod and laugh in agreement.

"Come on, Brian," Major chimes in. "If it weren't for plebes, where would we get our night-time snacks from? I don't know about you, but my mom hasn't sent me squat since I was at the prep, and that was a long friggin' time ago."

"Man, that sucks," Cadet O'Hara sympathizes.

"Not really," Major states. "I don't have to worry about carrying boxes from the mail room and whenever I need a snack, all I have to do is go by a plebe's room. There's nothing a plebe loves more than getting positive attention from an upperclassman. Plus my getting food from the plebes gives me an excuse to speak to them and see how they're doing."

"You're crazy, Major," Sara states as she shakes her head and squeezes Major's arm.

"I know," Major sarcastically replies.

As the group of cadet officers stands and casually talks among themselves, their battalion commander finally arrives.

"Hey, guys. Is everyone ready for the big day?" Cadet Donaldson states as he walks toward his commanders.

The group turns and quickly looks at Donaldson. They snicker then turn back around and continue with their conversation. Cadet Donaldson, a tad bit uncomfortable, joins his conversing commanders.

Donaldson attempts to join in on the conversation by saying, "The first sergeants should be here in about two minutes."

Cadet O'Hara looks down at his watch and says, raising his eyebrows, "You're right, Mike."

Major faces Donaldson and asks, "Putter's not going to be here, right?"

"No, he isn't," Cadet Donaldson replies. "He figured that since the battalion formations are split, he would just walk around and observe."

"Cool," Major says. "You all ready for your big speech?"

"Sure am!" Donaldson enthusiastically replies. "I've got it right here! You want to hear it?" he asks Major as he reaches his hand toward his back pocket.

"Naw, dawg. I'll just wait for the ceremony."

"Oh. Okay," Mike replies, somewhat disappointed, as he removes his hand from his back pocket.

Donaldson then turns and looks in the direction between the sally port that connects Washington Hall and Eisenhower Barracks.

"Look guys!" Donaldson shouts, pointing. "The new cadets are coming."

Jon pats Donaldson on the back, raises his eyebrows, and says, "Well, I guess you can give that speech now, huh?"

Donaldson stands there, not knowing how to react to Jon's comment. Seeing that Donaldson is not going to counter Jon's friendly attack, the commanders all separate and head for their respective company formation areas.

As Major and Sara begin to trot over to D-1's formation area, Major swings his sword in the air and shouts, "Let the games begin!"

Through the sally port, the new cadets of Company Alpha-1 are the first in line, led by their first sergeant. Major watches the procession impatiently. He bounces a little in anticipation of his new cadets' arrival. As Major waits, he watches. In the distance, a group of new cadets marches through the sally port that connects Bradley Long and Bradley Short Barracks. Major is unsure as to what company they are in because he cannot read the company's name off of its guidon, which is blowing lightly in the wind. All Major knows is that they are in Second Regiment, more exactly, Second Battalion, Second Regiment, due to the direction in which they are heading.

After a few minutes, Sara spots Dusty out in front of the new D-1 new cadets, marching out of the sally port. With a big smile on her face, Sara hits Major in the stomach with the back of her hand and says, "Here they come, Major!"

"Yeah," Major sighs.

"Hey," Sara begins. "I'm going to go back to the barracks and make sure that everything is ready for the new cadets' arrival."

"That'll work. I'll see you in a few minutes then," Major responds.

Sara leaves the Ducks' formation area and returns to Grant Barracks, the sound of multiple cadence calling echoing in the background.

To the cry of a loud, boisterous cadence, Dusty marches the D-1 new cadets into the company formation area. As the new cadets move into position, Major gets out of the way by standing up against Pershing Barracks. Once the new cadets are in their proper position, the first sergeant halts the formation and executes an about-face. Major places his sword back into its scabbard then marches to the front of the formation and faces his first sergeant.

Dusty renders a salute and says, "Sir, thirty-nine assigned, thirty-five present, four new cadets are at Michie Stadium for football practice."

Major softly says to Dusty so only he can hear, "Good work," then returns Dusty's salute. Immediately following, Major turns his head to the right and barks with a loud and powerful command voice, "Post!"

The first sergeant executes a right face and marches to the rear of the formation. As he steps off, Major gives the command of "Parade rest!" to his new cadets. The new cadets snap to the position of parade rest and silently stand in place, waiting for further commands.

Mike Donaldson, who is standing at the head of the battalion formation, watches all of the companies move into position. Noticing that all of the company commanders have their new cadets at the position of parade rest, Mike moves to the position of attention and shouts, "Battalion!"

The company commanders, in unison, snap to the position of attention, wait one second, cock their heads to the right, then shout, "Company!"

"Attention!" commands Cadet Captain Donaldson.

The entire battalion, minus the company commanders who are already at attention, briskly moves to the position of attention.

Once the entire battalion is at attention, Cadet Captain Donaldson gives the preparatory command of "Officers draw!" With the command given, the company commanders simultaneously take their scabbard with their left hand and grab their sword handle with their right, pulling the sword out approximately two inches.

On Cadet Captain Donaldson's command of "Sabers!" the commanders pull their swords out of their scabbards and bring their hand down to their right side with the sword pointing skyward.

"Report!" Cadet Captain Donaldson commands.

As each company commander renders his accountability report to the battalion commander, they first raise their sword handle to eye level, the sword canted at a forty-five-degree angle. Once the company commanders drop their salute, they then render the report.

"Alpha Company: thirty-eight assigned, thirty-seven present!"

"The Barbarians have forty assigned and thirty-seven present!"

"Commandos: thirty-nine assigned, thirty-nine present!"

"The Mighty Ducks have thirty-nine assigned and thirty-five present!"

"Stand at!" Cadet Captain Donaldson commands.

The commanders shout, "Stand at!"

"Ease!"

The Battalion moves to the position of parade rest then turns their heads toward Donaldson's direction. The company commanders do the same, except that they only place their left hand in the small of their backs and drop their swords to a forty-five degree angle: blade pointing toward the ground.

Cdt. Capt. Mike Donaldson, at this very moment, feels more pride than he ever had his entire life. Here he is in the middle of a crowd of people whom he leads who are supposedly intrigued on every word that he says. Mike walks out to the middle of his formation. As he does so, he reaches into his back pocket and takes out his preplanned speech.

Before he speaks, Mike slowly spins around and takes a quick look at his battalion. Inwardly, he smiles, but outwardly, he shows little, if any, emotion.

"Good afternoon, new cadets!"

"Good afternoon, sir!" the new cadets loudly respond.

"Today, you begin the second phase on your path toward graduation. You are all a success because you made it out of Beast Barracks alive. Be proud in the battalion that you are now in. Our companies are the oldest of the corps and hold the most tradition. Consider it an honor to be a part of First Battalion, First Regiment. During the remainder of the week, your companies will prepare you for acceptance so that you can truly become a part of the corps and hopefully, in four years, join the Long Gray Line."

Cadet Captain Donaldson, having finished his speech, refolds the paper and returns it to his back pocket. He then returns to his original position at the head of the battalion and immediately goes to the position of attention.

"Battalion!" Donaldson commands.

"Company!"

"Attention! Company Commanders, take charge of your units."

The commanders salute Cadet Captain Donaldson then execute an about-face, facing their new cadets.

Major, now facing his Ducks, shouts, "First Sergeant!"

Dusty quickly marches to the front of the formation and stands between it and Major.

"Get the kids over to the company area so we can get this show on the road," Major says to Dusty as he is saluting.

"Roger that," Dusty replies with a big grin on his face, rendering the salute, then quickly dropping it.

Major steps off and away from the formation and jogs toward Grant Barracks in anticipation of the little ceremony that he had planned for his new cadets.

Standing on the side of the road between Pershing and Grant Barracks is Sara. As Major approaches her, he notices that Sara does not look too pleased.

"What's up?" Major asks.

"Let me show you," Sara gruffly states as she leads Major to Grant Barracks.

As Major and Sara cross the street, he looks at Grant Barracks and no longer needs Sara to explain to him what the problem is. On the sidewalk, Major's entire company stands, instead of on the stoops and in the formation that they were supposed to be in. The reason: Second Battalion, First Regiment decided to take it upon itself to occupy all of Grant Barracks for their new-cadet introduction. There are cadets standing shoulder to shoulder on D-1's stoops and cadets standing an arm's length apart on the balcony overhang. For a new cadet, it is an ominous sight, but for Major it is nothing more than an eyesore.

Major is furious, but he controls his emotions enough to only clinch his fists. He says to himself, *I know they did this 'cause we're the only company in First Battalion living over here. This is intolerable! I don't care if they hold their formations here every day. This is my company area, and no one is allowed to occupy my barracks unless I say so, and God knows I didn't give anyone a go on this cluster!*

Once on the other side of the street, Sara, who by this time is quite upset, quickly turns around, faces Major, and says, "You see?"

"Yeah, I do," Major calmly replies. "Don't worry though. I'll deal with this. Go let the first sergeant know what's going on and tell him to stand fast on the road."

"All right," Sara replies as she runs off to meet the first sergeant across the street.

With Sara gone, Major walks over to his idle and perturbed company and says, "Don't worry. This mess is getting straightened out right now. PLs, platoon sergeants, come with me!"

Major marches onto Grant Area, his platoon leaders and platoon sergeants following close behind. Major is focused and determined. There is only one thing on his mind, and that is to get the Second Battalion slugs out of his company area.

The small yet determined group march up the middle stairs onto the stoop. Major steps forward and sternly states, "I want all of you out of my company area right now!" He looks up at the balcony overhang where there are numerous cadets standing, points to them, and shouts, "That goes for you too!"

The cadets on the overhang look bewilderedly at one another for a second, not really sure as to what is going on, then climb through the windows, abandoning their positions. Those on the stoop, however, are not so anxious to leave.

As the cadets from the overhang make their way downstairs onto the stoop below, a cadet officer from Second Battalion approaches Major and says, "Hey, Johnson, our battalion's holding its indoctrination ceremony right now. Can you wait another ten minutes or so?"

"No! We can't!" Major sternly states. "No one came to me, my XO, or my first sergeant, asking us if they could use D-1's portion of Grant Barracks."

"Well, I'm asking you now."

"Well, since you're asking, the answer is no! I want everyone off my stoop now! It would be better if you do it rather than me. You know what I'm saying?"

"Yeah, yeah," the cadet officer replies, pissed at the fact that he has to follow Cadet Johnson's orders.

As the cadets of Second Battalion leave the Ducks' area, Major turns to his lower-level chain of command and says with a smile on his face, "That wasn't too bad, was it?"

"No, but I was waiting for you to hit that dude, though," Cadet Brian Christopher, Major's First Platoon platoon leader, jokingly states.

"You know it would've been on if I did," Major replies, elbowing Brian in the chest.

Major looks out over the road and signals for Sara to have the first sergeant to continue marching the new cadets into position. Major then turns back to his chain of command and says, "Let's do this."

The platoon leaders and platoon sergeants run off of the stoops and inform their platoons that it is time to perform the ceremony. The yucks move up onto the stoops and everyone else falls into two lines, starting at the base of the middle steps, forming a gauntlet.

━━━━━━━━━━━━━━━━━━━━

Watching D-1 reclaim their company area is E-1's company commander, Cdt. Capt. Stephen George. He is not pleased as to what is occurring. His battalion, which consists of companies E-1, F-1, G-1, and H-1, had planned for days on their new-cadet indoctrination ceremony, and now Cadet Johnson has just ruined it.

Cadet George says to himself, *I'm going to have to have a word with Johnson!* He steps away from his company area and down the stairs into D-1's area, more commonly known as Duckland.

Major, who is standing on the far side of the stoops closest to the road, notices Cadet George coming toward him. He says to himself, *Uh oh. George doesn't look too happy. Let me go talk to him.*

Major leaves his position and meets Cadet George half way, shouting, "Curious George! How's it going?"

"What's going on, Johnson?" Cadet George opens.

"Nothing. Just getting ready for my new cadets' arrival."

"Well, you know that you've ruined Second Battalion's ceremony, right?"

Major places his hands on his hips and looks around and out toward Grant Area where Second Battalion's commander is still speaking to his cadets. "I guess it looks that way. Huh, George?" Major counters.

Major then thinks to himself, *I'm going to have to flip this on George so he understands where I'm coming from.*

Major continues as if no thought has run through his head. He places his arm around Cadet George's shoulder and calmly states, "Look at it like this, George. You'd be pissed as hell if I, or any other commander, had taken over your company area. Right?"

"You're damn right!"

"Of course I am. So look at the situation from my perspective. I come to my company area and find a mess load of cadets from other companies occupying my barracks. There was only one thing I could do, and that was to clear them out of my AO (area of operation). As far as I was concerned, I had no other option."

"I guess you're right, but I still don't like what you've done, Johnson. You've singlehandedly ruined three days' worth of preparation."

"Well, maybe if you all would have prepared properly, like gotten in contact with me, then we wouldn't be in this mess to begin with. Anyway, you don't have to like what I've done. All you can do is accept it."

"Well, I'm still going to have a word with my battalion commander about this."

"You do that. You know where I live. Now if you don't mind, I have new cadets to indoctrinate into the ways of Duckdom." Major removes his arm off of Cadet George then turns his back to him and goes over to speak to Joe about the remainder of the day.

Cadet George drops his head in defeat and leaves Duckland. He heads back to his company area, upset at the fact that he lost an argument to Cadet Johnson—an argument that he could not have won because D-1 was in the right and Johnson never backs down to anyone.

■————————————————————————■

The yearlings are all assembled on the stoops in a single line. The backs of their heels are up against the wall. The remainder of the company stands down on ground level in two single file lines, beginning at the base of the middle steps, thus forming a gauntlet.

Seeing that everyone is in position, Major signals to his training sergeant to start playing the music. Second Battalion has finally finished their ceremony, so Major does not have to worry about bothering them any further. The music of choice is the *1812 Overture*, while the new cadets timidly stand in the gauntlet, followed by George Thorogood's "Bad to the Bone" once all of the new cadets have paired up with their team leaders.

The first sergeant marches the new cadets to the sidewalk's edge on the Grant Barracks side of the road then brings them to a halt. He then gives them the command of "Files from the left, column half left!"

Simultaneously, the new cadet in the first column turns his head to the left and loudly sounds off with "Column half left!" while the three new cadets at the head of the other three columns sound off with, "Stand fast!"

"March!" the first sergeant commands.

Upon the command, the first new cadet marches forward, followed by the new cadets that are behind him. Through the gauntlet, the new cadets march. The first new cadet marches up the steps and onto the stoops. The new cadet that was behind the first new cadet halts at the bottom of the steps, thus trapping all of the new cadets within the gauntlet.

When the first new cadet marches up the steps and onto the stoops, she snaps to the position of parade rest and shouts, "Corporal, New Cadet Robertson reports!"

Upon the new cadet's report, a yearling assigned as New Cadet Robertson's team leader steps away from the wall and strides over to her. He gets in her face, looks her dead in the eye, and coldly states, "Come with me."

Red Bank, New Jersey

Killer is out working in his garden in the backyard. He has just returned from picking up his daughter Angie from the sitter's. Angie now plays in the yard as Killer works. Working out in the yard calms Killer. He likes the outdoors and enjoys gardening, something he picked up from his grandmother. Today, Killer decided to make a stone path encircling his garden. Instead of buying stones from a hardware store, as most people are likely to do, Killer drove up to Bear Mountain Park in the Palisades and personally selected rocks.

As Killer digs, his portable telephone that he had placed on the deck rings. Angie hears the phone as well and says, "Daddy. Daddy. The phone's ringing."

"Can you get the phone for Daddy, baby?" Killer says to Angie as he places his shovel down onto the ground.

"Okay." Angie drops the orange Nerf football that she was playing with then scurries up the deck steps and snatches the portable telephone up with her tiny hands. She runs to her daddy, lifts the telephone high over her head, and says, "Here, Daddy."

"Thanks, baby." Instead of taking the phone from out of Angie's hands, Killer snatches her up into his arms. Killer has caller ID, so when he looks at the display screen above the telephone buttons, he knows that it is Mac who is calling. Killer pushes the talk button, and Angie holds the phone to his ear as he begins to speak. "What's up, Mac? What're you up to?"

Hearing that it is Big Mac on the other end of the telephone, Angie takes the telephone away from Killer's ear and puts it up against her own. She then yells and giggles, "Hi, Uncle Doug!"

"Hey, Angie! How's my favorite girl?" Mac happily responds.

Mac does not have any children, so he treats Killer and Sharon's kids as though they were his nephews and niece.

"I'm great! I'm playing with Daddy today," Angie joyfully responds.

"That's great, princess. Are you having fun?"

"Uh huh. When Daddy stops playing with his rocks, we're going to play football."

"Really? Well, make sure you let your daddy win. You know how he gets when he loses."

"You're so funny, Uncle Doug."

Mac laughs at Angie's comment then says, "All right, baby, let me talk to your daddy now."

"Okay," Angie responds. She then places the receiver back onto her father's ear.

"So how's it going, brother?" Killer asks Mac.

"I'm chill. Just relaxing and trying to enjoy our time off. You know?" Mac replies.

"I hear you. I'm out here in the yard working in the garden, decided to build myself a stone path around the garden's perimeter."

"The things you do to relax. I party, and you work."

Both men laugh at Mac's statement.

"Well," Mac continues, "I was just calling to see how you and the family are doing."

"If you really want to know, how about coming over for dinner tonight? I'm cooking."

"What are we having?"

"Not really sure yet. I'll surprise you," Killer cynically responds.

"Well, whatever. As long as I'm not cooking, then it's all good."

"Yeah, I bet it is." After a brief silence, Killer continues. "How's eight sound?"

"That'll work."

"Then I'll see you at eight."

"Eight it is, then."

1600 Hours: West Point

The day is finally beginning to unwind. All of the cadets are performing their duties and ensuring that the new cadets get moved and settled into their rooms. Major and Joe, who have been quite busy today with supervising the day's activities and going to meetings, are in their room, enjoying peaceful solitude.

Major lays on his couch, his head propped up on the armrest by his pillow. Joe is lying in his bed. The two cadets are not sleeping, just laying there, relaxing, or, as Major likes to call it, meditating.

As he rests, Major has a brainstorm. Suddenly he sits up and says to Joe, "Hey, Joe. I've got a great idea."

"What is it?" Joe asks, still lying in bed with his eyes shut.

"Let's have Duck tryouts."

"Duck tryouts? What do you mean?"

"Think about it. We need a plebe to be the Duck, right?"

"Yeah."

"Well, the only way we can choose one and be fair about it is to have some form of a competition like tryouts."

Now that he is now in depth in a conversation, Joe sits up in his bed and swings his feet onto the floor.

"That doesn't sound too bad. What do you have in mind?" Joe asks as he straightens his back out.

"We can make some type of mini obstacle course and then have them dance."

"Dance?"

"Yes, dance. Think about it. If you're the Duck, you've got to know how to shake a tail feather," Major jokingly states.

"I guess you're right," Joe replies, laughing.

"What're the new cadets doing right now?"

"I don't know. Let me check." Joe gets up from his bed and walks over to his desk to check the training schedule. After a few seconds of perusing the training schedule, Joe looks over at Major, who is still on the couch, and says, "The new cadets don't have anything until dinner."

"Money!" Major shouts as he stands up from off of the couch. "I'm going to have the CCQ (cadet in charge of quarters) round up all of the new cadets and have them form up on the stoops," Major informs Joe as he puts his shoes back on."

"All right. I'll get the first sergeant and meet you out there," Joe replies as Major steps out of the room.

Major walks down the hall and turns right into the orderly room where the CCQ's desk is located. On duty today is third classman Cdt. Cpl. Shannon Gold.

Seeing Major enter the orderly room, Cadet Gold, with a huge grin on her face, says, "Hi, Major. How're you doing?"

"I'm good, Gold. You?"

"I'm okay, except for the fact that I'm on the Q."

"We've all been there," Major replies with his hands on his hips and a slight chuckle.

Major walks over to the CCQ desk, places both hands on it, and says to Cadet Gold, "I need you to round up all of the new cadets and have them form up on the stoops."

"Okay," Cadet Gold replies. She writes in the CCQ log that Cadet Johnson ordered her to form the new cadets up on the stoops then stands up and walks away from the desk. As she moves she turns toward Major and asks, "You don't mind me asking what this is about, do you?"

"Not at all," Major happily states. "I'm having Duck tryouts!"

"Oh! This should be fun!" Cadet Gold declares as she exits the orderly room on her way to retrieve the D-1 new cadets from their rooms.

Major steps out of the orderly room, behind Cadet Gold and runs into Joe and Dusty. Dusty is carrying the Duck suit and the Duck head. The Duck is the oldest mascot in the corps. Even more so, the Duck head is the most sought-after prize that a plebe from an outside company can attain. Major knows this and has a plan to counter any attempts by overzealous plebes and yucks from taking his Duck head.

Seeing Joe and Dusty, Major says to them as he begins to spring upstairs, "I'm going to go get Sara. Gold's rounding the plebes up right now. I'll meet you guys out there in a sec."

"All right," Joe replies as he and Dusty walk past Major and out onto the stoops.

Springing up the stairs, Major shouts, "Sara, Sara!" He quickly gets to the top of the stairs, where Major finds Sara standing in her doorway, waiting for him.

"What's up, Major?" Sara asks.

"We're holding Duck tryouts out on the stoops. Come on out."

"Ooh! This should be fun!" Sara excitingly responds.

Sara and Major run down the stairs and out onto the stoops, finding all of the new cadets lined up against the wall and Joe, Dusty, and Cadet Gold conversing with some of the new cadets.

When Dusty sees Major walk out onto the stoops, he shouts, "Fourth Class! Attention!"

On his command, all of the new cadets snap to the position of attention.

"Thanks, First Sergeant," Major says to Dusty. Major looks at the new cadets lined up against the wall and realizes that all thirty-five of his new cadets are not present. Sensing that something may be up, Major turns to Cadet Gold and asks her, "Gold, is this it?"

"These were the only new cadets that were in their rooms," Cadet Gold nervously answers.

"Ah, no big deal. They're probably out with their team leaders. Their loss, I guess," Major nonchalantly responds. "First Sergeant, give me a count real quick."

"Yes, sir," Dusty replies. Dusty walks to the middle of the new cadet line then gives the command of "Count! Off!"

Upon the command, all of the new cadets, except for the first one in line, turn their heads to the right. The first new cadet in line then shouts, "One!" the second, "Two!" and so on down the line. Immediately before the new cadets sound off with their numbers, they snap their heads back to the front. The last new cadet in line to sound off with his number shouts, "Twenty-four!"

Once the count is complete, Major faces the new cadets then calmly gives them the command of "At ease."

Upon the command, the new cadets relax their bodies, but they keep their hands behind their backs and their eyes on their company commander.

Major gingerly paces back and forth down the new cadet line. "Did Cadet Gold inform you all as to why I ordered you guys out here?" Major asks.

"No, sir," the new cadets respond in unison.

"Well, let me tell you then. I need a Duck mascot. Now it's not enough for me to just pick someone to be the Duck. Not anyone is capable of being the Duck. Understand that the Duck is the most notorious mascot in the corps. You have a reputation to uphold. Because it takes a special person to be the Duck, I decided that the best way to choose one of you to be the Duck is to have tryouts."

Major takes another trip down the line of new cadets and realizes that they are all wearing their white-over-gray uniform. Recognizing the need to change for the tryouts, Major says to the new cadets, "I want you guys to go upstairs and put on gym A. Be back in five minutes. Fall out."

With the command, the new cadets rush up to their rooms to change into their gym-A uniform. The gym-A uniform is what cadets wear for PT (physical training) or just whenever they want to relax.

After only about two minutes, two new cadets return from their rooms and fall back in onto the wall.

Major, who is sitting on the stoop's ledge, says to the two new cadets, "Hey! You two! I want you guys to go into the study room and bring six chairs out."

"Yes, sir!" the two new cadets shout. They leap from off of the wall and sprint past Major and his staff to retrieve chairs from the study room.

Both new cadets return to the stoops with a chair in both hands. As they return, Major orders, "Place the chairs down there." Major points to Grant Area.

The two new cadets do as they are ordered then return to the study room to retrieve one chair apiece. On their way back to the study room, Major bounces off of the ledge and goes down to Grant Area. He takes the chairs and evenly separates them so there is enough room for a full-grown person to weave through them.

While still separating the chairs, the two new cadets return with the last two chairs. As the new cadets step foot onto Grant Area, Majors tells them, "Put those at the end, fellas. Make sure they're spaced like the others."

After placing the final two chairs at the end of the line, the two new cadets return to the wall, where the remainder of the D-1 new cadets stand, waiting.

Major walks back up onto the stoops then gives the order of "At ease" to the new cadets, who immediately stand at ease.

"All right guys," Major begins, "Who wants to be the Duck?"

All twenty-four fists shoot out horizontal to the ground, all except for three.

Major walks over to the closest new cadet who does not have a fist out. The new cadet is no more than five feet, two inches tall. Major stands directly over her and asks, "What's your name, new cadet?"

"Sir, my name is New Cadet Rogers."

"Well, New Cadet Rogers, why don't you want to be the Duck?"

"Sir, I have cross-country practice every day. I do not believe that I will have time to do it."

"You know, if you did have the honor of being the Duck, it wouldn't interfere with cross-country."

"Sir, I also have really bad shin splints."

"I can't force you to try out because this is supposed to be fun, so how about I make you head of my enforcers."

"What's that, sir?"

"As head enforcer, you're the one who ensures that my Duck has proper protection whenever it makes a public appearance; like spirit rallies, and whatnot. I want at least six of you guys with the Duck at all times, carrying broomsticks. Do you think you can handle it?"

"Yes, sir!" New Cadet Rogers pridefully boasts with a large grin beaming across her face.

"We'll see," Major replies with a slight laugh under his breath. He then turns to the other two new cadets who do not want to be the Duck and asks them, "What's ya'lls story?"

A new cadet at the far end of the line answers, "No excuse, sir."

The other, who stands three spaces to the left of New Cadet Rogers, states, "Sir, I will tryout."

"Well, good," Major says to the former reluctant new cadet that is nearest him.

Major walks to the end of the line and faces the new cadet who still does not want to make an attempt at becoming the Duck.

"I say this," Major begins, "This is all for fun. I can't make you tryout, but if you don't want to, at least be an enforcer. All right?"

"Yes, sir," the new cadet replies.

"Good then," Major states, patting the new cadet on the shoulder. Major walks to the middle of the new-cadet line and states, "Fall in around me, guys."

The new cadets step away from the wall and crowd around Major.

"Here's what we're going to do for the tryouts."

Major forces his way through the new-cadet crowd and returns to Grant Area. Turning back to the new cadets, Major begins his explanation as to how the Duck tryouts are going to work.

"At the command of 'Go'," Major starts, "I want you to run through these chairs in a weave."

As Major instructs the new cadets, he walks through the obstacle. Standing at the end of the weave of chairs, Major points to the ground then to the stoops then continues his instruction. "Once you get here, I want you all to sprint back to the starting line then dance. Do not stop dancing until I tell you to. Is that understood?"

"Yes, sir!" the new cadets shout in affirmation.

Major jogs back up onto the stoops. Then, with his arms wide open toward the new cadets, he shouts, "So who's first?"

All of the new cadets jump up and down with great anticipation and desire to go first through the obstacle. Seeing that the new cadets are so enthralled in the upcoming event, Major makes matters easier on himself by randomly selecting a new cadet to go first.

Major places his hand on the shoulder of a male new cadet, who stands at five feet, eight inches tall, and says, "You're up!"

Major then turns his head to Joe and Dusty and says to them, "Let's get this kid in the suit."

Dusty and Joe, with the Duck suit in hand, walk over to where Major and the cluster of new cadets stand. As Major, Joe, and Dusty help the new cadet into the suit, Dusty asks him, "What is your name, new cadet?"

With the suit fully on, the new cadet boastfully replies, "First Sergeant, my name is New Cadet Zemory!"

"It's a good thing you know who I am, huh, New Cadet Zemory?" Dusty asks.

"Yes, sir!"

"All right, Zemory, let's see what you can do," Major declares.

Joe and Major help New Cadet Zemory down the stairs and onto Grant Area. Leaving New Cadet Zemory at the starting line of the obstacle course, Major and Joe return to the stoops.

Major turns to the impatiently waiting new cadets and shouts, "Let's get hype!"

Instantly, the new cadets begin to yell and cheer. As they cheer in jubilation, Major shouts down to New Cadet Zemory and says, "On your mark! Get set! Go!"

On "Go!" New Cadet Zemory starts the obstacle course. He weaves through the chairs, knocking down two with the Ducktail. When New Cadet Zemory reaches the end of the chairs, he sprints back down the right side of the chairs then dances. New Cadet Zemory throws his arms out and flaps them as if he were a giant eagle, while at the same time, bending his knees, while opening and closing them in time with the arm flapping.

As New Cadet Zemory performs the Duck tryout, all of the new cadets cheer him on. Major, Joe, Sara, Dusty and Cadet Gold laugh at the spectacle and the fact that the new cadets are enjoying the Duck tryouts. They are not laughing at the new cadets. They are laughing with them.

Dancing, Major shouts down to New Cadet Zemory, "Shake a tail feather, Zem!"

Hearing his company commander, New Cadet Zemory complies by bending forward at the waist and his knees then commences to fervently shake his butt. New Cadet Zemory's actions cause a large roar of cheers from his fellow Ducks who are watching on the stoops.

■————————————————■

After New Cadet Zemory's run through the makeshift obstacle course, several other new cadets run through, as well. The commotion that the Ducks are making attracts much attention to their activity. Numerous cadets who reside in Grant barracks walk out onto the stoops and peer out of their windows to view the Duck new cadets running around acting crazy.

Walking down the road between Pershing and Grant barracks is Captain Randall, a TAC from Second Regiment. Walking alongside him, but not with him, is a first sergeant from the same regiment. Captain Randall notices the cluster of new cadets lined up against the wall of Grant barracks and what appears to be a new cadet running through some chairs in Grant area. Captain Randall assumes that it is a new cadet because upperclassmen do not wear company mascot outfits. The other assumption that Captain Randall makes is that the upperclassmen are hazing the new cadets. If there is one thing that

Captain Randall cannot tolerate, it is the unnecessary hazing of fourth class cadets.

Upset at the actions that he is witnessing, Captain Randall motions for the first sergeant to come to his side. Captain Randall then points at Grant barracks and orders the first sergeant, "Go over there and tell them that when I walk back in this direction in five minutes, they better have ceased their activities."

Captain Randall continues in his previous direction toward Grant Hall, probably to get a sandwich. The first sergeant who Captain Randall gave the order to walks over to Grant barracks to deliver the ill-fated message.

———————————————————

Cheering his new cadets on, Major looks over to his right and notices a captain that he recognizes as a TAC from Second Regiment (he cannot remember his name though) watching what is going on in Grant Area. Uninterested in the officer, Major returns his attention to his new cadets. A few seconds later, he looks back to his right and notices the cow that was next to the TAC walking onto his stoops and the TAC walking away toward Thayer Road.

Curious as to why this cow is in his company AO, Major approaches him and asks, "What's up man?"

"Are you D-1's CO?" the first sergeant asks.

"Yeah, I am. What's up?"

"Well," the first sergeant snidely replies, "a captain has ordered me to tell you that if you don't cease with your present activities, then he's going to come over here and take care of the situation personally."

Major takes great offense to the first sergeant's message and the tone of voice that he is taking with him. Instead of blowing up at the misguided cow, Major takes two steps toward him and calmly, yet sternly, states, "Do you see what's going on here?" Major waves his hand over Grant barracks and area, illustrating the fact that everyone is enjoying themselves. "Not a single new cadet is being hazed. Look at them. They are all happy as hell and enjoying themselves. Now I want you to go back to that captain and tell him that everything is okay in my AO. If he isn't satisfied with that response, he can come over here and speak with me personally."

"I'll let him know that."

"Oh, and one more thing. I don't care who you're carrying a message for, but when you speak to a first class cadet, and in this case a company commander, you better show a little more respect and change the attitude in your voice real quick. Is that understood, First Sergeant?"

"Yes, it is," the first sergeant nervously answers. He is a bit shaken at the fact that Cadet Johnson actually corrected him on his obvious show of disrespect.

With the message delivered and Major's response given, the first sergeant leaves Grant barracks and continues on the path he was on before the captain had pulled him to the side.

———————◼—————————◼

Dustin, Sara, and Joe witness the altercation between Major and the first sergeant but did not interfere. As Joe says, "It's best that Major handles this guy on his own. It's what makes him a CO."

Sara and Dustin nod in agreement.

Once the first sergeant departs from Duckland, Major turns around and looks up at Sara, Dustin, and Joe. He then throws his hands up in the air and shouts, "Did you all see that? You have got to be kidding me?"

Joe, Dustin, and Sara walk over to where Major is standing, so he does not have to shout over the roar of the Duck tryout spectators.

"What was that all about anyway?" Joe asks.

"I guess some TAC saw the Duck tryouts from over there and thought that we were hazing our new cadets," Major explains as he quickly points to the chains next to the road.

"How could he think that?" Sara interjects. "Everyone's laughing and having a good time."

"I know," Major responds. "That's why I'm not worried about it."

"You think that TAC'll come over here and say something?" Dustin asks.

"Not sure, but I'm not really worried about it," Major answers. "We're not doing anything wrong, plus Captain Weiss'll have our backs on this."

"Yeah, he will," Joe agrees.

As the four cadets converse on the situation that had just occurred, Dustin looks out at the road and spots the TAC peering into Grant Area. "Hey look!" Dustin exclaims. "He's back."

Major, Sara, and Joe turn and face the road, eyeing the TAC watching the Duck tryouts.

"You think he'll come over?" Joe asks.

"Don't know. All we can do is wait," Major replies.

Covertly watching the TAC, the four cadets notice that instead of him walking over to the company area, the TAC simply eyeballs them and walks away from Grant and heads for Central Area.

"Well, that was a close one," says Sara.

"Yeah. Thank God!" Major exclaims. "The last thing I needed to deal with was some prick TAC. You know what I'm saying?"

"I hear you on that one," Joe affirms.

Having just dodged a possible near-butt chewing, Major, Joe, Sara, and Dusty turn their attention back to the Duck tryouts. By this time, the Duck yearlings are now out of their rooms and assisting the new cadets with the Duck tryouts, allowing the chain of command to sit back and enjoy the show.

Red Bank, New Jersey

Killer, finished with his garden project for the day, reclines in his black leather La-Z-Boy, drinking a giant cup of grape Kool-Aid and watching an episode of *The Cosby Show*. Angie is taking a nap, so he does not have to worry about being disturbed while he rests. His boys, Doug and Pete, are home from school. They are upstairs in their bedroom doing their homework. Killer enjoys helping Doug and Pete with their homework, but he allows them to go through it themselves first before he checks it and helps them correct their mistakes. Since Doug and Pete have football practice today, Killer will probably have to help them with their homework afterward.

Killer hears footsteps running around upstairs then some pattering going down the stairs. "Daaaad!" Killer hears Doug shout as he runs down the stairs. "Me and Pete are ready to got to practice now."

"All right!" Killer shouts back. He gets up from out of the La-Z-Boy. By this time, Doug is in the den with his father, holding his pads and his helmet in his hands. "You and your brother go wait for me in the yard. I'll go get your sister."

"Don't worry about that, Dad. Pistol already got her," Doug replies.

Pistol is what Killer and Doug call Pete, in homage to the great basketball player, Pistol Pete Marovich.

"You guys are too much," Killer chuckles, putting Doug in a headlock. Killer releases the hold as they walk out of the den together.

As father and son head for the front door, they witness Pete struggling down the stairs with Angie holding onto his left hand. "Don't leave without us, Dad," Pete says as he struggles to hold both his football equipment and help his little sister down the stairs.

"Come on now," Killer replies. "How can I leave without the Pistol?"

"Beats me," Pistol sarcastically responds as he shakes his head from side to side.

Pete and Angie finally make it down the stairs and chase after their dad and big brother out of the house. The family walks out to the black Suburban that is parked in the driveway. Killer hits the unlock button on his key ring. While Doug opens the passenger side door to let himself in, Killer opens the back door. Pete scurries in and throws his equipment onto the floor behind the driver's seat while Killer picks Angie up. Once Pete is set in his seat, Killer hands Angie to him, and together they secure her in her car seat.

After safely placing Angie in her car seat, Killer shuts the door and gets in on his side of the Suburban. With everyone buckled in, Killer turns his head to the back seat and shouts, "You guys ready?"

"Yeah!" all of the kids reply in unison as they back out of the driveway.

2005 Hours

An evening in the Stewart household is not like most, at least not when Killer is home, and definitely not when Mac is over for dinner.

When the two of them get together, combined with the energy of Killer's two sons, nothing but trouble is bound to happen. Since Doug and Pete have finished correcting their homework, they are free to wrestle with their dad and their Uncle Doug.

The relationship between Mac and the Stewart children is a very tight bond. So much so that it is only natural that they call him Uncle. Also because of the close bond that Mac and Killer share, it was only natural for Killer to make Mac the godfather to his children.

Doug is Mac's namesake. On their third assignment together, Mac saved Killer's life, and on that day, he swore on his grandfather's grave that if he survived the ordeal that he would name his first son after Big Mac. Needless to say, ten years later the Killer is still alive, and his oldest son's name is Douglas. Of course, that is not the story that Killer told Sharon.

There are many things that Killer loves about Mac. Though Mac is very carefree and loves to have a good time whenever his schedule permits, he is always punctual and never breaks an appointment unless he has contacted the individual he was going to meet first. Being that it is now 8:05 PM and Mac has been at the Stewart residence for about fifteen minutes, everyone can eat dinner.

"Soup's on!" Killer shouts from the kitchen.

"All right! Let's get our grub on!" Mac exclaims as he lifts Doug and Pete from off of the ground and carries them underneath both of his arms. Mac and the boys were wrestling before the dinner bell interrupted the match.

"Yeah!" the boys cheer.

Sharon, while placing Angela into her high chair, says to Mac, "You know, Mac, those boys're going to get you someday?"

"Don't count on it, sis. They may become bigger and stronger than me, but I guarantee you that they will never be able to overpower their Uncle Doug. Ain't that right, boys?" Mac jokingly states as he rubs Pete's and Doug's head.

"No," Pete replies as he attempts to shove Mac.

"That's right!" Doug affirms. "We'll get you in your sleep if we have to."

As Mac takes his seat, he leans across the table toward Doug and Pete and answers, "Didn't your daddy tell you? I sleep with my eyes open."

Doug and Pete look at their Uncle Doug then at each other with a perplexed look on their face.

Doug then sits up in his chair and addresses his dad. "Dad, is that true? Can Uncle Doug really sleep with his eyes open?"

"I don't know, son," Killer replies as he places the steaks and the sweet potatoes on the table. "When Mac and I are on the road and sharing a hotel room, the last thing I ever think of doing is gazing into his big brown eyes at night." Killer faces Mac and nods his head ever so slightly.

When Killer walks by Sharon, she lightly slaps him on the butt and says, "What am I going to do with you two?"

"I know this. You can't sell me. I have a lifetime-guaranteed contract. Now what you do with that fool over there is up to you," Killer smartly replies as he retrieves the broccoli and the Kool-Aid off of the kitchen counter and places them on the table. He then takes a seat at the head of the table, opposite Sharon.

"You're just full of jokes tonight, huh, funny man?" Mac laughingly retorts.

"You know it," Killer replies, pointing at Mac. After a few moments of laughter, Killer asks Mac, "Would you say grace, please?"

"Certainly," Mac replies.

Everyone seated at the table, including Angela, takes a hand as Mac opens with a word of prayer. "Dear Lord, I thank you for allowing us to gather together once again in your name. Thank you for allowing us to share this meal together as a family. Please, Lord, bless the hands that prepared this meal, help it to be nutritious and strengthen our bodies. In your Son's name, we pray, good bread, good meat, dear God, let's eat. Amen."

With the prayer said, they all lift up their heads and attack the food.

As Sharon fixes Angela's plate, she says to Mac, in reference to his grace, "You're too much."

"I know," Mac sarcastically responds. "Why do you think I'm still single?"

"It can't be because of your charm. Can it?" Sharon rebuts.

"Ooh. That was good counselor," Mac replies. He then faces Killer and says, "You see your wife down here knocking me out verbally, right?"

Killer throws his hands up in the air and answers, "Hey, man. You're on your own. I've got to sleep with that woman, remember?"

The three adults laugh at the conversation. Doug and Pete, on the other hand, look at one another confused. They have heard everything that their parents and their uncle Doug have said at the table thus far but have no idea what the joke is all about.

Doug leans over and whispers in Pete's ear, "Grown-up stuff."

"Yeah, grown-up stuff," Pete affirms, shoving a giant piece of steak into his mouth.

19 AUGUST 1999

0830 Hours: A Serbian Veterans' Hospital in Belgrade, Serbia

Colonel Drasneb sits in the chair in his hospital room, patiently waiting for his nurse to arrive and take him to rehab. As he waits, his mind is focused on the same thing that it has been on since he was brought to the hospital—how he allowed the Americans to take his victory out from under his feet.

Finally, after five past the hour, the nurse arrives with a wheel chair to take Colonel Drasneb to his daily rehabilitation session.

"You're late!" Colonel Drasneb barks as the nurse approaches him.

"I apologize, sir. I was held up with another patient."

"I don't want to hear your excuses! I only want to see you performing your duties efficiently and in a proper manner, especially when it comes to my care and well-being. Do you understand what I am telling you?"

"Yes, sir. I do."

With his near-regular scolding complete, the nurse rolls the wheelchair beside Colonel Drasneb. He leans forward and attempts to aid Colonel Drasneb into the wheelchair.

Suddenly, Colonel Drasneb blurts, "What have I told you the past week and a half? I can get my damn self into this God-forsaken chair without your help!"

"I know, sir," the nurse timidly responds, "but as I told you all of those other times, it's hospital policy. I'm just doing my job."

As the nurse speaks, Colonel Drasneb, with great effort and sheer will power, throws himself into his wheelchair. The nurse just stands there and shakes his head at the fact that he has to put up with this overbearing old son of a bitch every other day.

Once comfortably positioned in his wheelchair, Colonel Drasneb shouts, "Let's go, Togly! You have a schedule to keep."

At Colonel Drasneb's command, Togly quickly pushes him out of the room and rolls him down the hall to the rehabilitation room. As Togly grudgingly pushes Colonel Drasneb down the hall, Colonel Drasneb shouts at people to get out of their way. Everyone leaps out of the way, not out of respect for Colonel Drasneb, but for the simple fact that they do not want to get run over by an old man in a wheelchair. Most of the hospital residents and nurses ignore Colonel Drasneb's boorish manner. Though he is a war hero, they feel that they do not have to tolerate Colonel Drasneb's rude behavior. Unlike Togly, they have the great fortune of not having to directly deal with Colonel Drasneb on a day-to-day basis.

Taking Colonel Drasneb to his regular rehab sessions is the worst part of Togly's day. He hates the fact that he has to constantly listen to Colonel Drasneb's bickering, chastising, and straight rudeness. Fortunately for Togly, he spends no more than ten minutes at a time with Colonel Drasneb. If Togly were to spend more time with Colonel Drasneb, he would probably kill himself.

Having reached the rehabilitation room, Togly rolls Colonel Drasneb beside a bench and locks the wheels in place in order to keep Colonel Drasneb's wheelchair from moving as he positions himself onto the bench. Togly would help Colonel Drasneb onto the bench, but Colonel Drasneb is a very proud man who does not like assistance when it is not necessary.

The rehabilitation room is approximately the size of half a basketball court. It contains four large inflatable rubber balls, three sets of parallel bars, free weights, and jump ropes. Because Colonel Drasneb is rehabilitating his hip, he works with the parallel bars, which allows him to determine how much he can distribute on his bad hip.

With Colonel Drasneb beside the bench, Togly commences to exit the rehabilitation room. As he reaches the double doors, Colonel Drasneb says, "I'll see you Monday, Togly."

Togly simply waves his right hand in the air without a verbal response. He walks out of the rehabilitation room, upset at the fact that he has once again allowed Colonel Drasneb to ruin yet another good day. Thankfully though, Colonel Drasneb will be leaving the hospital in another two weeks, then life will be back to normal.

Sitting beside the bench, Colonel Drasneb grips his wheelchair's armrests then pushes his arms straight up. With his body physically out of the chair, Colonel Drasneb swings his legs out from in front of the wheel chair, thus using his body's momentum to place himself on the wooden bench.

Once on the bench, Colonel Drasneb shouts, "Katarina! I may have all day, but I would like to begin my rehab on time!"

Katarina, Colonel Drasneb's physical therapist, who is sitting in her small cubicle-sized office, slowly raises her head at the sound of Colonel Drasneb's squelching. As is most of the hospital staff, Katarina is accustomed to Colonel Drasneb's overbearing ways. Katarina straightens out her desk then rises from her desk, exiting her office, and heads for the rehabilitation room.

As soon as Colonel Drasneb spots Katarina stepping out of her office, he relaxes his demeanor and states, "You are late, my dear."

Whenever Colonel Drasneb deals with women, he tends to soften up a bit. Though he is still gruff in his mannerisms, Colonel Drasneb has his own personal way of flirting. Every man has to have a soft side.

"As you said, sir, we have all day," Katarina counters. "The last time I checked, you are not going anywhere for another two weeks."

"Like always, my dear, you are correct, but I would like to get this torture session over with as soon as possible."

Katarina grabs a walker that is leaning up against a wall and hands it to Colonel Drasneb. "Come on, sir, five laps. You know the route."

Begrudgingly, Colonel Drasneb forces himself up from off of the bench and places all of his body weight onto the walker. With his feet steady, Colonel Drasneb slowly and carefully walks around the outer perimeter of the rehabilitation room. Colonel Drasneb knows that it is important for him to work as hard as he can during his rehab sessions, but the pain is excruciating. The only thing that keeps him from quitting is the fact that he will someday walk without assistance from any devices or a feeble cane.

One step after another, one foot in front of the other, Colonel Drasneb takes his time, ensuring that he does not lose his balance and fall to the ground as he had done the first few times he had used the walker during his rehab.

Looking up at Katarina, who is watching him carefully, Colonel Drasneb, panting, states, "I swear to God you're trying to kill me, Katarina."

"Come now, Colonel. You're a war hero. If I were to kill you, I would give you the respect enough to kill you quickly, not torture you, as I am doing now."

"How kind of you, dear," Colonel Drasneb jests. He and Katarina both laugh as Colonel Drasneb sluggishly continues with his laps.

West Point

The early morning commenced with a SAMI, one of the most dreaded events in all of the corps because cadets, especially plebes, stay up to all hours of the night cleaning their rooms and ensuring that everything is positioned and situated as per the United States Corps of Cadets regulations.

Last night, after the rest of the corps had finished practicing for the Acceptance Day parade, Major and his platoon leaders, along with Joe giving instruction, continued practicing. What is significant about their additional practice time is that all of the corps was released from drill and ceremony much later than it should have, nearly missing dinner. Because of the late release, the cadets spent much less time before taps to prepare their rooms for the SAMI.

With the SAMI having concluded, the cadets prepare themselves for the Acceptance Day parade. Standing out on the stoops, Major, Joe, and Dusty discuss how the SAMI went in their company.

"I didn't realize we had so many plebe football players in the company," Major states.

"Yeah. No kidding," Joe agrees. "There's usually one or two, three at the most, but four's rare."

"Their rooms were a mess and hardly any of their stuff was put away!" Dusty interjects.

Hearing the first sergeant's words shock Joe and Major. They both snap their heads toward Dusty and look at one another with extremely curious looks on their faces.

"What are you talking about?" Joe asks Dusty.

"Their room appearance," Dusty answers. "It was piss poor!"

"You're right, First Sergeant," Major responds. "Their rooms weren't all that great, but look at the time constraint they were under."

"That's right," Joe jumps in. "They didn't get down here until last night. Their roommates should have squared their stuff away for them."

"Plus," Major adds, "Bradshaw was in the hospital all last night and didn't get back to the company area until about seven this morning."

"No disrespect, sir, but those excuses are not good enough," Dusty explains. "The football players should have accomplished the mission, no matter what the circumstances."

Following the first sergeant's words, Joe asks him, "Weren't you on the football team your plebe year?"

"Yes, I was."

"Well, how did you get your room in order? Did you do it all yourself, or did your roommates help you?"

"They helped me out, of course."

"That's our point, Dust," Joe exclaims. "We aren't saying that we're going to give the plebe football players any slack just because of the sport they play, but at the same time, you have to understand the situation that they are presently in. Now if there's anyone you should be upset with, it's their roommates for not looking out for their buddies. You know what we're saying?"

"Yeah. I guess I do," Dusty pouts.

"Don't get down on yourself, First Sergeant," Major says to Dusty, placing his arm around him. "This is all a learning experience. Me, the TO, and yourself, every day we're learning what it takes to be a good leader. It's not an overnight process. If that were the case, then there'd be no need for this great institution of higher learning that we attend. Now would there?"

"No. I guess not," Dusty soberly answers.

Dusty knows that Major is correct in that becoming a good leader takes time, but he does not agree with him or Joe on the plebe football-player situation. As much as Dusty would love to push the issue, he knows that his efforts would be futile and that he will not get anywhere by arguing with the company commander.

As Major speaks to Dusty, Joe notices a male and female cadet walk out of the last division in Grant Barracks.

Joe gets Major's attention and says, "Hey, Major, isn't that Natalie Hole?"

Cadet Natalie Hole is the deputy brigade commander, which means that she is West Point's second highest-ranking cadet. Major has known Cadet Hole since they were in the same psychology class the first semester of their plebe year. Though Major gets along well with most people, he and Cadet Hole did not end that semester as friends. Then again, they did not end the semester as enemies either.

Major turns around and faces the street. He eyes Cadet Hole and the trailing male cadet then angrily states, "It sure is! What the hell is she doing in my barracks? She didn't contact anyone, did she?"

Joe and Dusty look at one another then nod their heads from side to side.

"I didn't think so," Major acknowledges. "I'm going to go over to the CQ and see if she checked in there. First Sergeant, go find out what rooms she went to."

"Yes, sir," Dusty replies as he heads for the thirty-second division.

Major and Joe run to the orderly room and confront the CQ, Cdt. Cpl. Shane Richards.

"Hey, Shane. Did the deputy brigade commander stop by here any time this morning?"

"No, Major. She didn't," Cadet Richards replies.

Major wants to shout out an expletive at the top of his lugs, but he controls his frustration. Instead, he faces Joe and says, "Can you believe this crap!?"

"Yeah, I can," Joe simply answers.

"Well, I'm definitely going to handle this before the day's over."

Major and Joe are upset over Cadet Natalie Hole's actions because she did not follow proper protocol. As Major's superior, she has the right to walk through the Ducks' barracks whenever she pleases, but she has to inform the commander first; thus, Major should have been made aware that Cadet Hole was going to visit the Duck barracks. Cadet Hole did no such thing. Instead, she took it upon herself to inspect the Ducks' AO without giving Major word of her presence. Also, she did her walk through after the SAMI had concluded.

"We should go over to the thirty-second division and see what the first sergeant may have found out," Joe suggests to Major.

"Yeah. Let's go."

Joe and Major exit the orderly room and jog over to the thirty-second division. As they enter, Major and Joe hear the first sergeant ripping into a new cadet. Smartly, Major and Joe dart up the stairs and follow the sound of the first sergeant's loud mouth.

Approaching the room, Major and Joe spot the first sergeant speaking gruffly to one of the new cadet football players. The football player, New Cadet Jason Bradshaw, is standing in the doorway, locked up at the position of attention.

"What's going on here, First Sergeant?" Major asks Dusty as he stands next to him.

"Sir! This new cadet's room is ate the hell up, and he was out of uniform during the SAMI!"

Major steps in front of the first sergeant and tells New Cadet Bradshaw, "At ease."

Upon Major's command, New Cadet Bradshaw instantly moves to the position of at ease. Standing in front of New Cadet Bradshaw, Major quickly notices that he is six feet, three inches tall and weighs at least 250 pounds.

"You're a big one, huh, Bradshaw?" Major jokes.

"Yes, sir. They grow 'em big in Texas."

"So I've been told," Major chuckles. He then continues. "Tell me, Bradshaw. Did Cadet Hole inspect your room just a little while ago?"

"Yes, sir."

"How'd it go?"

"Not well, sir."

"What did she say was wrong with your room?" Major asks as he takes New Cadet Bradshaw's inspection clipboard from off of the sidewall beside the door.

"Sir, Cadet Hole said that my room was a disaster area and that it was a disgrace to my classmates and the corps."

"Did she?" Major softly states as he rubs his chin inquisitively. "Anything else?"

"Yes, sir. She told me that I was out of uniform."

Major simply shakes his head at New Cadet Bradshaw's report. "All right, Bradshaw. Don't worry about anything that went on between you two. So you know, she was in the wrong. She inspected your room ten minutes after the SAMI had ended, and I am assuming that you started getting undressed afterward. Am I correct?"

"Yes, sir. I did not want to get my white shirt dirty while I was shining my shoes."

"That's what I figured. Also, we understand why your room is still not together yet. About what time did you get back from the hospital?"

"Seven, sir."

"All right then. How're you feeling, now?"

"I feel fine, sir."

"Good. Make sure you take care of yourself. You've got a tough practice ahead of you today."

"Yes, sir."

"Oh, also tell my brother I said what's up and that I'll be at the scrimmage."

"Your brother, sir?"

"Yeah. Will Johnson?"

"Will's your little brother, sir?"

"Yep."

"That's cool, sir. I'll tell him you said hey."

"Good then. I'll see you at formation, Bradshaw."

"We own the pond, sir!" New Cadet Bradshaw shouts as Major leave the room.

Major turns and points to New Cadet Bradshaw's roommate and states, "Good job, Bell, in teaching Bradshaw my greeting!"

"Yes, sir!" New Cadet Bell proudly replies. "We own the pond, sir!"

Major exits the room and begins walking down the small hallway and down the stairs. Joe follows closely behind him. "First Sergeant, we need to talk," Major calmly states as he heads for the stoops.

As soon as the three cadets reach the stoops, Dusty opens with, "Sir, I do not understand why you were so lenient with that new cadet."

"First Sergeant, the boy was in the hospital all night, for God's sakes."

"I don't know, sir," the first sergeant says with his hands up in the air in frustration. "I see I can't win this one."

"That's your problem, Dust. This isn't a win-lose situation. It's about doing what's right and what's fair. In Bradshaw's case, we can't get upset with him because of the situation that he was in. But forget about all of that, we need to deal with Natalie coming through our barracks without giving me word first."

"What are you talking about, sir?" Dusty asks. "She's the deputy brigade commander. She can do pretty much whatever she wants."

"That's where you're wrong, Dusty," Joe jumps in. "She may be the second highest-ranking cadet in the corps, but when it's all said and done, she's still a cadet, just like you and me. She has to follow the regs just like the rest of us."

"That's right, Dust. The problem I have with Natalie is the fact that she walked through my barracks without contacting me or my XO. I don't care how high ranking you are, if you walk through someone's barracks, protocol states that you contact the commander of that unit first. In this case, me."

"I see your point, CO. What are you going to do about it?"

"I'd love to go tell her what's up right now, but I'm going to do it the right way and use my chain of command. I'm going to let Donaldson know what's up and ensure that he informs Putter."

"There's nothing I can do?" Dusty asks.

"Naw. I've got this. Just make sure everyone's ready for the parade."

"Roger," Dusty replies as he leaves Joe and Major and heads for his room.

Once Dusty gets out of ear shot range, Major states, "You've got to love that kid."

"Yeah. He'll make a great first sergeant, but he's a little too high strung," Joe replies.

"Yeah, he is, but he'll grow out of it hopefully, sooner than later."

"Come on. Let's go take a nap before this parade," Joe states.

"Yeah. I need one," Major agrees.

Joe and Major head for their room to take a quick power nap. If there is one thing that all cadets master before they graduate, it is the art of utilizing any amount of time, no matter how small, to get a good nap in.

0950 Hours

Joe wakes up from his nap to the sound of his miniature alarm clock ringing in his ear. Whenever Joe takes a nap, he lies his alarm clock on his pillow beside his head. He shuts the alarm off then rolls out of bed. Joe places his feet on the rug and slowly stands up.

"Hey, Major. Time to get up."

"I got you," Major groggily answers as he sits up from the top bunk.

Major leaps to the floor and quickly moves to his work desk where his stereo is located. He turns the stereo on and throws the volume nearly all the way up.

Hearing the loud music, Major happily states, "Now I'm awake."

"Yeah. You and the entire barracks," Joe says under his breath.

Joe and Major both commence in getting dressed for the parade. Because Joe is the training officer and has to grade a company in Third Regiment, he wears his white-over-gray uniform, which consists of a white heavy, short-sleeved shirt and a pair of gray wool pants with a black stripe along the seams. Joe's standing as a first class cadet requires him to also wear a red sash during parades.

Major, who obviously is parading today, puts on his full dress over white, which consists of the wool full dress coat with brass buttons down the front, a pair of heavily starched white pants, and white gloves. Because he is a first class cadet, Major also has to wear a red sash around his waist. Also, Major's rank as a cadet captain requires him to carry his sword and wear peacock feathers in his parade hat.

Joe finishes getting dressed before Major due to the fact that his uniform is not nearly as complicated as Major's.

Major has his pants and full dress top on but is having trouble getting his sash and sword properly around his waist. Seeing that Joe is done, Major asks him, "Hey, dawg. Give a brother some help?"

"Yeah, of course."

Joe walks over to Major, who is standing next to the couch. He grabs Major's saber belt from off of the couch and places the sheath into its holder. Next, Joe raises the saber belt over Major's head, while Major ducks, raises his right arm high into the air, then sticks his head through the hole. Joe places the saber belt upon Major's left shoulder. With the saber belt properly applied to Major's person, Joe straightens out Major's brass, ensuring that it is opposite the direction of 'port arms' and placed tightly beneath the second button.

"Stick your arms out," Joe instructs.

Major throws his arms out to his side, as Joe takes Major's red sash from off of the couch and hooks it around Major's waist, ensuring that the two bunches of tassel hang down Major's left side. Fully dressed, minus his white gloves, Major steps in front of the mirror to look himself over.

"God, I look good!" Major proclaims.

"Oh please," Joe replies. "Here. Take your hat." Joe hands Major his parade hat from out of his wardrobe.

Major slips his white gloves on, then snatches his sword from off of the couch with his right hand.

"Let's roll," Major says as he throws the door open.

The two roommates depart from their room and head toward the company's parade formation area. As Major and Joe walk, they hear the bustling of cadets scrambling to get ready for the parade and a host of plebes calling minutes.

At the formation area, Major and Joe stand around and speak among their friends, classmates, and fellow ducks. The cadets talk about many different subjects, as they wait for the parade to commence: the upcoming school year, the newly acquired plebes, and what they are going to do tonight, for those who can leave post.

Everyone is anxious for the parade to begin. Not too many cadets like parades and those who do would never dare admit such a thing. Minus the new cadets, Major is probably one of the few cadets who is actually looking forward to today's parade.

The only position Major has ever wanted, as a first class cadet, is that of company commander. As far as Major is concerned, company command is the ideal position; in that, one has over one hundred soldiers to lead (129 to be exact) and is able to interact with the plebes at a personal level. The combination of influencing and molding the plebes is Major's biggest motivator for wanting to be a company commander. Major thinks back to how particular firsties influenced and looked out for him when he was a plebe. He wants to do the same for the plebes as well, and the best way to do it is as a company commander because as the old saying goes, "That's where the rubber meets the road."

Major's other motivator for wanting to be a company commander is to mentor and motivate the young black cadets within the corps. Major wants them to know that there is someone out there who understands what they are going through. When Major was a plebe, his regimental command sergeant major, Ernest Lewis, was a great influence and inspiration to him professionally. Not only was Cdt. Lewis Major's regimental command sergeant major, he was also one of his junior varsity basketball coaches. Cadet Lewis was a good mentor and friend. The following year, Cadet Lewis went on to become Major's regimental commander for third regiment, the Wolfpack.

Major has a passion for giving back—for wanting to help others in ways in which he was helped in the past. Being a company commander is one of Major's outlets in reaching out to the young cadets in the corps.

Speaking with some Duck firsties in the rear of the formation, Joe casually looks at his watch and says to his friends, "Well, guys, it's time to get this thing over with. See you at the barbecue."

Joe quickly walks to the front of formation and says to Major, "You guys are ready."

"Hell yeah, we are!" Major exclaims, waving his sword in the air.

Joe smiles as he leaves Central Area and heads for the Plain." During every parade, all of the company training officers stand on the side of the Plain to grade a preassigned company on its drilling aptitude. Never does a training officer grade his own company, though he wish he could.

In front of the Duck formation, the battalion staff moves to the position of attention. The respective commanders for the Axemen,

Barbarians, and Commandos all follow suit and order their companies to move to the position of attention. Seeing the companies fall in signals Major to do the same.

Major faces his company and shouts, "It's game time!" then snaps to the position of attention.

"Company!" Major shouts.

Instantly, the guidon bearer, Cdt. Sgt. Henry Stein, raises the guidon high into the air.

"Attention!" Major follows loudly.

Simultaneously, Company Delta-1 sharply moves to the position of attention, and Cadet Stein places the guidon back onto the ground.

Major then commands, "Right shoulder, arms!"

Upon command, the underclassmen bring their M14 rifles to right shoulder arms.

The Ducks wait about thirty seconds before Charlie Company, who stands directly in front of them, begins to march forward. As the Commandos move, Major orders the Ducks, "Forward, march!"

As the Ducks step off, Major executes a quick about-face and leads his company out through Eisenhower Barracks' middle sally-port and onto the plain, marching to the beat of a loud bass drum.

Marching through the sally port, Major eyes the large crowd that is assembled on the Plain to witness the Acceptance Day parade. The number of people in attendance is so great that many are forced to stand crowded to the far sides; some even brought lawn chairs. The majority of those in attendance came to support the new cadets as they officially join the Corps of Cadets. Many though are tourists who are simply interested in watching a West Point parade.

To the far right of the Plain, stand the Hell Cats, the official West Point band. The Hell Cats comprise of regular army noncommissioned officers. They play at all of the parades and other formal West Point functions to include assisting the cadet band during home football games.

All thirty-two companies march out onto the Plain. A parade where every company participates is referred to as a double regimental parade. During a double regimental parade, the companies fall in a column one behind another from companies A through D and E through H. The order of the columns is determined by the companies' battalion and regimental status. Since the Ducks are in First Battalion, First Regiment, their position is in the rear of the first column.

About forty feet from D-1's position, Major spins around and shouts, "Guide on line!"

Immediately, a second class cadet to the far left of the second row jumps out of formation and runs to D-1's position on the Plain. The cow's job is to mark his company's position, ensuring that the commander does not march his company too far or too close to any of the other companies.

Major marches the Ducks to where the cow stands then gives the command, "Mark time, march!"

D-1 marches in place upon receipt of the command.

After a few seconds of ensuring that the company is properly aligned, Major then gives the order of "Company, halt!"

The Ducks cease marching and now stand at the position of attention, except for the fact that they are still holding their weapon at right shoulder arms.

Major does an about-face then commands, "Order, arms!"

The underclassmen smoothly bring their weapons to their side and now stand at the proper position of attention.

Next, Major shouts, "Parade, rest!"

The Ducks snap to the position of parade rest. With the Ducks at parade rest, Major executes an about-face and moves to the position of parade rest as well.

As the Ducks stand at parade rest, they wait for the remainder of the corps to fall into position. After about five additional minutes, the entire Corps of Cadets stands on the Plain in front of the great American public at the position of parade rest.

Across from the corps, on the opposite side of the Plain, stand the new cadets. They marched onto the Plain the same time as the remainder of the corps. The Plain is a large grass field that is roughly two football fields in length. The military academy conducts all of its parades and official award ceremonies on the Plain. It is located directly in front of Eisenhower and MacArthur Barracks. To the rear center of the Plain stands a majestic statue of a war imaged George Washington riding his horse.

Now that the entire corps is assembled on the Plain, the brigade S-1, Cdt. Capt. Bethany Jung, runs through a series of procedures that has the assembled formation constantly moving between parade rest and the position of attention—saluting the Colors, saluting the reviewing party, and issuing an accountability report, to name a few.

After all of the pomp and circumstance, Cadet Jung executes an about-face. Instantly, the brigade commander, Cdt. Capt. Stanley Roberts, marches forward and steps in front of Cadet Jung, who then immediately salutes her commander. Cadet Roberts returns his S-1's salute then orders her to return to the brigade formation.

Cadet Roberts executes an about-face, the four thousand members of the Corps of Cadets staring back at him. Over the loud speaker, a voice announces the Hell Cats, as they perform a song, marching down and back in the middle of the length of the Plain.

Once the Hell Cats return to their original position, Cadet Roberts executes another about face, then gives his executive officer a command. The brigade XO salutes Cadet Roberts then executes an about-face, as well. He faces the giant mass of new cadets who are nearing their time to join the corps and the company executive officers, who marched the new cadets out onto the Plain.

The brigade XO commands the company executive officers, "Join your units!"

Upon the command, the company executive officers render a salute then lead their respective groups of new cadets to their company formations.

Marching toward their companies, the new cadets fall in to the rear of their formations, where there is a large gap left open for them. Behind the new cadets in the formation is a row of first class cadets. Now having officially joined their companies, the new cadets are no longer new cadets; they are now official members of the United States Corps of Cadets. The newly accepted cadets are fourth class cadets and hold the rank of cadet private, but to all of the upperclassmen and old grads the world over, the cadet privates are simply known as plebes.

Once all of the plebes are properly in position, Cadet Roberts commands, "Pass and review!"

The under three classes all slightly rattle their bayonets, signifying their happiness in nearly ending yet another parade. The rattling gives off a very distinctive sound like that of tapping a pin on a piece of tin, which generally makes a light sound, except for the fact that over three thousand cadets are doing the rattling.

While the underclassmen rattle their bayonets, the immense crowd cheers at the acceptance of yet another class of cadets joining the corps: the Class of 2003.

After Cadet Roberts's command, Cadet Putter also commands his regiment, "Pass and review!"

Hearing Cadet Putter's command, Major executes an about-face then orders the Ducks, "Right shoulder, arms!"

The underclassmen bring their weapons up to right shoulder arms. Upon execution, Major then shouts, "Forward, march!"

The Ducks step off as they had marched out onto the Plain behind Company C-1. Immediately upon stepping off, the Ducks turn right by executing a column right. They march forward about fifteen paces before Major gives the command to turn left, ten feet from the fence. At the fence, families stand with clear signs of joy and approval of the Acceptance Day parade.

Marching alongside of the fence, there are only two things that Major can hear—the band and people cheering. Major has a very loud voice when he needs to use it, but the outside noise is so loud that he can barely hear himself shout his commands.

Thank God for the guidon, Major briefly thinks.

Major thanks God for the guidon because it is what the cadets use to signal them when to execute "Eyes, right" and "Ready, front." Without the guidon, the cadets would have no idea as to when to execute the commands.

Marching forward another thirty feet, Major gives the Ducks the command to turn left. As they turn, the upperclassmen softly, yet sternly, tell everyone to carefully straighten themselves out. Where the Ducks are marching now is the most important aspect of the parade. They are commencing to march through the "shoot," which is where the cadets march in front of the reviewing party, the official party, and the brigade staff.

On the ground, at the beginning of the shoot, is a small red flag that is no more than a foot high. The red flag marks the location where the commanders need to have their companies at eyes right. Having practiced for nearly five hours the other day, Major knows exactly when to give his company the command of "Eyes right."

As Major gets to about ten feet from the red flag, Major shouts at the top of his lungs, "Ready! Eyes, right!"

Upon the command "Ready," Major and his platoon leaders simultaneously raise the grip of their swords to eye level and cocked outward at a forty-five degree angle. On "Eyes," Cadet Stein thrusts the guidon high into the air, signaling to the Ducks that the next command of "Right" is coming up next. Also, the Ducks silently say "Eyes" to better prepare themselves and their buddies that the next command is coming. Once Major shouts "Right," at the same time Cadet Stein quickly drops the guidon horizontal to the ground, and all of the Ducks, including Major, snap their heads to the right, facing the review stands.

As the Ducks march through the shoot, the cadet on the PA system announces, "Leading Company Delta-1 is the company commander, Cdt. Capt. Milton Aynes Johnson of Woodbridge, Virginia."

Hearing his name over the roar of the crowd, Major discreetly smiles in satisfaction, knowing that he has finally accomplished a goal that has taken him three years to attain.

1145 Hours

The Acceptance Day parade has ended. Most of the companies are having barbecues and cookouts in their company areas. The Ducks are one such company; except when the Ducks have a barbecue, they go all out. Today, the Ducks are grilling not just hamburgers and hot dogs like everyone else, but also chicken and steak fajitas.

Major is not presently at the Duck barbecue. Instead, he is up in Cadet Donaldson's room, discussing what had occurred concerning Cadet Hole's untimely visit to D-1's barracks.

"I'm pissed as hell, Mike!" Major blurts. "Personally, I would take care of this myself, but I figured it would be better if I used my chain of command. That's why I'm talking to you."

"I'm glad you came to me first," Mike replies. "I agree with you wholeheartedly. Natalie shouldn't have gone through your barracks without an escort or at least informing you ahead of time."

As Mike speaks to Major, Major paces the room in disgust.

"I'll talk to Putter about this today," Mike continues. "I'll let you know what he says. All right?"

"Yeah. Let me know what he says because it'll get ugly if I'm forced to deal with it myself," Major states.

Mike changes the subject by stating, "I heard you guys looked pretty good today."

"That's what they tell me," Major boasts. "Of course, my PLs and I did practice an extra hour after dinner last night."

"Really?"

"Sure did."

Mike turns away from Major and walks to his sink. "You're not going to like what I have to tell you."

"What's that?" Major asks.

"Brigade staff got their SAMI canceled because of how long we all had drill practice yesterday."

"You're kidding me, right?"

"I wish I were."

"That's the kind of mess I hate, Major angrily states." Friggin' brigade staff taking advantage of their position. I know they didn't try to get SAMI canceled for the rest of the corps. Shoot! Me and my PLs were out practicing longer than anyone. That's all right though. I'll talk to my man Stan about this. He's going to know that I'm disappointed and upset about this."

"Do what you have to do," Mike states, "but don't get anyone too riled up."

"Don't worry. I'm going to rock the boat, but I won't tip it over. Stan's my boy, after all," Major adamantly states as he leaves Cadet Donaldson's room.

1215 Hours

Major has finally had an opportunity to change out of his full dress uniform. In its place, he wears his gym-A uniform with his socks up to his knees and last year's basketball team practice shoes. Major wears his socks up to his knees because that is how young black men generally wear them where he is from—the Washington, DC, metropolitan area.

Dressed, Major runs out of his room and onto the stoops to join his company in its barbecue.

"Somebody hook me up with a fajita and a burger!" Major joyfully shouts.

"Steak or chicken, sir?" one of the plebes who is standing beside the grill asks Major in reference to the fajita.

"Steak, Clancy! Gotta get all of the protein I can."

"What about your burger, sir?"

"I want everything on that joint."

"Yes, sir." The plebe grabs a second plate and fixes his and his commander a plate of food.

As the plebe prepares Major's plate, Major stands at the edge of the stoops and waves everyone in closer to him. "Everyone listen up real quick!"

The Ducks cease with their conversations and focus their attention on their company commander.

"I know you all have plans today, especially the cows and firsties, but I want everyone to go up to Michie today and watch some of the scrimmage. We all need to support our Duck football players!"

"What about the swim team?" a female Duck in the crowd shouts.

"When you guys have a meet, we'll be there too!"

Everyone bursts with laughter.

"That's all I wanted to say. Oh yeah. Don't forget to thank Melly Mel for this tight barbecue. This joint's another example of the Ducks being the best friggin' company in the corps. I've got to go see my brother and my family up at Michie. I'll see y'all there."

Major runs down off of the stoops and jogs over to the grill. The plebe who was preparing Major's food hands him his plate.

Major acknowledges the plebe's action with "Thanks, Clance."

"We own the pond, sir!" Cadet Private Clancy shouts as his company commander runs out of Grant Area with a burger in his mouth.

"We own the pond" is Major's official greeting for his plebes. Major chose the phrase because, as he figures, if the Ducks are the best company at West Point, then one can equate West Point to a pond. Thus, the Ducks own the pond. Major is very big in instilling a sense of pride in his plebes. It is very important to Major that the Duck plebes are truly proud about being Ducks.

Major crosses the street and runs between Pershing and Bradley Barracks into Central Area. He heads for Central Guard Room in hopes that the duty driver will give him a ride up to Michie Stadium.

Central Guard Room is where the cadets who are on guard for the day hold their post. At a minimum, there is a cadet officer and cadet noncommissioned officer pulling guard at all times. There are other guard posts and locations throughout West Point, but Central Guard Room serves as the headquarters.

As Major approaches Central Guard Room, he slows down his pace to a slight trot. Major leaps onto the steps and swings the door open and enters.

Inside, he finds two cadets sitting behind a four-foot-high counter, reading a book. Major steps up to the counter then commences to lay his entire body weight onto the countertop.

"Hey, Rob," Major says to the cadet officer in charge, who happens to also be a personal acquaintance. "Can the duty driver swing me up to Michie real quick?"

"Yeah. That shouldn't be a problem. He has to make a run up to the hospital in about five minutes. You can go with him when he goes on his run," Rob replies. He then turns to the cadet sergeant in charge and says, "Make an announcement for the duty driver to come down here."

"All right," the cadet sergeant in charge dryly responds as he places his book down and sluggishly rises from his seat.

As the cadet sergeant in charge walks over to the microphone, Rob places all of the telephone receivers off of their hooks to ensure that none of them ring while he makes his announcement.

With his hand on the mic, the cadet sergeant in charge announces, "Attention, all cadets. Attention, all cadets. Will the duty driver report to Central Guard Room. I repeat. Will the duty driver report to Central Guard Room. Out."

"Thanks, man. I appreciate it," Major graciously states to the cadet sergeant in charge as he completes his announcement.

"Shoot, man. I know how it is," the cadet sergeant in charge acknowledges, nodding his head in the air as he plops himself back into his seat.

After about five minutes or so, the duty driver, another cadet sergeant, strides into Central Guard Room. As he steps up to the counter, Rob says to him, "I need you to go to the hospital and pick someone up. On your way, take Major up to Michie."

"No problem," the duty driver responds.

"Good looking out, Rob. I'll see you," Major states, shaking Rob's hand.

"Anytime," Rob responds as Major and the duty driver step out of Central Guard Room.

Major and the duty driver get into the light blue, Ford, van that is parked beside Central Guard Room. The duty driver starts the engine, then carefully backs up: honking his horn twice to ensure that those who are walking know that he is backing up. The duty driver takes he and Major out of Central Area, driving alongside a cliff that is the western border of Cadet Area. On top of the cliff sits the Cadet Chapel, which overlooks all of West Point.

The duty driver passes alongside Arvin Gym, then swings a left and up a small hill. At the top of the hill, the duty driver takes another left and drives up a bigger hill, passing the Cadet Chapel on their left, once again. Passing the Cadet Chapel, the street veers to the right, as Major and the duty driver pass Lusk Reservoir to the left. Driving alongside Lusk Reservoir, the duty driver and Major are now between Michie Stadium and Lusk Reservoir.

Seeing the next corner on the right, Major says to the duty driver, "Hey man, let me out over there." Major points to a small parking lot and a large asphalt area that is marked with yellow lines, signaling for no one to park there.

The duty driver turns into the no parking area and lets Major out of the van.

"Thanks, man," Major states as he jumps out of the passenger's seat.

The duty driver takes off for the hospital, while Major runs into the stadium and heads for the home side.

On the football field is the entire army football team, running through various position drills. Among the numerous players is Major's little brother, William Stewart Johnson, one of several plebes vying for one of the few open slots on the team.

In the stands sit many parents, most of them the parents of the plebes who are attempting to make a name for themselves on the practice field today. The other parents are those of the already established players. The latter group of parents attends the majority of their sons' scrimmages and games, home and away.

Intermingled within the small crowd of parents are Major and Will's parents, Col. and Mrs. Sydney and Helen Johnson. Seeing his parents sitting on the fourth row of the fifty-yard line, Major walks over to them.

"Nice to see you guys made it," Major says to his parents as he approaches them.

"Well, we figured that since we have a couple of sons doing things up at West Point, we'd come up for a visit," Colonel Johnson sarcastically replies as he extends forward and shakes his son's hand.

After shaking his father's hand, Major gives his mother a hug then sits a row in front of his parents.

"How's Dubs look?" Major asks his parents in reference to Will.

"Will looks really good, like he belongs out there," Mrs. Johnson proudly answers.

Major and his dad shake their heads, not at the fact that Will is doing well, but at Mrs. Johnson's ability to critique her youngest son's football-playing ability. Though Mrs. Johnson has attended a many football game between her two sons, her analysis of her sons' abilities, no matter the sport or activity, is purely emotional. When it comes to her sons' extra curricular activities, to Mrs. Johnson, her boys can do no wrong. Don't tell that to Major and Will though, they will simply laugh because to them, their mother is the hardest woman in the world to please.

Major and his parents sit and watch the practice. As time progresses, the football team moves from individual drills to an intersquad scrimmage. An intersquad scrimmage is when the team plays among themselves and the head coach stops the play of the game whenever he feels necessary to give instruction to his players.

During army football intersquad scrimmages, the teams are divided between the offense and the defense. The offense attempts to score, and the defense works on stopping the offense in the hopes of scoring in the process, if possible.

At the beginning of the scrimmage, head coach Larry Hughes has his first team offense and defense out on the field. After a few drives, Coach Hughes begins to substitute other players into the scrimmage in order to test their abilities. As the scrimmage proceeds, Coach Hughes allows his assistants to substitute the players in on their own. With about fifteen minutes into the scrimmage, Will is finally given the signal to go out onto the field.

Will lines up against the number 2 receiver, Cdt. Sgt. Thomas Oman. The center snaps the ball to the quarterback. Cadet Oman takes off from the line of scrimmage and runs a slot route. Will stays right on Cadet Oman's hip. Sequentially, the quarterback drops back three steps and releases a pass intended for Cadet Oman. Will, anticipating the pass, is able to get a hand in and deflect the pass, thus forcing an incompletion. The defense becomes very excited and commences in letting Will know how proud they are of his play-making ability. With the play dead, Will's defensive back coach, Steven Sullivan, calls him back to the sideline. Sprinting off of the field and back to the sideline, Will's defensive teammates slap him on his helmet and on his shoulder pads, congratulating him for a well-executed play.

"Good job, Will!" Coach Sullivan shouts as Will sprints off of the field. "Keep up the intensity!"

Will nods his head several times in acknowledgment to Coach Sullivan's comment.

The scrimmage continues on for another hour or so. Happy at what he sees, Coach Hughes blows his whistle, signaling for the team to cease with the scrimmage. The players halt in their tracks, and the head strength coach, Arnold Scott, takes over practice and leads the team through a series of stretches.

Coach Scott is better known as "Satan" for his ability to inflict large amounts of pain in the weight room. Arnold is good at what he does, but some players dread having him run them through a lift because they know that they are going to leave the weight room feeling as though they had gone through a torture session.

Having stretched for about ten minutes, Coach Scott blows his whistle, signaling that the stretching is complete. The players leap up from off of the ground and run to their position coaches, who briefly speak with their respective players. After the position coaches' huddle, the entire team falls in around Coach Hughes.

Surrounded by his hardworking team, Coach Hughes states, "I am very pleased with what I've seen today. You all worked extremely hard. The intensity that I witnessed today is what I want to see at every practice, whether it's raining out or cold as hell. For you plebes, the coaches and I will let you know where you stand with the team Monday at three thirty. Whether you make the team or not, I want you young men to know that you all did an exceptional job out on this football field. If you ever need anything of me, don't hesitate to ask."

The plebes all look at one another and their upper-class teammates, some knowing that they will not return to the team, others unsure as to where they stand on the depth chart, and a few who know that they will return Monday, pads on and ready to go.

"Bring it in!" Coach Hughes shouts.

The players come in tight around their head coach with their helmets high in the air, pointed at Coach Hughes.

"One. Two. Three!" Coach Hughes again shouts.

Everyone surrounding Coach Hughes loudly cries, "Army!"

With the huddle complete, practice is now officially over. The players slowly walk off of the field, exhausted beyond belief. Those players who have friends and family present, in which Will is among, head for the stands.

As the players head for the stands, Major rises from his seat to meet Will at the concrete wall that separates the football field from the stands. Waiting for his little brother, many of Major's friends and acquaintances say, "What's up?" as they pass him by.

One of Major's good friends, Cdt. JT Roberts, walks toward him. Seeing each other from among the crowd, JT shouts, "Major!"

Major immediately follows with a loud and boisterous, "JT!"

JT steps off the field and into the stands. Major walks over to JT and the two close friends embrace.

Releasing their grip on one another, JT asks, "You still going to 'boken with us tonight?"

"I'm going to have to meet you all down there later tonight," Major answers. "The family and I are going to grab dinner after the Dubs showers."

"Oh yeah. I don't know why I forgot about that."

"Shoot. You want to come? I figure we'll get to Hoboken by nine. It's not like you'll be missing anything. You know?"

"Sure. Why not? I'll let Ed know when he shows up. He should be here in a little while."

"Cool then. Bring my brother out with you. We'll meet you at the steps, like always."

"All right, dawg. I'll see you in a bit," JT states as he and Major shake hands. JT then trots off for the locker room. As he passes the Johnson's, JT waves to them and shouts, "Hey, Colonel and Mrs. Johnson!"

"Are you coming to dinner with us tonight, JT?" Mrs. Johnson asks.

"Yes, ma'am. I'm going to go shower now. I'll see you in a few minutes."

With JT gone, Major turns his full attention to his little brother. "You looked pretty good out there, boy. Reminds me of myself back in the day."

"Anyway," Will snidely counters.

Major slaps Will in the back of the head in response to his smart-aleck remark.

Will gets in Major's face then sarcastically states, "You better be glad most of your boys are on this team, or I'd beat you down right here."

"Yeah, you would." Major laughs. "Come on. Let's go see Mom and Dad."

Major and Will turn from the concrete wall and walk up the bleachers to their parents, who are sitting patiently. With her youngest son in front of her, Mrs. Johnson leaps up from her seat and gives Will a giant hug. Mrs. Johnson's grip is so tight that Will begins to squirm.

"Let go of the boy, Helen. You're killing him," Colonel Johnson interjects.

Mrs. Johnson releases her grip and steps back. "I'm sorry, baby," she says to Will. "I didn't think that I'd miss you so much."

"You should be used to this by now," Major says to his mother.

"Yeah. She probably misses someone doing all of the work around the house," Will adds. The two brothers laugh and give each other a pound.

"Where's the brat?" Will asks his parents in reference to his and Major's fourteen-year-old little sister, Jasmine.

"She's still at Dear's," Colonel Johnson answers.

Dear is the name that Major gave his maternal grandmother when he was about two years old. Major is not fully sure why he started calling his maternal grandmother Dear, but it has stuck throughout the years.

"Cool," Will simply replies. "I'm going to go to the locker room now. I'll see you guys in a little bit."

"All right then. Go shower up," Colonel Johnson states as Will leaves the stands and runs off to the locker room.

23 AUGUST 1999

0630 Hours: Grant Barracks, West Point

There is not a more monotonous period than a weekday morning at the United States Military Academy. At 0620 hours, the fourth class cadets awaken to perform their morning duties such as cleaning the bathrooms and the orderly room and memorizing their knowledge—the meals of the day and the front page and sports page of the *Washington Post*, to name two.

One duty that the plebes perform every school day is *calling minutes*. Calling minutes alerts the cadets to when it is time to head down to both breakfast and lunch formations and Thursday spirit-dinner formations. The upper-class cadets use the plebes as a human alarm clock. The very experienced are able to wake up at the two-minute warning and make it down to breakfast formation on time, but usually without a moment to spare.

The manner in which the plebes call minutes is as follows. They stand beneath a predetermined clock in a hallway. With seven minutes until formation, the plebes call five minutes. They call the minutes up until two minutes to formation. The manner in which they call the minutes is somewhat annoying to some but is necessary.

At the top of their lungs, the plebes yell, "Attention, all cadets! There are five minutes until assembly for breakfast formation! The uniform is 'as for class'! Five minutes remaining!"

As stated, the plebes repeat this statement up until the two-minute warning. At two minutes, they call, "Attention, all cadets! There are two minutes until assembly for breakfast formation! The uniform is as for class! Do not forget your lights! Two minutes remaining!" Now the reason the plebes announce, "Do not forget your lights,' is because during the days before electricity, cadets were not allowed to leave their kerosene lamps on while they were away from their rooms for an extended period of time—a precaution to prevent fires from breaking out in the barracks.

Major does not wait for the plebes to call the minutes as his signal to head down to formation, though there are some days that he wished that he did. As the D-1 company commander, Major feels that it is his duty to be at formation the same time as his non minute-calling plebes, ten minutes prior to fall in. Instead of rolling out of bed at 0645 hours, he wakes up at 0630 hours. Fifteen minutes does not seem like much to most people, but those extra minutes of sleep can do wonders for a person throughout the day.

With 0630 hours shining bright on his alarm clock and the hip-hop sounds of Hot 97 FM sounding moderately in the room, Major awakens from a restful slumber. Simultaneously, he rolls over and sits up in the top bunk, springs off, and lands on the persian rug that he took from his parents' basement for his room. Lucky for Major, as a first class cadet, he is allowed a rug in his room because God knows that the floor is freezing cold in the morning, something one does not wish to encounter first thing in the morning.

"What day is it?" Major asks, somewhat bewilderedly.

"It's Monday," Joe answers.

"Man, I could have sworn I slept through an entire day already. Oh well."

Major steps to his desk and takes a seat behind his desk to check his e-mail. At the same time, Major bends down underneath his desk to get his socks and shoes.

"Hey, boy! Your girl called last night while you were out," Major jokingly says to Joe.

"Shut up with that. You know that girl bugs the hell out of me. I get sick of just looking at her," Joe defends.

"Relax, Joey. She didn't ask about you. She just wanted to know how she should go about writing that law paper. I hooked her up. You finish yours yet?"

"Naw. I'm going to knock it out tonight."

"I finished it yesterday. It wasn't too bad."

Major rises from behind his desk and walks over to the medicine cabinet to retrieve his toothbrush and toothpaste. He then turns and heads for the bedroom door to go to the bathroom.

On his way out the door, Major sarcastically asks Joe, "You need anything when I get back?"

"Yeah. How about your mom?" Joe rebuts.

"How about your girlfriend so we can both share?" Major replies as he leaves the bathroom to brush his teeth. Major would brush his teeth in his room, but he and Joe hate having to clean their sink every day.

On the way back to his room, Major notices one of his plebes briskly move into the orderly room. He decides to see if this plebe has done his duty and read the newspaper yet.

"Hey, Miles!" Major shouts to the plebe.

The plebe halts in his tracks, does an about-face, and strides over to where Major stands. "Yes, sir?"

"What's going on in the world today?"

"Sir, today in the *Washington Post*, it was reported that First Lieutenant Perez, Chief Warrant Officer Anderson, and Sergeant Burns are still missing in action. Their last known duty was flying a top-secret surveillance mission over a Serbian outpost last week. Military analysts say that—"

"That's good Miles. Go on and do whatever it was you were doing."

"We own the pond, sir!" barks Cadet Private Miles.

"You better believe it!" Major boastfully replies.

Miles returns to the direction from which he came while Major returns to his room.

"Hey, Joe. You remember that dude Perez over in H-2 who graduated in '97?" Major asks as he enters the room.

"Yeah. He was a firstie on the baseball team when I was a manager our plebe year. Why you ask, anyway?"

"'Cause his helicopter was shot down over in Serbia last week."

"Yeah, I know. Shit like that really pisses me off!"

"I hear you. He's probably all right though. He'll get rescued like that air force guy did a few years back."

"Yeah. You're probably right. I mean, hell! This isn't Vietnam or anything. The Marines'll find Mark and bring him home like they always do," Joe agrees, though his face does not hide his feelings of uncertainty.

0900 Hours: A Serbian Army Interrogation Building, Belgrade, Serbia

"I am sick and tired of the Americans getting in the way all of the time! Why can't they just leave us alone? What concern of theirs is it if we unify Yugoslavia?"

"None, Colonel."

"I know this, but we need to figure out why," Colonel Drasneb states as he leans back in his chair and ponders.

After a few moments of deep thought, Colonel Drasneb rises from his seat and paces around his office. There is a slight limp in his step from his war wound. Thought of as a crutch, Colonel Drasneb now uses his injury as a motivator toward continuing his great service to his nation. In a way, he takes great pride in his injury. His battle against the Americans was the last offensive that Serbia took in an attempt to push further into Croatia. Colonel Drasneb heard that Serbia is ceasing all military actions against Croatia. Now Serbia has turned its focus to reclaiming lands from Bosnia.

Colonel Drasneb turns to the lieutenant in his office and says, "Bring me prisoner number 53877."

"Yes, colonel." The lieutenant leaves Colonel Drasneb's office and heads toward the cell block, which is five floors beneath the building— the better to ensure that no one escapes. The lieutenant climbs down the dank and musty staircase and hangs a right. Four doors down is the holding cell of First Lieutenant Perez.

The Serb lieutenant has one of the guards unlock the iron cell door. Together, they enter. Inside the cell awaits 1st Lt. Marcus Perez. His continence is neither happy nor relatively upset. Of course, he has little reason to be happy, except for the fact that he is still alive. In place of his flight suit, First Lieutenant Perez wears a simple, thin, gray-colored pair of pants and top that resemble a pair of pajamas. Most POWs sit in their cells and think of loved ones and recite verses or phrases that they may have memorized sometime during their lives. First Lieutenant Perez does as well, but he also works to maintain his strength by doing various forms of push-ups and abdominal work.

When the Serb lieutenant and the guard enter First Lieutenant Perez's cell, they find him with his feet elevated on his cot, doing push-ups.

To get First Lieutenant Perez's attention, the Serb lieutenant storms up to him, stands over his head, and barks, "Get the hell up and come with me!"

First Lieutenant Perez does not speak Serbo-Croatian and therefore does not understand what the Serb lieutenant has just said to him, but he is smart enough to know when someone is ordering him around. He quickly drops his feet to the ground and jumps up from off of the floor. He then stands at a modified position of attention. He does not stand fully erect because he does not feel obliged to give the Serb lieutenant any respect.

For his obvious show of disrespect, the Serb lieutenant punches him in the stomach. "That is what you get for your continued lack of respect, you worthless American!" the Serb lieutenant bellows as First Lieutenant Perez buckles over from the immense pain of the Serb lieutenant's cheap shot.

First Lieutenant Perez slowly picks himself up from off of the cold concrete floor. On his feet, the guard grabs him and slams him up against the wall. The Serb lieutenant presses him on the wall, while the guard then proceeds to throw shackles on him. Spinning him around, the Serb lieutenant then pushes him out of the cell and down the hallway. With First Lieutenant Perez properly restrained, the guard returns to his post at the cell-block entrance. The Serb lieutenant forces First Lieutenant Perez up the musty staircase to the interrogation room where Colonel Drasneb waits.

Approaching the interrogation room, a guard standing at the entrance opens the door for the Serb lieutenant. As soon as the guard opens the interrogation room door, the Serb lieutenant shoves First

Lieutenant Perez inside. From the force and the lack of coordination from the shackles on his feet, First Lieutenant Perez runs into a chair that is at the end of a table and tumbles hard to the floor.

Colonel Drasneb stands at the far end of the interrogation room and observes the occurrence. He laughs to himself. Colonel Drasneb takes great pleasure in seeing and hearing of Americans making fools of themselves, whether it is intentional or not.

"Thank you, Lieutenant Howitzky. You may go now," Colonel Drasneb states to the Serb lieutenant.

Lieutenant Howitzky snaps to attention and salutes Colonel Drasneb. In kind, Colonel Drasneb returns the salute. Lieutenant Howitzky drops his salute, does an about-face, then exits the interrogation room. Upon leaving, the guard shuts the door behind Lieutenant Howitzky.

With the lieutenant out of the interrogation room and having complete privacy, Colonel Drasneb leans over the table on the opposite side from where First Lieutenant Perez is. "Good morning, Lieutenant. Please take a seat," Colonel Drasneb invites First Lieutenant Perez in his best English.

"If you say so," First Lieutenant Perez cynically replies as he clumsily picks himself up from off of the floor. His fall to the ground did not hurt too bad, but at times, he has trouble standing up when his feet are shackled together because the chains get tangled and his feet are too close together.

Colonel Drasneb walks around to the other end of the table and takes a hard look at his prisoner. He paces around First Lieutenant Perez, looking to discover anything that he may have missed during the previous sessions. Investigating, Colonel Drasneb notices a bit of color peaking out from underneath First Lieutenant Perez's left sleeve. Slowly, yet assuredly, Colonel Drasneb moves his hand over First Lieutenant Perez's left shoulder and rolls up the short sleeve.

"What is this a tattoo of?" Colonel Drasneb asks.

"It's my school crest," First Lieutenant Perez answers.

"University?"

"Humph. Hardly. I went to a military academy."

"Military academy, huh? How many of you go there?"

"What do you mean by 'how many of you'?"

"Who in the American army attends this university?"

At that moment, Colonel Drasneb kneels down and gazes more intently at the crest, closely studying it. Upon glaring at the crest, he sees two words and whispers, "West Point."

"Yeah, that's the name of the place," First Lieutenant Perez mumbles under his breath.

"Yes, I have heard of it," Colonel Drasneb counters, rubbing his head. He then continues, "So as I asked before, how many of America's soldiers attend this West Point?"

"The few and the proud," First Lieutenant Perez sarcastically replies.

From First Lieutenant Perez's smart-aleck comment, Colonel Drasneb immediately becomes upset and in a show of intimidation, he throws his face in front of First Lieutenant Perez's, to where their nose are nearly touching.

"Do not test my patience, Lieutenant!" Colonel Drasneb growls.

"No one's testing your patience, sir. It's just that you're asking me open-ended questions, which allow me to fill them in with my natural wit and humor."

Colonel Drasneb moves away from First Lieutenant Perez and turns his back from him, taking a moment to collect himself. He thinks, *This American is very disrespectful, but he has information that may be quite valuable to me and Serbia. What should I do?*

Colonel Drasneb finally calms down then turns back around and pulls up a seat next to First Lieutenant Perez. "So, Lieutenant, how many graduated with you?"

"I don't know. I didn't count."

Controlling his temper, Colonel Drasneb replies, "Of course you know. You went there. You know how many graduated with you?"

"Well, a little less than a thousand of us graduate each year."

"So close to a thousand of your country's best officers graduate from this West Point every year?"

"That's what I said."

"So for simplicity's sake, about one fourth of America's officers graduate from the West Point Military Academy?"

"That sounds about right," First Lieutenant Perez answers, who is not really sure where Colonel Drasneb is going with his line of questioning.

The Serbs do not treat him too bad. The guards and the junior officers get their pop shots in every once and a while, but over all, he is treated well. It is nothing that he cannot handle due in part to his SERE (Search, Escape, Rescue, and Evasion) training. Those instructors kicked his butt and broke a few bones in the process. All he has to account for now is a bruised hip and a bump on his head. It could be worse. It definitely beats being a POW in Cambodia or Vietnam.

Colonel Drasneb rises from his seat and walks over to a small shelf that is next to the window on the far end of the room. He reaches for a silver-colored flask, raises it in the air, and asks, "Would you like some scotch, Lieutenant?"

A bit surprised, First Lieutenant Perez answers, "I wouldn't mind a little pull, sir."

First Lieutenant Perez is unsure as to why his captor is being so generous all of a sudden. He realizes though that a couple of sips of scotch sure beats the hell out of drinking water that makes New Jersey's water taste like it comes from a mountain spring.

Colonel Drasneb smiles, pouring First Lieutenant Perez a small glass. Handing the lieutenant the drink, he asks him, "So, Lieutenant, tell me about this West Point."

"Well…" and so First Lieutenant Perez tells Colonel Drasneb of his life at West Point and the history of the school. To him, it is a lot better talking about the Point than Colonel Drasneb constantly interrogating him about reconnaissance flights and helicopter schematics.

1533 Hours

"So, Colonel, I hear you have some very important information for me. Knowing you, I know that it is some good intel. Making you chief interrogator was the best thing that I've done in a while. So let me have it," Major General Bruscev boasts as he rubs his hands together like a child receiving an expected Christmas gift.

"Sir, I have a plan that can ensure the extermination of one fourth of the American army's officer corps for the next four years," Colonel Drasneb proudly boasts, puffing his chest out with pride.

"I knew this would be good. Please, continue."

"After interviewing prisoner number 53877, I was able to assess a method that could lead to the crippling of the American army through the deaths of one fourth of their officer corps."

"Yes, yes. You have already said that. Get on to the good part."

"Yes, sir. I'm getting there. I am naming the operation *Quarter*. The goal is to kill the cadets that attend West Point, America's supreme military academy."

On hearing Colonel Drasneb's words, Major General Bruscev slowly raises his head, his eyes quickly opening as wide as his lids will allow. "West Point! The United States Military Academy? If you are able to pull off this operation, do you understand the effect that this will have on the Americans? Their army will be crippled beyond belief. The destruction of morale alone would enable us to be victorious and push the Americans and those Muslim dogs out of our rightful lands."

"That is my point exactly, sir."

"One thing though, Colonel. General Kradvit graduated from West Point, therefore, we must ensure that this operation remains secret. If he finds out, there is a possibility that he will send word to the Americans."

"Sir, wouldn't that be considered treason?"

"Technically yes, but with the severity of your possible operation, our country's politicians will probably look the other way if General Kradvit informs the Americans of your plans. Their thinking being that he is not harming Serbia's goals but, instead, is preventing a possible war crime from occurring. Understand?"

"Yes, sir. I understand fully."

"Now, Drasneb, explain to me this master plan of yours."

And so Colonel Drasneb, in minimal detail, briefs his plans for Operation Quarter to Major General Bruscev. He has not had time to formulate a conclusive plan to date.

With Colonel Drasneb finishing his brief, Major General Bruscev states, "That sounds pretty concrete, Drasneb. You have my permission to form your special unit, but let me remind you to keep this secret. No one but you, your special unit, and I can know of Operation Quarter. All right?"

"Yes, sir."

"Good. If this works the way that you plan, the Americans will no longer be a thorn in our side. And maybe they'll finally take the Serbian Army seriously. You'll be greatly rewarded for your success—medals and that promotion you should have received four years ago. Of course, if you fail, the government will deny any knowledge of Operation Quarter. You will be forced to retire, but not in disgrace though. I respect a man who takes personal risks for his country. Do you have any questions of me?"

"No, sir."

"Well then. I want you to report back to me two weeks from today to fully brief me on the operation—maps, schematics, the budget, everything."

"I'll get right on it, sir."

"All right then. I'll see you in two months." Major General Bruscev rises from his seat and extends his hand toward Colonel Drasneb, who firmly grasps it, smiling slightly.

With the meeting complete, Colonel Drasneb salutes Major General Bruscev then exits the general's office. Walking down the hallway, Colonel Drasneb feels very jovial, a far contrast to how he usually feels. Colonel Drasneb has not felt this good in a very long time. *It's funny*, Colonel Drasneb thinks to himself. *My leg no longer seems to bother me as much as it usually does. Maybe this second chance at life has renewed my strength both physically and psychologically.* Colonel Drasneb strides out of the headquarters building, whistling an old song that he has not thought of since he was a young boy.

27 AUGUST, 1999

1545 Hours: West Point

All of D-1's twenty-five excited first class cadets stand outside of the orderly room patiently waiting. Today marks an extremely important day for all cadets—the day they receive their class rings. The weekend long ceremony, which commences this Friday with the first class cadets receiving their rings, is known as Ring Weekend. According to West Point lore, the Ring Weekend formal is the second most influential formal in the United States—second only to the official presidential inaugural ball.

The uniform for the ring ceremony is india whites with red sash, a top and bottom tailored from a thin cotton material. India whites is a popular uniform among cadets because of its comfort; unfortunately, they only have two opportunities to ever wear it.

Joe looks at his watch and, realizing that it is three forty-five, says to Major, "It's time."

"All right. Let's do this," Major states as he strides through the small crowd of firsties.

Major leads his classmates out of the barracks and out onto Grant Area where D-1's plebes, wearing white over gray and under arms, await in a row at the bottom of the middle stairwell at the position of parade rest.

As the D-1 firsties approach the top of the stairwell, the first sergeant commands, "Fourth class! Attention!"

Instantly, the D-1 plebes snap to the position of attention. An instant before Major reaches the first two plebes, they snap to the position of present arms, thus saluting Major as he passes. Walking through the gauntlet, each set of plebes snaps to present arms as Major and the D-1 firsties proudly pass through. Once the final D-1 firstie proudly strides through the plebe gauntlet, they all walk together to the apron for their 1600 hour formation of all of West Point's first class cadets.

Trotting to catch up with Sara, Major states, "That went pretty well, huh?"

Of all of the firsties in his company, Sara's opinion on company matters means the most to Major.

"It was a nice little added touch for Ring Weekend," Sara replies. "I don't think any other companies had a ceremony like ours."

"I doubt anyone else did either, but then again, there isn't another CO like me!"

"That's the truth," Sara retorts, laughing and jabbing Major on the shoulder.

At the apron, all of the first class cadets in the corps are loosely assembled in preparation for the Ring Weekend ceremonial formation. Between Eisenhower and Mac Arthur statues, the firsties form up: Company A-1 beside Eisenhower statue and Company H-4 beside Mac Arthur statue. The firsties fall in based upon alphabetical order, except for the company ring and crest representatives and the company commanders. The ring and crest reps and company commanders fall in to the front of their respective company formations.

With all of the first class cadets having formed up, they execute a left face and march to Trophy Point. As Major marches among his fellow Ducks, he thinks to himself, *There couldn't be a better day for this ceremony.*

Major is more than correct. High overhead in the sky above, there is not a cloud in sight. The sun shines bright, illuminating the horizon. Its rays reflecting off of the Hudson River as it slowly ripples down stream.

Trophy Point sits in a small pocket overlooking the Hudson River to the north. On a pleasant day, such as this one, the scene from Trophy Point is quite picturesque. For the ring ceremony, the first class cadets stand within the bowl of Trophy Point, while onlookers fervently watch on the edge above. Those viewing the sacred West

Point ceremony are an amalgam of tourists, family, friends, girlfriends, and fiancées.

Standing at the position of attention, all of the first class cadets wait with a great deal of bottled-up impatience to receive their rings. To a West Point graduate, the class ring is one of the most cherished possessions that one owns. Most old grads revere their ring more than their diploma. For West Point graduates, the class ring represents prestige and honor—that they have accomplished something that many strive for but few attain.

As the ring ceremony progresses, the tactical officers receive a box containing their respective company's rings. Major stands proudly waiting to receive his ring. Joyfully nervous, Major bounces lightly on his toes, just enough to shake the nerves off, but not obvious enough for anyone else to detect.

Being the Duck company commander, Major is the first one in his company to receive his ring. Gripping his black velvet ring box, Major thinks, *I can't believe this day is really here. I knew I'd get this, but God, this is friggin' unreal!*

Upon receiving their class rings, the superintendent of the military academy, Lt. Gen. Christopher Holiday, commands the first class cadets, "Don your rings!"

Hearing the order, the firsties open their boxes to great amazement. Within their boxes sits the most beautiful object that their eyes have ever seen. Full of joy and a high sense of accomplishment, the first class cadets take their rings out of their boxes and place them on their ring fingers.

Major gazes at his ring. Its majesty brightly shines, as though purposefully projecting its grand esteem. A sense of joy rushes through Major's entire being, a feeling which he has never felt before.

Major takes his ring into the palm of his hand and closely examines it. His eyes slowly inspect its every crevice and dimension. On one side of Major's ring, as with all of the class rings, lies West Point's crest: a bold bald eagle with its majestic wings outstretched. Beneath the eagle lies the helmet of the ancient Greek goddess Athena. Beneath the eagle's left wing are inscribed Douglas MacArthur's famous words: Duty, Honor, Country. And beneath the eagle's right wing are the words *West Point* and the year of the military academy's founding, *MDCCCII* (1802).

Major turns his ring over and pridefully peers at his class crest: a West Point first class cadet and an army officer saluting one another with their sabers, with the American flag waving proudly in the background. A majestic eagle is perched above the army officer. To the left of the eagle is emblazoned the year *2000*, signifying Major's graduating class. Below, stamped on a shield is *MM* (2000), and etched on a scroll is the Class of 2000's motto, With Honor in Hand.

Major slowly slips his ring onto his left hand ring finger. Unexpectedly, a surge of energy courses through Major's body, as though his ring now serves as a new power source. Major clinches his fist in acknowledgement of his great achievement.

Once all of the first class cadets have placed their rings on their fingers, Lieutenant General Holiday dismisses them, thus ending the ring ceremony. With the ceremony complete, Major says a few quick hellos to a few of his friends then takes off in a dead sprint for his room. He and some of his friends have a six forty-five train to catch from the town of Garrison heading to New York City. Garrison is a small town across the Hudson River from West Point.

Major darts and dashes through the immense crowd of spectators. At the road's edge, he jogs as he watches for the oncoming traffic. The road clear, Major crosses, picking his speed back up. Major sprints down the sidewalk, passing Thayer statue.

As Major approaches MacArthur statue, he notices a very large crowd of plebes and a few mingling yearlings. Major knows exactly what they are waiting for—him and all of the other oncoming firsties.

A very old tradition at the United States Military Academy is the recitation of the "Ring Poop," given by the plebes to the firsties upon reception of their class rings. The plebes will literally attack a firstie in their attempt to recite the "Ring Poop." The plebes get down on one knee and crowd around the firstie, saying,

> *Sir, what a beautiful ring! What a crass mass of brass and glass! What a bold mold of rolled gold! What a cool jewel you got from the school! See how it sparkles and shines! May I touch it, sir? May I touch it please, sir?*

Major knows that if he slows down, the plebes will maul him until they have recited the "Ring Poop." Fortunately, he is faster than all of the waiting plebes.

As Major approaches the hungry gang of waiting plebes, Major hears a yuck shout, "There's one! Get him!"

Upon the command, the plebe mob jumps to and immediately chases after Major. He runs past the plebes, tapping into his innate speed to burst through the small mob. The plebes though are quite persistent. They chase Major all the way to the Normandy sally port, which separates Eisenhower Barracks from Washington Hall. As Major sprints through Normandy sally port, the plebe mob ends its chase and regroups at Mac Arthur statue.

At the other end of Normandy sally port, waiting for unsuspecting firsties, stands another yearling. As Major slows his pace down some, he sees this yearling and says to himself, *God help me. Not again.*

As soon as Major and the waiting yearling lock eyes, the yearling shouts, "Hey! Over here! A firstie!"

Standing outside of Bradley Short Barracks, a large group of plebes chases Major down, causing him to pick his pace back up to a full sprint. Major outruns these plebes, but much to his chagrin, another gang of plebes standing alongside Pershing Barracks cut him off from his destination. Major, finally realizing that he cannot win, stops in his tracks and allows the plebes to recite the "Ring Poop."

While the plebes begin to recite the "Ring Poop," Major shouts, "I've got to make a train, guys! Walk with me."

Major's idea was a nice one, but the plebe mob is so large that they are unable, or unwilling, to move with him.

Patiently, Major waits as the plebes recite the "Ring Poop." Once they have completed their dastardly task, the plebes leave Major in search of another unsuspecting firstie.

Free of the plebe mob, Major continues on his path in a dead sprint to Grant Barracks. Fifty meters from Grant Barracks, Major spots most of his plebe Ducks anxiously waiting for him on the other side of the road. Seeing his plebes, Major says to himself, *I have to let my plebes recite the "Ring Poop." They are my soldiers for crying out loud.*

Seeing their commander running at full speed across the street, one of the Duck plebes from among the group shouts, "There's the commander!"

In a great fervor, the D-1 plebes encircle Major. Full of pride, Major makes a fist with his ring hand (left) and thrusts it high into the air. The plebe Ducks, loud and proud, recite the "Ring Poop" for their commander.

"Oh my god, sir! What a beautiful ring! What a beautiful mass of brass and glass! What a bold mold of rolled gold. What a cool jewel you got from the school! It must have cost you a fortune! See how it sparkles and shines? May I touch it? May I touch it please, sir?"

Having completed the "Ring Poop," the plebes take a few steps away from their company commander. Looking at his plebes with great pride, Major says to them, "You guys make me proud! I hope your weekend is as good as mine's going to be!"

Finished speaking, Major runs into Grant Area. Leaving his plebes, they all shout, "We own the pond, sir!"

Major leaps to the top of the stoops in a single bound and loudly replies to his glowing plebes with a fist high in the air, "Hell yeah, we do!"

Goat Park, Harlem, New York

Goat Park is dedicated to the New York City playground basketball legend Harold "the Goat" Manigault and is home to many great street ballers as well as college and NBA superstars. Basketball players come from all over the world to play at Goat Park to prove their skills and abilities on the court against the best street ballers.

Today, Goat Park is hosting a youth basketball tournament for ages twelve to fifteen years old. Hundreds of people are in attendance from the local community and from throughout the New York tristate area. Among the ecstatic small crowd are Mac and Killer. They regularly attend these tournaments because they love good, exciting basketball, plus it allows them to talk shop without worrying about anyone listening in on and comprehending their conversations.

"I really needed this leave," Killer opens.

"I hear you, bro," Mac chimes. "I love what we do, but a man can only go so long before he needs a break. I don't know how you do it sometimes."

"What do you mean?"

"Well, think about it. You have a family. Me? I have no one depending on me. I'm my on person. I mean, sure. I have my dad and all, but it isn't too hard to make him think that I have another job other than what we are actually doing for a living."

"I see what you're saying. It is getting tough to come up with lie after lie to explain to Sharon why I'm away so often. The whole 'sales convention' and 'training session' lines are really getting old."

"What are you going to do about it?"

"Not sure. God knows I don't want to quit. What we do is a part of me. I don't think I'd be the same if I had to do something else."

"I hear you, Killer. X has been bugging me a lot lately, trying to get me to be his head of security."

"Does he even need a head of security?"

"Not now, but he's getting ready to blow up real soon."

"Really?"

"Yeah. He told me that a couple of movie directors have gotten in touch with him about some roles."

"That's nice, man. You think he'll get into the movies?"

"From the way he was talking last week, I know he will."

"Well, if he does blow up like you think he will, he's probably going to need a head of security."

"Yeah, I guess he will, but I'm stuck like you are."

"How so?"

"My job is my life. It's what I do because it's what I do best. I know I'd make a great body guard, but there's nothing like the rush I get when we're out on a job."

"I know what you're saying. I love my wife and kids more than anything, and they give me the greatest joy, but there's no feeling like the adrenaline rush I get when I end someone's life."

"That's why you're the Killer."

"That's right."

The two friends laugh as they return their focus to the basketball game. Watching a very close game between a team from a Boys and Girls Club and one sponsored by a local athletic store, one of the fifteen year olds on the Boys and Girls Club team steals the ball from the opposing point guard at the top of the key. The young man speeds past the point guard and pushes the ball ahead of him. All alone, at the other end of the court, the young man leaps high into the air, spins around, then does a one hand jam. Everyone in the crowd, sitting and standing, jumps up and cheer at the spectacular sight that they had just witnessed. Ecstatic, some people even run out onto the court to congratulate the young man by slapping him on his butt with towels and lightly banging his chest with their fists.

"That kid's the future, right there," Killer calmly states.

"Naw, dawg. I've met the future. That boy's the second coming."

"Yeah, he is," Killer agrees. "Like Earl Monroe."

Enjoying each other's company and the basketball game, both Mac and Killer's cell phones ring.

"Damn it!" Mac exclaims. "I'm trying to enjoy the game.

Both men reach into their pockets and retrieve their cellular phones. Looking at the screen, Mac and Killer notice that the incoming call is coming in as an unknown number. Seeing the phrase, Mac and Killer know that the call is from "J."

Simultaneously, Mac and Killer answer their phones. "What do you want, J?" Mac opens. "The Killer and I are trying to enjoy a basketball game."

"I apologize for cutting into your personal time," J explains, "but I need you guys to get back here."

"What do you mean, get back here?" Killer asks.

"I need you guys to come back to headquarters. I have a mission for you two," J states.

"We're still on break, J," Killer says.

"I know this, gentlemen, but I need you guys here for this one. I need my best operatives, and unfortunately, that means you two."

"You're pissing us off, J," Killer mumbles under his breath. "What am I supposed to say to my family?"

"You're a smart man, Killer. You will figure it out. Now there is no room for discussion here. Your tickets are waiting for you at Newark, the last flight out tonight. You know the airline," J firmly explains to Mac and Killer. He then hangs up his telephone, leaving Mac and Killer sitting in the bleachers, staring at one another in disbelief.

"Can you believe that?" Mac angrily blurts.

Killer just sits there in silence. He is unsure of what to say at the moment, let alone tell his family.

"Come on, Killer. We've got to get going," Mac states as he rises from his seat.

"Yeah. We've got to go," Killer coldly replies, following Mac out of the bleachers.

Forcing their way through the immense crowd, Killer and Mac exit Goat Park.

At the front entrance, Mac and Killer turn and face one another. Mac grasps Killer's shoulder and states, "I'll see you at nine, brother."

"Yeah. Nine," Killer replies.

Mac loosens his grip and walks down the street toward a subway terminal. As he steps off, he faces Killer again and shouts, "I'm sorry, man!"

Throwing his left arm up in the air, Killer silently replies, "Yeah. Me too."

Killer turns down the street and heads for a train terminal. He has to go home and explain to his family why he has to leave so abruptly. Fortunately, he has a two-hour train ride to figure something out.

28 AUGUST 1999

0800 Hours: Paris, France

"So, J, I hope this is important? We're supposed to be on our off cycle, remember?" Mac complains.

"I know, Mac. I apologize for the inconvenience, but I got a call from a potential client who has a very lucrative job for us. It is by far the most delicate job we have ever gotten a contract for. I need my best men for this one, so I called in you and the Killer," J explains as he points to Killer.

"Humph…" shrugs Mac. "What is it we have to do now?"

"I'm glad you asked. As I stated earlier, this job is as delicate as they come. Here, take a second to read this."

J tosses a manila envelope across his desk. Mac leans over and picks it up from off of the reflective mahogany desk. He carefully breaks the wax seal and smoothly removes the documents. While skimming through the pages, Mac's face contorts and transforms as his eyes move quickly over the words. Suddenly he throws the papers back onto J's desk.

"Hell no!" Mac barks. "There's no way we're doing this job! I mean, God don't we have any sense of morality left?"

Mac's words stammer together. He does not understand why Black Jack would even think about taking a job like this.

Killer leans forward and retrieves the manila envelope from off of J's desk. As J and Mac continue their argument, Killer quickly yet studiously thumbs through the contents of the envelope. Killer finishes reading the documents then carefully places them back onto J's desk. He then calmly leaves J's office and heads for the bathroom.

"Listen, Mac. I know how you are feeling. You and the Killer are both United States war veterans. Your feelings are clearly understandable, but do not think of the cadets as noncombatants. Their entire purpose is to lead soldiers into combat. Think of this as only a job, and you'll be fine," J desperately attempts to explain to Mac.

"This doesn't sit right with me, J. We may just be training these fools, but our training is leading to the deaths of some kids! Kids, J!"

"Obviously, you're going to need some time to think this over. How about this then? Take the packet with you. You and Killer do a little research. Come back in a couple of days or so, and talk with me about it. All right? Do not lose any sleep over this."

"Yeah, whatever. We'll figure something out. We always do," Mac soberly responds.

Mac heads for the door when J suddenly says, "Oh, I almost forgot. There's five million US dollars in it for each of you."

Mac abruptly stops in his tracks and quickly spins around. "Five mil?"

"Yep," J replies.

"Hmmm…I'm going to have to take that into consideration," Mac comments as he departs the room.

As Mac leaves J's office, he spots Killer slowly walking down the hallway toward him. Killer sees Mac as well and raises his right hand in the air.

"Where'd you run off to, brother?" Mac asks.

"I needed to step out for a while and splash some water on my face," Killer answers with a slight chill in his voice.

"You read that piece of shit, didn't you?"

"Sure did. Made me sick to my stomach."

"Yeah. Me too."

"Did I miss anything while I was out?"

Instead of answering Killer's question, Mac walks away from him and over to a plate-glass window, looking down onto the street below.

"What do you do this for, bro?" Mac asks Killer.

"What do you mean?" Killer responds.

"You have a beautiful wife and three great kids. Why don't you go straight?"

"I don't know. I love what we do. I don't know how I could go straight after all of this time. Plus, if I were to tell Sharon what we really do, she would take it pretty hard. She thinks I'm at another sales convention right now." Killer sighs and continues, saying, "I am getting tired of all of the lying."

Mac fans the manila envelope in the air. "This job brings in five mil a piece. When we're done, I think you should get out."

"Yeah, maybe you're right."

"Come on. Let's go handle this one. I'll talk to J later," Mac solemnly states as he walks back over to Killer.

"All right then, but I really need to go home for a while, get my head straight and all."

"That's cool, bro. I understand," Mac replies. "When do you think you'll be back?"

"September 6."

"Well, I guess we better get you back to the airport and get you a flight back home. I'll hold things down here 'til you get back."

Mac hails down a cab. After a brief moment, a white Peugeot pulls over to the curb. The two friends climb in and head for the airport with a million thoughts racing through their heads, One of family and loved ones, the other a feeling of loss as though his soul is fading away.

———————◆————————◆

Back in the Black Jack headquarters building, J is running the recent events through his head.

Drasneb *said that he wanted my best! Well, damn it! He is definitely going to get that in Mac and Killer. I just did not think that they loved their country enough to really care.*

While J contemplates his decision, his telephone rings. J picks up the receiver and says, "Hello?"

"Yes, J. It is good to hear your voice," the voice on the other end states.

"Colonel Drasneb. I did not expect you to call so promptly."

"Well, I did not want to waste any time. I have this thing about sticking with my timetables. So being that this is a business call and not social, allow me to skip the pleasantries and get right to the point. Have you assigned me my two men yet?"

"Yes, I have."

"Good. See to it that they arrive in Belgrade on September 14. That is all for now. I will be in touch." Colonel Drasneb hangs up on his end.

"Before you go, we do need to discuss something about this contract."

"What is it? I need to take care of some business."

"This Serb-to-French translation of the word *train*, which I then had to translate to English, does not sit well with me."

"How so? It is apparently clear to me. You agreed to supply me with two men to lead my mission."

"Hold on now. What do you mean by lead?"

"J, I am surprised by your inquiry. You are supposed to be an intelligent man. Maybe you are slipping some in your old age. Who knows? Either way, when I say 'lead my mission,' that is exactly what I mean."

"You!"

"Now, J, if you had an issue with the contract, you should have made sure you truly knew what you were getting your men into."

J takes a moment to gather himself. He cannot believe what a mess he got Mac and Killer into. Due to the structure of the contract, it is now apparent that Mac and Killer must not only train Colonel Drasneb's men but must also lead the mission. That means that they will play a direct role in killing West Point cadets.

"Okay, Drasneb, you are correct. Mac and Killer must follow through with the contract. I will make sure they do so. I promise you this though. If you make it out alive, we are no longer doing business with one another. I may have lost a step or two in my old age, but whatever honor you may have had thirty years ago is now gone."

J ends his conversation with Colonel Drasneb by hanging up the phone.

"That arrogant son of a bitch!" J angrily mumbles under his breath. "I hope Mac and Killer can see it through."

1500 Hours: The Serbian Army Interrogation Building, Belgrade, Serbia

In a small colorless room, a group of five men sit chatting among themselves. They patiently wait for Colonel Drasneb to come and brief them on their new mission. None are aware of the details concerning the mission. All they know is that the mission is at the highest levels of top secret and that its success could mean the turn of the war in their favor.

Most of the men know one another through their service in the army. As they wait patiently, the five men converse about their army experiences and their triumphs during the war.

Outside of the room, beside the entrance, Colonel Drasneb listens to the men speak among themselves. A slight smile appears on his face, the pleasure coming from the fact that the men are all getting along.

It is good that the men enjoy one another, Colonel Drasneb pleasantly thinks to himself. *It will make training more bearable and increase our likelihood of success.*

After a few moments of silent thought, Colonel Drasneb decides that it is time to enter the room and begin his brief.

"Good afternoon, gentlemen. I have called you all here today for a very special and utmost important mission. Some of you I know personally, and others by your professional reputations. This mission, if successful, will make you national heroes. If we fail, then your careers are over. If for whatever reason you do not wish to participate in this mission, speak now. Your decision will not be held against you, and your nonparticipation will not be added to your record. Otherwise, you're in it for the long haul."

Colonel Drasneb's statement causes the room to go silent. Each man looks at one another to see who is going to walk out. Much to their relief, no one leaves the room. After a brief moment, the men prepare to take notes as they anticipate the remainder of Colonel Drasneb's speech.

"Good," Colonel Drasneb satisfyingly replies. "Let us continue. Now as you have all noticed, the highest-ranking person in this room other than myself is a captain. I did this to ensure that there is as little butt kissing as possible. I have come to learn through my years of military service that the higher in rank you achieve, the more prevalent the butt kissing. Why do you think I'm still a colonel after all of these years? Now that I got my little philosophy out of the way, I want you to take a look at each other around the room. From this moment on, you are all equal in terms of rank, but not in pay. Your pay is still whatever it currently is. This also goes in hand with what I said previously. Your new title while under my command is *expert*. Each of you will command a team containing five men. I am allowing you to form your own units. I do not need to tell you what caliber of men is required for a mission of this importance. Because this mission is so important, you must ensure that you would place your lives in your men's hands. The dangers involved with this mission are so high that it may come down to them saving your lives."

The men all nod their heads, understanding where Colonel Drasneb is coming from in relation to selecting the men who will serve under them. Sluggishly, Colonel Drasneb begins pacing around the room.

As he walks, the men follow him with their eyes. Colonel Drasneb stops at the other end of the room then humbly says, "Your training will be led by mercenaries."

All of the men grimace at Colonel Drasneb's words. They, as true soldiers, have no respect for mercenaries. As far as they are concerned, men who kill for the sole purpose of earning a paycheck have no honor. They do not trust mercenaries for the simple fact that there is no one to regulate their activities or their actions. Mercenaries have no code. They simply kill any and everything for money and have little, if any, remorse of the repercussions of their actions.

Empathizing with his men, Colonel Drasneb assures, "I know that none of you agree with my decision, but these men have skills that we need in order for us to accomplish our mission. We truly need their specialties and expertise if we are to achieve success. Do not worry about the mercenaries. I am only hiring two, and I will have constant security on them at all times. They will not be able to go to the toilet with my knowing it. I have personally handled their acquisition. I know someone who owed me a favor."

The men sit in their seats feeling quite perplexed. They cannot fathom why any mission that they are participating in would need to utilize mercenaries for the mission to be successful. After a little thought though, they all come to generally the same conclusion: that Colonel Drasneb knows what is best for the mission and that they are going to just have to trust him, even if it means training alongside a couple of dirty, dishonorable mercenaries.

Colonel Drasneb notices his men's discomfort over the information, so he concludes, "If there are no questions, you all may leave?"

The men begin to rise from their seats when a first sergeant raises his hand and asks, "Colonel Drasneb, sir, may I ask a question?"

"Certainly."

The first sergeant sits straight in his seat and states, "Sir, I believe I speak for everyone in the room when I say that I feel very uncomfortable having to work with a couple of dishonorable mercenaries. Because of my misgivings, I am curious as to how far into the operation the mercenaries will take part?"

"That is a good question, Expert Setaudarg," Colonel Drasneb affirms, stressing Setaudarg's title of expert. He refers to the first sergeant as expert to emphasize to his men that he views all of them as equals, whether they are senior noncommissioned officers or officers. "The two mercenaries will train us, as you already know, but they will also take part in the operation."

Expert Setaudarg uneasily squirms in his seat. The other experts also show slight negative reactions to Colonel Drasneb's answer.

Colonel Drasneb, aware of their noticeable discomfort with his latest announcement, then states, "As soon as we move further along in our series of briefs prior to the training phase of the mission, you will all understand why I am utilizing the two mercenaries during the mission's execution phase. I am sad to say, but our success depends upon their aide during the execution phase. Does everyone understand?"

The experts all reply yes but still do not favor Colonel Drasneb's decision. Nonetheless, there is nothing they can do to reverse it. All they can do is trust Colonel Drasneb's wisdom on the issue and follow their orders to the letter.

"So are their any other questions?" Colonel Drasneb asks.

No one replies.

"All right then," Colonel Drasneb continues. "This meeting is now concluded. You may all leave. My office will get in contact with you in a few days. Your first priority is to recruit your men. You have two weeks to do so. As soon as you have formed your teams, contact me. You are all dismissed."

Walking down the hall, the experts silently discuss among themselves what their mission may be and if it truly is as important as Colonel Drasneb is stressing. They all are still in complete disbelief that they are going to have to work alongside mercenaries. None of the men have ever had any association with any mercenaries, but they have heard rumors and tales of distrust and sheer villainy on the battlefield. Men with no honor have no compassion.

30 AUGUST 1999

1230 Hours: West Point

In 1929, Washington Hall was constructed on the old gymnasium site, which sat between Central and North Barracks. Washington Hall, its original three wings emanating from the main entrance and its high ceiling supported by deep cross beams, is magnificently set off by T. Loftin Johnson's mural, which covers the entire south wall. The mural depicts in brilliant color twenty great battles and great generals in world history.

A worthy counterpart to the mural is the beautiful stained-glass window in the west wall that portrays the life of George Washington. The flags of the fifty states, one territory, and the District of Columbia, presented for display in the dining hall by the National Guard Association in observance of the academy's sesquicentennial, were replaced in 1971 by a gift of new flags from the West Point chapter of the Daughters of the United States Army.

The keystone of the 1964 expansion program was the three-wing addition to Washington Hall. The dining hall was extended to the front onto the Plain in a mirror image of the three existing wings, thus allowing the entire Corps of Cadets to still sit together and eat family-style meals. This design is how Washington Hall stands today. The front of the old Washington Hall was preserved in place and now stands at the center of the dining hall as the hub, with the six wings extending from it. The hub is now referred to as the poop deck, where the brigade S-1 makes announcements to the Corps of Cadets.

The poop deck is referred to as such because it is where the cadet brigade S-1 makes her announcements during breakfast, lunch, and Thursday-night spirit dinners. The word *poop* means information or knowledge, and *deck* refers to the fact that when announcements are made from the poop deck, the individual stands out on a large balcony that faces both the front and the back of the mess hall.

Carved into the granite-and-limestone front of this massive structure are the Great Seal of the United States, George Washington's coat of arms, and scenes depicting the genius of George Washington. The string course of carved figures depicting the evolution of warfare was removed from Old North Barracks and preserved in Washington Hall. Replicas of early American colonial flags and flags showing the evolution of the American flag are also on display, hanging high overhead along the sides of the mess hall's wings.

Other than the mess hall, there are numerous USCC (United States Corps of Cadets) agencies and support activities located in Washington Hall. The chaplains' offices are located on the first floor. The commandant, his staff, and the Department of Military Instruction are located just above the mess hall on the fourth and fifth floors. The offices and classrooms of the Department of Geography and Environmental Engineering and the Department of Foreign Languages occupy the remaining area of the fourth, fifth, and sixth floors. Foreign-language laboratories and classrooms are located where cadet uniforms were once manufactured on the fourth floor of old Washington Hall.

Washington Hall is where the cadets eat their daily meals—breakfast, lunch, and dinner. Each company has designated seating within the six wings. One wing, which is located in the far back, directly behind the poop deck, is known as the corps squad section. The corps squad section is where the football team, basketball team, and all other in-season athletic teams eat.

When Major enters the mess hall with his company, instead of eating with them, as all of the other company commanders do, he goes over to the Corps Squad Section to eat with his teammates. Major could eat with his fellow Ducks especially since the basketball team's traditional season has not yet begun, but he cares deeply that a deep bond is maintained and strengthened in preparation for what he and his teammates anticipate will be a record-breaking season.

Each table in the mess hall seats ten people, two at the perspective ends and four on the two sides. The head of the table is referred to as the table com's position, where the highest-ranking cadet sits. The basketball team has four tables, one of which Major is a table com. The remainder of the seats at Major's table are filled by another firstie, two cows, two yucks, and four plebes.

Lunch ends every day in the same manner: the brigade S-1 making her announcements then concluding them by either saying, "Please continue eating" or "Brigade, rest." After doing so, the first class cadets are permitted to leave the mess hall. The three under classes are not permitted to leave until their "light" comes on. The light hangs on the two sides of the poop deck and resembles an old-fashioned streetlight. The light has three circular yellow lights inside that flash signaling when the three under classes are permitted to leave.

Once the brigade S-1 finishes making her announcements, Major stands up, puts his right hand on the back of the chair, and simultaneously slides the chair underneath him and hops over it.

"I'll see you guys at practice. I have to go to a meeting with my new RTO (regimental tactical officer)," Major says as he leaves his table.

Major strides out of the Corps Squad Section toward the poop deck. On his way up the stairs to the DFL (Department of Foreign Languages) lecture room, Major runs into the other three company commanders in his battalion.

"Hey, BC. Have you met the new RTO yet?" Major asks Cdt. Brian Charles.

"No, I haven't. Putter probably has though. Being that he's the regimental commander, and all," Cadet Charles, A-1's commander, replies.

"Yeah. I heard he saw a little combat over in Croatia," Cdt. Capt. Rick Peterson, C-1's commander, adds to the conversation.

"That's cool," Major responds.

"I hope he's better than Clemson was. That dude was a prick!" B-1's company commander, Cdt. Capt. Jon O'Hara, exclaims.

The four company commanders all acknowledge Jon's statement with giant head nods and some snickering.

They reach the fifth floor of Washington Hall, where the DFL lecture room is located. The four commanders step out of the elevator, hang a left, and casually stroll down the hallway. They enter the room, and sit in the front middle seats. The commanders would love to sit more toward the back or the sides of the lecture room, but they know that they would probably just have to move down to the front anyway. Besides, there are only going to be fourteen cadets in the meeting, so there is no point in sitting in the back anyway.

As the four company commanders wait for the RTO and the regimental commander, they sit and chatter about many things except for company business. First battalion's commanders are known for their laid-back nature. They keep their lives and, more importantly, the lives of the cadets under their charge as stress free as possible. Some do not approve of their leadership approach, but they get the job done well, and at the end of the day, that is all that matters.

As first battalion's commanders converse among themselves, the other cadets who have to attend the meeting enter the room. Everyone says hello to one another as they sit.

After a few minutes of waiting, First regiment's commander, Cdt. Capt. Albert Putter enters the room, stands at the position of attention, and says, "The regimental tactical officer."

On command, the company and battalion commanders jump to their feet and stand at the position of attention.

The RTO casually enters the room and says, "Sit down, sit down." Upon the RTO's orders, the commanders take their seats. "Gentlemen," the RTO begins, "thank you for showing up for this little meeting. Not that you all had much of a choice."

Everyone laughs at the RTO's statement mostly because they know that he is right; they did not have a choice in attending the meeting. If they had a choice, most of them would all be taking a nap right now.

"I am Lt. Col. Al Turner, and I am very proud to be your regimental TAC. This is just an introduction so I can see your faces and you mine. A little about myself. I'm a '79 grad and was in Company E-3. Go, Eagles! I'm not going to bore y'all with too many details about my career. If you want details, stop by the office sometime, and I'll tell some stories. For those of you who are wondering, yes, I have seen combat. I just came back from the Balkans—very intense. Now down to business. I am not a micromanager. I am very hands off. You do your jobs and ensure that your companies meet and exceed the standards, and you won't have to worry about me. I am all about spirit and motivation. Please, keep me motivated! As long as I am motivated, I am happy. Cadet Johnson, I've already heard of some of the stuff that you and the Ducks have been doing. Keep it up. We are by far the best regiment in the corps, and it's time that we let everyone know it. That's all I have for you. Any questions?"

None of the commanders raise their hands. Though they have a good feeling about Lieutenant Colonel Turner and his approach to leadership and his role as their RTO, they would rather go do other things than extend the meeting out any longer.

"No questions, huh? I understand, fellas. I was there once. All right then, you guys can get the hell out of here if you want. Remember, if you want to talk, my door is always open. First and proud!"

The commanders jump to their feet and stand at attention. Lieutenant Colonel Turner motions them to relax, which they do. The commanders slowly leave the lecture room in small groups.

Instead of leaving right away, Major walks over to Lieutenant Colonel Turner to speak to him. "Hey, sir, do you know Coach O'Hara?"

"Yeah, I sure do. We were in the same company way back when. How's he doing anyway?"

"He's good, sir."

"And the team?"

"We're doing really well, sir. If we keep our heads on straight, we should have no problem making it to the tournament this year."

"That's good to hear. As you probably know, our team wasn't too bad back in my day."

"Trust me, sir. I hear about it all the time."

"I bet you do," Lieutenant Colonel Turner responds with a soft laugh.

After a short pause, Major asks, "Sir, is it all right if I stop by your office sometime?"

"Certainly. If I'm not in, just leave a message on my desk. Better yet, e-mail me the morning you want to stop by so I can make sure my calendar's clear."

"Roger, sir. I'll do that." Major looks at his watch then looks back up at Lieutenant Colonel Turner. "Sir, I've got to get going now."

"All right then. I look forward to your visit." Lieutenant Colonel Turner extends his hand. Major firmly grasps it then departs the lecture room.

3 SEPTEMBER 1999

0945 Hours: West Point

West Point's academic schedule is broken up by One and Two Days. An hour after lunch each day is dedicated to a particular form of training and instruction. One Days belong to the Dean; thus, on One Days, cadets are either taking a major exam, are in a lab, or are sitting in on an academic lecture.

Two Days belong to the Commandant. Two Days is when cadets receive various forms of military and tactical classroom instruction. They also lead and participate in respect and honor classes.

On the days when there is nothing scheduled during a Dean's or Commandant's Hour, the cadets have that time to themselves. Many, especially the Corps Squad cadets, use that free time to run errands and schedule appointments: i.e. eye exams, dental, etc.

Major strolls down one of the fourth floor hallways of Washington Hall. Since he has the third hour off every Two day, he decided that he would take Lieutenant Colonel Turner up on his word and pay him a visit. Major reaches Lieutenant Colonel Turner's office door, steps to its right side, then gives it three hard, loud knocks.

"Enter," Lieutenant Colonel Turner loudly responds.

Major enters the office, stops three paces from in front of Lieutenant Colonel Turner's desk, salutes, and says, "Cadet Johnson repo—"

Lieutenant Colonel Turner interrupts Major in mid speech. "Take a seat, Cadet Johnson."

"Yes, sir."

As Major sits in the chair to the front right of Lieutenant Colonel Turner's desk, Lieutenant Colonel Turner asks, "What do your friends call you, Cadet Johnson?"

"Major, sir."

"Well, Major, what made you want to come by my office today?"

"Well, sir, you told us in the meeting to stop by whenever, so here I am."

"I'm glad you stopped by then. It's funny. A commander will always tell his soldiers that he has an open-door policy, but very few will ever take their commander up on the invitation and when they do, it's usually to whine or complain about things that they could've used their chain of command for," Lieutenant Colonel Turner explains. He then leans slightly over his desk and asks Major, "So what can I do you for today, young man?"

"Well, sir, I wanted to know about your last battle. I knew a guy who was over there in Croatia, and I was thinking that you might know him."

"What's your friend's name?"

"Marcus Perez."

Lieutenant Colonel Turner leans back in his swivel chair and ponders for a second. "Is he the same lieutenant who was captured by the Serbs a few months ago?"

"Yes, sir."

"I'm sorry to say that I don't know him. I knew his battalion commander though. He and I went to CGSC (Command General Staff College) together."

"That's all right, sir. I was just curious."

"You still want to know about the battle?"

"Yes, sir."

"Good then. Go over to that shelf"—Lieutenant Colonel Turner points to a bookshelf to his front left near the office door—"and get me that notebook."

Major raises up and quickly goes over to the bookshelf and retrieves a black notebook that has on its cover a gold drawing of a bulldog carrying an M16A2 assault rifle, a bone in its mouth, a Kevlar on its head, and wearing BDU (battle dress uniform) pants and a pair of black jungle boots.

"This the one, sir?" Major asks.

"Yep. That's the one."

Major takes the notebook and hands it over to Lieutenant Colonel Turner, who then opens it to about the middle.

"Come around here and take a look at this," he tells Major.

Major moves over to the side of the desk where Lieutenant Colonel Turner is sitting. Inside the notebook are numerous pages describing Lieutenant Colonel Turner's tour of duty in Croatia. He turns to the third tab in the notebook, which is the twenty-fourth page that begins the description and explanation of his sole battle and victory against the Serbs. Lieutenant Colonel Turner then flips through a few pages further and stops on page 30. Once there, he points to a map that is covered with drawings and a terrain sketch.

"This battle scheme here is what I call Illegal Alien. I tell you. I never thought that I was ever going to use it. I hate war and everything to do with it, but when you're able to win as decisively as we did that day, you can't help but get a huge adrenaline rush."

Major leans forward to get a better look at the map. Highly intrigued in Lieutenant Colonel Turner's exploits, he asks, "How decisive was your victory, sir?"

"Here. Take this." Lieutenant Colonel Turner hands Major the notebook, who then returns to his seat in front of Lieutenant Colonel Turner's desk.

Once Major sits, Lieutenant Colonel Turner continues, "Follow along in there as I explain to you what happened that day."

Lieutenant Colonel Turner leans back in his chair and begins telling Major his story of Illegal Alien and how he and his battalion humiliated and destroyed a Serb infantry brigade.

6 SEPTEMBER 2000

1030 Hours: West Point

Major wakes up from his regular post-breakfast morning nap. Usually, he only takes a two-hour nap on One days, but since he had a third hour class drop, he was able to take advantage of the extra time and get some much needed sleep. Balancing his time between his command, basketball, and classes has caused Major to go to bed at night much later than in semesters past.

Hearing his alarm clock sound, Major slowly sits up in his bed, throws his feet over the side, then carefully leaps off his bunk, softly landing on the floor. Major takes a seat behind his desk and retrieves his low quarters from under his bed. He then walks over to the alarm clock and turns it off. Almost wide awake but still a bit sleepy eyed, Major turns on the stereo. Whenever Major takes a serious nap, as he has just done, he usually listens to *The Chronic* to get his blood flowing and to fully wake himself up. *The Chronic* is the hip-hop album produced by Dr. Dre that put Death Row Records on the map.

Major grabs his long-sleeved as-for-class shirt from the back of his chair, throws it on, and buttons it up. He then picks his tie up from off of his desk and puts it on. Next, Major grabs his black letter sweater, which hangs on the back of his chair as well. Finally, Major lifts his SE 401 book, notebook, and garrison cap, which are all neatly stacked on one another, off of his desk then concludes his pre-class preparation by striding out of his room and heads for Mahan Hall.

As Major walks out of Grant Area, he runs into one of his best friends, Edward Winner, between Pershing and Grant Barracks.

"Uhhhh!" Ed yells loud enough that everyone in a fifty-meter radius can hear.

Major responds equally as loud with, "Special Ed!"

Standing at the bottom of the side steps of Pershing Barracks, Major waits for Ed to saunter down the stairs.

When Ed reaches ground level, he and Major give each other a pound then continue their slow and monotonous trip to class.

"What's up, boy?" Ed asks.

"Nothing, man. Just going to class," Major answers.

"You ready for tonight?"

"Hell yes!"

"Good. Everyone's going to be down at the Firstie Club at eight."

The Firstie Club, or the First Class Club as it is known by its proper name, is the sports bar at West Point for the first class cadets. Many cadets refer to the Firstie Club as the Slug. Though all first class cadets may frequent the Firstie Club, only those who are at least twenty-one years of age may drink alcoholic beverages—New York state law.

"That'll work. I'm going over to Colonel Wood's house for dinner at about six or so, though. Mrs. Wood's fixing me enchiladas tonight for my birthday."

"That's cool. You just make sure you're at the Slug at eight."

"No problem, brother. I'll be there."

"All right then. I'll see you at eight then."

"Most definitely. I'll see you."

Major and Ed shake hands and embrace as they end their conversation then part ways, Major for Mahan Hall and Ed for Thayer Hall.

1230 Hours: Paris, France

Every early afternoon, unless they are working a job, Mac and Killer eat a heavy lunch. However, what Big Mac considers a heavy lunch, the average person would consider a gluttonous amount of food. After their hearty lunch, Killer and Mac return to J's office to discuss their new contract. The two men ride the elevator up to the twenty-fifth floor, get off, and then storm down the hallway toward J's office.

As they approach Marie's desk, Mac barks at her, "Is J in?"

"Yes, he is," Marie replies, "but he's very busy."

Mac and Killer do not wait for Marie to page J. They instead storm past her desk.

Marie jumps up from behind her desk and yells, "You two cannot go in there now!"

Marie's warning is to no avail since Mac and Killer are inside J's office by the time she finishes her words. Inside the office, J is on the telephone and taking some form of notes as well.

Mac and Killer throw the doors open and bash into J's office. Swiftly, they place themselves in front of J's desk. Killer then boldly states, "We'll do the job, J, but after this, we want out. No more jobs— *nothing*. We want to be totally out of the system and go straight."

Hearing Killer's words, J looks up and says to the individual on the other end of the telephone, "I will call you back in an hour." J then proceeds to hang up the telephone.

"Your words are more true than you know," J responds.

"How so, J?" Mac asks as he attempts to calm down.

"Well, it seems that the contract which the three of us have already committed ourselves to has you and Killer doing more than just training Drasneb's men. You are leading the entire operation."

J's words thrust into Mac and Killer's hearts, causing their bodies to freeze. For a brief moment, they are without words, though their minds are racing. Mac and Killer's emotions flood in a combination of rage and disbelief. Never have they felt as though they were trapped into a corner as they are now.

Finally able to formulate some words and gather his thoughts, Killer asks, "What do you mean we are leading the entire operation, J?"

J rises to is feet and begins to pace behind his desk, solemnly saying, "Gentlemen, I take full responsibility for this. Somehow, we did not properly translate the word *lead*. I don't know if it was from Serb to French or French to English, but somehow we didn't get it right. This has never happened before. I have no words, and I know it will not suffice or make up for my flagrant error, but I truly am sorry."

"You're sorry?" Mac explodes. "How about you screwed the hell up, J!"

"Seriously, J!' Killer interjects. "Now we go from training Drasneb's men in killing the cadets to leading the operation. Jesus help us!"

J stops pacing and faces Killer and Mac, saying, "There is nothing I can do to get you out of the contract, but what I can do is double your pay. I know that it doesn't ease your conscience and won't help you sleep better at night, but it is the only gesture I can hand you."

"Okay, J," Killer calmly states, "We'll continue on without protest, but we want out after this. The money's right, but more importantly, we don't feel too good about this one. Killing cadets? Give me a break, J. They're just kids! I don't care what they'll become in the future. Right now, they're still innocent."

"I'm tired of talking, J. Just give us the entire file so we can get this over with," Mac demands with his right hand extended.

J opens his top drawer and pulls out a packet that is nearly two inches thick and slides it to Mac, who retrieves it and hands it to Killer. Mac and Killer shake their heads at J in disappointment as they slowly leave his office.

J sits down behind his desk and flips through his Rolodex to the *D* section. He picks up the telephone and dials a number. At the second ring, someone on the other end answers. J says in his best Serbo-Croatian, "May I speak to Colonel Drasneb, please?"

"May I ask who is speaking?"

"Tell him it's his French colleague," J replies.

"One moment please, sir."

There is silence for a few moments until it is broken by Colonel Drasneb's voice. "J, I am very pleased to hear from you. I hope that you are not calling to renege on my contract."

"No, Drasneb. I'm just calling to reconfirm with you that my men will be in Belgrade in five days, as you requested."

"Very good. I need to get this operation off of the ground as soon as possible."

"You do need to know one thing though. My guys are extremely uneasy about doing this mission. Don't get me wrong, they'll do it because they are professionals and they always complete a contract, but the ethics of your mission is bothering them."

"Should I expect any problems from them?"

"No. Of course not."

"Good, but if I do have any problems with your men, I know what the fine print says: 'Exterminate if operatives breech contract.'"

1805 Hours: At the Home of Colonel and Mrs. Wood, West Point

"Hey! It's the birthday boy!" Mrs. Wood happily shouts as Major enters the Woods' home and into the kitchen through the back entrance.

"Thank you. Thank you," Major comically replies, waving his hands in the air like a congenial politician. He walks over to Mrs. Wood and they give each other a big hug.

"You ready for dinner, Major?" Mrs. Wood asks.

"Come on, ma'am. You know I'm always ready to eat."

"Don't I know it," Mrs. Wood responds with a huge grin and shake of the head. Mrs. Wood moves to the stove and checks on the enchiladas. "They should be ready in about ten minutes."

"Good. Good," Major responds as he rubs his hands together.

"The Big Guy should be home any minute now."

The Big Guy who Mrs. Wood is referring to is her husband, Col. Harold Wood, the head of the Department of Foreign Languages. There are many reasons why Mrs. Wood refers to her husband as big guy. The most evident to Major, and everyone else who has ever met Colonel Wood, is the fact that Colonel Wood stands six feet, ten inches tall. Colonel Wood played on West Point's basketball team way back when Bobby Knight was the head coach.

Mrs. Wood and Major sit down at the kitchen table and chat about everything from cadet life to Major's personal life. "So, Major, any big plans for tonight?"

"Yes, ma'am. I'm meeting some of my friends down at the Firstie Club at eight."

"That should be fun. Anyone that I know?"

"I think Jimmy and Martin are going."

Mrs. Wood's eyes widen as she says, "Oh, I know you guys are going to have a good time tonight if Jimmy's going to be there."

"If you only knew, ma'am," Major replies as he and Mrs. Wood laugh.

As Mrs. Wood begins to ask Major, "So how are you doing with the young ladies?"

Saving Major from embarrassment, Colonel Wood strolls into the kitchen. When he enters, he ducks down a few inches to ensure that he does not bump his head.

"So how's the birthday boy doing today?" Colonel Wood asks as he enters the kitchen.

Mrs. Wood rises from the table. Colonel Wood bends forward and gives his wife an "it's good to be home" kiss. Bending over is necessary because Colonel Wood is nearly two feet taller than Mrs. Wood. Major gets up from his seat as the couple briefly shares in each other's affection. Colonel Wood then turns his attention over to Major and embraces him.

"Let me go up stairs and get out of these clothes, then we can eat," Colonel Wood informs.

"Roger that, sir," Major replies.

Colonel Wood leaves the kitchen and heads upstairs for his room to take off of his class A uniform and put on something that is a little more comfortable.

While Colonel Wood changes, Mrs. Wood and Major continue with their conversation.

"As I asked you before Woody stepped in, how are you doing with the young ladies?" Mrs. Wood asks Major for a second time.

"I'm doing all right, ma'am. No girlfriend as you know, but there are a couple of prospects," Major answers.

Major does not mind conversing in personal matters of this nature with Mrs. Wood. To Major, Mrs. Wood is like a second mom and a cool aunt all rolled into one. The Woods have mentored and sponsored Major since he was a plebe. They make it a point to bring in all of the basketball team, both guys and girls, and mentor them. The Woods also sponsor their army friends' children and those of Colonel Wood's classmates.

"Well, that's good. You're still young, so you don't have to worry about having a girlfriend now. There's plenty of time for that," Mrs. Wood instructs.

"Oh," Major enthusiastically begins, "I almost forgot to tell you. I'm going to the Miss America pageant this Saturday."

"That's exciting!" Mrs. Wood happily responds as she clasps her hands together. "How are you able to do that?"

"Well, my friend Ed went to high school with the current Miss New Jersey. JT met her through Ed and became friends with her a couple of years back. Anyway, she asked him to go, so he's bringing me and Gabe along."

"You must be excited?"

"You have no idea."

"Maybe you'll find yourself a girlfriend down there. There will definitely be a lot of beautiful young ladies for you to choose from."

If Major was white, he would be blushing at Mrs. Wood's comments.

"With your charm and your full dress gray uniform on," Mrs. Wood continues, "how can they resist you?"

"Come on, ma'am," Major bashfully replies.

"Well, it's true."

Colonel Wood returns back down to the kitchen from changing. In place of his class A uniform, he is wearing a pair of black baggy sweat pants and a North Carolina Tar Heels sweatshirt. He wears the sweatshirt because it is the university where he received his doctorate.

"So what did I miss?" Colonel Wood asks as he slaps Major on the back.

"Major's going to the Miss America pageant Saturday," Mrs. Wood happily informs her husband.

"Are you?" Colonel Wood responds with surprise. "Those girls are in for a good time, huh?"

"Yes, sir," Major answers.

Mrs. Wood gets up from her seat to check the enchiladas. As soon as she reaches the stove, Will and Matt enter the kitchen. Matt is a third class cadet who is on the football team with Major's little brother, Will. Matt's father, General Schultz, is a close friend and classmate of Colonel Wood. Major looked out for Matt last year when he was a plebe.

"It's about time you two got here," Colonel Wood says to Matt and Will as they enter the kitchen. Colonel Wood raises both of his hands in the air and Matt and Will follow through with a high five.

"We just got out of practice, sir," Matt responds.

"Yeah, sir," Will adds. "We didn't even take the sports shuttle. We walked down. Figured it would be faster."

"Which it was," Matt concludes.

"Well, you guys made it down here just in time because it's time to eat," Mrs. Wood says to everyone as she pulls the enchiladas out from the oven. "Will, you get the plates, Matt, the silverware."

"Yes, ma'am," Mat and Will respond in unison.

Mat and Will perform their assigned tasks, while Major gets the glasses and fills them all with ice except for his because he does not like ice.

"What are you going to drink tonight, Major, beer or wine?" Colonel Wood asks.

"I'm going to have plenty of beer tonight, sir, so I'll take some wine," Major answers Colonel Wood.

"Wine it is," Colonel Wood responds as he goes to the back covered deck to retrieve a bottle of red wine that he had received as a gift during his trip two months ago to École Spéciale Militaire de Saint-Cyr, France's military academy.

As the head of the Department of Foreign Languages, Colonel Wood regularly visits the military institutes of the allies of the United States and their perspective allies. Occasionally, Mrs. Wood is able to accompany him on his trips. The trip to France was one such occasion.

As Colonel Wood reaches for the red French wine that is stored in a cupboard next to the refrigerator, Cdt. Jimmy Hazel enters the house through the back door. Jimmy is one of Major's closest friends. Standing six feet, five inches tall and weighing a solid 255 pounds, Jimmy is the starting power forward on the men's varsity basketball team. Major and Jimmy have played together and have been friends ever since they attended the United States Military Academy Preparatory School.

"Hey, sir!" Jimmy cheerfully bellows with a big grin on his face. "What's for dinner?"

"Mexican," Colonel Wood answers.

"You know, it's funny, sir. I was sitting in my room, and all of a sudden this strong message bombarded my thoughts. It kept saying over and over again, *Enchiladas. Enchiladas.*"

"Come on, Jimmy, let's go eat," Colonel Wood says laughing as he puts his arm around Jimmy's shoulder.

Colonel Wood goes into the dining room, while Jimmy gets a plate, fork, and a glass from the kitchen cabinets. With his eating utensils in hand, Jimmy happily enters the dining room—happy because he is getting yet another free meal.

As soon as he enters the dining room, Major blurts out, "I see you got my e-mail, dawg."

"I thought you were having deep thoughts in your room, Jimmy?" Colonel Wood sarcastically attacks Jimmy.

"So it was subliminal, sir," Jimmy rebuts as he takes a seat next to Matt with his back to the fireplace. Major, because it is his birthday, sits at the head of the table, Colonel Wood sits opposite of him, and Will and Mrs. Wood sit opposite of Matt and Jimmy.

"So," Colonel Wood begins, "who's going to say the prayer?"

Colonel Wood, along with Major, Jimmy, Mrs. Wood, and Matt have a finger on their respective noses. Placing a finger on the nose is a new Wood house tradition that one of their sponsored cadets, Cadet First Classman Janet Hill, instituted late last semester. Whoever is the last one to place their finger on their nose has to say the prayer for the meal. Being a plebe, Will has not quite caught on to the tradition yet; thus he is obligated to say grace.

"Ah man!" Will says after realizing that everyone has a finger on their nose except for him. "Oh well," he continues. "I don't have a problem saying grace."

"Like you have a choice, little man," Jimmy retorts.

Everyone laughs.

After a second to compose themselves, they all take hands and bow their heads. Will then commences with grace.

"Dear Lord," Will begins, "thank you for allowing us to gather together once again. Thank you for this meal. Help it nourish and strengthen our bodies. Bless the hands that prepared it. Most importantly, thank you for my brother being able to celebrate another birthday. In Jesus's name we pray. Amen."

With the prayer over, everyone lifts their heads and releases each other's hands.

Colonel Wood then says, "Let's eat!"

Major reaches for the enchiladas first. Everyone else follows suit as Colonel Wood pours him, Jimmy, Major, and Mrs. Wood a glass of wine. Matt and Will's glasses are already filled with cran-raspberry juice.

With all of the plates full of enchiladas and salad, everyone begins to dig in.

After taking one bite, Jimmy quickly lifts his head and boasts, "Once again, Mrs. Wood, you have outdone yourself."

"Why, thank you, Jimmy," Mrs. Wood approvingly replies.

Matt, Will, and Major shake their heads at Jimmy's cheesy comment. Jimmy has a habit of purposely kissing up to Mrs. Wood every chance he gets. He does it all for fun.

"So what's new in the corps?" Colonel Wood asks the cadets.

"Well, sir, CID (civilian investigation division) finally arrested the guys who broke into the C-Store," Major answers.

The C-Store, or the Cadet Store as it is formally known, is a two-story store where only cadets and military personnel are permitted to shop. Most cadets refer to it as the C-Mall. The C-Store sells many high-value items, such as clothing, electronic equipment, and jewelry, at low, discounted prices. One of the many items that cadets like to purchase from the C-Store before they graduate are Rolex watches because they cannot get a better deal anywhere else.

"Do you know who it was?" Colonel Wood intuitively asks.

"Not a clue," Major says. "All I know is that they're a couple of cows."

"Yeah, sir," Jimmy adds. "Those fools got caught because they messed up trying to get rid of their merchandise."

"How so?" Mrs. Wood asks.

"From what I heard," Major continues, "they went to a pawnshop to sell the Rolexes, but Rolex had already put out a list of all of the serial numbers of the stolen watches. When they attempted to sell the watches, the guy at the pawnshop realized that they were stolen and called the cops."

"That's a shame," Mrs. Wood states as she shakes her head.

"It sure is, ma'am," Jimmy answers. "Those two idiots pulled off a near-perfect robbery but weren't smart enough to get rid of the stuff without getting caught."

"It just goes to show," Major chimes in, "that there's no such thing as a smart criminal. They only exist in comic books. That's why there'll never be a Lex Luthor in real life because criminals have this weird itch to get caught."

"Well said, old boy," Jimmy jokingly states as he taps his glass with a knife.

With good conversation and company and immersed in a family-like atmosphere, everyone enthusiastically eats their dinner as they tell random jokes and stories of their lives at West Point.

While chewing on a large piece of his enchilada, Major looks down at his watch and notices the time. "Ah man!" he blurts. "It's seven-fifty. We've got to get going, nut."

Major and Jimmy leap from the table and prepare to exit the dining room.

"Have a good time, guys," Mrs. Wood says to Major and Jimmy as they begin to leave. "Don't worry, ma'am. Good times are all I have," Jimmy answers with a giant grin on his face as he and Major exit through the front door and head across the street and down the hill toward the Firstie Club for Major's birthday bash.

1955 Hours: Paris, France

It is a late evening tonight for J. Usually, he leaves for home no later than five thirty in the afternoon. Tonight is not a typical night. As he sits and thinks, he begins to come to the realization that the mission he had given Mac and Killer truly is unethical.

J contemplates to himself, *I cannot believe I put Mac and Killer in this uneasy predicament. The mess with the whole translation thing in the contract isn't even the point. The fact that I have them involved with someone like Drasneb is bad enough. I will never be able to make up for this.*

No one knows better than I as to how hard it's been for them to fulfill some of their contracts, especially the ones against US targets. Now I've sent them into the fire and have forced them to kill some kids. On top of all of that, my conversation with Colonel Drasneb wasn't very positive either, though he'd probably disagree.

J stands up from his chair and walks over to his file cabinet. He opens the top drawer and looks under *C.* In the *C* section, he pulls out a blank copy of his company's official contract. With the contract in hand, he returns to his desk and flops back into his chair. J glances over the contract and carries his eyes down to the bottom where he reads the clause that is bothering him the most: "Exterminate if operatives breech the contract."

What have I done? J broods. *I've just sent Mac and Killer to their deaths. There's no way Drasneb's going to let them live after they fulfill their contract. I just know Mac and Killer are going to do something to force Drasneb's hand.*

J throws his elbows on his desk and lays his shaking head in his hands. For a long moment, J is unsure of how to remedy the situation.

After pulling himself together, J flips through his Rolodex and pulls out Killer's and Mac's emergency telephone numbers. He dials the two numbers on his digital phone then waits for a response.

"What do you want, J?" Mac answers.

Mac knows that it is J who is calling because only he, Killer, and one other person has this particular cell phone number. Also, both J and Mac's telephones have a scrambler, which allows Mac to recognize whoever is calling through the series of codes that the telephone screen displays.

As Mac finishes his question, Killer answers his cell phone as well. "What do you need, J?" Killer asks.

"Douglas, Amos," J begins, "first, I want to apologize to you."

"Whoa! This has got to be good," Killer interrupts. "You just called us by our actual names. Are you feeling all right?"

"No, I'm not," J answers. "I should never have accepted that contract from Colonel Drasneb. You guys are right about the morality issue. I think we may be a little more ethically wrong than we traditionally are. What's bothering me the most though is the fact that I believe

Drasneb's going to get rid of you two right after you fulfill your end of the contract."

"Are you serious?" Killer questions.

"As serious as I ever have been," J soberly retorts.

"You have got to be kidding me!" Mac shouts. "Are you telling me that we've just signed our death sentences? Don't tell me that, J!"

"I deeply apologize, gentlemen. That's the way the cards were dealt. There was neither nothing that I could have done to predict Colonel Drasneb's intentions nor anything I can do to subvert his future actions. If I do anything, I and the company will lose all of our credibility," J explains.

"We understand that side of the business, J," Killer responds. "But what are you going to do to ensure that Mac and I get our money?"

"Yeah! What about our money?" Mac assists.

"You are still going to receive your money," J begins to explain to Mac and Killer. "Like always, as soon as you arrive at the airport in preparation for your mission destination, two-thirds of your payment will be electronically transferred to your accounts. Once the money goes through, I will call you. If it does not go through, you know not to board the plane."

"That's all fine and good, J," Killer interrupts, "but what about the other third? Since Drasneb's planning to kill us, he obviously isn't planning on paying us. Not that he'll be alive to make the payment."

"That's a good question," J acknowledges. "You make it out of this alive, and I will give you the final third of your payment."

"That will work. Our lives are in your hands. Make sure you handle your business," Killer replies. "And don't worry. We'll get the job done no matter how bad things get down the stretch."

"I know you will, and I greatly appreciate it. Hang in there, Mac. Things will get better," J says as he hangs up his telephone.

J steps out from behind his desk then reaches down and lifts his black alligator-leather brief case from off of the gray carpeted floor. He drags himself over to his coat closest then slips on his blazer on the way out of his office door.

All that is on J's mind as he heads for the parking garage is, *I am tired as hell, but I don't think I'm going to be able to sleep at all tonight.*

8 SEPTEMBER 1999

1140 Hours: West Point

The poop deck reaches all the way to the mess hall's high ceiling, which is roughly sixty feet high give or take a few feet. The two balconies are fifteen feet off of the ground, allowing those looking over its edge to see everyone in the mess hall very clearly. Between the two balconies is a dining area with a table that seats ten. In this small area is an oil painting of a majestic George Washington.

On both sides of the poop deck, there is a stairwell that leads to the fourth, fifth, and sixth floors of Washington Hall. Washington Hall and MacArthur and Eisenhower Barracks are all connected to one another, with MacArthur to the north and Eisenhower to the south. The series of hallways that connect the three structures is known as the web. Most of the cadets who reside between the fourth and sixth floors of Eisenhower and MacArthur Barracks climb these stairs every day going to and from their rooms.

At least once a week, very important world and national figures visit the military academy to observe and take note as to how West Point trains and educates its cadets. Among most circles, West Point is revered as the number 1 leadership school in the world. Those who visit come so that they may take a little something back to better their institutions or organizations. When these people come to visit, they go to the mess hall for lunch. Before they and the corps eat though, the cadet brigade S-1 introduces them to the corps immediately before the command of "Take seats."

Today the brigade S-1, Cdt. Capt. Bethany Jung, has the luxury of introducing a VIP to the corps.

"Attention to orders!" Cadet Jung announces. "The corps is pleased to have as its guest today Gen. Yoly Molachka, commander in chief of the Croatian Army."

Immediately, the corps bursts out with a thunderous cheer. Many cadets bang pots and pitchers in jubilation, while others throw their garrison caps and napkins up in the air. It is tradition for the cadets to cheer loudly whenever a VIP comes to lunch. Most cadets do not really care who the visitor is, but cheering is tradition, and it is actually kind of fun, so they stick with it. Cheering for the VIPs is one old West Point tradition that most cadets do not mind continuing.

Seeing the corps' jovial admiration gives the Croatian general a warm feeling of acceptance. He thinks to himself, *It's a good thing that the Americans are fighting on our side. I couldn't imagine having an enemy with such spirit and energy as the Americans.*

While General Molachka waves to the jubilant corps, his aide, who is standing three steps behind, looks down at his cell phone and notices that he has just received an urgent message that he must check. Unfortunately, the message is going to have to wait until after all of the festivities have ended for the day. The general finishes waving to the corps then follows the brigade S-1, who escorts them down the poop-deck stairs and back onto the main mess hall floor. The official party hangs a left and heads for the D wing.

As they walk by the backside of the poop deck, General Molachka's aide says, "Sir, I believe this would be an excellent location for a picture."

The general rubs his chin and replies, "I agree, Alex. Take our picture here."

Alex has Cadet Roberts, Cadet Jung, and Lieutenant General Holiday stand with General Molachka underneath the poop deck, facing the corps squad section. He takes a picture, then one extra, in case the first does not develop properly.

Lt. Gen. Christopher Holiday, the superintendent of the United States Military Academy, escorts General Molachka around West Point, taking him to all of the academic buildings, military training areas, and historical points of interest. As the two generals walk, Maj. Alex Petrova takes photographs of all of the buildings and the active cadets moving sporadically to and from their various destinations.

"General Holiday, your campus here is very beautiful. I wish my country had a school of leadership of such high caliber and surrounded by such a beautiful landscape," General Molachka happily states. "My wife will love all of the pictures that my aide is taking."

"She certainly will, General Molachka. After dinner, I will take you out to my garden. She'll love to see pictures of that as well."

"She certainly will."

"You know that if you want a more advanced military academy, our country can help you with that."

"Really? Well, we're going to have to look into that."

"At dinner tonight, I will introduce you to Colonel Wood, the head of our foreign language department. He regularly travels to our allied countries, critiquing military academies and assessing their war-fighting effectiveness."

"I look forward to meeting him."

The two generals and their entourages walk past Eisenhower statue toward Thayer Hall to finish the remainder of General Molachka's tour.

1300 Hours

Major sits in Captain Weiss's office for one of their regular training meetings. Major and Captain Weiss for the moment, discuss random events and stories unrelated to the company. As they converse, Captain Weiss changes his seat position several times from behind his main desk to his computer desk, which is positioned in an L shape.

Captain Weiss returns to his original position behind his main desk and refaces Major. He pulls out his calendar and asks, "We're still having the dining-in next Tuesday?"

"Yes, sir. Were we able to get the com?"

"Yes, we were. I spoke to his aide yesterday to confirm. He'll be a few minutes late, but he will definitely be there. Did you send all of the invitations out?"

"Yes, sir. I did. Mostly everyone's responded. Colonel Wood told me last night that he and Mrs. Wood are coming."

"Good. I think this dining-in will be very successful."

"I know it will." Major begins to laugh slightly.

Captain Weiss, seeing Major laugh, curiously asks him, "What's so funny, Major?"

"Colonel Wood has something planned for the dining-in, sir, but I can't tell you what it is."

"I guess I shouldn't even ask, but knowing Colonel Wood, it has to be something good. I guess I'll just have to wait."

"Trust me, sir, you'll like it." Major looks down at his watch and realizes that he has to hurry up and get ready for his workout and shoot around with Coach O'Hara. "Sir, I've got to get going. I have to get up to the gym."

2300 Hours

"Alex, is this line secure?"

"No, sir. It is not."

"Then I will be brief," Colonel Drasneb states. "Do you have your ingredients for dinner?"

"Yes, sir. I followed your list to the letter. When do you want me to arrive for dinner?"

"I will call and let you know before your brothers and I arrive at our friend's house."

Colonel Drasneb hangs the telephone up and returns to completing the plans for the training phase of his mission.

13 SEP 1999

1030 Hours: Paris, France

J walks into his office. He does not feel any better about himself, but he is reassured in the fact that he believes that he may have a plan to ensure that Mac and Killer receive the entirety of their payment for the contract that they signed to aide Colonel Drasneb in his ill-fated mission.

As J quickly strides past his secretary, a forty-something-year-old blonde who is rather attractive for her age, he tells her, "Marie, hold all of my calls until I say otherwise."

"Yes, J," Marie answers as J enters his office.

J shuts the door behind him and heads straight for his desk, where he grabs his Rolodex to retrieve Colonel Drasneb's telephone number. He hurriedly dials the number and waits four brings before Colonel Drasneb answers on the other end.

"Hello," Colonel Drasneb states.

"Drasneb, this is J," J coldly replies.

"Good afternoon, J, or should I say good morning. It is still morning in Paris, is it not?"

"Yes, it is," J confirms. "Let us stop with the pleasantries, Drasneb. I am calling to check up with you to ensure that you are going to pay my men all of their money. Since you are so well versed in our contract, I assume that you still plan on upholding your end."

"Oh, of course, J. Is there any reason why I would not pay your employees for their services?"

"No. There is not. Just remember, two-thirds now and the other third as soon as your entire team arrives at the designated training site. If they do not receive the entirety of their payment at that time, then you have breached the contract and they are no longer obligated to complete your mission. Do you understand that, Colonel?"

"Of course I understand, J. I have no reason to cheat your men from their hard-earned money. If they're as good as you say they are, then I know that it is money well spent. As a matter of fact, I was just getting ready to wire the money to their accounts just as you called."

"Very well then. Mr. Stewart and Mr. Pollard are now at the airport, waiting for my call. They will be very pleased to hear that you are honoring your end of the contract."

"I am a soldier, J. There is nothing I cherish more than honor. I would never go against my word with an ally." *Fortunately, these two mercenaries are not my allies, but mere tools*, Colonel Drasneb silently says to himself.

"See that you do not break the contract in this case, Colonel. I will call you from time to time to check on my men's status. J, out."

J hangs up the telephone. He is furious but controls his temper enough not to slam the receiver. J knows that Colonel Drasneb is lying. What makes J even more upset is the fact that he cannot call Colonel Drasneb out on his future deception. No matter how much he may dislike Colonel Drasneb, J must still maintain a certain level of professionalism with him. J has no power to avert the course on which he has placed Mac and Killer. Fortunately, Mac and Killer are two of the smartest men that he knows, and they should be able to come out of all of this alive and in one piece God willing.

Paris International Airport

Mac and Killer sit in front of their departure gate, awaiting their telephone call from J informing them that Colonel Drasneb has wired the first two-thirds of their payment to their accounts. Without the money, Mac and Killer will not board the plane. Even if Colonel Drasneb were to attempt to pay them at a later date, they still would neither accept the money nor take on the mission anytime in the future. As far as they are concerned, their services are a one-shot attempt. If the possible employer does not get it right the first time, he does not receive a second.

The plane that Mac and Killer plan on boarding connects in Prague. When it lands, they do not have to depart the plane but do have to wait half an hour. Their plane will then take off and depart for Belgrade.

Mac walks over to the window and watches the tech crews prepare the plane for departure. Ever since Mac was a kid, he has been fascinated with airplanes. He would have given anything to have become a naval combat pilot, but he and high school did not get along. Mac did not see the importance in making good grades; that was left for the smart kids. All he cared about was keeping his grades high enough to play football and wrestle every season and talking to girls.

A few months before Mac's high school graduation, his father sat him down one day and told him, "Son, I love you, and because I do, I'm letting you know that after you graduate, you can no longer live here unless you're going to college."

Mac sat on the couch flabbergasted. For the first time in his life, he was forced to make a mature decision that could have life-changing effects. He never imagined not living at home. For some reason, he had assumed that he would be able to stay at home for a few years, at least until after he got himself situated. That plan was out the window.

After a few moments of complete and utter shock, Mac's father continued. "So, Doug, do you have a plan? Your grades suck, but you can still go to the community college. It's never too late to turn your life around especially since you're still young."

"I don't know. I haven't really given it much thought. I know I don't want to go to college. I can't take another four years of school."

Mac's eyes follow the path of a plane as it takes off. He laughs slightly at the thought of the conversation he and his father had so many years ago.

To appease his father, though he really did not have much of a choice, Mac joined the United States Marine Corps. When he and his father went to speak with the recruiter, Mac asked him if he could fly fighter planes. The recruiter, a five-foot-ten overly muscular gunnery sergeant, informed him that only officers and warrant officers are pilots. NCOs and enlisted personnel take care of the aircraft. Mac did not take the news very well. Mostly though, he was disappointed with himself because he knew that being an officer meant having to go to college, which he stubbornly did not want to do.

Reacting to Mac's emotions, his father simply cants his head to the left and gives him the "I told you so look." At first, that made Mac feel even worse as though he had let not only himself down, but his father as well. Surprisingly, his father then placed his hand on Mac's shoulder, brings him in close, and says, "Mac, whatever decision you make, I will support you because I know that in the long run, you will be successful in whatever it is you decide to do."

With a feeling of relief and a little less pressure, Mac signed his enlistment contract as an infantryman—a decision that he never regrets, except when he spies a fighter plane streaking through the sky.

Mac's father knows that he resigned from the Marine Corps ten years ago, but he would definitely blow a gasket if he knew that his son was not head of security at a South Bronx high school but, instead, was one of the highest-paid, most-asked-for mercenaries in the business. Mac silently chuckles to himself of his father getting pissed off.

As Mac stands by the window reminiscing, Killer walks over to a corner for some privacy. He whips his cell phone out from his inside blazer pocket and pushes a series of buttons until he gets to a screen that contains a highlighted row that reads FAM. Killer presses the green button on his cell phone so he can call home and speak with his family.

Waiting for his telephone to ring, Killer begins reflecting on his life and how his "job" affects his family's life. He and his wife, Sharon, have no secrets. They share everything, except for the fact that she believes that her husband is a prominent small-arms salesman who happens to take extended trips about every two months. For the eight years that they have been married, Killer's profession has been an utter lie to his wife. As much as Killer wants to tell Sharon what he really does, he cannot get over the possibility of his six-year-old son, David, going to the playground and saying, "My daddy can beat your daddy up 'cause he's a mercenary." Killer laughs heartily at the thought.

After a series of three rings, a female voice answers the telephone on the other end. "Hey, baby. I figured you would call about now," Sharon states, happy to hear her husband's voice.

"Yeah. I'm waiting to board the plane now," Killer replies.

"I still can't believe you're going to be away for almost three months," Sharon disappointingly voices. "You've never been gone this long before."

"I know, hon," Killer agrees, shaking his head. "I don't like being away from you and the kids for so long either." Killer drops his head in silence for a brief moment, thinking of the right words to say to his wife. The thought of the payment for his upcoming job excites him into telling Sharon, "Baby, I promise you that this will be my last business trip. I swear."

While speaking to Sharon, Killer's cell phone receives a beep, signifying an incoming call. Since he is speaking with Sharon, and Mac is standing beside the window within eye view, Killer knows that J is the one who is calling him.

Whenever J calls Mac and Killer, he always does a three-way call with them. J's method is the procedure that he uses with all of his operatives. His philosophy behind calling both men simultaneously ensures that the men do not feel as if he is favoring one over the other. When J calls both men, he knows that they are both getting the same information. This protects both him and his operatives.

Instead of answering the call, Killer looks up at Mac, who is also inconspicuously looking at Killer. Mac nods to Killer in recognition of the incoming call. He slips his cell phone from out of his left front pants pocket and answers the call.

"We got the money, J?" Mac gruffly asks.

"The Killer's talking to Sharon?" J asks instead of answering Mac's question.

"Yeah, the Killer's saying his good-byes. Now back to the matter at hand. Do we have the money or not?"

"Yes, we do."

"Good. I guess me and the Killer can get on the plane now, huh?"

"I guess so."

"God. I never thought that I would end up in Serbia. What a worthless country. I can't believe I'm doing this. Oh well. I guess I'm going to have to think of this as just another job, no matter how morally wrong our actions may be."

"You'll be all right. Of course, I don't need to tell you to watch each other's backs. I have a bad feeling Colonel Drasneb's going to do his best to exterminate you and the Killer after you've accomplished your end of the mission."

"We know, J. And don't worry, we'll be back to collect our pension checks as soon as this is all over," Mac jokingly states as he hangs up his cell phone.

Mac slips his cell phone back into his pants pocket then proceeds to walk over to where Killer is standing, still speaking with his wife.

Before Mac can reach Killer's location, Killer spots him coming toward him, so he concludes his conversation with Sharon by saying, "Hey, babe, my plane is getting ready to board. I've got to go now. I'll give you a call sometime tomorrow. Love you."

"I love you too, baby. Take care."

Killer closes his cell phone and places it back into his inside blazer pocket. He then turns to Mac and says, "We got the money, huh?"

"How'd you know?" Mac curiously asks.

"Well, the way I figure it, if we hadn't, you would either have punched the window in disgust or clinched your fist and thrown it in the air with that quick snap that you like to do whenever you're excited. After you hung up with J, you didn't react at all, so I know that the money's sitting in our accounts."

"God, you're good. That's why you're my partner." Mac places his arm around Killer and continues, "Come on. Let's get on this plane before we change our minds."

"Yeah. No kidding," Killer responds.

"You tell Sharon yet?" Mac asks

"I told her that this was it. I'm going to wait to tell her what 'it' is after we get back. Some news isn't meant for the telephone. You know what I'm saying?"

"Yeah. I hear you, brother. You're definitely a better man than me."

As Mac and Killer speak, they hear over the intercom the flight attendant at the front desk announce, "All first-class passengers and those requiring assistance, please report to the front of the line to board the flight."

"Hey. At least we're flying first-class," Mac cynically smirks.

"Yeah, like every other job we do," Killer sarcastically replies. He gets up from his seat and slaps Mac in the chest with the back of his hand.

Laughing, the two friends easily walk through the cluster of people and board their plane unhindered.

1530 Hours: Belgrade International Airport, Belgrade, Serbia

"Mr. Pollard, Mr. Stewart, it is a pleasure and an honor to meet you. Your employer speaks very highly of you, and from what I have read and heard, your skills and expertise will be truly useful to me and my cause," Colonel Drasneb boastfully states to Mac and Killer.

"That's nice and all, sir," Mac coldly states, "but we aren't here for pleasantries. This is purely business. The less we get to know one another, the better off we all are. Do we have an understanding, sir?"

"Yes. Very, clear," Colonel Drasneb answers with an obvious attitude change. *This is very good*, Colonel Drasneb thinks to himself. *This will make it a lot easier for me to kill them when I am finished using them.*

"All right gentlemen. Follow me, this way. The car is right out front," Colonel Drasneb says to Mac and Killer as he leads the way through the crowded airport terminal.

Mac and Killer follow Colonel Drasneb out of the airport, carefully scanning the area for anything out of the ordinary. They do this out of force of habit. Too many times have they had to know the layout of a supposed friend's area of operation; old habits are hard to break.

The three men approach a waiting black Mercedes limousine that is idling in front of the main entrance. Standing beside the Mercedes, at the position of attention, is a uniformed soldier. Mac and Killer notice that the Mercedes is bullet proof from head to toe, including the windows and the windshield. As if programmed, the driver opens the doors for them, and the three men enter the limousine. Mac and Killer move all the way over and sit on the far side of the limousine, facing each other.

"So, gentlemen," Colonel Drasneb opens as they begin moving, "am I to assume that your employer briefed you on the mission and gave you the packets that I had prepared?"

"Yes, sir," Killer answers as he sips on a Coke and stares out of the window. He drinks from the can, not from a glass—less chance of his Coke containing any poisons. Plus there is nothing more that Killer hates than a bad Coke.

Colonel Drasneb notices Killer staring out of the window and states, "Oh, you have never been to our lovely country before, have you?"

"No, sir. We have not," Mac quickly answers.

"Oh, it is so beautiful during this time of the year, especially in the countryside. The way the leaves change color and blend with the mountains is quite lovely."

"Must be nice," Mac softly and sarcastically retorts.

Colonel Drasneb eyes Mac wearily as he thinks to himself, *These two are trouble. I'm glad I already have my plan in place for them.*

The entire situation is sitting bad with Mac. It is apparent that Colonel Drasneb is not being totally straight with him and Killer on this job. Mac reminds himself to speak with Killer about his unease later—at a secure location, of course.

Driving through the streets of Belgrade, Killer notices all of the anti-US propaganda that is prevalent. He wonders what his purpose is for this job. *Why am I doing this?* he asks himself. *I love my country. It's been good to me for the most part. I mean, shoot, I still have my identity back home. My wife thinks that I'm a friggin' salesman for God's sake! I do this for the money and the rush, not for any special cause. I don't like this situation one bit. Mac and I are going to have to talk. He needs to know what's up.*

The black Mercedes pulls alongside a hotel and comes to a stop. The valet manning the main entrance quickly moves to the Mercedes and opens the rear passenger door.

"Here we are, gentlemen," Colonel Drasneb states as the valet opens the door. "My driver will be here in the morning at nine to take you to the initial in brief with the remainder of the team."

"All right, sir," Killer replies. "We'll be here waiting."

Mac and Killer exit the Mercedes. The valet attempts to carry their bags for them, but they are hastily snatched from his hands. The valet gives Mac and Killer a funny look. Killer gives him the evil eye, forcing the valet to return to his post and aid other hotel patrons.

1900 Hours: Eisenhower Barracks, West Point

Will has nearly completed his daily routine of waking up, eating, going to classes, eating, football practice, and now eating. Having eaten dinner with his teammates, which is mandatory for all football players, Will heads for his barracks with a few of his teammates. As they climb the high stairs of Eisenhower Barracks, the teammates part ways, until Will reaches the fifth floor, where he is now alone for the remainder of the journey.

Will's room is near the middle of the hallway, almost directly in front of the CQ desk. As he heads for his room, an upperclassman stops Will.

"Where you off to, Cadet Johnson?"

Will stops his forward progress and faces the speaking upperclassman. "I am going to my room, sir."

"That's funny," the upperclassman sarcastically responds, "because last I checked, all of your classmates were in the duty room performing their evening duties. Why aren't you helping them? You must be a get over. Is that what you are, Johnson?"

"No, sir."

"You must be since you're hanging out here in the hallway in your corps squad sweats."

"Sir, I was coming—" the upperclassman cuts Will off in midsentence.

"Shut up! Is that one of your four responses?"

"No, sir."

"I think you've forgotten them. What are they?"

"'Yes, sir.' 'No, sir.' 'No excuse, sir.' 'Sir, I do not understand.'"

"At least you know that." The upperclassman brashly paces in front of Will, who remains locked up at the position of attention.

"Since you are a buddy dick and a corps squad get over, I want you to report to my room every night at 1830 hours with my laundry and mail. I want you there even if there is nothing to deliver. Do you understand me?"

"Yes, sir. Sir, may I make a statement?"

"What is it Johnson?"

"Sir, I cannot make it at 1830 hours."

"You better make it happen," the upperclassman states, getting in Will's face.

"But, sir, I don't—"

"I don't want to hear your excuses, Johnson. Do you understand me? You need to figure out real quick what's important, football or the corps. Now get out of my face!"

"Where Eagles dare," Will states as the upperclassman turns his back on Will and continues down the hall.

Will walks to his room and slams the door behind him. "I hate that dude! I've got something for his punk ass!"

"What's wrong, Will?" asks Cadet Private Gram, one of Will's roommates.

"That punk Carson just hazed me for not helping out with duties!"

"But you don't get back from practice in time to help."

"Yeah, no kidding. I tried telling him that, but all he wanted to hear were the four responses. That's all right though. I've got something for him."

"What are you going to do?"

"I'm calling my brother." Will snatches his telephone receiver and dials Major's number.

After four rings, the answering machine picks up. Much to his dismay, Will is forced to leave a message: "Hey, bro. It's Will. Call me as soon as you get this. I've got a problem."

Will hangs up the telephone and sits down. He broods in his chair for a few moments then leaps up and coldly states, "Forget this. I can't wait for my brother to call me back. I'm going to go find him myself."

Will bursts out of his room and races out of Eisenhower Barracks. Once outside in Central Area, Will does not run to Grant Barracks but, instead, boldly walks with a sense of determination stamped on his face. Focused on his mission, Will does not greet any upperclassmen as they pass him by.

In Grant Area, Will leaps up the first set of stairs that he reaches and heads for Major's division. Approaching Major's door, Will sees that it is shut, as it usually is, which could mean many things. Major could be sleeping, which is highly unlikely at this time of the day. He could be doing his homework; yeah, right, he could be on the phone with some girls, which is highly plausible, or Major could be in a meeting with someone, which is more than likely the case. Will quickly contemplates all of these scenarios but really does not care which one is occurring on the other end of the door. As far as Will is concerned, he has a problem and his big brother needs to fix it.

Will throws Major's door open and suddenly realizes that he has just walked in on one of his brother's regular meetings with his executive staff.

A little embarrassed, Will softly states, "My bad. I didn't know you were having a meeting. I'll come back later."

"Don't worry about it," Major replies. "What's the word?"

"Can we talk in private?" Will asks.

"Sure." Major spins in his chair and faces Sara, Dusty, and Joe, and states, "Hey. Can you guys excuse us?"

"Yeah. No problem," Sara answers for the group.

"Thanks. Give me about fifteen minutes."

As the three cadets exit the room, Major asks his little brother, "So what's the problem, bro?"

"The problem is that this punk yuck in my company's messing with me because I play football!" Will blurts as he pounces in the room.

Major shakes his head and lets out a deep breath. "All right. Tell me what happened from start to finish."

Will plops himself down on the couch and tells his story.

"I was coming back from dinner at around seven like I always do. Anyway, I walked by this yuck, and he asked me why I'm not helping my classmates out with evening duties."

Major interrupts Will. "What's the yuck's name?"

"Carson. Paul Carson."

"All right. Keep going."

"Right. So anyway, this guy tells me that because I'm not helping with duties, I'm a corps squad get over. Now he wants me to deliver his laundry and mail every night at six thirty."

"You can't do that. You're just getting out of practice some nights at that time."

"I know. That's what I tried to tell him, but all he said was, 'Make it happen.'"

"God! This crap really pisses me off!" Major spins in his chair a couple of times, pondering on how he is to aide his little brother. Major stops spinning and says to Will, "Go back to your room. I'll handle this my way. Don't worry. Consider your problem solved."

"What are you going to do?"

"Don't worry about it. Just understand that I've got this handled."

"Cool. Thanks a lot, bro."

Major and Will simultaneously rise from their seats and walk toward one another. The two brothers shake hands then embrace.

As they release, Major tells Will to "Let them know they can come back in now" in reference to Sara, Joe, and Dusty.

"Aight," Will replies as he leaves Major's room.

A couple of seconds later, Joe, Dusty, and Sara return to the room.

"What was that all about?" Joe asks.

"Some punk yuck's messing with my brother because he doesn't help out with evening duties."

"Well, shouldn't he be helping?" Sara asks.

"Sara, you know good and well football players don't make it back in time for evening duties."

"Yeah. I guess you're right," Sara agrees.

"So what are you going to do about it, sir?" Dusty asks.

"I'm not sure. What do you guys think?"

"Personally, I'd beat the hell out of him if he messed with my brother, but you can't do that," Dusty suggests.

"What company's your brother in?" Joe asks.

"E-3. Why you ask?"

"That's what I thought. Will's first sergeant was my first semester plebe when we were yucks," Joe answers.

"Get out of here!" Major replies, surprised at Joe's announcement. "Make that call then."

"I'm on it."

Joe goes over to his desk and picks up his telephone receiver. As Joe speaks to the cadet on the other end, he turns his back on everyone in the room.

After a brief conversation, Joe turns back around and states, "She's on her way."

"Good deal. We'll keep on with our meeting until she gets here."

The four cadets continue their meeting, to pass the time. With only a little over ten minutes having passed, they all hear a light knock on the door.

"Enter!" Major shouts, as he always responds when someone knocks on his door.

The door slowly opens, and a short blond-haired girl wearing gym A steps into the room. She quickly glances over the room and spots one familiar face.

"You wanted to see me, Joe," she states, still standing in the doorway.

"Yeah. Come on in. Take a seat." Joe directs the E-3 first sergeant to the couch, where she sits beside Sara.

Major stands up from his seat and walks over toward their visitor. He extends his hand and says to her, "How're you doing? I'm Milton Johnson. Will's big brother."

"Wow. You guys look almost exactly alike, except for the height," the E-3 first sergeant answers as she extends her hand and firmly shakes Major's.

"What's your first name? I see your last name is Reid, but I don't deal with last names if I can help it or unless you have a cool last name, which you don't have, no disrespect."

"None taken. It's Tara."

"Good deal then, Tara," Major begins, returning to his swivel chair. "The reason I brought you here is because there seems to be a slight problem within your company, and I want to bring it to your attention."

Tara leans forward to see Major's face more clearly and replies, "What problem is that?"

"You have a yuck in your company who's running around harassing corps squad plebes, namely football players."

"Really? Well, what's this yuck doing, exactly?"

Major sits up, straightens his back up, and coldly states, "He locked my brother up in the hallway after dinner and messed with him about being a buddy dick. The yuck then went on and ordered my brother to report to his room every night at 1830 hours with laundry and mail. Now I'm coming to you because you are the first sergeant. I could have easily have gone over to Ike and handled this my own way, but instead, I wanted to handle this the right way. Understand that if the harassment does not cease, then I will be forced to talk to this punk myself."

Cadet Reid squirms in her seat and affirms, "I understand, and thank you for coming to me first. So I can handle this properly, who's the yearling that you're referring to?"

"Paul Carson," Major answers.

"Are you sure? He's one of my best team leaders."

"Well, obviously he isn't if he's harassing corps squad plebes."

Feeling a little uncomfortable, Cadet Reid stands up and says, "Thanks again for keeping me informed. I'll look into this."

"You do that."

Cadet Reid leaves the room with her head down, thinking to herself, *That arrogant prick! Who does he think he is telling me how to run my company? Johnson's just going to have to suck it up and take whatever Paul is dishing out.*

"That went pretty well," Sara acclaims as the door shuts.

"If you say so," Major states. "I don't think she's going to do anything about it."

"You don't?" Dusty asks.

"Not at all. It would be one thing if she were a friend of mine or knew me in some capacity, but she doesn't. She could care less about what I have to say. Think about it like this: if someone were to come to you and tell you to ensure that some kid isn't getting hazed anymore, would you put a stop to it?"

"Probably not," Dusty responds.

Major rises from his seat and replies, "I didn't think so."

Major picks up his telephone receiver and dials a series of numbers. After three rings, a voice on the other end says, "Yeah."

"Hey, Will. It's me. Just finished speaking to your first sergeant. Everything should be good to go, but if it isn't by tomorrow, you let me know. All right?"

"Yeah. Thanks a lot, bro."

"No problem. That's what I'm here for. Now finish your homework. Peace." Major hangs up the telephone.

14 SEPTEMBER, 1999

0930 Hours: Belgrade, Serbia

Gathered in a small conference room are Colonel Drasneb and his specially selected experts. As they wait for Mac and Killer's arrival, they discuss some of the minor intricacies of the mission, mainly personnel matters.

After a short wait, Mac and Killer enter the conference room. The room quickly fills with absolute silence. No thoughts run through the experts' heads as Mac and Killer enter the room. They are astonished at Killer's shear massiveness. His entire body seems to fill the entire room. Killer, on the other hand, is an intimidating figure due to his face. He holds an expression as though death has no affect on him.

The look that the experts read from Killer's expression is one of "I can kill you all with ease then go play with some little kids in the park without a second thought."

Killer and Mac smoothly make their way for the back of the conference room, where Colonel Drasneb stands smiling. Colonel Drasneb smiles because he finally is able to envision his plan coming to fruition. Approaching Colonel Drasneb, Killer moves to his right side and Mac stands to his left.

Now that everyone is present for his in-brief, Colonel Drasneb opens, in his best English, with "Look around the room, gentlemen. Understand that the mission will not achieve success without full participation and cooperation from everyone standing in this room. There is one other who is in our aid, but we will all have the pleasure of meeting his acquaintance in the near future."

Colonel Drasneb walks to the front of the conference room then picks up where he left off. Pointing to every man in the room, he loudly states, "We have no choice but to quickly rely upon one another's skills and attributes. Trust equals victory. You see these two men here"—Colonel Drasneb waves his hand past Killer and Mac—"they may not be our countrymen, but they are behind our cause. They understand and believe whole heartedly in the purpose of our mission. Without their assistance and participation, we cannot achieve our goal—the elimination of America from our lands."

Colonel Drasneb's words cause the room to fill with applause from everyone listening, everyone except Mac and Killer.

Once the applause cease, Colonel Drasneb says, "You may all take your seats now."

All of the men sit down in their designated seat as Colonel Drasneb slowly paces around the large wooden conference table.

With everyone seated, Colonel Drasneb continues. "Gentlemen, this meeting today is merely a chance for all of us to meet. The formal briefing will take place tomorrow, as you have listed in your itineraries."

Colonel Drasneb walks over to Killer and Mac's seats and stands behind them. Placing a hand on each of their shoulders, Colonel Drasneb continues his monologue. "I will begin by introducing these two fine gentlemen. Please, Mr. Stewart, Mr. Pollard, stand up and tell us something about yourselves."

Mac and Killer rise from their seats. Killer is the first to speak.

"As you all know, my last name is Stewart. My friends call me Killer, which is short for my mother's maiden name: Man Killer. I am half Cherokee and half Irish. What can I say, I'm a little mixed up."

Some of the experts in the room lightly chuckle at Killer's subtle joke.

A bit loosened up, Killer looks at Mac and says, "You have anything to say, brother?"

"Not at this time," Mac coldly states, staring everyone down in the room.

"Hmm. The strong-and-silent type," Colonel Drasneb comments. "Reminds me of myself when I was young and full of vigor."

All of the experts laugh at Colonel Drasneb's analysis of Mac. Killer even lets out a small chuckle. Mac looks at him with disdain. Killer returns a look, signaling to Mac that he needs to calm down and relax. Mac takes his seat then folds his arms and stares out ahead of him.

Once both Mac and Killer have seated, each expert, in a clockwise direction, introduces himself and proudly explains how grateful they are to Colonel Drasneb for selecting them for his top-secret mission.

As the experts speak, Mac thinks to himself, *I cannot believe these fools. They actually believe that they're doing a great service. To and for whom, I'll never know, 'cause God knows that if for some unknown reason we're able to pull this mission off, it sure as hell isn't going to help Serbia out any. If anything, it's going to cause 'em some serious pain.* Mac smiles at his final thought of his country's possible response if the mission is a success.

1745 Hours: West Point

Major stands in the mess hall with several other Ducks, in their full dress uniforms, waiting for the rest of the company and the invited guests to arrive. Most cadets do not like dining-ins for the simple fact that they have to wear their full dress, but they do love the food. It is much better than the regular dinner meal. As the invited guests and the remainder of the Ducks slowly arrive in small packs, Major greets them, and then they enter Regimental Room, where the dining-in will take place.

Captain Weiss arrives and asks Major, "How's everything looking?"

"Pretty good, sir," Major replies. "Everyone's pretty much here."

"Great. Has Colonel Wood shown up yet? I'm really curious what he's going to do tonight."

Major laughs. "Not yet, sir, but I'm expecting him shortly."

"All right then," Captain Weiss says as he begins to enter the Regimental Room.

Interrupting Captain Weiss, Major states, "Oh, I almost forgot, sir. General Erickson is still going to be a little late. His aide, Major Thomas, stopped by a while ago. He said we should eat when we're ready. He'll catch up with us when he gets here."

"Good. I was wondering that myself. I'll see you inside."

"Roger, sir,"

Still standing outside of Regimental Room entrance, Mrs. Wood approaches Major and states, motioning to the mess hall's main entrance lobby, "The Big Guy's out there. Go check him out real quick. I'm going to go in and seat myself."

"Yes, ma'am," Major smilingly replies, walking toward the main entrance of the mess hall.

Major steps out into the lobby to find a very tall Duck-suit-wearing man sitting in a wheelchair. Major laughs at the sight. Even if he did not know that Colonel Wood was the one in the wheelchair, it is too obvious for anyone not to know. Colonel Wood's legs are not suited for the wheelchair. His knees practically touch his chest, plus the Duck suit pants legs go halfway up his calves.

"This is too much, sir," Major laughingly comments.

"Now I can say that I am a real Duck," Colonel Wood replies. "You're next, man."

"Yes, sir."

"You go on ahead of me," Colonel Wood says. "I'll follow behind you."

"Roger, sir," Major answers shaking his head in disbelief at what he is witnessing.

Major leads the way back into the mess hall and into Regimental Room, where all in attendance patiently sit, waiting for Major to arrive so the dining-in can begin. Major enters the room and stands behind his seat. Most of the Ducks and guests do not pay any attention to Major because all of their attention is focused on the weird creature that follows behind him.

Captain Weiss, who stands next to Major, leans to his right and asks, "Is that Colonel Wood?"

"Yes, sir. It is."

Captain Weiss and those at his and Major's table burst out in laughter.

Once the disguised Colonel Wood is situated at his table, Major stands at the position of attention and barks, "Post the colors."

Upon the command, five cadets march into the regimental room. The two flank cadets carry M14 assault rifles at port arms. The cadet to the left carries the army flag, the cadet at the center carries the US flag, and the cadet to the right carries the USMA flag.

As the colors enter the regimental room, everyone faces in their direction. As the colors move forward, everyone moves with them, ensuring that they face the colors at all times.

The colors march in front of Major and come to a halt when the US flag is in front of him. The colors then execute a right face. Facing Major, he salutes the colors. The color sergeant then gives the order for the colors to continue with the ceremony. Having posted the colors, the color guard marches out of the regimental room, wait a few seconds, then quietly reenter the regimental room and sit at the rear.

With the colors posted and everyone situated within the regimental room, Cdt. Sgt. Adam Skelton, the company military NCO, steps to the front of the room. Cadet Skelton is famous for the fact that his father is none other than the brigade tactical officer (BTO) , Colonel Skelton. He used to catch a lot of flack his plebe and yuck years for it, but Cadet Skelton's good-dude status among the corps is solidified due to his nature and interactions with his fellow cadets and soccer teammates. Major calls Cadet Skelton "Biscuit" because of his round size. He is not fat, just short and stocky.

"Good evening, everyone," Cadet Skelton opens. "We are going to open the dining-in with the reading of the rules of the mess."

Cadet Skelton reads the several rules to the attendees. Each rule read is followed by a host of laughter. The rules of the mess are not serious rules by any means. They are created to add a sense of fun to the dining-in. The rules of the mess, along with dining-ins, is an old army tradition.

Having read the rules of the mess, Cadet Skelton's officer counterpart, the company security officer, Cdt. Lt. Adam Reese, steps forward and stands behind a table that has a large water-filled punch bowl on top of it.

"Good evening, distinguished guests and fellow Ducks," Cadet Reese opens. "We will now perform the ceremony of the grog."

The best way to describe the *grog* is as a concoction of many different substances. Grogs are like snowflakes; there are never two identical ones. The contents used to make the grog stem from the traditions and personalities of the unit and its members. Like the dining-in and the rules of the mess, the grog is also an old army tradition. The only difference between the grog that the Ducks are preparing to make and a traditional army grog is the absence of alcohol.

Cadet Reese stands before the small crowd, preparing the grog. First, he adds Nestle Quik chocolate powder then some dirt from a football cleat, followed by half a bottle of Texas Pete hot sauce and a few squirts of Gulden's mustard. Cadet Reese then tosses in two sweaty gym socks, retrieves them from the bowl then wrings them out into the bowl. Everyone grimaces and laughs simultaneously.

For the final touch, Adam holds up a presweetened container of tropical punch Kool-Aid and says with a big grin on his face, "And for the final ingredient to the grog, I add our illustrious commander's favorite beverage, Kool-Aid, not because we love him so much, but because we expect him to drink at least half of this bowl before the night's over."

The room fills with laughter. Captain Weiss slaps Major on the back. Many of the Ducks point at him and laugh. Major simply shakes his head and softly says, laughing, "God help me."

Nearly an hour goes by. The Ducks have nearly completed eating their meal, consisting of prime rid, fresh green beans, scalloped potatoes, and baked rolls. With his connections in the mess hall, Major has extra rolls brought to his table. It is not because he likes rolls so much but the fact that he loves to eat and the rolls are all that he can receive in extra quantities.

The commandant of cadets, Brig. Gen. Randall T. Erickson, enters the regimental room. Aware that Brigadier General Erickson is approaching their table, Captain Weiss and Major both rise to their feet to greet him.

Brigadier General Erickson shakes Captain Weiss and Major's hands and states, "Sorry I'm late, guys. I got here as fast as I could. The intramural championships for Third Regiment kept me busy."

"No problem, sir. We understand," Captain Weiss replies.

Brigadier General Erickson takes his seat. Captain Weiss and Major follow suit. With Brigadier General Erickson, one of the waiters brings him a plate. As Brigadier General Erickson quickly devours his meal, the remainder of the attendees starts on their dessert.

In the process of eating his dessert, Captain Weiss looks at his watch and realizes that it is past 1930 hours—study barracks. Knowing that the dining-in is cutting into the designated cadet study period, Captain Weiss leans toward Major and whispers, "It's past seven thirty. You need to introduce the com. Keep his introduction short though due to the time constraint."

"Roger, sir," Major replies. He wipes his mouth with his napkin then rises from his seat.

Major stands behind the lectern before the small crowd and begins his introduction of the commandant by recognizing all of the invited guests, in rank order. Having done so, he formally introduces Brigadier General Erickson to the audience.

With the brief introduction complete, the room fills with applause as Brigadier General Erickson makes his way to the front. Standing beside the lectern, Brigadier General Erickson and Major shake hands. Major then returns to his seat.

"Good evening, everyone," Brigadier General Erickson opens, waving to the small crowd. "It is an honor to speak before you this evening. You are the first group of cadets that I have had the privilege of speaking to in a formal setting. Other than the brigade tactical department's dining-in last week, this is the first speech I have rendered at West Point. D-1 is one of the oldest companies in the corps—full of honor and tradition. As leaders among the corps, it is imperative that each of you continues to uphold the tradition of Duty, Honor, Country, which has been passed down through the years. As you grow and mature and move further in your leadership growth here at the Point, remember to always have compassion for those you lead.

"A compassionate leader is an effective leader. Without compassion, one cannot truly grasp the strengths and limitations of those of whom he leads. Compassion for your soldiers gives you the ability to properly weigh the costs in executing missions. Understand though that compassion does not equal coddling. As a leader, you are forced to make difficult decisions, some that may mean the death to some of your soldiers. Compassion will enable you to take the proper course of action by eliminating unnecessary risks. Though you know that some of your soldiers may not make it home, you will be able to take comfort in the fact that you did all that you could to ensure that you have the means of getting them home safely, for example, giving your soldiers the proper training that they need to achieve mission success.

"D-1, always remember that your soldiers come first. Instill in them the same level of compassion that you have for them. Do that and they will follow you to hell and back. Continue to uphold the traditions of the corps. Go Army!"

Upon Brigadier General Erickson's completion of his speech, the room fills with applause and everyone rises to their feet. Major pulls a bag out from under his seat and walks toward Brigadier General Erickson.

While shaking hands with Brigadier General Erickson, Major states, "Sir, on behalf of the Ducks, we would like to thank you for your inspirational words on compassion and how it is an effective leadership tool. All of the cadets here will certainly take your words and apply them as leaders in the corps and the army." A few applause ring through the room. Major pauses for a moment then continues. "Now, sir, I know that you did not have the honor of being a Duck while you were a cadet, so we would like to present you with a company T-shirt and make you an honorary Duck."

Major pulls the neatly folded T-shirt out of the bag and hands it to Brigadier General Erickson, who then unfolds it to see what it looks like on the front. Brigadier General Erickson laughs at what he sees. He turns the shirt around so everyone else in the room can see it as well. The non-cadets in the audience laugh at the T-shirt and the cadets laugh because everyone else is laughing. The reason everyone is laughing is because the T-shirt depicts a rubber ducky in the middle of the chest that says "Go, Ducks!" on the top and the company motto "Bad to the bone" beneath it.

Still laughing, Brigadier General Erickson shakes Major's hand again and states, "You're right, Major, I didn't have the honor of being a Duck back in my day. I will wear this shirt with pride…in my house."

Major laughs and replies, "I understand, sir." After a short pause, Major faces the audience and proclaims, "This concludes the dining-in. Retire the colors."

The color guard posts, retrieves the colors, then exit the regimental room. With the colors gone, everyone relaxes and slowly follows suit, especially the plebes and yearlings who have to be in their rooms studying at this time. While the underclassmen leave, some of the upperclassmen and the invited guests stay behind to mingle.

Mrs. Wood departs from her table and heads for where Major and Brigadier General Erickson stand. "I have to get a picture of the two of you together," she happily states.

"Yes, ma'am," Major replies with a bashful grin on his face.

"Hold the shirt up, Randy," Mrs. Wood says to the com as she peers through her camera.

Brigadier General Erickson laughs. He takes one end of the shirt and Major grabs hold of the other end. Mrs. Wood snaps her photo, smiles, then says, "Very good. This one'll make it in the history books someday."

Belgrade, Serbia

Walking in a serene park in the middle of the city, Mac and Killer talk to one another with relative privacy.

"We had to get out of that hotel," Killer states. "God knows that place was bugged."

"Yeah, I know," Mac replies. "There are also two spooks following us."

Killer inconspicuously looks about the area. "Yep," he acknowledges.

"I don't like this one bit," Mac angrily, yet quietly, states.

"Yeah. Me neither."

"This doesn't sit well with me at all. I never signed on so that I could betray my country. Do you realize that if we're caught we'll be executed for treason? We can't do this!" Mac exclaims.

"I know, but what choice do we have? We can't just up and cancel out on the contract. If we do, that Drasneb bastard'll kill us for sure."

"Yeah, I know. Our only option is to ride the wave and get off right before it crashes. We're smart guys. We'll come up with something," Mac jokingly states. "In the meantime, let's get something to eat."

"Good idea. I'm hungry as hell."

The two mercenaries continue their walk through the park. After hanging a left past a giant oak, Mac takes a seat on the edge of a statue of the famous late Yugoslav President, Josep Broz Tito.

Killer walks over to a bench about thirty feet away from the Tito statue and sits next to an old wino, who is in a very stuporous state and reeks of garbage. Killer places his arm around the wino, leans over, and says, "Tell Drasneb he needs to find better spooks. You guys are worse than those dudes in the James Bond movies."

The wino throws his head up suddenly, jumps to his feet, and walks off as if nothing surprising had just happened.

Across the way, Mac has a newspaper in his hands, pretending to read it since he does not know how to read a lick of Serbo-Croatian. He watches the wino stumble over to a man who is walking a dog and whisper something in his ear. Mac is too far to hear but is smart enough to know that the wino just tipped the man off to the fact that he and Killer are aware of their presence.

Mac rises off of the statue and walks over to the bench where Killer is sitting. Laughing, he says, "That was funny as hell, bro. That's some mess I would've pulled."

"I know," Killer laughingly replies. "That's why I did it. I can't wait to see Drasneb's reaction when we meet with him tomorrow during that training op prep."

"He's going to really want to kill us after the stunt we just pulled."

"Oh well. At least we'll die laughing."

Killer and Mac rise from the park bench and walk back in the direction from where they came. Turning right past the same oak, they spot the man with the dog who the wino had spoken.

As they pass the man, Mac slaps him on the butt, winks, and says, "We'll be seeing you."

■———————————■

"Sir, the Americans that you hired have identified the men that I had following them."

"Is that so?" Colonel Drasneb replies with a devilish smile on his face. "Well, it was inevitable. My friend said that they were good. I guess he wasn't kidding, huh?"

"No, sir. I guess not."

Colonel Drasneb rises from his chair and stairs out over the city bellow while formulating what he should do with the two Americans. He knows that he needs their skills and expertise, but he now knows that they are a liability.

"Sir?"

"Yes, what is it?" Colonel Drasneb annoyingly answers.

"What should I have my men do?"

"Well," Colonel Drasneb begins with a long pause, "since they already know that we are suspicious of them, it would be redundant of us to spy on them. On the other hand, we can't have a couple of American mercenaries running around our beloved capital. Now can we?"

"No, sir. We cannot"

"Place two of your best men on the detail. Same orders as before."

"Yes, sir. Anything else?"

"No. That will be all. You can go now. I need to think," Colonel Drasneb retorts as he sits back in his chair.

The young officer leaves the room as Colonel Drasneb turns, faces the window, and reclines back in his chair. He now has to figure out how to use the Americans,] while at the same time expend of them as soon as they execute the mission. Until that day arrives, Colonel Drasneb has to ensure that the Americans do not realize that they are expendable. Though very difficult, they do have the ability to escape from the country if they feel the need to. God help him if they do.

Colonel Drasneb sits up and turns back around. He pulls out a manila folder and begins dialing a sequence of numbers. The line is secure, so he does not have to worry about anyone listening in on his conversation—his government or his enemies. The telephone rings four times, and a man with a thick Russian accent answers.

"Hello?"

"Gurgtzy. This is Colonel Drasneb," he responds in his best Russian.

"Ah, Colonel. It is good to hear from you. We were getting a little worried over here. We were not sure if you were still coming."

"Of course, I am coming. My men and I will be there in two days. I am calling to confirm and ensure that you are ready for us."

"Yes. We are ready for you. The training facilities are all in place. My staff is already there, preparing for your arrival."

"Well then. I guess I'll see you in two weeks."

"Until then, Colonel."

"Until then."

Colonel Drasneb places the telephone back on the receiver then picks it back up and dials another set of numbers. This time, instead of a person answering, he gets a voice-mail message. After the message finishes playing, Colonel Drasneb states, "Call your dad. It's time to prepare dinner," then hangs up.

15 SEPTEMBER 1999

0900 Hours: Belgrade, Serbia

Mac and Killer stand outside of the main entrance to their hotel, waiting for Colonel Drasneb's car to come by and pick them up. They have been standing outside for nearly fifteen minutes.

Unless on the job, where timing is everything, Mac and Killer always arrive fifteen minutes early. For instance, if they have to meet with J back at their Paris headquarters, they arrive at Marie's desk fifteen minutes prior to the meeting. Being on time is quite crucial to Mac and Killer's lives. Besides that, Mac gets very frustrated when he is forced to wait for anything or anyone for an extended period of time.

Killer first formed his great level of time discipline from his mother when he was a young boy. She always told him, "To be fifteen minutes early is to be on time. To be on time is to be late." Her rationale behind her little-time philosophy is based upon the fact that if one is fifteen minutes early, it gives them a cushion just in case things do not go as planned, which is what usually happens in many cases.

As the two mercenaries stand on the edge of the street, a brisk wind blows by. Killer stiffens slightly, causing him to button his cashmere coat as far as it will go. Mac just stands there, uninhibited by the breeze.

Killer looks down at his watch and states, "The car's late. It was on time yesterday."

"What'd you expect? A certain level of consistency?" Mac replies.

"I guess not. You would think though that with how important this job is to Drasneb, he would have us at his little meeting on time."

"True."

As the two friends converse about the car's lateness, a black Mercedes turns the corner and pulls up in front of them.

"It's about time," Mac blurts as the car comes to a screeching halt. Killer and Mac step into the car and sit comfortably, waiting to arrive at their destination. The drive is not too long. It is the end of rush hour, so they hit little traffic. Their travel time is slowed down some, but the traffic is nothing like it is in the New York City or Washington, DC, metropolitan areas.

After driving for nearly fifteen minutes, the black Mercedes comes to a stop in front of Colonel Drasneb's building. A couple of seconds later, the rear passenger door opens from the outside. Mac and Killer step out of the Mercedes and head directly for the main entrance. Ten feet from the entrance, two soldiers standing on both sides of the double doors opens them for the two mercenaries. With Mac and Killer inside the building, the two soldiers shut the doors behind them then escort Mac and Killer up to the conference room.

Mac and Killer enter the conference room, where the experts are already seated and ready for the meeting to begin.

Seeing Mac and Killer, Colonel Drasneb springs from his seat and shouts with his arms open, "Gentlemen! I apologize for your delay. There was an accident, which slowed my car's arrival time down. I apologize for the inconvenience. I hope it was not too cold outside for you."

The experts laugh on cue. Mac gives Colonel Drasneb the evil eye in return for his cynical comment. Colonel Drasneb does not catch Mac's hateful look, much to Mac's good fortune.

As Mac and Killer walk to their seats, some of the experts give them funny looks. Killer pays them no mind, but Mac once again flashes the evil eye to every expert who is not looking at him in a respectful manner. All of the experts notice Mac's hateful look and are taken aback by it.

The one thought that now flows through every expert's mind is, *I don't care what Colonel Drasneb says. These two mercenaries do not believe in our cause.*

With Mac and Killer seated, Colonel Drasneb motions for his assistant who stands to his left to hand packets out to all of those who are seated at the conference table. As the men receive their packet, they immediately open it up and peruse through it.

When Mac receives his packet, he does not open it.

Killer takes his packet from Colonel Drasneb's assistant and says, "Thanks."

Colonel Drasneb, noticing that everyone has a packet, states, "Read through the packet on your own for a few minutes. We will then discuss it and answer any questions that you may have."

After a couple of minutes, Killer looks at Colonel Drasneb and asks, "Colonel Drasneb, your training schedule for training phase is nearly nonexistent. Also, with this mission being solely based upon West Point's mess hall, why is there not any mention of plans or schematics of the place?"

"Very good question, Mr. Stewart," Colonel Drasneb replies. He focuses on his experts and says, "See, gentlemen, why I hired these two men? Look how quickly Mr. Stewart picked up upon what seems to be a mistake on my part."

Colonel Drasneb rises form his seat and begins pacing around the room. He then continues speaking. "To answer your question, Mr. Stewart, the training phase contains holes because you and Mr. Pollard are going to fill them."

Mac raises his head and looks at Colonel Drasneb with a questioning look.

Colonel Drasneb replies to Mac's look by stating, "Yes, Mr. Pollard. You and Mr. Stewart will plan nearly every aspect of our training. It only makes sense since you two are the experts in killing. No pun intended."

The experts laugh. Mac and Killer do not. They look at one another dumbfounded.

"Colonel Drasneb continues. "You will receive some assistance though once we get to Russia. To answer your second question, Mr. Stewart, another will join us a day after we arrive at the training site. He will have with him the mess hall schematics as well as a layout of West Point and some photographs to better assist your planning."

"You must be out of your mind," Mac states. "You expect us to plan this little crusade of yours? We were under the impression that we were here solely for execution purposes. Now you're telling us that we have to be the masterminds behind this bullshit!"

Killer squeezes Mac's knee to calm him down.

Colonel Drasneb slowly walks toward Mac and asks, "This is not a problem for you, is it, Mr. Pollard?"

Not waiting for Mac to reply, Killer quickly asks, "Colonel Drasneb, we have twelve days until departure, correct?"

Colonel Drasneb was expecting Mac to lose his composure and make a regretful comment. He is a little taken aback by Killer speaking out instead of Mac. *These two seem to read each other's minds*, Colonel Drasneb thinks. *I'm going to have more trouble than I thought of when to make my move.*

Colonel Drasneb steps out of his brief personal thoughts and answers Killer. "Yes, Mr. Stewart. We leave for Russia in twelve days."

"Well then," Killer replies, "Mac and I have more than enough time to plan the training for the mission. We'll have it ready for your final approval when we step onto the plane. We are flying, right?"

"Of course," Colonel Drasneb answers.

"That's what I expected. Mac and I can fully brief your men once we get to Russia and complete the remainder of the plans once the other guy arrives with the schematics. How's that sound to you?"

"That sounds great."

"Good." Killer looks down at his watch, not to read the time but merely as an action. "Since Mac and I have all of this planning to do, we're going to leave now. You know how to get into contact with us if you need us, sir."

Killer and Mac rise from their seats, packets in hand, then quickly exit the conference room. The two same guards stand outside in the hallway and escort Mac and Killer down to the main entrance doors. The guards open the doors for Mac and Killer, who then promptly head for the Mercedes. Once inside, the Mercedes pulls away and takes Mac and Killer to their hotel.

1815 Hours: West Point

Major is over at the Woods' home once again, treating himself to yet another free dinner. This time though, it is like most evenings when he goes to visit the Woods on a school night—just he and Colonel and Mrs. Wood hanging out at the kitchen table swapping stories and telling jokes.

For dinner tonight, they are having steaks, wild rice, and salad. Usually, Mrs. Wood prepares the main course and Colonel Wood handles the salad (he loves making salads), but ever since he bought his George Foreman Grill, Colonel Wood has been cooking more frequently. Tonight is one such night. Colonel Wood throws the steaks on the grill then sprinkles some seasoning on them. Major makes the salads and fills the glasses with ice except for his because he does not like ice. With the food ready, Major and Colonel and Mrs. Wood take a seat at the kitchen table.

While they eat, Colonel Wood looks up at Major and says, "Have you worn the Duck suit yet?"

"No, sir. I haven't," Major answers.

"You know, you can't truly be a Duck unless you wear the suit, right?"

"No, sir, I didn't know that," Major curiously answers.

"That's right. I know that you're the CO, and that's good, but to become an official Duck, you have to wear the suit, and I don't mean in your room where no one will see you. You have to wear it out in formation."

"Formation, sir? Are you sure about that? I'll get killed."

The reason Major is worried about wearing the Duck suit is because of D-1's notoriety throughout the corps, much of which stems from the Duck suit. The Duck head is the most coveted company mascot head in the corps. Whenever a D-1 plebe wears the Duck suit out to a spirit rally, that individual has to be escorted by at least six other plebes—all of whom are carrying broom sticks—and a couple of yucks to ensure that no one gets hurt. It is a dangerous job, sometimes suicidal, being the D-1 Duck.

After Major recovers from his brief shock, he says to Colonel Wood, "All right, sir. I'll do it. I may get killed, but you're right. I have to show my kids that I wouldn't have them do anything that I myself am not willing to do."

"There you go!" Colonel Wood excitingly states. "When are you going to do it?"

"I don't know. This Thursday, I guess. Since it's a spirit dinner and all. I'll wear it to formation and lead the company into the mess hall in it."

Colonel Wood claps his hands together and says, "Me and Sally'll be there."

"Yeah!" Mrs. Wood echoes, "And I'll bring the camera so we can get some pictures of you."

"Oh, won't that be great," Major sarcastically replies. "All I need is evidence."

The three laugh as they continue eating their meal. Major thinks to himself, *My god! What have I gotten myself into? I'm definitely going to have a fight on my hands.*

16 SEPTEMBER 1999

1000 Hours: Belgrade, Serbia

Mac and Killer's morning routine is dependent upon the phase of their respective mission and the terrain and environment in which they inhabit. Being that they are in the planning phase of a mission in a relatively nonhostile environment, Mac and Killer are able to do two things that they love best: workout and run.

Mac and Killer woke up at six in the morning and immediately ran ten miles. After their run, they returned to their rooms to do various forms of push-ups, sit-ups, crunches, flutter kicks, and manual-resistance neck and lat raises.

Now complete with their workouts, showers, and breakfast, Mac and Killer sit in their room and finally begin planning the training for the mission.

"Well," Killer begins, "since we're planning the training for this mess, I guess this means that we determine how the mission runs, huh?"

"I guess so," Mac grunts.

"You still pissed?" Killer asks, knowing the answer to the question. "Aren't you?"

"Of course, I am, but if we act as we feel around these dudes, they're going to get sick of us real soon. The last thing I need is a bullet in the back of my head. You know what I'm saying?"

"I hear you, bro."

"So you're going to play the game, right?"

"Yeah, but you can't make me smile around these fools."

"No one's asking you to. Remember, we do this job, then that's it. We're out, or at least I am."

"You're really going to get out, huh?"

"Yeah. The double life, lying to my wife and kids thing, isn't working out as I had thought."

"You going to tell Sharon?"

"The truth?"

"Of course."

"Everything?"

"No. She doesn't need to know everything. Tough as she is, I don't think she could handle the entire truth. I think Angie can though. And the boys, well, you know how they'd react."

"Yeah, I do," Mac laughs.

"I'll tell Sharon what I do and for how long, but that's it." Killer pauses for a second, then his mind finally jumps. "Damn it! I can't tell her without telling her about you!"

"That's all right, dawg. That thought crossed my mind back in Paris when you first had doubts."

"You don't mind me telling her?"

"How can I not? You're my best friend. You're like a brother to me. If revealing to your family what we do is going to relieve some burden off your chest, then do what you've got to do."

"Man, I really appreciate that."

"No prob. What are brothers for?"

Mac and Killer simultaneously squeeze each other's shoulders and nod.

With the quick bonding moment passed, Mac says, "All right. Let's get this nonsense underway."

"Definitely."

Having straightened out their personal problems—for the time being, that is—Mac and Killer get underway in planning the training for Colonel Drasneb's mission. The task itself is very easy: secure an area and its hostiles then destroy something within the perimeter. Colonel Drasneb's mission is the first that Mac and Killer have worked alongside regular soldiers from another country. The additional soldiers allow Mac and Killer to free themselves up during the execution phase. They do have one question though. The mission, though somewhat complicated due to the number of unknown factors, is an easy one that they can execute alone. So why so many personnel assigned to the mission?

1800 Hours: West Point

Major has returned from basketball practice and sits on his couch somewhat nervous. Sara and Dusty enter the room, Dusty carrying the Duck suit in his hands.

"Are you sure you want to do this, sir?" Dusty asks.

"Not really," Major honestly answers, "but it's like Colonel Wood said that I can't have my soldiers do something that I myself am not willing to do. You know?"

"I hear you," Dusty agrees.

Sara stands there laughing.

Major looks at her and replies, "What's so funny?"

Sara continues laughing and states, "I can't wait to see everyone's face when they see you in that thing."

"Ha ha," Major cynically replies.

Major gets up from off of the couch. Dusty hands him the Duck suit, and Major proceeds to get dressed. While dressing, Joe bursts into the room and says, "The yucks are all ready for you out on the stoops."

Major takes the Duck head from Dusty, places it on his head and replies, "Let's do this. One final touch before we go though." Major bends down and lifts the left pants leg up to his knee. Standing back up, he boldly states, "Now I'm ready."

Major leads the way out of his room. He is a little nervous, but fortunately, no one can see that through the Duck suit. Major steps out onto the stoops where fifteen of his yearlings wait.

"You ready for this, Major?" one of the yucks asks.

"Hell yeah!" Major shouts.

The yucks surround Major on all sides, ensuring that no one passes through them to harm their undercover commander. As Major walks, he notices everyone's reaction to his wearing the suit. No one outside of D-1 knows that he is the one wearing the Duck suit, but they are aware that something different is occurring due to the extra protection that the Duck is receiving this evening.

One of Major's friends, Cdt. Lt. Maleka Bird realizes that it is Major in the Duck suit because of the pants leg and his signature knee-high socks.

"That's got to be Major in the Duck suit," Cadet Bird informs a small group of her friends. "That fool is crazy."

Major and his oversized entourage enter Central Area. They all move to their respective platoon areas, while Major stands in the front of the company, as he always does prior to formation. As he idly stands, Major realizes that violence is about to ensue.

All of a sudden from all sides, Major hears a loud, "Get the Duck!"

Instantly, an overwhelming swarm of plebes from First Battalion and from Second Regiment rush Major like bees on honey. The odds are squarely against the Ducks. Major and his company find themselves forced to defend themselves against nearly a quarter of the population of the Corps of Cadets.

As the fighting rages on, Major is hit from behind with such a force that the Duck head is knocked from off of his shoulders. An attacking plebe scoops the Duck head up from off of the ground. Without warning, one of Major's yucks, Cadet Corporal Emirs tackles the helpless plebe onto the asphalt. Cadet Emirs quickly leaps up from off of the plebe, snatches the Duck head off the ground, hands it back to Major, and states, "Here you go."

Major retrieves the Duck head and returns it onto his own. After a few more minutes of fighting, another plebe breaks through the defending Duck yearlings and, unbeknown to Major, steals the Duck head from off of his head.

With the riot having gone on for over five minutes, Major had finally had enough. In retaliation, Major snatches the plebe and spins him around so that they are now face-to-face, their noses nearly touching. The plebe's eyes widen in fright. Without hesitation, Major shakes the life out of the plebe, thus causing him to drop the Duck head.

Major glares into the scared plebe's eyes and snarls, "Do you know who I am? Do you?"

"Yes, sir," the plebe frighteningly replies.

"You tell your little friends then to get out of my AO before we really hurt somebody! You understand?"

"Yes, sir," the plebe answers with a tremble in his voice.

Major releases the plebe, who then runs away, shouting something to his classmates that Major is unable to make out. After a couple of seconds, the mob ceases its violent activities against the Ducks with them returning to their company areas.

As the plebes scurry off, another D-1 yearling hands the Duck head back to Major. "Thanks, Jake," Major graciously states.

"No problem," Jake replies, returning to his platoon formation.

Major stares at the Duck head's face for a brief moment and thinks to himself, *This was wild. I never thought I'd do something crazy like this. Fighting off over a regiment's worth of plebes. Too nice.*

Major places the Duck head back onto his shoulders, moves to the position of attention, then falls his company in.

God! I love this! Major thinks as his company, the Mighty Dirty Ducks, move to the position of attention.

17 SEPTEMBER 1999

1930 Hours: West Point

Major sits silently in his room. It is a rare moment when he is able to focus on his homework and not have to deal with any company business. Because he knows that company business is bound to come across his desk at any given moment, Major takes full advantage of the free time that he has to do his SE 420 Drill Problems.

While Major works on one of the problems in his textbook, his telephone rings.

"Goddawg!" Major says under his breath. He then thinks to himself, *I can't get any work done around here.*

Major picks up the telephone receiver and coldly states, "Hello?"

"Milt. I need you, bro," a familiar voice frantically replies.

"Will? What's the word?"

"That punk Carson's got me again. He's now making me report to his room at five thirty every morning and hazing the hell out of me! I can't take this mess, bro!"

Hearing Will's plea greatly disturbs Major. Even more so, it pisses him off tremendously. Major has never understood why or how some cadets get off on making life miserable for plebes. Major knows what he has to do.

"Don't worry, bro," Major answers Will. "I'm going to handle this personally. I'll be by your room in five minuets." Major immediately hangs up the telephone receiver then darts out of his room.

■————————————■

On the first floor of Ike Barracks near the Central Guard Room, Major stands by the elevator, waiting for it to take its slow trip down to him. During the duty day, cadets are not permitted to ride the elevator. After 1600 hours though, at the completion of the duty day for the West Point faculty and staff, cadets are permitted to ride the elevators—all except for plebes. Plebes are not permitted to ride the elevators until after recognition, which occurs the Thursday before spring break in March. Of course, the rule does not stop all cadets from riding the elevators when they get a chance, upperclassmen and plebes alike.

The elevator doors finally open. Major jumps in then pushes the five button numerous times. The doors finally shut, and the elevator slowly creeps up. After only a short trip, the doors open again, but not on the fifth floor. Several cadets walk in, laughing and talking about something that Major is not paying much attention to. Respectfully, Major nods his head to say hello. Some of the cadets among the group return his greeting by saying hello.

"You guys know I'm going up, right?" Major says to the group

"Yeah," one of the cadets answers, "but it's easier to ride up then all the way down, instead of waiting for the elevator to go down."

Major laughs, remembering the days when he too lived in Eisenhower Barracks and had to deal with its dastardly elevator. "I hear you, man," Major agrees.

Arriving on the fifth floor, Major states, "This is me." He makes his way through the cadets and steps out into the hallway, hanging a left toward Will's room.

Major enters Will's room, let's the door slam behind him, and shouts, "What's up, fellas?"

Will's roommates, cadet privates Walter Gram and Harley Richard turn from their desks and reply, "Hey, Major! How's it going?"

"Chillin'. You know how I do," Major answers. "Just here to take care of a little business. You know what I'm saying?"

Walter and Harley nod their heads in compliance.

Major walks over to Will, who is also sitting at his desk, and asks, "So where's this punk's room?"

"It's down the hall across from the second bathroom on the other end of the hall," Will bluntly states.

"I'll be back." Major leaves the plebes' room and heads straight for Cadet Carson's room. When Major arrives, he does not knock. He simply walks in, swinging the door open in a blatant but controlled emotional display of anger.

Entering unannounced, Cadet Carson flinches in surprise. He was not expecting any visitors, and if he were, he would have expected a knock on his door.

"Can I help you?" Cadet Carson asks, standing up from behind his desk.

"Yes, you can," Major replies. "I hear you're giving corps squad plebes a hard time."

"So what if I am?"

Major laughs at Cadet Carson's cynicism. "You're definitely making this easier for me. That's for sure."

Cadet Carson gives Major a funny look.

"Let me explain something to you, Carson," Major continues. "My brother is not your verbal punching bag. If you have a professional problem with him, then you deal with it in a professional manner. The fact that you don't like his football practice schedule is not grounds for you harassing him and making his life tougher than it already is. What! Do you get your rocks off hazing plebes and wasting their time?" Major pauses briefly then continues, saying, "This is when you speak."

Cadet Carson jumps back slightly then answers Major. "No. I don't think he's pulling his weight. When the plebes are doing duties, he's eating dinner or just coming back from dinner."

Major shakes his head in frustration. "You obviously have no concept of how things work around here. My brother, as well as the other corps squad athletes, works a hundred times harder than you ever will. While you're taking naps in the afternoon, he's lifting weights until he reaches muscle failure. He's running until he wants to throw up. He's hitting people and getting hit. And then when you do wake up from your nap, he's doing it all over again. You need to thank him and all of the other corps squad athletes who sacrifice their time and their bodies for this school. We all do something to make West Point great. Some of us drill, others play sports, others debate. Some even sing. The fact of the matter is you need to respect them all. Just because you don't see my brother working hard doesn't mean he isn't. What! Do you honestly think that the football team plays on Saturdays and hangs out in the locker room watching TV and playing video games the rest of the week? Don't tell me you're that dumb? Please, don't tell me that!"

Major turns his back to Cadet Carson and heads for the door. He then spins around and marches back to where Cadet Carson's location. Major stands nearly nose to nose with Cadet Carson and glares into his eyes, sternly saying, "Oh, and understand this. If I discover that you're messing with my brother or any of the other plebes in this company, know that I will deal with you in such a manner that will make this little exchange look pleasant. Don't take this as a threat 'cause it's definitely a promise. Do you understand where I'm coming from?"

"Yeah. I got you," Cadet Carson solemnly replies.

"I don't think I heard you correctly. We're not friends. Is that how you speak to a cadet officer?"

Perturbed, Cadet Carson coldly replies, "Yes, sir. I understand you completely."

"Good. I hope we don't have to visit this issue again." Major heads for the door again and says on his way out, "Hey, Carson. You may have pissed me the hell off by messing with my brother, but I don't take this personally. You shouldn't either. It's only business."

Major, now finished with his business with Cadet Carson, returns to Will's room.

As Major enters the room, Will jumps from his seat and asks, "So did you give it to him?"

"Of course I did. I had that dude shaking."

Will, Walter, and Harley cheer and give each other high fives.

"I don't expect him to be cool with you or anything. Shoot! He may not even speak to you again, but he sure as hell won't be messing with you anymore."

"I appreciate this, bro," Will graciously states. He and Major shake hands and hug.

"It's no problem. Just make sure you're doing your part to help out when you can, all right?"

"I will."

"Cool. All right then, fellas. I'm out. I'll holler at you later."

18 SEPTEMBER 1999

1000 Hours

It is yet another Saturday, and once again, the Corps of Cadets has just completed another SAMI. Major, having finished his inspection rounds with the training officer and the first sergeant, returns to his and Joe's room to get out of his uniform. Entering the room, Major and Joe discover Gabe and JT lounging on their couch.

"Let's go, Major! We're ready to roll!" Gabe shouts.

"I just got done with SAMI, dawg. Give me a minute," Major replies as he begins unbuttoning his white shirt.

"Major, are you ready for this?" JT excitingly asks.

"Hell yes!" Major exclaims.

As Major speaks, numerous cadets enter the room.

Joe stands up from his desk in response to the barrage and asks the incoming cadets, "What do you guys want?"

One of the cadets answers up and says, "We just wanted to know if it is cool if we start the cookout now."

Major, who at this time is sitting in his chair, intermixed among his "soldiers," quickly responds with "When have I ever put restrictions on starting a cookout?"

"Never."

"Well, then…"

"We just wanted to make sure because of the SAMI and all."

"It's all good," Major replies. "I understand."

"Yeah," Joe chimes in. "The SAMI's over now."

"Great. We'll get going then." The group of Ducks scurries out of the room and leaves the four first classmen to themselves.

With the door shut, Major jumps up from his seat and darts over to his wardrobe. He opens the top sliding door and pulls out his West Point basketball garment bag. Major hangs the garment bag on the wardrobe door then pulls his full dress over white uniform from out of the wardrobe.

Seeing Major pack his full dress over white, JT asks, "Hey, Major, are you really sure we should take our full dress?"

"Hell yes!" Major replies as he walks to the bed. "How many times must I explain it to you? Every other dude at the pageant's going to be wearing a tux or suit of some sort. If we wear our full dress, we're going to stand out. Plus, we look good in that bad boy. Am I right?"

"Yeah, you're right, but I don't know…"

Major interrupts JT in midsentence, "Just trust me on this one, all right?"

"All right, but you better be right."

Major simply shakes his head at JT's doubt.

With his low quarters in hand, Major places them into his garment bag as well. Major then grabs a shirt from the back of his wardrobe, places it into the garment bag, then zips it up.

Major turns to JT and Gabe and says, "You guys go get dressed. I'll meet you at Mac turn around."

"That'll work," Gabe states as he and JT stand up. "We'll see you in fifteen minutes?"

"Yeah, that'll work. I'm going to see if Theo can give me a lift up to the lots."

"All right then," JT replies. "We'll see you."

JT and Gabe leave Major's room and quickly return to their own in MacArthur Barracks.

Once JT and Gabe leave the room, Joe asks, "Where're you guys going?"

"The Miss America Pageant," Major simply answers.

"Are you serious?" Joe exclaims.

Joe cannot comprehend the fact that his commander, roommate, and friend is going to the Miss America Pageant.

"Hell yeah!" Major excitingly replies, in response to Joe's excitement.

"How'd you guys pull that off?"

"You know Ed Winner. Well, a friend of his from high school, Mary London, is the current Miss New Jersey. Anyway, she and JT met plebe year and became friends. Gabe got a chance to meet her last spring when he and JT went to party with her at Princeton. I couldn't go because of basketball."

"That's cool, man. I know you guys are going to have a great time."

"You better believe it," Major states as he slips his gray pants off and replaces them with a pair of jeans.

Major takes a seat behind his desk and grabs his telephone receiver. After dialing a series of numbers and three rings, a groggy voice answers from the other end.

"Hello?" the groggy voice asks.

"Theo, it's Major."

"Hey, Major. What's up?"

"Do you have the van down here?"

"Yeah. What's up?"

"Well, I was wondering if you could give me a quick lift up to the lots if it's no problem."

"Yeah. It's no problem. I needed to get my car anyway. This gives me a good excuse to get out of bed."

"Well, I'm glad I'm helping you out too."

"It's no problem, man. How soon can you meet me?"

"Five minutes."

"Cool. I'm parked next to Central Guard Room."

"All right. I'll be there. Peace."

Major hangs up the telephone after speaking with the head basketball manager. He then squats and pulls a black Nike athletic bag out from underneath the bunk beds. In it, he grabs a pair of mid-length brown Timberland boots. Up from off of the floor, but now sitting on Joe's bed, Major slips his boots on. With the bag in between his legs, Major leans forward and chooses one of his several Army Basketball T-shirts to wear. While throwing the T-shirt on, Major kicks the bag back under his bed with the heel of his boot.

Fully dressed, Major says to Joe, "I'll tell you all about it when I get back."

"You better," Joe exclaims as Major bursts out of the room.

Theo hangs up the telephone after speaking with Major and rolls out of bed.

Thank God Major called me, or I'd have been in bed all day, Theo thinks to himself as he reaches for his running shoes from underneath his bed.

Theo does not have to go through a complicated clothes-changing process since he always sleeps in his gym A.

I don't know what I'm going to get into this weekend, let alone today, Theo continues to ponder, *but I may as well get my car from the lots, better now than later.*

Theo grabs his keys from out of an overly large coffee mug. Before leaving his room, Theo looks out his bedroom window. His room, which is located on the sixth floor of Bradley Barracks, gives him a perfect view of Central Area.

Good, Theo says to himself. *Major's not down there yet.*

Theo checks for Major because Major has this uncanny ability to be somewhere either first or early.

Seeing that Major is not in Central Area, Theo turns from the window and leaves his room. Since it is a weekend, Theo heads for the elevator instead of taking the stairs. Since his regiment's MAMI (maintenance AM inspection) has been over for almost an hour, Theo figures that his duty day is over.

After what seems an eternity, the elevator finally makes its way to the sixth floor. As soon as the doors open, Theo leaps in, presses the number one button, and sporadically pushes the "close door" button, just in case his interpretation of the reg is incorrect.

On the first floor, Theo exits the elevator, turns right, and steps out of Bradley Barracks underneath the cover of the overhang that connects Bradley Long and Bradley Short. Turning right into Central Area, Theo heads for his van.

Theo refers to the team van as his own for many reasons. During the season, Theo parks the van in Cadet Area for easy access wherever he can find a parking place. Coach O'Hara entrusts Theo with the keys, so he keeps them until Coach asks for them back, which is not until the season is over. Theo does not break the regs with the van, but he definitely takes full advantage of it, as he is currently undertaking with Major.

Theo's plan is to park the van in his parking space in the lots, so that whenever he returns, whether it is from pass or just OPPs (off-post privileges), he'll be able to get back to Cadet Area without having to walk.

Stepping out from underneath the overhang, Theo spots Major walking from between Pershing and Bradley Barracks.

Man! Theo inwardly shouts. *How does he do it?*

Theo continues his course to the van, and as he figured, Major arrives at the van before him. Though Major beat Theo by only three steps, he was still first, nonetheless.

"How do you do it?" Theo asks Major as the two teammates shake hands.

"Do what?" Major curiously asks.

"Never mind," Theo sighs with a grin as the two teammates jump into the van.

With a quick drive up to the lots, Theo pulls into F lot, which is located behind Crystal Arena. All of the firsties on the basketball team park in F lot because of its convenience, especially during weekend practices. The only problem with F lot is the fact that cadets cannot park there, let alone any other lot except for the Triple A lot, which is exclusive to team captains and football players during home football games. Like everything though, there is a way around that regulation as well.

Theo parks his van, and he and Major jump out.

As Major trots over to his 4Runner, he shouts to Theo, "Thanks, dawg. I appreciate it."

"No problem," Theo replies as he gingerly walks to his cherry red Fire Bird.

In their rooms, JT and Gabe sporadically pack their bags for their big trip.

"You think Major's right about us wearing our full dress?" JT asks.

"I say we trust him on this one," Gabe answers. "I think he's right. If anything, we will definitely set ourselves apart from all the other guys who'll be there. I know this though."

"What's that?"

"He better be on time getting down here!"

"He will. When have you known him to be late?"

"That is true."

The two roommates finish packing their bags in preparation for their big night. Gabe and JT do a quick double check to ensure they do not leave anything important behind, such as their tickets to the pageant, then leave their room.

Stepping outside of their barracks, Gabe and JT run into an already-waiting Major, who is sitting in his 4Runner with the door open and his music blasting loud enough for his pleasure, but low enough that the MPs will not mess with him about it.

"How long have you been out here, Major?" Gabe asks.

"Not long," Major replies.

"Well, let's roll then!" Gabe exclaims

Gabe jumps into the front seat, and JT gets in the back.

"You know how to get down to Atlantic City, right?" JT asks Major.

"Yeah," Major answers as he pulls out of Cadet Area. "It's an hour south of the prep. Plus, I went down there once with one of my uncles a couple of years back. I still remember how to get down there."

"Good," JT states, leaning back in his seat.

As the three friends pass through Thayer gate, exiting West Point from the south, JT leans forward and asks, "Have you eaten yet?"

"Not since breakfast," Major answers.

"Let's stop at Mickey D's real quick. I'm hungry."

"Hold your hunger for a little while. I want to get some distance between us and school," Major responds to JT's request while quickly passing by the Highland Falls McDonald's.

"I hear you on that, Major," Gabe agrees. "Can't you wait a while, JT?"

"I guess I have no choice now," JT mopes.

"Hey. I need to fill up, but I'm going to wait until we get to Jersey. The gas is cheaper there. When I pull over to fill up, we'll get something to eat real quick, all right?" Major states in the spirit of compromise.

"Yeah. That'll work," JT agrees.

Forty-five minutes into the ride, Major, Gabe, and JT are just over one quarter of the way to their destination: Atlantic City, New Jersey, home of the Miss America Pageant, among other things. They travel on the Garden State Parkway, an always busy, usually crowded interstate thruway. When traveling on the Garden State Parkway, one must ensure that he has a lot of change because of the numerous tolls. Each toll is thirty-five cents. Between Atlantic City and the Garden State Parkway's northern New York border, there are nine tolls.

After the second toll on the right side, there is a rest stop of sorts that contains an Exxon and a McDonald's.

Seeing the giant McDonald's sign from the parkway, JT quickly sits up and shouts, hey, Major, let's pull over here!"

"Cool. That'll work."

Major pulls over to the far right lane then exits off of the Garden State Parkway. Slowly driving into the parking area, the three friends are confronted with a mob of cars and families.

Aware of how long the line in McDonald's may be, Major says to JT and Gabe, "You guys go in and stand in line. I'll fill up and meet you guys inside."

"What do you want?" Gabe asks Major.

"Get me the Big Mac meal."

"Super size?"

"Naw. Just the regular joint. Get me a Hi-C with no ice and get it to go."

"All right," Gabe says as he and JT jump out of the 4Runner and walk into the overcrowded McDonald's.

Major pulls off and waits in the Exxon line to fill his tank. After what seems an eternity—but is only about ten minutes—it is finally Major's turn to receive service.

Parked alongside the gas pump, the gas attendant steps beside Major. With the attendant in hearing and eye distance, Major says to him, "Fill it up, regular."

The gas attendant immediately fills Major's 4Runner up with regular gasoline. The reason Major does not pump his own gas is because he is not allowed to. In the state of New Jersey, all gas stations are full service. The policy has been in effect for as long as Major can remember. He asked his Uncle Jack, who has lived in Linden, New Jersey, since the late fifties, why all of the gas stations are full service. His Uncle Jack informed him that the policy exists to keep the unemployment rate down.

As Uncle Jack explained, "The more people you have pumping gas, the less people you have living out on the streets."

Major understood.

With his gas tank filled, Major hands the attendant his American Express card. Two minutes later, the attendant returns Major's card and hands him the receipt for his signature.

After signing the receipt, Major says, "Thanks, man."

"No problem," the gas attendant replies as Major slowly rolls away.

Pulling into the McDonald's parking lot, Major thinks to himself, *They ought to be done by now.*

Major parks then heads into the McDonald's. Entering, he immediately spots JT and Gabe from among the immense crowd. Why? Because Gabe is by far the tallest and largest person inside, second in size only to JT proportionately. Gabe stands at six feet, six inches tall and weighs about 260 pounds. JT is six seven and weighs 225 pounds. To his friends and teammates, JT is known as Dr. Swoll and Big Swoll, among other similar names, out of respect of his size and power.

Major eases his way through the thick crowd. Standing beside Gabe and JT, Major states, "You've got to be kidding me."

"I know. I didn't think it would take this long," Gabe frustratingly states.

Slowly but surely, the line moves. The three friends move closer and closer to the front of the line. With only one lady standing between them and the counter, Gabe states, "Finally."

JT and Major simply laugh.

In and out of a good daydream, Major hears something that sparks his interest. He turns his attention to the conversation between the lady in front of them and the cashier.

"Welcome to McDonald's. May I take your order?" the cashier asks.

"Yes. I would like three cheese burgers with no meat and onions."

"No meat?" the cashier asks bewilderedly.

"Yes. No meat."

"Okay," the cashier replies without a semblance of concern.

Overhearing the order, Major takes a mental step back and says to himself, *I can't believe what I just heard!*

Major then elbows Gabe in the stomach and says, "Did you just hear this lady's order?"

"No. What's up?" Gabe replies.

"She just ordered three cheese burgers with no meat and onions."

"You're kidding me. Right?"

"I wish I were. She just friggin' ordered three cheese sandwiches," Major laughingly states.

"Hey, JT! You hear this?" Gabe says loudly. "The woman in front of us just ordered three cheese burgers but told the guy to hold the burger!"

"Huh?" JT responds, dumbfounded as to what Gabe has told him had just transpired between the cashier and the lady in front of them.

As the three friends laugh and converse on the bizarre event, the lady finally receives her order and slowly moves to rejoin her family.

Stepping up to the head of the line, Major leans on the counter and says to the cashier, "Hey, dude, I can't believe you just sold that lady three cheese burgers with no meat. You could have given her a discount or something. I mean, goddawg, she just bought three cheese sandwiches with ketchup."

"I hear you, man," the cashier replies. "I'm just trying to do my job. You know?"

"Yeah. I hear you," Major retorts. He then quickly places orders for him, JT, and Gabe, supersizing each of them because they have not eaten since breakfast.

1600 Hours: Atlantic City, New Jersey

After an easy drive down the Garden State Parkway, Major, Gabe, and JT arrive in Atlantic City. Though the drive was smooth and without any troubles, it seemed to take the three friends forever to reach their destination, mostly due to their great anticipation of the event to come—the Miss America Pageant.

"We've made it!" JT shouts as Major drives them through the main casino district.

"Yeah, we have," Major agrees, "but now we need to find ourselves a cheap hotel room."

"That shouldn't be too hard," JT replies. "Look at all of the hotels!" The bright lights and tall buildings mesmerize JT. It is obvious to Gabe and Major that JT is quickly falling in love with Atlantic City as if it was a beautiful woman who just so happens to have a lot of money as well.

"There may be a lot of hotels, JT," Gabe intercedes, "but they've got to be expensive as hell. I mean, look at the price of that one over there."

Major and JT look to their left and eye a small hole in the wall hotel that is priced at $999 per night.

"You've got to be kidding me!" Major shouts. "There've got to be cheaper spots further away from the casino area."

"Well, we have time," JT calmly responds.

"Cool. We'll take a drive and see what we can find," Major states as he turns left away from the casino district.

Driving endlessly from one street to another, the three friends come to the conclusion that they are not going to be able to find a reasonably priced hotel near the casino district, let alone further away.

Frustrated in their search, Gabe says, "Let's just head back and find something nearby."

"I guess we have no choice," Major states as he speeds through a yellow light. "Start looking for places, preferably on the right side of the road. I don't want to have to fight this traffic trying to get across the street."

With their heads thrown out of the windows, Gabe and JT scour the streets for hotels.

Having not looked for a hotel long, Gabe shouts, "Right here, Major! Right here!"

Major slams on his breaks and makes a sharp right turn into a small parking lot.

"Goddawg, Gabe! Give a brother some warning first," Major states as he pulls the 4Runner into a parking space.

"Sorry, man. I saw this place right when we were passing by it," Gabe apologizes. He then jumps out of the front seat and says, "I'll put the room on my card. Stay here until I get back. If they see that there's more than just me, they may try to charge us more for the room."

"All right," JT responds as Gabe walks to the front of the hotel. JT then states, "This place is a dump."

"You ain't kidding," Major agrees. "I can't believe this place is going to run us over a hundred dollars."

The hotel where Gabe, JT, and Major are preparing to stay is connected to a pawnshop. Outside, in the parking lot, lie several discarded beer cans and bottles as well as trash. The hotel is in dire need of a new paint job. The paint is chipped in several places and is severely fading.

Being somewhat optimistic, Major states, "This isn't too bad. I've seen worst."

"I guess so," JT cynically replies.

As the two friends sit and converse about the evening's upcoming event, Gabe returns to the 4Runner. Seeing Gabe approach them, JT and Major jump out of the 4Runner and head for the back to retrieve their bags.

"Our room's up there," Gabe says, pointing to the second floor. "Twenty-four."

JT, Gabe, and Major quickly grab their bags then head for their room.

Climbing up the grimy steps, JT says to his friends, "Let's go walk around some. I've never been in a casino before."

"You haven't?" Major asks.

"Never."

"Well, I guess we're going to have to go take a walk along the boardwalk then," Major answers.

"And get something to eat!" Gabe chimes in.

"Yeah, and that too," Major agrees.

Reaching room 24, Gabe pulls the key from out of his pocket and unlocks the door. Standing in the doorway, the three cadets realize that their room is not too standard, or at least not theirs. Looking down at the floor, they notice that the carpet is soiled in several places. Soiled from what? They do not know.

They walk into the room and throw their bags onto the bed. JT looks at the television and states, "That TV looks like it's older than me."

Gabe does a quick look around and spots cracks in the two mirrors, one in the first half of the bathroom and the other above the dresser. "I can't believe we're paying a hundred dollars for this dump!"

"This place is ghetto!" Major protests. "I'm going to go check out the bathroom. I'll be darned if I'm not able to take my bubble bath."

While in school, Major is only able to take showers, but whenever he goes home or is on the road for a basketball game, he always takes a bath. Major always makes it a point to take a bubble bath whenever the opportunity presents itself.

Major walks into the bathroom and shouts, "You've got to be kidding me!"

"What's up, Major?" Gabe asks.

"This tub is disgusting. I don't think I'll be taking a bath in this bad boy."

JT walks in behind Major and shakes his head saying, "I'm glad I brought my shower shoes."

Looking into the bathtub, Major and JT have come to the conclusion that it is not fit for human use, or at least not for an extended period of time.

"I guess your going to have to force yourself to take a shower," JT consoles, placing his hand on Major's shoulder.

"Yeah," Major replies as he walks out of the bathroom.

JT follows behind Major, then states. "Hey! Let's go walk around some. I want to see Atlantic City."

"That's cool," Gabe comments.

"Yeah," Major agrees. "Sounds good to me."

The three friends immediately stop what they are doing and exit their room.

Gabe, JT, and Major spend an hour and a half quickly sightseeing Atlantic City's major points of interest. They walked through Caesar's Palace and the Trump Casino, where JT was amazed at all of the money that was moving from hand to hand. After walking quickly through the two casinos—and without gambling—the three friends take a walk along the boardwalk. Having seen all they had cared to see and knowing that they were on the clock, Major, Gabe, and JT head for a small mom and pop restaurant to get a quick bite to eat for dinner.

On the walk back to their hotel, JT begins a conversation. "Major, are you really sure about us wearing full dress?"

"How many times do I have to tell you that we are going to be the shiznits up in their tonight," Major excitingly replies.

"I don't know, man," JT contests. "Just the fact that everyone's going to know that we're cadets."

"I feel you, bro," Major sympathizes. "When I take pass, I don't want people knowing that I'm a cadet either, unless it happens to come up in a conversation, but look at it like this: civilians love cadets, especially the type of people that're going to be out tonight."

"Yeah, I guess you're right," JT states, giving up the battle.

"Of course, I'm right!" Major boasts. "Plus, we didn't bring suits anyway, so we don't have a choice but to wear our full dress."

"Ah ha!" Gabe laughs. "He got you, JT!"

"Yeah, yeah, yeah," JT pouts.

The three friends laugh their way back to the hotel to prepare for the big night that lies ahead of them.

———————◆———————

Fully dressed, JT, Major, and Gabe look themselves over in the mirror, making final adjustments to their uniform. The last thing they want to occur is for their full dress uniforms not to look their very best.

"God, we look good!" Major shouts.

"I have to give it to you, Major," Gabe states. "You made the right call."

"Yeah you did," JT agrees. "I wasn't too sure about us wearing full dress and all, but now that I look at us, we look pretty good."

"That's right! We're going to be the best-looking dudes up in there tonight," Major struts.

Finished checking each other off and ensuring that their uniforms are up to standard, Major, JT, and Gabe prepare to leave the room.

"Let's rock and roll, fellas," Major states as he heads for the door.

"Don't forget the cameras," JT remarks.

"Ah man. Good looking out," Major states. He runs back to his bag, which is located at the far side of the room, and retrieves his small disposable AAFES camera.

"All right. I'm ready now," Major says as he trots to catch up with Gabe and JT who are already outside of the room. Major shuts the door behind him and catches up with his friends. "Let's do this, fellas."

The three friends walk down the hotel steps and head toward the Atlantic City Convention Center, home of the Miss America Pageant.

"We've got some time to spare," Gabe states as they enter Caesar's Palace. "Let's go to the bar for a little while."

"Sounds good to me," Major agrees.

"I could take back a couple myself," JT chimes in.

The three cadets step into Caesar's Palace like they own the place. They cut through the casino, taking the fastest route to the escalator. As they quickly pass through the casino, people from all directions turn their attention to the three finely dressed young men. The three cadets stick out among the immense crowd like flowers in the desert.

Reaching the escalator, Major, Gabe, and JT ride it down to the boardwalk level where the bar is located. Following Gabe, Major and JT head for the bar.

The bar is not overly crowded. There are only two bartenders working tonight, suggesting that the casino is not expecting any overwhelming business. Patronizing the bar are only a small handful of people. Some are sitting at the bar, others at small tables that circle the bar. Gabe, JT, and Major stand on the far side of the bar and face the casino exit onto the boardwalk.

"What do you guys want?" Gabe asks.

"I'll take a Long Island," Major states.

"I'll take one too," JT seconds.

JT and Major lean up against the bar, waiting for their drinks.

Gabe leans over the bar to get one of the bartenders' attention.

One of the bartenders, a cute thirty-something-year-old woman walks over to Gabe and asks, "What can I get for you, sir?"

"I'll have three Long Island iced teas," Gabe states.

The bartender takes the order and quickly prepares the drinks. Sitting next to Gabe is an old man in his midsixties. He's dressed in a dingy, faded blue jeans outfit. Gabe takes a glance at the old man and comes to the conclusion that he is intoxicated.

The old man points to the bartender and says to her, "Put those drinks on my tab." He then looks at Gabe and says to him, "You boys are drinking on me tonight."

With a big grin on his face, Gabe says to the old man, "Thanks a lot, sir. I really appreciate it."

The old man thrusts his right hand out. Gabe takes the old man's hand and firmly shakes it.

While JT and Major wait for their drinks, three women, two in their forties and the other in her early thirties, call them over to their table.

"You young men here for the pageant?" one of the women asks.

JT and Major instantly turn their attention to the three beautiful women. "Yes, ma'am," JT happily replies. He then goes into a long-drawn-out explanation as to why he, Major, and Gabe made the trip down to Atlantic City to attend the Miss America Pageant.

As JT converse with the lovely ladies, Gabe gets Major's attention. "Hey, I've got your drinks."

Major turns around toward the bar to take his and JT's drinks. Lifting the glasses from off of the bar, the old man waves to Major. Understanding the gesture, Major returns the greeting with, "Thanks, sir."

The old man tips his glass to Major.

Major turns back around as JT is concluding his monologue. "Here's your drink."

"Thanks, Major."

Continuing the conversation, one of the women asks, "So what are these uniforms for?" motioning her hand in the direction of JT and Major's full dress uniform.

"Well, ma'am," Major answers, "we're first class cadets at the United States Military Academy at West Point."

"Ohhh. West Point." The ladies blush.

"I wish I would have brought my daughter here," one of the forty-something ladies states, sitting up in her seat and straightening out her back. "I'd let you take her out."

"So would I," the other states. "If I were twenty years younger, I'd date you myself."

Major and JT stand there awestruck. They are not accustomed to receiving such accolades from women. Instead of verbally responding, they simply return the kind words with two large smiles. Major and JT also smile because they have no idea of what to say in response to what they have just heard.

"You guys are going to be the hit tonight," one of the ladies boasts.

"Oh yes. The girls are going to love you guys," her friend chimes in.

JT asks, "Where are you ladies from?"

"Oh, we're from Idaho," one of the lovely ladies answers.

Another follows with "Where are you young men from?"

"Well, ma'am," Major quickly replies, "to make a long story short, my father's a Marine. I've moved around a bit. I consider northern Virginia home, DC metro area."

JT jumps back into the conversation, responding with "And I'm from the great state of Texas."

As Major, JT, and the three lovely ladies from Idaho converse and sip on their drinks, Gabe slides his way into the group, a drink in both hands.

"A little thirsty there, huh, bro?" Major sarcastically asks Gabe.

"You know it," Gabe replies with a giant grin. He then turns his attention to the ladies and says, "You ladies look very beautiful this evening."

"Why, thank you," they happily respond.

"You ladies should allow us to escort you to the pageant," Gabe romantically requests.

"Oh, we would love that," a lovely lady replies, her friends giggling, "but we don't want to impose. If you gentlemen escort us, the other young ladies will think that you're taken for."

"She's right, Gabe," Major wholeheartedly agrees.

Continuing in their fun conversation, two other less-attractive women approach the group. Both of the unattractive women are intoxicated as well. One of the said women reaches into her black pocket book, which resembles more of a backpack than a purse, and pulls out a camera.

She leans beside the old man and asks, "Would you take a picture of me and my friend with those three cadets over there."

"Certainly," the old man replies.

The two women rudely break into the group and force themselves around Major, Gabe, and JT, shoving the other women in the process.

"Everyone say cheese," the old man shouts.

Major, who is not one to smile in pictures, joins along with the group and smiles for the camera.

"Take another one. Take another one," one of the unattractive women states.

The old man obeys the command and snaps away.

The two women, squirming and moving in an attempt to get closer to Gabe, JT, and Major, knock over the younger of the Idaho lady's drink, causing it to spill all over her outfit.

Highly upset with the debacle, the younger Idaho lady sternly states, "I believe you women have taken enough pictures!"

Realizing the trouble that they have caused, the two unattractive women offer to buy the younger Idaho lady another drink. She refuses then gives her a look that forces them to scurry to the other side of the bar.

As the scuffle clears, JT looks down at his watch and realizes that it is time for them to go. "Hey guys. We've got an hour to show time. Let's start heading over."

"All right," Major responds.

The three friends slowly walk out of the bar. As they do so, Major says to the lovely ladies, "It was very nice to meet you."

"Likewise," one of the ladies cheerfully responds.

"Other than the spilled drink, it was lovely," the younger lady answers.

"We'll see you inside," the other lady states.

Gabe takes a bow and states, "Ladies, it was an honor to meet you."

On that note, Major, JT, and Gabe exit the bar and casino and step out onto the boardwalk. With a quick thirty-some-second walk through a very dense crowd, the three friends reach the Atlantic City Convention Center, which is conveniently next to the casino.

Inside of the convention center, Major, Gabe, and JT carefully force their way through the crowd to the ticket check-in. After having their tickets cut, the three Cadets walk through with great anticipation.

Having only walked a few steps, JT notices someone familiar.

Immediately, the familiar individual notices JT and Gabe as well. As they walk toward each other, the familiar individual shakes their hands then says, "Hey, fellas! How're you guys doing?" Major stands behind Gabe and JT as they converse with the individual.

"We're great!" JT and Gabe exclaim.

"How about you? What are you doing here?" JT follows.

"My fiancée's Miss Ohio."

Hearing that, the three friends all look at one another with approval.

The familiar individual continues, "So, what are you guys doing here?"

"Our friend, Ms. Mary London, is Miss New Jersey. We're here supporting her."

"Well, that's great. It was great seeing you guys again. Have fun. I'll see you inside." The familiar individual shakes all three of their hands, turns, then disappears into the crowd.

As they watch the familiar individual leave, Major grabs JT by the shoulder and asks, "That was James Mellon, wasn't it?"

"Sure was," Gabe answers instead.

"He's Class of '96. How'd you guys know him?" Major asks again.

"We met him during our recruiting visit," JT replies.

"Oh yeah. That's right. He seemed pretty cool."

"Yeah," Gabe agrees. "I can't believe he's engaged to Miss Ohio."

Saying that, Major raises his left hand, on which he wears his class ring. Gabe and JT follow suit. They then bring their fists together and nod their head ever so slightly.

Continuing their walk through the convention center, Major, JT, and Gabe are continuously stopped by groups of women to have their picture taken with the three handsome cadets. Being the gentlemen that they are, neither cadet refuses.

Reaching the auditorium, Gabe, JT, and Major find their seats and wait patiently. As they do, those sitting around them strike up several conversations, and as at the bar, yet another old man buys them each a drink. Suddenly the lights go out and the pageant begins, introduced by a barrage of smiling beautiful women.

With the pageant complete, Major, JT, and Gabe walk out of the stands and stand around at floor level. As they stand, the excited immense crowd quickly dissipates out of the civic center.

Unsure of what to do next, the three friends stand and converse.

"I swear to God I fell in love fifty-one times," Major boasts.

"You're not kidding," Gabe agrees. "I knew the girls would be beautiful, but not like that."

The three of them simply shake their heads.

"So what do we do next?" Major asks. "We didn't quite plan for anything afterward."

"I want to go see Mary," JT quickly states.

"How are we going to do that?" Gabe asks.

"Not sure," JT replies.

While JT and Gabe exchange words, Major gracefully spins around and notices a small crowd gathered at the far-left end of the stage. "Hey, fellas," Major states, "let's check out over there." Major points to the crowd.

"Something's got to be going on over there," Gabe says.

Gabe and JT follow Major toward the far end of the stage. After only a few paces though, JT busts past Major and Gabe and trots over to the crowd ahead of his friends.

When they reach the crowd, they realize what a great treasure they had discovered. JT, Gabe, and Major quickly realize that the small crowd exists to greet the Miss America contestants as they exit the backstage area through guarded partitions.

JT slithers his way to the front in order to get ahold of Mary when she walks by. Gabe and Major stand among the crowd, but more toward the back.

As they wait for Mary to pass, Major recognizes a familiar face walk through the partitions. Major slaps Gabe on the back and says, "Gabe. It's Judge Judy."

In unison, the two friends shout, "Hey, Judge Judy!"

Hearing the two young men shout at her, Judge Judy turns, smiles, and returns their greeting with a wave.

Having Judge Judy waive at them causes Major and Gabe to become very excited.

"This is cool, man!" Gabe exclaims.

Before Major and Gabe have a chance to calm down, Major spots yet another familiar woman walk through the partitions. Realizing who it is, Major becomes truly excited, probably more excited than he has been all night.

Major elbows Gabe in the stomach and whispers, "Gabe, it's Tia Carrera."

"Where! Where!" Gabe shouts, jumping up and down.

"Over there!" Major points.

Finally seeing the most beautiful woman in the civic center, Gabe shouts, "We're not worthy! We're not worthy!"

Aggravated by Gabe's immature yelling, Major sternly says to him, "Cut that out, man. That makes us look immature."

Realizing his small blunder, Gabe replies, "Sorry, Major. I got caught up in the moment."

"It's all good, dawg," Major returns, squeezing his friend's shoulder.

As Tia Carrera passes by, Major and Gabe breathe a sigh of relief.

"I have now fallen in love fifty-two times tonight," Major comments.

"I'm with you on that," Gabe agrees.

"She is definitely a ten," Major continues.

"Yeah. A ten," Gabe again agrees.

"You know, Tia Carrera's only the second ten I've ever seen."

"Who's the other?" Gabe asks.

"Lieutenant Colonel Jackman's wife."

"Who's that?"

"He was my Arabic instructor. His wife's Lebanese."

As Major describes Mrs. Jackman's beauty to Gabe, JT stands impatiently waiting beside the partitions, anxiously waiting for Mary to pass. Standing among the crowd with immense anticipation, JT carefully watches the Miss America contestants stroll by him.

Before he is able to lose faith in finding his friend, JT hears a shout. "JT! JT!"

"Mary!" JT shouts.

Mary quickly moves to where JT stands and embrace as though they had not seen one another in years.

Gabe and Major see Mary standing with JT and so quickly make their way over to their position.

Major takes his disposable camera and snaps a surprise photo of JT and Mary embracing.

After the photo is taken, Gabe boasts, "Hey, Mary. You did great tonight! We were rooting for you!"

"Thanks a lot, Gabe. I really appreciate you guys coming down here to support me."

JT hands Major his camera and says, "Take our picture, Major."

Acknowledging his friend's request, Major takes the camera from JT. Mary and JT then hug one another, giving Major his cue to snap away.

Mary releases her hold on JT then says to the three cadets, "I am so glad you guys came."

"I told you we'd come, didn't I?" JT states.

"Yes, you did," Mary happily replies.

JT turns to Major and says, "Mary, this is Major."

"Oh, you're Major," Mary replies. She extends her hand, and she and Major shake. "I've heard so much about you. Thank you for coming."

"No problem," Major simply states with a slight smile on his face.

Mary gives JT, Gabe, and Major a hug then states, "I've got to get going."

"All right. We'll see you, Mary," JT says as Mary walks off.

"Bye, Mary," Gabe and Major say in unison.

Once again, the three friends find themselves stuck with nothing to do and unsure as to where they should go next. Major looks to his left and notices that security is not guarding the backstage area very well. It is obvious that the guards are not from the Atlantic City Police Department. They are regular civilians who wear maroon blazers as security jackets. None of the guards is of any great size. In fact, all of the security personnel seem to be quite small. As Major takes all of this information in, he notices that people with VIP passes hanging from around their necks are entering the backstage area at their own leisure. Also, there are only three people guarding the entrance, which makes for easy access for anyone who looks like they belong but truly do not.

Major, standing on Gabe's left side, who is actually closest to the backstage entrance, whispers to Gabe, "Start sidestepping. We need to get in there."

Gabe does as Major instructs. The two friends carefully step to the left until they are at the edge of the entrance. Realizing that JT was not in sync with he and Gabe's plan, Major walks over to JT and grabs him.

"Come on, bro. We're going backstage."

JT follows Major to the backstage entrance. Instead of stopping and looking conspicuous, the three cadets walk in as though they had always had access to the backstage area.

Standing alone for only thirty seconds backstage, the friends are surprisingly met by an elegantly dressed elderly man who asks them, "West Point?"

"Yes, sir," Gabe answers.

"I thought so. The uniforms are a dead giveaway," the elderly man jokes. "You boys do look good tonight," he continues. "What brings you guys to the pageant?"

"We're supporting our friend, Mary London, Miss New Jersey," JT boasts.

"Ah yes," the elderly man comments. "She did quite well this evening."

The guys nod their heads in agreement.

"So do you boys have any plans for this evening?" the elderly gentleman asks.

"No, sir," Major answers. "We're kind of winging it tonight."

"Well, once you're done down here, come up to the sixth floor. Tell them Mr. Lees invited you."

"Yes, sir," Major replies.

"Good then," Mr. Lees states as two women come to his side. "I'll see you boys up there later on tonight."

Mr. Lees walks off with a cool, composed look on his face, while the two beautiful women follow close behind.

As soon as Mr. Lees leaves, another elderly gentleman walks up to Major and Gabe. JT is a few feet away, speaking with a small group of young women.

"So you gentlemen go to West Point, huh?" the elderly man asks, knowing the answer to his own question.

"Yes, sir," Gabe answers.

"I'm a World War II vet."

"Really, sir? What branch of service were you in?" Major asks.

"I was in the Coast Guard."

"The Coast Guard?"

Major and Gabe are taken aback by the gentleman's reply. They both have studied the military arts and done plenty of self-reading on World War II. Tonight is the first time they have ever heard of any members of the Coast Guard serving during World War II.

"That's right, the Coast Guard. We patrolled the entire Atlantic coastline, intercepting German U-boats."

"That's cool, sir," Gabe excitedly states.

Major nods his head in agreement.

While the elderly gentleman entertains Gabe and Major with his World War II stories, Major notices a black stretch limousine pull up behind him. Having seen many limousines in his day, Major, as well as everyone else for that matter, pays it no mind.

Continuing his World War II stories with Major and Gabe, the elderly gentleman's son enters the group. The son, who is a Vietnam vet, then decides to share a couple of his own war stories with the two highly engaged West Point cadets.

As Major listens to the Vietnam stories, he senses a presence behind him. He turns around and sees a man standing only five feet away from him, placing a black leather bag into the trunk of the limousine.

Immediately realizing who it is, Major lightly hits Gabe with the back of his hand and says, "Gabe! Dawg! It's Donny Osmond! It's Donny Osmond!"

As soon as the words leave Major's lips, the Coast Guard vet's wife practically throws Major to the side and grabs a hold of Donny Osmond.

Though Major is by no means a Donny Osmond fan, he is a little perturbed that he lost his opportunity to get a picture with him. To substitute his moment in the spotlight, Major takes a picture of Donnie Osmond and the extremely jovial older lady.

The crowd around Donny Osmond increases with every second. As the crowd swells, Major and Gabe step more to the left of the limousine. While they watch the excitement surround Donny Osmond, Gabe and Major notice this overly large gray-haired man walk to the limousine door and open it.

Major and Gabe turn their attention from the large gray-haired man to the left. Again, they are shocked by who they see walking toward the opened limousine—Marie Osmond.

Excited beyond belief, Major opens his arms wide and shouts, "Marie!"

Standing only ten feet away from Gabe and Major, Marie quickly turns, faces them, opens her arms wide, and shouts, "Hey!"

Major and Gabe in unison return Marie's greeting with a loud and boisterous, "Hey!"

Before Major and Gabe have a chance to react and actually meet Marie Osmond, a little girl no older than twelve slips by them and asks her for an autograph.

While Marie signs the autograph, the crowd swoons around her. This time though, Major and Gabe stand their ground in the hopes of being able to get a picture with Marie Osmond. Unfortunately, those plans are for not. As soon as Marie signs the little girl's autograph, the gray-haired man, who happens to be her and Donnie's bodyguard, rushes Marie into the limousine, where Donny patiently waits. The bodyguard slams the door and quickly enters the front passenger side.

As the limousine drives off, Major solemnly states, "Well, at least we have our memories."

"Yeah," Gabe agrees, squeezing Major's shoulder.

With the crowd dissipated, JT is finally able to rejoin his friends. The three of them quickly hash out the stories and experience that had occurred to one another.

As the three friends converse among themselves, a young lady in her early twenties approaches them and asks, "Can I get a picture with you guys?"

"Of course," the three cadets emphatically reply.

Moving in front of the three cadets, the girl introduces herself. "My name's Danielle Sanchez. I'm the reigning Miss Philadelphia."

"Wow! That's a great accomplishment!" JT praises. He then suggests, "Hey, let's salute for the picture."

Upon JT's suggestion, the three cadets all salute for the picture.

Seeing the cadets salute, Danielle says, "That's cool. Can you show me how to do that?"

"Here you go," JT states. "It's like this." JT takes Danielle's right arm and straightens it out. He then has her bend at the elbow and raises her hand to her eyebrow. JT takes his hand, brings her fingers together, then moves her hand so that the tips of the index and middle fingers are touching the end of her eyebrow.

Now that Danielle is saluting, another picture is taken. Tired of standing around and not participating in any of the fun, Danielle's six girlfriends jump in and have their pictures taken with Gabe, Major, and JT as well.

After several pictures are taken, the small group of women, accompanied by Danielle's seemingly overprotective boyfriend, says their good-byes to the three cadets. Major, Gabe, and JT return the gesture as the young ladies leisurely stroll off.

"That was fun," Gabe states as he looks around the backstage area, noticing that everyone is dispersing from the area.

"Seems like this party's over," Major comments.

"What do you guys want to do now?" JT asks.

"Well, we can't just stand around here and look stupid. I know that," Gabe retorts.

"Gabe's right," Major agrees. "We can't go out the way we came in 'cause that'll make it look as though we don't belong." Major looks up to his far front and notices a large group of people riding an escalator. "Let's go up there," Major suggests, pointing to the moving stream of people.

"Where's that going to take us?" JT asks.

"Beats me," Major replies, "but they obviously know where the hell they're going."

"All right then," Gabe chimes in, "let's go."

Gabe, Major, and JT easily make their way to the escalator and patiently ride it up to the next floor. As the people in front of them step off, so do they.

In front of JT, Gabe, and Major is an entrance to a large ballroom. All of the people in front of them enter without restraint. The three cadets, on the other hand, are not so fortunate.

A short white-haired elderly man dressed in a black tuxedo and wearing a security earpiece steps in front of the three friends' path and asks, "What can I do you gentlemen for?"

Major, who stands in front of Gabe and JT, states, "We would like to enter the ballroom, sir. We are here in support of our friend, Mary London, who is the reigning Miss New Jersey."

"Really," the elderly security guard coolly states. He then follows with, "So what are these uniforms about?"

"Sir," Major replies, "we are first class cadets at the United States Military Academy at West Point."

"Where is West Point?" the security guard asks.

Somewhat frustrated with the game that the security guard is playing with him, Major answers, "Sir, West Point is sixty-four miles north of New York City, off the western bank of the Hudson River."

The security guard laughs slightly then states, "Fellas, I am a retired first sergeant in the army."

"Really!" Gabe exclaims. "That's great!"

"Let me go talk to my manager and see what I can do," the elderly gentleman states. He walks about ten paces away from Major, Gabe, and JT then abruptly turns around in mid stride.

Seeing his sudden turn around and knowing that the first sergeant did not speak to his manager, Gabe, JT, and Major look at one another, bewilderedly.

Returning to the front entrance of the ballroom where Major, JT, and Gabe patiently wait, the retired first sergeant states, "You know, you guys are supposed to have a VIP pass to enter this room."

"Really, sir. We didn't know that," Major answers honestly.

"Yes, but I'm going to let you guys in, anyway," the first sergeant replies with a small grin on his face.

"Oh, thank you, sir! Thank you!" JT blurts.

"No problem, fellas. Make sure you boys are on your best behavior."

"On our honor, sir!" Major excitingly states.

As the first sergeant unhooks the chain, he states, "You boys have a great time!"

"We will, sir!" the three friends reply as they enter the ballroom.

In the ballroom are the contestants' families and friends. Also present are the runners up from each state's pageant. Though there are numerous people present, the ballroom is by no means filled to capacity. Taking up the majority of the ballroom's space are round tables where every state congregates around their contestant.

Entering the ballroom, JT quickly jumps out in front of Gabe and Major, stating, "We have to find Mary." "Well, that shouldn't be too hard," Gabe replies, "since all of the tables have a sign with each state's name on it."

JT quickly finds the New Jersey table. Gabe and Major simply follow JT instead of trying to force their way through people.

Arriving at the New Jersey table, Gabe and Major find JT hugging Mary once again. Major and Gabe stand to the side and converse with Mary's boyfriend, Troy Stevens, and his dad. While they wait for the pageantry frenzy to calm down around Mary, the four men discuss the stock market, money management, and Troy's father having wanted him to attend West Point similar to himself (he attended the Citadel). Troy graduated from Princeton—not too bad.

After the small group surrounding Mary settles some, Gabe and Major walk over to congratulate her.

Seeing Major and Gabe, Mary meets them halfway then states with tears in her eyes, "Thanks again for coming out and supporting me."

"I told you we'd be here, didn't I?" JT sarcastically remarks.

"Yes, you did," Mary replies.

"It was a privilege just being here," Major says, holding Mary's hand. "I'm glad I could make it."

Mary follows Major's comment by giving him a big hug. She then steps over to Gabe and gives him a hug as well.

Once Major and Gabe finish congratulating Mary, they leave JT at the New Jersey table to socialize with the entirety of Mary's supportive family members and friends.

"I want to go congratulate Miss Iowa," Gabe informs Major as they slowly step away from the New Jersey group.

"That's cool. I'll go with you," Major states, stepping to the side so Gabe can lead the way through the somewhat thick crowd.

The Iowa table is located at the far end and toward the right of the ballroom. Fortunately, for Major and Gabe, the ballroom is not too large, so they do not have too much trouble making the short trek. About twenty or so feet from the Iowa table, Major takes a look to his left. What, or better yet whom, Major sees causes him to take a mental step back. He is awestruck by the beauty which his eyes behold.

I knew that she was beautiful like all of the other girls, but goddawg! I didn't know that she was this beautiful, Major thinks to himself, though he feels as though the entire world can hear his thoughts at the present.

Standing in the apex of a small crowd is the vision, which has suddenly grasped Major's attention. Who seems to be the most beautiful woman that Major has ever seen is now his entire focus. The ballroom lights reflect off of her, causing a slight glimmer to permeate from her soft brown skin. The entire crowd surrounding her is entirely enraptured by her presence.

Struck by a burst of courage, Major decides to act upon his emotions. He lightly taps Gabe on the shoulder and says, "Hey, dawg. I'm going to go over to the Indiana table."

Gabe turns around and asks, "For what?"

"There's something I have to do," Major answers. "God help me though. I can't believe I'm going to do this."

Gabe looks over to where Major's focusing his attention. Realizing what Major is motivating himself to do, Gabe states, "You only live once, Major. Do your thing, man." Gabe slams his hands on Major's shoulders.

Major nods his head in agreement then turns left and heads for the Indiana table. He walks tall and proud, though his nerves cause him to shake on the inside. Major is not known for being courageous in the realm of women, but he feels very determined.

I have to take advantage of the situation, Major encourages himself as he walks toward the Indiana crowd. *I may never have another opportunity like this again.*

Major now stands on the verge of the Indiana crowd, unsure of what his next act should be. He attempts to move deeper through the crowd but decides against it. There are so many of Miss Indiana's family and friends present that Major feels it would be rude to push his way through just to speak to a girl who does not know him.

Stopping in his tracks, still among the crowd, Miss Indiana turns and faces Major's direction. For a brief moment, their eyes lock. Major's heart races as the reality of the moment hits him square in his chest. He feels as though she is running through his thoughts.

It takes all of Major's willpower to restrain himself from going over to Miss Indiana. He so badly wants to introduce himself, but for reasons he does not comprehend, he does not. Instead, to acknowledge Miss Indiana's glance, Major simply waves, nods his head, smiles, and then turns away.

Meeting Major between the Iowa and Indiana tables stands Gabe. "So how'd it go?" Gabe asks.

"I couldn't do it," Major regretfully responds.

Gabe looks at Major funny, then replies, "Why not?"

"I don't know."

"Were you scared?"

"I was at first."

"At first?"

"Yeah. At first, I couldn't do it, but when our eyes locked, it was all good."

"So why didn't you talk to her then?"

"I didn't want to be rude, going through her family and friends and whatnot."

"I guess so," Gabe replies, shaking his head in disappointment.

"Yeah. Well, let's go get JT."

"All right."

Gabe and Major make their way back to the New Jersey group. Because JT is still engrossed in conversation, Major and Gabe decide to turn their attention to the activity taking place within the ballroom.

Besides the Miss America contestants celebrating with their family and friends at their individual states' tables, there is also a big band playing on the stage. In the front center of the ballroom, a few couples dance to the melodic jazz that the band bellows.

In the front-left corner of the ballroom, the newly crowned Miss America holds a small press conference. Gabe and Major decide against watching the press conference, knowing they will not be on television.

As Major and Gabe soak up the atmosphere, they hear a familiar face say, "So you boys having a great time tonight?"

The two friends turn around to find James Mellon standing behind them.

"Hey, Jim!" Gabe boasts. "Karen did great!"

"Thanks, Gabe," James replies. "What about you, Major?"

"Man, I've fallen in love fifty-one times. Fifty-two if you include Tia Carrera," Major answers with a huge grin on his face.

Jim laughs. "I hear you on that, brother." Jim then looks over his shoulder and notices his fiancée and the remainder of the Ohio group leaving. "Hey, fellas, I've got to get going. Gabe, it was great seeing you again. Major, it was nice meeting you. You guys have fun tonight."

The three men firmly shake hands. Jim walks off and rejoins his fiancée, Karen Sanders.

"Dang it!" Major blurts as he and Gabe watch Jim leave the ballroom.

"What's wrong?" Gabe asks.

"We should've asked Jim what he was getting into tonight."

"Man! You're right."

"Oh well, it's too late for that. Let's go get JT and get out of here."

"I'll get him."

Gabe walks over to the New Jersey group, which is beginning to disperse from the ballroom. He motions JT to come on.

JT catches the signal, says one final good-bye to Mary and her mother, then follows Gabe over to where Major patiently waits.

Together again, the three cadets make their way for the ballroom exit. Walking down the hallway, there is no longer a crowd. There are small groups exiting the convention center, along with Major, JT, and Gabe, but none of the groups are numerous enough to cause any congestion.

JT, Gabe, and Major step out onto the boardwalk and make their way for the Trump casino. After about only five steps, they are confronted by two extremely small elderly men.

"Your uniforms look very good on you," one of the gentlemen states, looking at the cadets' uniforms over.

"Yes. Yes. They sure do," the other interjects. "Tell me, are they comfortable?"

"Very, sir, except for this collar," JT states, pulling his collar out so he can breathe.

While the two gentlemen look Major, Gabe, and JT over, the three cadets look at one another bewilderedly. They have no idea as to why these two little old men are so interested in their uniforms.

"You young men are probably wondering who we are, are you not?" one of the gentlemen asks, as though he is reading the three Cadets' minds.

"Yes, sir, we are," Gabe responds.

"We are your tailors," the two gentlemen reply in unison.

"Ohhhhh," Major, Gabe, and JT answer together.

"That's cool," Major follows.

As the two gentlemen discuss the art and nuance of West Point tailoring, their wives approach from the rear. Aware that their wives are ready to leave, the men shake hands and depart in opposite directions.

Major, Gabe, and JT walk into the lower lobby of the Trump casino, where they had previously drank at the bar.

"So what are we going to do now?" JT asks.

"We're going to go to that party that Mr. Lees invited us to," Major quickly states, leading the way up the escalator.

JT and Gabe follow behind Major up the escalator to as many floors as it will take them. On the last floor they reach, the three cadets find an elevator and take it to the sixth floor.

The elevator doors open at the sixth floor and the three cadets step out. They are unsure as to where they should go in relation to the party, but fortunately, there is only one way for them to go—left. By force, they turn left and follow the hallway until it nearly ends.

As they walk down the hallway, JT, Gabe, and Major cross paths with the retired first sergeant who had aided them in getting into the ballroom earlier. He is walking in a stupored state with one woman under his right arm and two others under his left.

Noticing the three cadets in his path, the first sergeant loudly slurs, "You boys have a great evening! I know I am!"

"We sure will, sir!" Major returns as they all pass each other, waving and smiling.

Major, JT, and Gabe find themselves at the end of the hallway, which is nothing more than a large circular turnaround point. To the left, there is a large banquet hall containing several people.

"I guess this is it," Major states as he, Gabe, and JT stand outside of the door.

The three friends walk into the banquet, being careful not to attract any attention.

"Do you see Mr. Lees anywhere?" JT asks.

"I don't see him anywhere," Gabe answers.

Major looks at the far wall and spots a giant ABC sign. "Well, I guess this is the place," he states, pointing the sign out to JT and Gabe.

"Well, we need to find Mr. Lees," JT states.

The three cadets slowly walk to the back of the banquet in an attempt to locate Mr. Lees in a discreet manner. While looking, a woman in a silver sequined dress approaches them.

"Do you gentlemen have passes?"

"No, ma'am," Major answers. "We are cadets from the United States Military Academy. Mr. Lees invited us."

"Well, if you don't have a pass, I must ask you to leave," the woman sternly states.

"Even though Mr. Lees invited us?" Gabe desperately asks.

"I'm sorry, but only those with passes are invited," the women restates.

"Let's go, guys," Major says as he turns around and heads for the exit.

The woman follows closely behind the three cadets to ensure that they leave ABC's official Miss America after party.

As Major, JT, and Gabe reach the entrance from where they entered, Major looks over his right shoulder and spots Mr. Lees surrounded by a small crowd.

"There he is," Major states as he, Gabe, and JT are forced out of the door.

Standing on the outside of the party, JT states, "Let's go in there and let him know we're here."

"Naw," Major disagrees. "I don't want to cause a scene."

"Major's right, JT," Gabe agrees.

Major faces JT and says, "We had our fun, brother. Who else can say they did all we did tonight?"

JT nods his head with a giant smile on his face. "You're right, Major. Let's go to the club and finish the rest of the night off right. Who knows? Maybe we'll find a better party later on tonight."

"That's what I'm talking about," Gabe agrees.

"Fellas," Major replies, "I thought you knew. We are the party."

The three friends laugh as they walk away from the room and head for the elevators. Though the evening did not end as they would have liked, nonetheless, the three friends had just had one of the most memorable times of their lives.

19 SEPTEMBER 1999

1830 Hours: West Point

Once again, Major sits at the kitchen table with the Woods for another free dinner. Though he seems to eat more dinner meals at their house, the Woods do not mind Major eating dinner with them regularly. In fact, they love it.

"So," Mrs. Wood begins the conversation, "how was the pageant?"

"Oh my god, Mrs. Wood! You should've been there," Major opens. "I fell in love at least fifty-one times."

"Fifty-one times?" Colonel Wood asks with a nod of the head.

"Fifty states and DC," Major quickly responds.

"Ohh," Colonel Wood replies, fully understanding Major's comment.

Mrs. Wood leans forward toward Major and excitingly states, "You have to tell me all about it."

Major tells the Woods about his experience at the Miss America pageant. The Woods are at the edge of their seats as Major tells his story.

Ending his invigorating tale, Colonel Wood proudly states, "It's great to see you using your West Point experience to the fullest."

"Yes, sir," Major agrees.

"Imagine," Colonel Wood continues, "if you guys wouldn't have worn your uniforms, you wouldn't have had as great a time as you did."

"Roger that, sir," Major states with a big, bashful grin on his face.

"You guys must have looked so handsome," Mrs. Wood adds.

"Of course, we did," Major replies.

Mrs. Wood, already knowing the answer to her question, asks Major, "So you didn't speak to Terry?"

"No, ma'am."

"Why not?" Mrs. Wood asks again.

"As much as I wanted to, I didn't want to intrude."

"You should find some way of contacting her," Mrs. Wood proceeds.

"You think so?"

"Of course. What woman wouldn't want a handsome, intelligent young man like you to speak to her?"

Major shakes his head and laughs.

Mrs. Wood continues. "And the fact that you're a West Point cadet? What woman couldn't resist?"

"She's right, you know," Colonel Wood interjects.

Major ponders on the thought for a while then states, "You know, you're right. What do I have to lose? The worst she can say is no."

"Exactly," Colonel Wood agrees.

"I'm going to do that. Tonight," Major states.

The Woods take a break from picking on Major, and they all finally begin to eat dinner.

As Major eats, he thinks to himself, *This is crazy! I don't even know why she would write me back. Oh well. I have nothing to lose, right?*

———————◆———————

Back in his room, Major sits in his chair behind his desk and says to himself, *I need a second opinion before I actually do this.*

Major picks up his telephone receiver and dials a number. After two rings, a female voice answers.

"Hello," the voice says.

"Hey, Michelle," Major replies. "I'm glad you're in. I need to ask you a question."

"What's up?"

"This may sound a little weird, but I need a girl's opinion on this, and you were the first girl I thought of."

"Well…"

"How would you feel if you get a letter from some guy that you've never met, but he let's you know that he goes to West Point and whatnot and he just wanted to say hello and see if they could possibly get together or something?"

"It depends. How does he know me?"

"He saw you from a distance but was unable to speak to you because there was too big a crowd around you."

"Well, I think that would be sweet. What's this all about?"

"I saw this girl, Terry Boyd, Miss Indiana, at the Miss America pageant last night. I wanted to speak to her, but the opportunity didn't present itself, or at least I didn't think it did."

"Ahh. That's sweet. You should write her."

"I will. Thanks, babe."

"Any time."

"I'm going to get writing now. I'll talk to you tomorrow."

"Okay, Major. Bye."

"Peace."

Major hangs up the phone then turns his computer screen on and double clicks on the Netscape icon. The webpage instantly fills the screen and goes to the Yahoo homepage. Searching through the list of subjects, Major finds the directory and clicks on it. Major grabs his Miss America pageant book from off of the table behind him and turns to Terry Boyd's page. Finding her parent's name, he enters them into the spaces provided on the computer screen as well as the city and state in which they reside.

"I can't believe I'm doing this," Major mumbles. "This girl's going to think I'm crazy."

Major clicks on the Go button. After a few seconds, another screen appears, full of names and addresses. Major scrolls down through the screen and finds Terry's parents' home address.

"Here goes nothing," Major mumbles again.

Major copies the address on a sheet of paper then exits from the Internet. He grabs a sheet of paper, a pen, and a book then moves over to his couch. Propping his feet up on the table, Major begins his first attempt of writing to Terry.

Dear Terry,

My name is Milton Aynes Johnson, and I am a first class cadet at the United States Military Academy at West Point. You're probably wondering why I am writing you. I'd ask the same question if I were receiving a letter from someone I've never met.

Two of my friends and I attended the pageant this past Saturday in support of Mary London (Miss New Jersey). While in the ballroom, I spotted you through a crowd. I didn't want to approach you because you were with family and friends. My mother raised me better than that. Maybe I should have taken the risk, but I did not feel that it was appropriate for me to intrude at that time especially since I'm not from Indiana.

Well, I guess I'm taking a risk now. I figure, "Hey. Why not give it a shot." In a situation like this, I have everything to gain and nothing to lose.

It'd be great if you were able to write me back. I understand that you're busy, but who knows. Maybe I'll check my mail someday and see a letter from you. Who knows.

Respectfully Yours,
Milton A. Johnson

Finished with his rough draft, Major breathes a sigh of relief. "Well, it's done," he states aloud. Major reads the letter over to himself then makes the proper corrections. With the corrections made, Major transcribes the letter to a sheet of his formal West Point stationary. Major neatly folds the letter and carefully places it into an envelope. After licking and folding the envelope fold over, Major writes Terry's parents address as well as his own on the envelope.

Smiling, Major places the letter on his desk in a spot where he will not overlook it tomorrow morning.

"I guess I just took a Nestea plunge," Major states as he checks his inbox to check if there is any company business that he needs to attend to before starting his homework.

21 SEPTEMBER 1999

0930 Hours: Belgrade, Serbia

Mac and Killer sit in Colonel Drasneb's office to speak to him about the training that they have planned for the mission. Colonel Drasneb sits behind his desk, anticipating the brief that he is expecting to hear.

"So, gentlemen," Colonel Drasneb opens, "how does our training look?"

"Very good, sir," Killer answers. "There's just one thing though that we are not fully prepared to brief you yet."

Colonel Drasneb's face contorts. He is highly upset. He does not verbalize his anger, but his ill emotions are very evident on his face. "What is the reason for the delay?" Colonel Drasneb asks.

"It's nothing major, sir," Killer replies. "There're just some last-minute tweaking that Mac and I need to do in terms of the minute details. We have the schedule itself complete as well as the major training components. We are able to brief the experts today on the schedule itself. Once we get in the air tomorrow, Mac and I will be prepared to brief you on every aspect of training, minus the schematics and mission sight layout, of course."

Somewhat relieved, Colonel Drasneb states, "All right then. That will work. Let us go then."

The three men exit the office and step out into the hallway. Colonel Drasneb's office is located at the end of the hall. Mac and Killer, led by Colonel Drasneb, walk to the other end of the hall to the conference room.

Colonel Drasneb, Killer, and Mac walk into the conference room, where the Experts patiently wait. The Experts stand around the conference table: none of them seated. It is customary for lower ranking personnel to take their seats after the highest individual in the room.

Entering the conference room, Mac and Killer remain in the front, while Colonel Drasneb goes to the rear, where his seat is located. Colonel Drasneb takes his seat, and the experts follow, suit. Killer hands Colonel Drasneb's aide a stack of the training schedules, who then hands them out to the experts, starting with Colonel Drasneb.

Seeing that everyone has a copy of the schedule, Killer opens the brief with "Good morning, gentlemen. If you will turn to page 1, we will begin. We should be long. Please save all questions until the end."

Everyone turns his packet to page 1.

"There are six key areas that we are going to train on," Killer begins. "Small arms, explosives, cultural immersion, climbing, schematics, and driver's training."

Mac steps forward and continues. "For small arms, we are utilizing your current weaponry: the AK-47 assault rifle and the .45 mm handgun. We are using these weapons for merely defensive purposes only, for example, if we are attacked trying to escape."

Mac receives a few questionable looks from some of the experts. It is obvious that some do not agree.

Mac, unshaken by the experts' disapproval, continues with his portion of the brief. "In terms of explosives, we are utilizing TNT in the form of plastic explosives and clamor minds. The TNT is what we are using to destroy the mess hall. The clamor minds, as with the small arms, are only to be used in self-defense while escaping."

"Moving on to page 2," Killer continues, "we have the cultural immersion aspect of our training."

The experts turn to the second page. Killer waits for everyone before continuing. "Some of you may be surprised, but cultural immersion may be the hardest part of your training. I, along with the assistance of Colonel Drasneb's friend, will teach you basic English sentences and phrases. The goal of this training is to make you and your men appear as tourists, not soldiers, wearing civilian clothes."

Some of the experts chuckle at Killer's comment.

Killer smiles. He then continues, "This is imperative to our operation since you will be among the general population for two days prior to execution."

Mac steps forward and states, "Turn with me to page 3." After the experts turn to the next page, Mac continues with his portion of the brief. "The Killer and I will train you in the proper and most expedient climbing techniques. From the minimal knowledge that we have on the terrain that West Point sits on, we do know that there are several cliffs that may require climbing."

Colonel Drasneb raises his eyes from his packet. He is taken aback some due to the fact that he was unaware that Mac and Killer had any knowledge of West Point. It is something that he places in the back of his mind for the time being.

Mac takes a step back, and Killer steps forward again. "Turning to page 4," Killer says. He waits for the shuffling of pages to cease. "You see that the schematics page is blank. Mac and I cannot plan this aspect of our training until Colonel Drasneb's 'friend' meets us at the training site. He has the maps, pictures, and schematics that we require to formulate the actual plan. The same goes for our escape plan, which is posted on page 6."

The experts all turn their head and stare at Colonel Drasneb with a nonunderstanding look. Colonel Drasneb does not say a word. He simply nods his head in approval of Killer's information. The experts accept Colonel Drasneb's gesture and return to their previous positions.

With full attention back on him, Killer states, "Turning to page 5, you see that we will also have to do some driver's training. This will consist of testing your driving skills through different situations such as rush-hour traffic, rugged terrain, and opposing obstacles. You and your soldiers' driver's training will also consist of teaching you US driver's laws, especially those of New York state, which is the state where West Point is located, and New Jersey because some of you will fly into Newark airport, which is located in New Jersey. That completes our brief for the moment. We now open for questions."

One expert, sitting to the left of where Mac and Killer, stands and asks, "How many weeks are we training?"

"Good question," Killer replies. "We will train for seven weeks straight. We will have the weekends off in terms of training. We will remain on-site the entire time though. The last weekend before we depart for the US, we will take liberty at an unspecified location."

The experts shake their heads in approval of Killer's response.

Another expert stands and asks, "How long will we train each day?"

"Every weekday from Monday to Friday, we'll conduct physical training from five thirty to seven in the morning. From seven fifteen to eight, we will eat breakfast. From nine until twelve, we will conduct our first half of training for the day. Twelve to two in the afternoon is laid on for lunch. Two to five is dedicated to the second half of the day's training."

Another expert stands and asks, "To what level are you two involved in this mission?"

Mac steps forward, uncrossing his arms and placing them on his waist. "We are the trainers as well as the executors. You are here merely for support purposes—to ensure that the Killer and I are able to get in and get out undetected."

The question-asking expert slowly returns to his seat. Several of the other experts do not appreciate Mac's comment. They murmur among one another.

Killer and Mac lock eyes for a brief second. Mac reads the disappointment in Killer's eyes. He knows that he has just messed up. *You idiot!* Mac shouts internally. *You let your emotions show. Hopefully, you can make up for this slip up.*

As the experts continue to murmur among themselves, an expert jumps from his seat, facing Colonel Drasneb. The expert slams his hands on the table and shouts, "This is what we were afraid of, sir! We don't need these mercenary dogs to carry out your mission! We can do this on our own and achieve the level of success that you desire!"

"No. Unfortunately, we require Mr. Stewart and Mr. Pollard's assistance and knowledge to carry my mission out the way I intend. Do not worry. All will be taken care of and understood as we progress into our training."

Colonel Drasneb stands up and steps away from his seat. He places his hand on the upset expert's shoulder, softly forcing him to retake his seat. Colonel Drasneb then walks over to where Mac and Killer still stand and says, "That is all for today, gentlemen. I will see you all here in two days for the flight brief."

1845 Hours: West Point

Major returns to his room from dinner. Before he enters, he pokes his head into Dusty's room and asks, "What's up, man?"

Dusty, who is sitting at his desk with his head held down low, looks up at Major with a sober look on his face then lowers his head again.

Noticing that Dusty appears very distraught over something, Major asks him, "What's wrong, Dust?"

"It's the platoon sergeants," Dusty replies. He slams his hands down on his desk then stands to his feet. "They don't listen to me!"

Major steps out of the hallway and into Dusty's room, saying, "What do you mean they don't listen to you?"

Frustrated, Dusty paces very sporadically across his room. "They don't do what I tell them to do! They work at their own pace! Every time I give them a tasking, they blow me off!"

Major rubs his chin and states, "Really?"

"Yes! And I am getting sick and tired of dealing with them! I know you tell me to be calm, but if they mess up one more time, I'm going to lose it and go off on them!"

Leaning against the doorway, Major states, "Have them come by my room tomorrow at seven. You come too."

"What are you going to say?" Dusty inquires.

"I'm not sure yet, but I'll have something ready by the time you guys get here."

"Okay."

"Cool then. I'll see you." Major leaves Dusty's room and goes to his own to start his homework.

As Major enters his room, Joe, who is sitting on the couch cooking from a Crock-Pot, asks, "What was that all about?"

"Dust and the platoon sergeants aren't getting along.

"Huh?"

"The first sergeant doesn't feel that they're giving him the respect he deserves."

"Oh. You going to do anything about it?"

"Yeah. I've noticed some stuff myself, but I wanted to see if they'd work it out themselves. Obviously, they have not."

"So what are you going to do?"

"I'm going to have them come over tomorrow night and talk to them."

"You know what you're going to say?"

"Not sure yet. I'll figure it out when the time comes. Maybe I'll do this like some of my briefs."

Joe laughs. "This should be good then."

Major laughs as well. He then sticks his head out of the room and shouts, "Sara!"

Hearing her name called, Sara leaves her room and heads downstairs for Joe and Major's room.

"What's up, Major?" Sara asks as she enters the room.

"Tomorrow night, I'm having a little come to Jesus meeting with the first sergeant and the platoon sergeants at seven. I want you to sit in on it."

"Okay. Is that it?"

"Yeah."

"Okay. I'm going over to Orson's room. I'll stop by on my way back."

"Tell OG I said hey."

"I will," Sara replies as she walks out of the room.

22 SEPTEMBER 1999

1855 Hours: West Point

Major, Joe, Sara, and Dusty sit in Major and Joe's room, waiting for the arrival of the four platoon sergeants, cadet sergeants John McKinley, Debra Wales, Fred Klein, and Mark Hammer.

At exactly 1900 hours, three soft knocks are heard on the partially closed door.

"Enter!" Major shouts, spinning on his chair.

The four platoon sergeants slowly enter the room.

"Take a seat, guys," Major says.

Sara, who is sitting on the chair at Joe and Major's spare desk, rises from her seat and offers it to one of the platoon sergeants. Three of the platoon sergeants sit on the couch, and another sits in the offered seat. Dusty sits on the sink, Sara moves to the refrigerator, and Joe sits on his bed.

Seeing that everyone is situated, Major pushes away from his desk and positions himself between the desks and the beds in order to see everyone clearer.

Speaking directly to the platoon sergeants, Major asks them, "You guys know why I brought you all in here?"

None of the platoon sergeants reply.

"Well, the first sergeant doesn't feel that you guys're working to your potential. He doesn't feel as though you guys are respecting him in the proper manner or taking him seriously."

Major lifts a lever on his chair to make it go down. He then leans as far back in his chair as it will allow.

"Here's an analogy for you. I, as the company commander, am like God. The first sergeant's Jesus. He makes the way for me as Christ did for God. Now you guys, my platoon sergeants, are the disciples. I, as God, give the first sergeant wisdom and understanding, he then passes that knowledge on to you so that you can then pass that information on to your platoons. Understand that if the disciples don't listen to Jesus and do as he requests, then you all—and those under you, fail. Without Jesus, the first sergeant, we cannot be successful. Can you come straight to God? Of course, but God is busy and has a lot to do. It makes things a lot less complicated when we go through Jesus. Do you guys understand what I'm saying?"

Cadet Wales looks at Major with a funny look on her face and asks, "So you're saying that we're the twelve disciples?"

"Yeah."

Cadet Wales nods her head in understanding.

Dusty raises his hand and says, "I'm like Jesus? How?"

"Because I work through you. All of the information and instruction that you receive comes from me, in some manner or another. All it is is an analogy of information dissemination."

"Oh," Dusty replies. "I got you."

"Good. You guys have any questions?"

The platoon sergeants shake their heads no.

"All right then. We shouldn't have anymore problems then, should we?"

"No," the platoon sergeants answer in unison.

"Good deal. I'll see you guys tomorrow then."

Cadets McKinley, Wales, Klein, and Hammer rise from their seats and leave the room like ducks in a row. No pun intended.

23 SEPTEMBER 1999

0635 Hours: West Point

Major strolls out of Grant Barracks on his way to breakfast formation. He makes it a point to be the first upperclassman at formation. This gives him the opportunity to speak with his plebes and observe their training from their respective team leaders. As Major heads for the formation, several of his plebes quickly walk past him, greeting him with "We own the pond, sir!"

Reaching the formation, Major observes the yearlings and the plebes interact. It is the job of the yearlings to instruct the plebes and ensure that they learn their military knowledge. Formations are a venue that is used to do so.

As Major observes his formation, he slowly spins around, arms crossed, and faces Company A-1's formation. Much to his dismay, he witnesses a third class cadet yelling at a plebe.

I know that plebe, Major thinks to himself. *He plays ball with Will.*

Watching the example of improper discipline, Major is even more disturbed to see some of the cow's peers circle around the plebe. Some of them even get involved in the yelling spree.

What a friggin' shame, Major thinks to himself. *I be darned if that mess happens in my company!*

Major would intercede on the plebes behalf, but the cows have not broken any rules. They may have crossed the line in terms of professionalism, but in terms of the Corps of Cadets regulations, the cows are not doing anything illegal.

Disgusted at what he sees, Major turns away from A-1 and returns to his own formation in preparation for yet another scrumptious West Point breakfast.

Major leads his company to the mess hall for breakfast. He falls out of the formation and slowly walks up a series of steps to enter the mess hall. Walking up the steps, he notices the same cow from A-1 grilling the plebe.

"Is this dude ever going to stop?" Major rhetorically asks himself.

Still making his way into the mess hall, Major continues to watch the cow-plebe interaction. The plebe, who is displaying serious signs of disgust of the ill treatment that he is receiving, suddenly turns and steps away from the cow. The cow, shocked at the plebe's seemingly disrespectful action, grabs the plebe by the arm, spins him around, and forces the plebe's back up against the wall.

Several cadets jump back at what occurs before their eyes. Major, who is surprised at the cow's action, quickly moves to the cow's position. Major grabs the cow by the arm and spins him around.

Glaring into the cow's eyes, Major sternly states, "You can't touch that plebe in any manner. You're in the wrong now."

Major then forces the cow to the side, takes the plebe by the shoulder, and calmly says, "Come on, little brother. Let's go to breakfast."

The plebe steps away from the wall and walks with Major. The crowd that grew around them during all of the action makes way for Major and the plebe. Once through the crowd, it disperses, and the cadets return to their daily breakfast routine.

0930 Hours: Belgrade, Serbia

Colonel Drasneb's aide stands before the experts, Mac and Killer, and Colonel Drasneb, prepared to brief them on their upcoming flight in five days. "Good morning, gentlemen. I will not keep you all long. I know that you still have much to do in terms of preparation for our most glorious mission. On the twenty-seventh, at 0400 hours, we will meet at the airfield. The day prior, ensure that your men bring all of your gear to hangar number 8 so the flight crew can load it onto the planes. There will be three planes. Colonel Drasneb, Mr. Stewart, Mr. Pollard, myself, and the members of team one will travel on the first chalk. We will mark our gear in black. There is an example in the packets in front of you."

Everyone flips through the thin packet, searching for the example that the aide has just mentioned.

Continuing, Colonel Drasneb's aide states, "Teams 2 and 3 will ride in the second chalk. Your mark is red. Teams 4 and 5, you ride on the third chalk. Mark your bags with green."

Colonel Drasneb's aide flips to another slide and states, "Our travel time is about five hours. Due to the top-secret nature of our mission, we are not taking the most expedient route. This is to ensure that no one is following us. Once we land on the ground, Mr. Stewart and Mr. Pollard are in charge, under Colonel Drasneb's supervision, of course. Do not take any orders from the training-facility personnel. That concludes my brief. Are there any questions?"

"I have one," Killer asks. "What are we supposed to mark our equipment with?"

"I'm glad you asked that." The aide bends down and picks up a boxful of black, red, and green markers. He then passes the box around the room, saying, "Take your respective colors and pass the box back to the front."

With the box returned to the front, Colonel Drasneb's aide asks, "Are there any further questions?" The aide scans the room. Seeing no hands or acknowledgment from the experts that they have anymore questions, he states, "Since there are none, I will see you gentlemen, along with your teams, at the airfield in four days."

Acknowledging Colonel Drasneb, his aide further states, "Sir, do you have anything for your men?"

"No, I do not, Lieutenant. Thank you for the brief. Gentlemen, you are dismissed."

Upon the dismissal, the experts and Mac and Killer rise from their seats and head out of the conference room. As they exit, Colonel Drasneb walks beside his aide, who is packing his equipment and briefing materials.

Sensing Colonel Drasneb's presence beside him, the aide quickly rises to his feet. Colonel Drasneb steps very close to his aide and whispers in his ear, "I want Mr. Stewart and Mr. Pollard watch more intently this time."

"But they found us out last time, sir."

"I am aware of that. I do not care if they are aware or not. I just want to have an exact accountability of them at all times."

"Sir, are you afraid that they will sabotage your mission?"

"One can never be too sure, Lieutenant. One can never be too sure."

27 SEPTEMBER 1999

0100 Hours: At the outskirts of Belgrade, Serbia

Colonel Drasneb's men are all assembled and ready to move out to the training sight to begin the training phase of the mission. Because the entirety of the mission is top secret, the men board cargo planes for their departure. Killer and Mac sit in the front of the plane across from Colonel Drasneb so they can further discuss the plans for the training aspect of the mission.

"Sir, the site is prepared for our arrival?" Killer asks Colonel Drasneb.

"Yes, it is."

"Good because I want to get everything organized on the ground and meet with all of the site personnel before we begin tomorrow morning."

"That should not be a problem," Colonel Drasneb responds.

"All right then." Killer opens his satchel and pulls out a black folder. He hands it over to Colonel Drasneb. "Here is a copy of the training schedule."

Colonel Drasneb reads it over quickly and nods his head in agreement. "This is very good. I will stick with this. Do you have a backup plan?"

"I do, but I won't pull it out unless it's necessary."

"Understood." Colonel Drasneb reclines his seat back. "I'm going to take a nap now. We have a long flight ahead of us."

Killer turns to his left and faces Mac. "Well, that went easy enough."

"How else was it supposed to go?" Mac sarcastically asks.

"Funny."

"Two and a half months in Russia, huh?"

"Yep."

"God, I hate Russia."

"Yeah, me too, but at least we get the weekends off."

"Yeah," Mac chuckles. "I can't believe we're going to be using Russian equipment on this mission. I'd feel more secure using a bed sheet for a parachute than a Russian one."

"I feel you, but we've got to make the most of it. Think of it this way: we'll be home free by Christmas."

Mac smiles and sighs, "Happy thoughts." He too leans back and dozes off.

0400 Hours: Somewhere over Western Russia

The sky is dark and ominous, as though a storm were brewing. Though it is late morning, the dark heaviness of the sky makes the day look more like it is midnight. What is odd is that as dark as the sky is and as heavy as the clouds appear, there is no thunder and lightning as one would expect; yet again, if the sky were to open up with thunderous roars, it would not be a surprise to anyone around.

The small trail of planes flies low over the desolate terrain to avoid any turbulence. The planes were built during the early period of the Cold War, which gives the pilots reasons for concern. They have not flown into Russia since it officially abandoned its communist dogma. There is no reason for concern on the pilots' part, but usually, the mission commanders inform them of the reasoning behind their flights.

Colonel Drasneb, on the other hand, is of a different breed. He is very secretive. All the pilots know is that they are flying to a set of coordinates near the Volga River, drop the soldiers off, and pick them up in two and a half months at the same location. The pilots know not to ask too many questions. Colonel Drasneb has a reputation for being ruthless toward who do not follow his instruction to the letter. It is best prescribed to follow his orders and hold your head down when doing so. Asking the wrong questions can mean the end of one's career.

The Serbian cargo planes land softly on the runway. Standing outside to greet the Serbs are the training-site staff led by former USSR major Boris Gurgtzy. The lead plane comes to a stop in front of the welcome party. Colonel Drasneb leads his entourage out of his plane, followed by his aide and then Mac and Killer. Killer pulls a folder out of his satchel and hands it to Colonel Drasneb, who quickly looks at it and smiles.

"I hate this place," Colonel Drasneb quietly says to Mac and Killer. "The last time I was here, my men spent half of their time maintaining the facilities that we were using. Definitely a third-rate operation."

"Third rate, sir?" Colonel Drasneb's aide asks.

"Yes. Third rate. This place does not deserve second."

"Then why are we here, sir?" Killer smartly asks.

"Since this is a secret operation, I had to ensure that we went to a training site that no one would expect. This was the first place that came to mind."

"Understood," Killer agrees.

Colonel Drasneb and his three man entourage slowly yet assuredly meet Boris Gurgtzy about three hundred feet away from the airplane. Mac and Killer casually scan the area for anything out of the ordinary. They notice watchtowers placed apart about every two thousand yards, give or take one hundred feet. There is no noticeable barbed wire, but with a facility such as this one, there has to be some somewhere. They will look into that later.

As Colonel Drasneb and his entourage approach the Russian welcome party, Major Gurgtzy smilingly bursts, "Greetings, Colonel! Welcome to our beautiful country,"

"I have been to Russia many times, Gurgtzy. Beautiful it is not."

Gurgtzy scowls at Colonel Drasneb's remarks but quickly reclaims his emotions. Gurgtzy has to be on his best behavior for this training session. He is receiving less and less contracts every year. For reasons that he cannot put his finger on, the Libyan, Somali, and Afghan terrorist organizations are getting much more business than he and his Russian counterparts.

"Here is our training schedule," Colonel Drasneb says to Gurgtzy as he hands him a copy. "We are not going to commence training until tomorrow at 0800 hours. After breakfast, of course." He turns and approvingly nods at Killer.

"Why are you waiting until tomorrow?" Gurgtzy asks. "Aren't you wasting time by not beginning your training today?"

"No. We are not wasting time. We are better utilizing it." As Colonel Drasneb and his entourage walk past Gurgtzy and his party, Colonel Drasneb says to Gurgtzy, "How about you do your job and ensure that your facilities are ready for me and my men? That includes our meals. Allow us soldiers to train."

The Serbian party marches off to their quarters and leaves the Russians standing on the airstrip, twiddling their thumbs. Gurgtzy is highly upset with Colonel Drasneb's remarks and the Serbs' overall pompous attitude. What upsets Gurgtzy even more is the fact that there is nothing he can do about it. Gurgtzy knows that he needs the business, and the only way he can keep his training facility open is by appeasing pompous men like Drasneb.

As they walk further away from Gurgtzy and his personnel, Killer says to Colonel Drasneb, "Way to handle yourself back there, sir. You definitely set the tone for our training. I don't think we're going to have any problems with Gurgtzy and his people while we're here."

"That was my intent entirely, Mr. Stewart. The Russians may be our Slavic brothers and historical allies, but they have lost their focus and drive over the past five years. They have become soft and wilted. They all aspire to become Americans. What a shame." Colonel Drasneb shakes his head in shame and disgust.

"I hate to say this, sir, but I have to agree with you on that one," Mac chimes in. "Honestly, the Russians have always been overestimated—more bark than their bite. Excluding nukes, there's no way that they could sustain a long-term war with the US. They don't have sufficient resources and their weaponry and armament are second rate at best, contrary to popular Cold War propaganda."

"True. True," Colonel Drasneb agrees.

The three men, along with Colonel Drasneb's aide, who walks two steps and to the right of his commander, continue walking in silence toward their barracks. The aide would join in the conversation, but he knows that it is not his place to express his opinions unless asked—proper protocol and etiquette.

28 SEPTEMBER 1999

0830 Hours: Russian training camp

Mac and Killer sit in their tent, going over plans for the upcoming training that will take place next Monday. As they converse, Colonel Drasneb steps into their tent and asks, "Are you gentlemen going to accompany me to the tarmac to meet our friend?"

Without looking up, Mac coldly replies, "Your spy?"

"If that is what you wish to call him, then yes, my spy."

"We may as well," Killer states, rising to his feet. "We have to work intimately with him, so we may as well meet him at the most opportune time, which just happens to be now."

"I couldn't have said it better myself," Colonel Drasneb comments. Mac and Killer simply look at one another.

Colonel Drasneb turns and exits the tent. Killer follows. With Killer and Colonel Drasneb out of the tent, Mac slowly rises from off of his cot and follows behind the two men. Slowly, Mac catches up with Colonel Drasneb and Killer, who are conversing about something. About what? Mac does not know and does not care to know: At least not at the moment, anyway.

After about a ten-minute walk, the three men arrive at the airfield. They calmly stand there in silence, waiting for Colonel Drasneb's "friend" to arrive.

With another ten minutes having passed, Mac notices a small dark speck heading from out of the southwest. "Is that him?" Mac asks nonchalantly.

Looking at his watch, Colonel Drasneb replies, "It should be."

Larger and larger, the black speck grows, until it is obvious to the untrained eye that it is a prop plane. The plane taxis and parks fifty meters away from the waiting gentlemen. The engines cut off, and the propellers slowly come to a grinding halt. A slight moment later, the passenger door opens and a tall, decently shaped young man carrying nothing more than a duffel bag and a brown leather briefcase steps out of the plane. He turns around and shuts the door behind him.

The man slings the duffel bag over his shoulder and strides to where Colonel Drasneb stands. He places the duffel bag onto the ground, snaps to the position of attention, and salutes Colonel Drasneb, stating, "Sir, Major Petrova reporting as ordered."

Colonel Drasneb returns Major Petrova's salute then says, "It is good to see you again, Alex. Now we can begin our training."

"Yes, sir," Alex replies.

Gesturing toward Mac and Killer, Colonel Drasneb states, "These are the two Americans I was telling you about—Mr. Amos Stewart and Mr. Douglas Pollard."

"It is a pleasure to meet you, gentlemen," Alex politely says, sticking his hand out.

Killer firmly shakes Alex's hand. Mac glares at Alex, signaling to him that he does not want to be bothered with friendly gestures.

"You're friend is the brutish type. No?" Alex jokes to Killer.

"Yes, I am," Mac quickly answers.

"I see. Well, I guess we're going to have to do something about that. Aren't we?" Alex replies with a slight chuckle in his voice.

Mac glares at Alex with a puzzled look. He is unsure how to read Alex or what his angle is. Is he genuinely friendly, or is it all a ploy? Only time will tell.

Colonel Drasneb interrupts the conversation, saying, "Let us go now, gentlemen. You have much work ahead of you."

Killer, Alex, and Mac follow Colonel Drasneb back to the training area and into the plans tent.

Waiting inside the tent is Colonel Drasneb's aide. Alex approaches the lieutenant and tosses him his duffel bag, saying, "Take this to my tent. Place it under my cot with the open end facing away from the tent entrance."

"Yes, sir," the lieutenant replies, rushing out of the plans tent as ordered.

Colonel Drasneb stands in front of the training board, reading over the upcoming training events. He peruses the board very carefully. The other gentlemen stand, watching Colonel Drasneb. Neither of them is sure what he is looking for, nor do they show much concern.

Alex steps to the table that is in the center of the tent and places his satchel onto it. Hearing the action causes Colonel Drasneb to convert his attention from the training board to the center of the tent.

"Well," Colonel Drasneb begins, "I see you are going to get underway. I will go now and supervise my men to ensure that they are ready for tomorrow's training. The first day of training is always the most important." Colonel Drasneb exits the plans tent, leaving the entrance panels flapping behind him.

"Colonel Drasneb is a very interesting man, is he not?" Alex comments upon Colonel Drasneb's departure.

Taken aback some by Alex's comment, Killer replies, "Yeah, he is."

Mac stands there, waiting for another response from Alex. Alex does not reply. He simply removes the contents of his briefcase onto the table and begins shuffling through them.

"You need any help?" Killer asks.

Without pausing, Alex answers, "No, but thank you for asking. I will be ready shortly."

After a couple of minutes of organizing, Alex looks up from his pile of papers and states, "We can begin."

Killer and Mac stand on both sides of Alex in preparation of his brief. In front of them, Alex has a pile consisting of various papers, documents, photographs, and maps. The first item on the pile is a general photograph of West Point.

Before Alex begins his brief, he states, "I do not want to insult your intelligence, gentlemen, so if you know of or have any knowledge in anything that I am about to brief you on, simply let me know and we will move on."

Alex picks up the first photograph from on top of the pile, stating, "This, gentlemen, is West Point, or at least what the general public thinks of West Point."

The photograph that Alex holds is a picture of a cadet parade on the Plain with Eisenhower and MacArthur Barracks, Washington Hall, and the Cadet Chapel in the background.

"Those, gentlemen, are our targets," Alex comments, referring to the cadets in the photograph.

Alex places the photograph back onto the table facedown then retrieves a sheet of paper from the pile. "These are the numbers: how many cadets per class, how many in each of the barracks, etc." Alex hands the sheet to Mac then continues. "Crowd control is very easy. There are only just over four thousand of them, and they are always at the same place on any given day. Colonel Drasneb thinks that this mission is going to be difficult. On the contrary, because of their regular routine, this mission will probably be the easiest one that you ever execute."

"You think so too, huh?" Killer asks, a bit surprised at Alex's point of view on the mission.

"Of course. Having been there, I know for a fact that I could carry this out on my own," Alex confidently retorts.

Mac turns his head and faces Alex. He has not truly looked at Alex since he arrived earlier in the morning. "You sound pretty sure of yourself. So tell me this, since you're Colonel Drasneb's favorite lackey and all, why doesn't he just have you do this friggin' mission. Why involve me and the Killer?"

Alex gets in Mac's face and replies, "I do not know, friend. I collect information. That is my thing." Alex then smiles and says. "You know, Mr. Pollard, I like you. You're an honest man. So let me ask you a question."

Mac is somewhat shocked by Alex's boldness. *This guy has balls*, he thinks to himself. Mac then answers Alex. "What's your question?"

"Why accept the mission? I know you had a choice."

"Choice is relative," Mac simply replies.

"True, but whatever your reason, I pray that it is good enough for you."

Mac looks at Killer with a puzzled look. Killer returns the same facial expression. Neither man is sure on how to read Alex.

Killer reacts on his instincts and says, "Alex, if we're going to be working as close as we are, you've got to stop calling us gentlemen. I'm Amos or Killer, whichever works for you. That's Big Mac, Mac for short."

"Well, Killer, Mac, it is a pleasure to finally have an opportunity to work with true professionals." Alex throws his hand out, which Killer firmly shakes.

Alex then turns his hand to Mac. Unlike last time, Mac returns the gesture with a firm grip.

Mac then sternly states, "I get a good read from you, Alex. Stay the same, and we won't have any problems. Change, and you may find a lot more than you're able to handle. Understand?"

"Do not worry, Mac," Alex replies with a smile. "As you Americans say, what you see is what you get."

1815 Hours: West Point

Major and Ed have finished with basketball and lacrosse practice and now sit on the sports shuttle, riding down the hill to Cadet Area. The bus stops beside Bartlett Hall, and the cadets aboard rush off and head in several directions, most to the mess hall. Major and Ed do likewise, heading to the mess hall for dinner as they usually do.

Walking past Eisenhower Barracks, Ed suggests, "Let's go check our mail real quick."

"Aight," Major replies.

The two friends walk past the first mess hall rear entrance and turn right, down into a tunnel known as the Beat Air Force tunnel and into Washington basement. The Beat Air Force tunnel received its name due to a spirit mission that one of Major's friends, Lee Name, and several other cadets executed. Lee and his friends painted the words *Beat Air Force* on the tunnel walls. It looked so good that higher decided that it should stay. Everyone has referred to the tunnel by that name ever since.

In Washington basement, Ed and Major take the third right, turning into a large mailroom full of numerous mailboxes and an ATM machine. Ed and Major go to their respective mailbox and check their mail. Major usually checks his mail about once every other week because he never gets any mail except for his telephone and American Express Card bills—nothing to make Major's mail checking routine very enjoyable.

Major opens his mailbox and retrieves the small stack of mail that has accumulated in his box over the past couple of weeks. He carefully sifts through it, tossing out the junk in the nearby trashcan.

After a couple of tosses, Major comes across an envelope that causes him to pause. He stares at the envelope and realizes that the impossible has just happened. Major holds in his hands the response letter from Terry Boyd.

"Ed!" Major shouts. "She wrote me back!"

"Who, fool?" Ed shouts back.

"Terry!"

"Who?"

"You know. Terry Boyd, Miss Indiana."

"Ah man!" Ed rushes over to the other side of the mailroom where Major stands then says, "Open it up, and see what the letter says."

"Hold up."

Major carefully opens the envelope and slips the letter out from its envelope. Nervous, he opens the letter. It reads:

Milton,

Thanks so much for taking the time to write me a letter. I have been very busy making appearances since I got back from Miss America. I was able to get to know Mary at the pageant. She is a very lovely person. She's doing a really great job of staying in touch with all of the other contestants.

Hmmm…what can I tell you about myself? I graduated from Ball State University in Indiana this past May with a BA in Telecommunications. I want to become a news reporter and anchor, but right now, my full-time job is being Miss Indiana. I love to go out dancing, to the movies, and I'm a football and basketball fan. Other than that, my life is consumed with the pageant stuff right now. Fortunately, I enjoy it, but it's only

going to last another nine months, and then it's back to the real
world!

*Well, I hope you are doing well. My email address is daddys_*
girl@email.com if you want to reach me that way.

Take care!
Terry Boyd

"Wow, Major. That's nice," Ed quietly replies.

Major has no initial reaction. He slowly folds the letter then carefully slips it back into its envelope. Firmly gripping his mail, but not damaging Terry's letter, Major, from out of nowhere, leaps high in the air and shouts, "Yes!" then screams, "Woooo!"

Major bursts out of the mailroom, running at full speed, and continues to scream in the tunnel. Ed follows behind Major as best he can. Through shouting, Major and Ed rush into the mess hall head straight for where JT is sitting.

"Dawg!" Major excitingly shouts as he approaches JT. "She wrote me back!"

JT turns around in his seat and asks, "Who?"

"Terry!"

"You're kidding me, right?"

"Hell naw!" Major barks, fanning the letter in the air.

"Ah man! That's great!" JT happily replies, sharing in Major's joy.

Major turns to Ed and says, "Brother, I've got to go tell the Woods. You'll have to find someone else to eat with tonight." Major runs off and darts out of the mess hall.

Major sprints across North Area and runs through the sally port connecting Mac Short and Mac Long. He cuts left, with Mac Short to his left and the superintendent's garden to his right. Turning right, Major sprints past Arvin Gymnasium behind the superintendent and commandant's houses. Major keeps straight and runs behind what is known as Colonel's Row. Colonel's Row is where the senior colonels on post live. Reaching the Woods' home, Major slows his pace down some and darts into the kitchen.

"Hey, Major!" Mrs. Wood says upon Major's arrival. "You come for dinner?"

"Not tonight, ma'am. I came to show you this."

Major hands Mrs. Wood Terry's letter. Mrs. Wood carefully takes the letter from out of the envelope and quickly reads it.

"My goodness, Major!" Mrs. Wood hoots, "This is great!" Mrs. Wood hands the letter to her husband, who then reads it for himself.

"You go, man!" Colonel Wood states. He gives Major a high five. "So you going to e-mail her back?" Colonel Wood asks.

"Of course, sir!" Major replies.

"You should ask her up one weekend," Colonel Wood suggests.

"I will, sir. I just have to find a weekend when she's free. Hopefully, she'll want to come up here. Then again, I hope she'll be able to fit me into her calendar."

"A handsome young man like you?" Mrs. Wood states. "She can't help but say yes."

"I hope you're right, Mrs. Wood." Major looks at the clock and notices the time. "I've got to go now. I'll let you guys know how it goes."

"All right, man. We'll see you," Colonel Wood states.

Major and Colonel Wood do their special handshake. Major turns to give Mrs. Wood a big hug then leaves their home for the barracks.

2 OCTOBER 1999

1100 Hours: Russian Training Camp

"These guys aren't too bad," Killer states.

"Don't compliment them," Mac retorts.

"I'm only giving credit where credit is due," Killer defends.

"If you say so. Personally, they're no better than a bunch of army reservists," Mac disrespectfully replies.

"You're cold, brother."

"I have to be. It's the only way I can separate myself from the building madness."

"Building, huh?"

"Yeah, building."

"How so?"

"Because if we stop now, then the madness will not exist, but being that we can't, then the madness that we are producing is building exponentially."

"That's a big word—exponentially. You must be upset."

"Does it show?"

Killer laughs at Mac's cynical question. He knows that Mac is highly upset at the training that they are leading and the fact that they are the essential players in the execution of Colonel Drasneb's mission.

Mac and Killer sit atop a giant bolder in full view of an expansive, clear piece of land. The terrain is quite rocky but relatively flat. The only obstructions in the terrain are several large posts resembling telephone poles sticking out from the ground. During the preparation phase of training, Mac and Killer had the experts' men construct these posts. Their purpose: to train the men how to climb pillars without causing any damage to them. From the several hours of meetings with Alex, Mac and Killer became aware that climbing was going to be an important aspect in the mission's success.

As Killer and Mac observe training, Alex quietly walks up behind them and asks, "May I join you, gentlemen?"

Killer turns his head around and answers, "I hardly heard you walk up behind us. You may want to watch that left foot of yours. It drags some."

"Thank you," Alex replies. "I will remember that next time." He takes a seat beside Killer.

"What brings you out here?" Killer asks.

"I needed to get away from Colonel Drasneb for a while."

Mac lets a little smile show.

Alex observes Mac's quick emotional change, so he states, "I see you found that funny, my friend."

Quickly returning to his gruff demeanor, Mac replies, "I am not your friend. Colleagues, yes, friends, no, but to answer your question, yeah, that was funny."

Alex laughs. "I like you, Mac. You're an honest man."

Without looking at Alex, staring out onto the terrain, Mac replies, "I must not be too honest if I'm involved in this nonsense."

"That's a good assessment," Alex agrees, "but you should not judge yourself based on your works."

"How can I not when my work is all I have?" Mac retorts.

"True," Alex again agrees. "I guess you find yourself in a moral dilemma, huh?"

"You've got that right."

"So the money is your only motivation?"

"The majority of the time, yes."

"Interesting."

"How do you say?" Killer interjects.

"I am paid, as well, but my motivation does not come from my paycheck," Alex explains.

"What motivates you?" Mac asks.

"I cannot say, but understand that I hold a personal grudge against America, and when Colonel Drasneb offered me an

opportunity to strike my revenge, I could not turn his offer down."
"That's motivation for you," Mac comments.

All of the team members have finished their iterations of pole climbing and now stand at the base of their respective poles, awaiting further instructions from Mac and Killer.

"I believe your students are in need of further guidance," Alex points out to Mac and Killer.

"Yeah," Mac blurts as he and Killer rise from their comfortable perch.

Killer and Mac leap off of the boulder and walk over to the teams' position. Alex follows close behind.

Approaching the teams, Killer instructs, "All right, guys. It is now 1130 hours, time for lunch. We'll see you guys at one. That's all."

The team members depart from the training site and head for the chow tent. Some of the team members nod their heads at Mac, Killer, and Alex as they go on their way.

As the team members head off, Killer turns to Alex and asks, "You want to eat lunch with us?"

Mac shakes his head at Killer's open gesture of friendship to Alex.

With a huge smile on his face, Alex answers, "Yes. I would enjoy that. Thank you."

The three men leave the climbing training site as well and head for the chow tent, one of the few places Mac enjoys.

1300 Hours: West Point

The underclass members of the men's varsity basketball team wait at Grant turnaround for their firstie teammates to pick them up. Every year, on the first Saturday of October, since Coach O'Hara became the army's men's basketball coach in 1997, he has had the team over to his house for a barbecue. Coach uses the team barbecue to kick off the season and is the team's first official function, though it is not formal by any means.

Not waiting too long, the firstie ballers drive down and pick up their underclass teammates. Four vehicles, including Major's 4Runner and the team van, are filled to capacity. Theo, who is driving the team van, pulls out front and leads the caravan to Coach O'Hara's house.

Coach O'Hara lives in the small town of Cornwall, New York. From his house to West Point is about fifteen minutes. The trip would be much faster if there was not a small mountain standing between West Point and Cornwall. When the weather is good, like no rain or snow, the trip is fine, but when there is inclement weather, the trip is not for the faint of heart.

Theo leads the team out through Thayer gate, driving through Highland Falls. He then turns right and heads up a steep hill. After crossing an intersection, Theo merges onto US Route 9W. All of the firsties driving know how to get to Coach O'Hara's house, so as soon as they merge onto 9W, they all open up and race over the windy mountain road in an attempt to beat Theo. Their driving is by no means the safest, but to the cadets, it sure is fun.

Pulling in front of Coach O'Hara's house, everyone jumps out of their respective vehicles and freely enters.

"Glad to see you knuckleheads decided to show up," Coach O'Hara sarcastically barks at his players as they enter the house.

Jimmy walks up to the coach and replies, "Like we had a choice, Coach." Jimmy then slaps him on the back.

As the basketball players enter the kitchen, Coach O'Hara's wife, whom everyone calls T, says, "Make yourselves at home, guys. If you want something, take it. If you don't know where it is, ask."

"That's what I'm talking about, T!" Jimmy shouts, heading for the deck to hang out near the barbeque grill.

Major walks over to the refrigerator and looks for a noncarbonated drink. Major has been a frequent visitor to his coach's home and knows that they do not stock his favorite drink, Kool-Aid, but they do usually have some variety of juice and Gatorade.

While Major still has his head in the refrigerator, Coach O'Hara's youngest daughter, Leslie, walks up to him unexpectedly and says, "Hey, Major. Mom bought some Kool-Aid today."

"Get out of here!" Major replies, stepping back from the refrigerator.

"I'll make some for you real quick," Leslie states as she retrieves the Kool-Aid from one of the cupboards.

After a minute or two pass, Leslie states, "All done."

Leslie grabs a glass from out of a shelf and pours Major a glass. Leslie does not fill the glass with ice because she knows that Major does not like ice.

"Thanks," Major says while taking the glass from Leslie's hand. He immediately takes a giant gulp of the grape Kool-Aid. "So," Major asks, "what are you getting into tonight?"

"I don't know," Leslie answers. "I may go over to Jenny's later."

"That's cool. Tell her I said hey."

"I will. What about you? What're you doing? I know you're not staying around here all night."

Major laughs. "You're right about that. I'm linking up with some of my friends in Hoboken later."

T walks in on the conversation and interjects, "Hoboken, huh? Hanging out with the yuppies?"

"I never thought of it like that," Major replies, "but I guess you're right. I always have a good time though. That's all that matters."

"Very true," T agrees. She hears some commotion occurring behind her and in response says, "Let me see what's going on outside. Those boys can get crazy sometimes."

"Yeah, they can," Major jokingly states. He turns his attention back to Leslie and says, "Hey, go out there and get me Jimmy."

"Okay," Leslie replies.

Major walks over to Coach O'Hara, who is standing near the kitchen table. "Hey, Coach, did you bring the tape?"

"Sure did. It's on the TV."

"Thanks." Major leaves the coach and heads for the television.

On top of the television is a videotape of an Army versus Duke basketball game from Coach O'Hara's first year coaching, the 1997–1998 season. During that season, Major and the other current firsties on the team were yearlings. Though Army played Duke their plebe year, during the 1996–1997 season and has played other tough teams in the past, this Army-Duke game will always hold a special place in Major's heart.

Major takes the videotape from off of the television and slides it into the VCR. As he does so, Jimmy enters the den and says, "Leslie said you wanted me?"

Without turning around, Major replies, "Yeah. Coach brought the tape. Get the rest of the guys."

"Bet," Jimmy bursts as he returns to the deck to get the other firstie teammates.

A brief moment later, Jimmy returns with the other firstie teammates as well as a few other underclassmen.

As Jimmy takes a seat on one of the couches, he makes a cynical remark to Major. "You watch this game every chance you get. For once, I would like to see that game where we beat Navy our plebe year in the Patriot League tournament."

Major laughs. "You want to see that because you're the only one of us who played in that game. Some of us were still living the good life down in JV."

"All the comforts of varsity with none of the stress," one of the other firstie teammates states.

Everyone in the room laughs.

Major hits the play button on the VCR. Instantly, a shot of center court appears on the television. The room grows silent in mental preparation of the game. Of course, the silence ceases after tip off.

———————————◆———————————

The guys finish watching the Duke game. Jimmy jumps up and shouts, "Man, I love that game!"

"Listen to you," Major replies. "Every time we watch this game, you make some noise about watching it before I hit play, but once it's done, you get all excited like some little schoolgirl. You're a trip, dawg."

"Yeah man!" Jimmy shouts. "I'm hungry again. I'm getting some more to eat."

Everyone in the room rises from their comfortable positions. Major gets up with his teammates and follows them out onto the deck.

Outside, Major stretches his arms up into the air and says, "Thank God it isn't too cold out yet." Relaxed and enjoying the fresh air, Major steps to the grill and grabs himself a hamburger and some ribs.

"Hey, Major!" Coach Quarter shouts from the other end of the deck. "Make sure you save some food for the rest of the team!"

Everyone laughs at Coach Quarter's remark. Major, though he is not the largest guy on the basketball team, is known for his ability to eat any and everyone under the table, especially when the food is free, like pregame meals during away games.

Coach Quarter is Coach O'Hara's head assistant and the "big man" coach, which means that during practice, Coach Quarter focuses on the center and power-forward positions. Like Coach O'Hara, Coach Quarter is a USMA graduate, except that he graduated in 1981, two years after Coach O'Hara.

Laughing, Major returns with "Don't worry, coach! I'm going to leave some food for these kids. Some of them need it a lot more than I do!" Major finishes fixing his plate and plops himself down in one of the lounge chairs in the yard.

———————————————◆——————————————◆

After hanging out at Coach O'Haras's for nearly five hours, Major walks up to Theo and says, "Hey, bro. I'm about to roll. You got enough room in the van for the guys that I brought?"

"Yeah," Theo replies. "I've got 'em."

"'Preciate it." Major gives Theo a pound then walks away toward Coach O'Hara. He then grabs Coach O'Hara by the shoulder and says, "Thanks again, Coach."

"You leaving already?" Coach asks.

"Yeah. I'm meeting some of the fellas in Hoboken."

"Ahh. Have a good time."

With a huge grin on his face, Major states, "I shall."

Coach lightly slaps Major on the back as he exits the kitchen and heads for the front door. Before he exits the house, Major shouts, "Leslie! Brian!" I'll see you guys!"

Leslie and her younger brother, Brian, rush down the stairs to see Major off.

When Leslie and Brian reach the main floor, Major then says, "Tell Jennifer I said hey."

"I will," Leslie replies. "You going to Hoboken now?"

"Yep. I'll tell you all about it when I see you next. All right?"

"Okay," Leslie responds.

"See you, Brian."

"See you, Major."

Major waves to the kids and exits the house, jogging to his 4Runner. He jumps into the driver's seat and heads for US Route 9W south. After about a ten-minute drive up and over the mountain and through the town of Fort Montgomery, Major veers onto the Palisades Parkway, heading south for New Jersey.

There are many things that Major likes. One of them is speed. He has driven on the Palisades Parkway so many times that he knows where all of the New York State troopers' hiding places are. Passing by every vehicle that he approaches, Major ensures that he slows down to five miles per hour over the speed limit whenever he approaches a possible speed trap.

■————————————————————■

Driving for a little less than half an hour, Major enters the state of New Jersey. He picks up the pace some because the New Jersey State Troopers do not monitor their portion of the Palisades Parkway as fervently as New York. After driving for about another hour along the Hudson River through several New Jersey towns and hamlets, Major finally arrives in Hoboken: Frank Sinatra's hometown.

Unless it is about four in the morning, there always seems to be some form of traffic in Hoboken. Though Major knows his way around the city like the back of his hand, he has never had an easy time driving through. Major finds himself stuck behind a bus and is unable to pass it, so he simply accepts defeat and follows behind the bus as it turns right onto Washington Street. As Major takes a right turn, his cell phone rings.

Major answers his cell phone and hears a familiar voice shout from the other end, "Hey, fool! When're you getting here?" "I just got into town," Major replies. "I'll be there in about fifteen minutes."

"Aight, brother. I'll see you when you get here. Peace!"

"Peace." Major hangs up and returns his cell phone to its usual position.

Major drives through numerous blocks and up and down several streets, becoming a bit frustrated as his search for a parking spot on the street appears to become more and more futile. Major is about ready to give up his search and park in a garage, but suddenly he discovers a parking space, one that will not cause his 4Runner to be towed away the next morning.

Major quickly maneuvers his 4Runner into the parking spot, and having successfully parallel parked, he barks and then shouts, "I am the best parallel parker in the friggin' world!"

Major gets his stuff together then places his valuable items in positions where perspective thieves will not see them. He waits for a car to pass by then quickly jumps out of his 4Runner and heads for 123 Park Avenue.

As Major approaches his destination, he reaches for his keys, which he had placed in his left pocket. Major passes a synagogue, then makes the immediate right, through a small, black, iron gate. He walks down a set of steps and is about to place his key in the keyhole when he notices that the door is already unlocked.

Major gingerly walks into the apartment and places his black Nike bag on the floor in the hallway. Hearing noises, voices, and music coming from the backyard, Major quickly makes his way there.

Major leaps through the backdoor and springs up over the set of steps that lead to the backyard. Seeing everyone, Major throws is hands up in the air and shouts, "Now the party can begin!"

The eleven people present return Major's greeting. Major knows most of the friendly crowd, but four of the girls are unknown to him. He makes his way to them and immediately introduces himself.

"Evening, ladies. I'm Milton Johnson, but my friends refer to me as Major," Major states as he lightly shakes each of their hands.

"It's nice to meet you," one of the girls responds. "We heard a lot about you already."

"Really? Well whatever you heard is probably true, depending on who you heard it from," Major replies with a smile. He then states, "I'll speak to you ladies in a bit. I have to make my rounds."

"It was nice meeting you," another of the girls says as Major moves on to another small group.

Major approaches a five-foot-eight blonde who is speaking among a small group of guys who appear to be a few years younger than her. With great affection, Major stands behind the young woman and gives her a delicate squeeze.

"Hey, babe," the young lady says in response to Major's hug.

"Hey, love," Major replies.

"Glad you finally made it."

"You know the man had to come down and see his favorite girl," Major says, winking his right eye.

Major is speaking with Ed's older sister, Melissa. Major is closer to Melissa than he his with any other girl. They talk to one another about everything. Major and Melissa are so close that she and her roommate, Alison, gave him a key to their apartment a year ago so he could come and go in their apartment as he pleases.

The first time Major met Melisa his yearling year, he attempted to impress her, but to no avail. Back then, Major was only a little boy to Melissa, being that he was twenty-one and she was twenty-five. Now she looks at Major like a little brother. Some guys cannot catch a break.

Major refers to Alison as his hero for a special reason, but he only discusses that with his closest friends and usually when there is a drink in his hand. Major appreciates all of his friendships, but the one he has with Melissa and Alison is a special one.

Ed walks up to Major and breaks up his conversation with Melissa, saying, "It's about time you got here, fool."

"My bad, trick. I had that joint at Coach's house today."

"Oh yeah. I forgot."

"I knew you weren't going to let this joint start without me, bro."

"True. True."

The two young men who are more like brothers than friends embrace.

6 OCTOBER 1999

0900 Hours: Russian Training Camp

Alex is in Colonel Drasneb's tent, going over future plans for the mission.

"So, Alex. What do you think of my two mercenaries?"

"They are very knowledgeable," Alex answers.

"That is your only assessment?"

"Of course not, sir. They are true professionals as well."

Frustrated, Colonel Drasneb asks, "What about their attitudes toward our mission?"

"Sir, everyone can see that they do not want to be here, but as I stated, they are true professionals."

Colonel Drasneb shifts in his chair and asks, "You do not think they will compromise the mission?"

"As I stated, sir, they are professionals. They may not like what they have signed up for, but they respect the contract. They will follow the mission through to the end."

"What about Douglas Pollard?"

"Mac? It is obvious that he is disgruntled about the morality of the mission, but Killer will not allow him to lose his focus."

Colonel Drasneb's eyes jump up as he sternly asks, "When did you start calling them by their code names?"

"Do to our close working relationship, Killer felt it necessary to make the environment as light as possible."

"Did he?" Colonel Drasneb shakes his head and states, "You may go now. My aide will get you when I need you again."

"Yes, sir." Alex salutes Colonel Drasneb then departs the tent.

Those bastards! Colonel Drasneb angrily says to himself. *They really think that they are smart—making nice with Alex so that he may come to sympathize with their situation. I am going to have to keep a closer eye on them as well as Alex.* Colonel Drasneb slams his right fist on his desktop as he finishes his thought.

West Point

Major returns to his room from class. He places his books on his desk, pulls his chair out from underneath the desk then takes a seat. Major turns his computer screen on and moves his mouse around to turn off the screen saver. At the bottom-right corner of the screen, Major notices an envelope, symbolizing that there is a new e-mail message in his inbox.

Major pulls up his e-mail account, expecting yet another commander-related e-mail. Much to his surprise, he does not have a commander-related e-mail. Instead, there is an e-mail from Terry.

I don't believe this, Major thinks, shocked at what his eyes see.

Major double clicks on the message line and quickly reads the e-mail. Not able to completely fathom what is occurring, Major reads the message over again to ensure that he is not delusional.

Much to Major's relief, he is not mistaken. The e-mail truly is there. At the bottom of Terry's e-mail is her telephone number. Now Major is extremely excited.

With reality having struck him in the head like a sledgehammer, Major jumps up from out of his seat and shouts, "Hell, yeah!"

1300 Hours

Colonel Wood and Major depart from Mahan Hall after an honor class that was conducted for the firsties. Colonel Wood and Major are the last to leave. Most of the firsties have to rush to class, so they are unable to take their time.

As Colonel Wood and Major walk out of Mahan Hall, Colonel Wood says, "The class of '89 is having their tenth reunion next weekend."

"Roger, sir," Major responds.

"Do you know Captain Taylor?" Colonel Wood asks. "He works in the math department."

"I think so."

"Well, he's a Duck, and he wants to wear the suit Saturday."

Major gives Colonel Wood a funny look and replies, "Huh?"

"Yeah. He wants to surprise his classmates Saturday night by wearing the Duck suit."

Shaking his head, Major answers, "Roger, sir. I'll get someone to drop it off at the house sometime before then."

Major and Colonel Wood reach the road that runs between Grant and Pershing Barracks. They turn left then stop in front of Grant Area.

"What time are you going up to the gym, man?" Colonel Wood asks.

"I'll be up top a little after two," Major answers.

"I may stop by," Colonel Wood replies. "I'll see you if I do."

"All right, sir. I'll see you."

Major salutes Colonel Wood then shakes his hand.

11 OCTOBER 1999

1115 Hours: West Point

The week of the eleventh is the beginning of what is known as Beat Air Force Week. During Beat Air Force Week, the fourth class cadets pull pranks on the air force cadets who are attending West Point for the semester. There is also a push-up contest between the two academies, which West Point always wins. Beat Air Force Week ends after the army-air force game on Saturday.

Major stands in lunch formation with his back to his company. Having received the command of "Company commanders, take charge of your units and march them to the mess hall," Major does an about-face and faces the Ducks.

Major returns his saber then shouts, "Half right, face!"

The Ducks immediately execute a half right.

Major then commands, "Front leaning rest position, move!"

When the command of "Front leaning rest position" is given, the individuals receiving the command are supposed to quickly move to the push-up position, not the Ducks.

Instead of dropping to the ground, someone in the D-1 formation shouts, "Get him!"

Instantly, the plebes fall out of ranks and rush Major. Out of reflex, Major runs away from the plebes. Being the fastest person in the company, Major is able to pull away from his overly exuberant plebes but, instead, decides to run into the right corner of Pershing Barracks. Major allows his plebes to trap him in the corner.

I could run, but what would be the fun in that? Major thinks to himself.

The plebes corner Major and then grab a hold of him and thrust him over their heads.

One of the plebes shouts, "To the mess hall!"

Carrying Major over their heads, the plebes head for the mess hall, shouting, "Bad to the bone!"

In response, Major shouts, "Go Ducks!"

Together, Major and his plebes shout, "Bad to the bone! Go Ducks!" With his plebes still holding him high in the air, Major does push-ups, while his jubilant plebes jump in the air.

Major and his highly motivated plebes walk behind Second Battalion, Second Regiment's formation. They have formation five minutes after First Regiment, so inadvertently, the Ducks are disturbing their formation. Major thinks nothing of it. He notices a few ugly and curious looks from TACs and upper class cadets alike. Major pays them no mind. He is on a natural high in how much motivation his plebes are displaying.

When the jovial Ducks reach the steps of the mess hall, instead of placing Major on the ground, they throw him into the air three times.

With Major's feet safely on the ground, the plebes shout at the top of their lungs, "We own the pond, sir!"

"Hell yeah, we do!"

13 OCTOBER 1999

1914 Hours: West Point

Major sits on his couch, going through some paperwork that Captain Weiss had left for him in his inbox. Most of the paperwork is relatively unimportant information that Major can quickly and easily disseminate down to his first sergeant and executive officer, except for the memo on the current window-policy issue, but he will deal with that one later. Major drops the papers that are in his hand onto the table then grabs another stack of papers that is full of nothing but Article 10s (cadet delinquency reports) and flips through them rather rapidly. He gets up and walks the three-foot distance across the hall to his first sergeant's room.

"Hey, Dusty! These kids are coming over tonight for counseling, right?" Major asks as he waves the Article 10s in the air.

"Yes, they are, but I'll send them another e-mail, just in case."

"Cool."

As Major leaves, he sees one of the delinquent cadets walking down the hall.

"You're coming down to my room, right?" Major rhetorically asks.

"Yes, I am," the cadet responds.

Major enters his room, followed by the cadet. Major directs the cadet toward the couch as he sits in his desk chair.

"As you know," Major begins, "I have the PLs do most of the counseling for the Article 10s, but because of the nature of your offense, I decided to handle it myself. First, let's get all of the formalities out of the way."

Major reads the Article 10 to the delinquent cadet, Cdt. Cpl. John Morgan. Major asks Cadet Corporal Morgan if he wishes to appeal, but Morgan declines. Major then has him sign the Article 10.

Major sits back in his chair then leans forward, saying, "Morgan, this is not the first time your chain of command has had a problem with you in terms of respect. I like you. I think you're a great kid, but you need to learn to control what you say, how you say it, who you say it to, and, most importantly, when you say it. I know that you're prior service time and status as a ranger puts you head over heals over most cadets, but at the same time, you are still a third class cadet, and as such, you have to bite your upper lip sometimes and learn to take orders. You don't have to like your chain of command or even respect them as people, but you need to respect their rank and position. Put yourself in their position. You wouldn't want someone telling you off if you gave them an order. Would you?"

"No, I wouldn't."

"Exactly. Now I've already spoken to your platoon leader and platoon sergeant, and we've agreed that five hours of walking tours is sufficient enough of a punishment for your mistake. If you want to really make things better, you should go to your squad leader and apologize for what you said to her. You know what I'm saying?"

"Yeah."

"I hope so. You have anything to say?"

"Not really. It just bugs me that I have kids younger than me bossing me around. I have more military knowledge than some of them will ever have."

"I know you do, but what you need to do, if anything, is share that knowledge with people. That way, your chain of command will see that you care about your classmates and that the betterment of the company really means something to you. It's all about impressions."

"Yeah, I know. It's just frustrating sometimes."

"I know, but you've got to fight through it."

"I'll try."

"No. If you try, then you're already setting yourself up for failure. Think about it. If you try to do something, then you already know that there is a good chance that you'll fail at whatever it is you're attempting

15 OCTOBER 1999

1145 Hours: West Point

The entire class of 2000 convenes in Roscoe Robinson Auditorium. Robinson auditorium was known as South Auditorium up until Major's firstie year, when it was christened with its current name. Robinson Auditorium is dedicated in memory of Gen. Roscoe Robinson, a West Point graduate and the first black four-star general in the United States army.

Whenever the cadets meet in Robinson auditorium during commandant's hour, it is always for a speech or lecture of some sort. Nine times out of ten, the cadets are unaware as to who is going to speak. One thing is for sure though; a lot of napping, side talking, and homework doing will occur, no matter how important the speaker, even the president of the United States.

Major walks down to Robinson auditorium with a small group of friends. As he enters, he says his good-byes and heads for his company's area. During all lectures, the companies have to sit with one another; it is how higher is able to track accountability. Most cadets would skip a lecture if they had a chance in order to sleep. The brigade tactical department is highly aware of this fact.

Major and Joe make eye contact as Major heads for D-1's area. Joe waves Major in, signaling that he has a seat saved for him.

Major squeezes through the aisles and plops down in his seat. "Who's speaking today?" Major asks Joe, as he gets comfortable in his seat.

"I'm not sure. Some general, I think."

"Cool," Major replies, slouching in his seat until his knees are up against the seat in front of him.

While Major impatiently waits for the lecture to begin, Joe is busy accounting for all of the D-1 firsties.

Having completed one of his most hated tasks, Joe informs Major, "We've got everyone. They're not all sitting with us, but they're in here."

"Works for me," Major responds.

Joe sits down and waits as well.

With about ten minutes having past, the brigade commander steps out to the bottom middle of Robinson auditorium. Seeing his friend walk out, Major sits up in his seat, aware that everyone in attendance is about to stand to their feet.

The brigade commander faces his classmates and loudly commands, "On your feet!"

The entirety of Robinson auditorium rises to its feet and stands at the position of attention.

From the far left, a four-star general enters the auditorium. He walks over to the brigade commander and, out of earshot of everyone in Robinson auditorium, says something to him. The brigade commander salutes the general then takes his seat.

The general faces the standing crowd and says, "Everyone take your seats."

Everyone in the room quickly returns to their seated positions.

"How's everyone doing today?" the general asks.

No one really responds. The general laughs. Many of the cadets throw odd looks at one another, wondering why the general is laughing.

"A long time ago, when I was cadet, I sat right where you all are sitting right now, and the guest lecturer would always say, 'I'm going to be as brief as possible.' You know what? They never were, so here is my promise to you. I may not be brief, but I will stop speaking once I have lost your attention. Is that fair?" A large hoo-ha fills the auditorium.

Once the jubilation decreases, the general continues. "I am Gen. Michael Schultz. I have been told that I am supposed to speak to you all about leadership." General Schultz raises his head up and says, "Turn the screen on." The screen turns on and a giant classic army basketball team picture appears. "You see that guy down there, bottom row, fourth from the left?" General Schultz asks the crowd. "I graduated three years after that guy. You know who he is?"

Many scattered yes fill the auditorium.

"That's Coach Mike K, the head coach at Duke." General Schultz looks up again and says, "You can turn it off now." Returning his focus to the firsties, and with a grin on his face, General Schultz says, "I just wanted to show you guys that."

General Schultz begins to slowly pace from one end of Robinson auditorium to the other. Having seen the 1969 army basketball team picture strikes Major's interest. He sits up in his seat in anticipation of General Schultz's next set of words.

"Let me tell you all a little about myself," General Schultz says. "I am currently the commander of US forces in Korea. That simply means that I am the military leader of all military personnel located in South Korea. It's a good job. I like it." The crowd laughs.

"I am a '72 grad. I was not the smartest guy in the world, but I was a hell of a football player. For some strange reason, West Point thought I could make it academically, so I was recruited to play football. I started my last three years and was an All-American my firstie year."

General Schultz's words spark everyone's attention. He now has all of the firsties under his spell as he had planned.

"Let me tell you what leadership is all about," General Schultz continues. "It all boils down to one word—love. You have to love your soldiers more than you love yourself. Everything you do as a leader, you have to do to make your soldiers' lives better. One way you can make your soldiers' lives better is by not wasting their time.

"When I took over as the CG (commanding general) at Ft. Hood, units were rolling out to the field on a Wednesday and rolling back in on a Sunday or a Monday. During the weekdays, no real training was occurring. When I noticed this trend among all of my units, I asked the commanders why. None of them had a logical answer. You know what I did to remedy that situation? I disallowed all field-training exercises on weekends. Why? Because the soldiers need their weekends. It's the only time when they're able to do what they want and truly relax. You take that away from them, and their morale quickly disintegrates.

The only time I allowed a unit to train on a weekend was if they were prepping for a deployment or an NTC (National Training Center) rotation."

Major excitingly elbows Joe in the ribs several times in the ribs. "He's saying just how I think. It's all about the love."

"I hear you, man," Joe replies.

General Schultz continues his lecture. "The second change I made was creating a family day on Thursdays. Every Thursdays, soldiers are released from work at 1400 hours, in order to spend time with their families. This also allows the single soldiers to handle any business that they may have. I instituted this policy because every day, soldiers were going home at five, even six o'clock at night. When a soldier gets home at that time of the day, he hardly has any time to spend with his family. You will learn that if your soldiers' families are happy, then your soldiers are happy. This all makes for a cohesive unit because everyone's morale is high. If the home life is unpleasant, then there is a chance of your unit losing a certain level of its cohesiveness."

Still excited, Major says to Joe, "I want to work for this guy. It's like he's reading my mind or something."

"It's more like you're reading his," Joe rebuts.

"Very funny," Major replies.

Major and Joe silently converse on General Schultz's leadership philosophy, Joe continuously striking Major's every word.

With nearly an hour having passed, General Schultz says, "Well, I believe I have taken up enough of your time. I will see you all at the game tomorrow. Beat Southern Miss!"

16 OCTOBER 1999

0745 Hours: West Point

It is an early Saturday morning. A slight chill is in the air from the wind flowing down the Hudson River. The sun pushes its way through the cloudy sky, causing a pinkish hue to emanate over the horizon. Today is the perfect day for tourists to visit West Point. Then again, every day is a perfect day for tourists to visit West Point. The beautiful array of pastel colors in the sky alone makes for a great backdrop for any picture. Most of the cadets do not appreciate the lovely scenery that envelops them. When one sees beauty every day, he becomes accustomed to it and thus no longer appreciates it.

With today being a Saturday, West Point is going to be very busy, full of more tourists, family, friends, and, most importantly and enthusiastically, army football fans. Two public events occur on home football game Saturdays. Those are double regimental parades followed by an exciting football game. The stands at the parades are always full of tourists who are eager and intrigued by the aura that the United States Military Academy ensues and the family and friends of those cadets who are marching in that day's parade. March on for the parades usually commences at 1030 hours. After the parades, the other two regiments that did not parade march onto the football field and support the army team. The stands of Michie Stadium are always packed with enthusiastic fans and those cadets who marched on, all of whom represent the twelfth man.

For those few cadets who are members of the men's varsity basketball team, the thoughts of a Saturday morning do not ring with the enthusiasm of a parade or a football game, though many of them love football. To the basketball team, Saturday means morning practice, plain and simple. This Saturday is not any ordinary Saturday for the basketball team though. Today is their first official NCAA-sanctioned practice.

Major and three of his four firstie teammates, cadets Jimmy Hazel, Henry Lindbergh, and Martin Rowser, walk to the Holleder Center for their first official basketball practice of the year. Most major Division I universities have what is referred to as Midnight Madness, which marks the beginning of the official NCAA basketball season. The first practice is christened Midnight Madness because the practices are held at midnight and is viewed by a very large and spirited crowd.

During Midnight Madness, the basketball team runs through their drills and shows off to their fans and the media. Because West Point has taps at 2330 hours every weeknight and Sundays, the army basketball team is unable to have Midnight Madness, much to the dismay of the players, their fans, and the corps. In place of Midnight Madness, the NCAA allows the army basketball team to have double-session practices the Saturday prior to the official season, the first at 0830 hours and the second at 1400 hours.

The team has really been looking forward to the season getting under way. There was a time when a part of them dreaded the season beginning, but this year is different. This is the year that they go to the tournament. They have three returning starters and five seniors on the squad. Last year, the team finished fifth in the Patriot League with an overall record of 15–15. The last time an army basketball team went .500 in a season was during the 1985–1986 season when army's all-time leading scorer, Kevin Houston, was playing.

The defeats that the team suffered last year were relatively close. The greatest margin of defeat was by twenty-five to Duke. The score does not tell the true story of that game. Though Duke won decisively in terms of points on the board, those who watched the game know the true story. Duke earned every point that day. Army played one of the best games that they have played in a long time. During the first half, Army could not get their shots to fall, and were unable to work the ball down low. Army's leading scorer, power forward Jimmy Hazel, was only three for ten from the floor. The rest of the team did not fare well either. Major could not get into position to rebound and was smothered offensively, causing him to only shoot the ball five times. At the end of the first half, Duke led 36–15. The only thing that held Army's pride intact was their intense defense. Duke had to toil for every point scored.

The second half was another story all together. Coach O'Hara gave his team an intense, motivating speech that churned the blood of everyone in the locker room, including the managers who are always ready to play. When Army hit the floor to begin the second half, they maintained their same level of high intensity at the defensive end, but this time, they were able to incorporate their offense into the game. At the close of the game, Duke only outscored Army by four points. Though they lost, the army men's basketball team knew that they had just proven to the world that they were a squad that the world should not underestimate.

Major, Jimmy, Martin, and Henry walk together, very enthusiastic about their upcoming practice. They cross the street and walk with Lusk Reservoir to their left.

Lusk Reservoir is a part of West Point knowledge. All fourth class cadets are required to know how many gallons of water it holds—twenty-eight million when the spillway flows over. The slight chill in the air has caused the fog to flow over Lusk and off onto the road that is to the right of where the four teammates stroll. The fog is so thick that they are unable to see the water within the reservoir's walls.

Major, Jimmy, Henry, and Martin veer left around a slight bend, then cross the street toward Michie Stadium. Standing at the back gate in the direction of their path stand the MPs (military police) who are working today's football game. During home football games, the MPs are tasked with the responsibility of ensuring that traffic moves as smooth as possible and that the fans and pedestrians move from one place to another in a calm manner. The MPs are preparing for their accountability formation. While on game-day duty, the MPs are required to wear their class A uniform with highly spit-shined boots with laces. The MPs do not like this uniform; then again neither do many other soldiers too. When they reach the other side of the street, Major greets some of the MPs that are somewhat separated from the larger group. They return his greeting with a head nod.

The MPs get a bad reputation from the Corps of Cadets. Because the MPs are forced to do their job, they are required to not respect rank, status, or privilege; some cadets become upset when the MPs do their job, like enforcing rules and regulations that cadets do not follow. The MPs are not rude while performing their duties, but they are definitely stern and firm. They have to be when dealing with America's future leaders.

Passing the MPs, the four teammates walk to the far end of Michie Stadium. When they get to the intersection, they turn right and stride up a slight incline. At the top of the small hill, they cross the street and head toward the Holleder Center, home to both the men's and women's basketball teams and the ice hockey team. The basketball teams play in Crystal Arena, and the hockey team plays in Tate Rink.

The four firsties spring up the Holleder Center stairs to the far right doors of the main entrance of the sports arena. Just as Martin reaches for the door handle, Jimmy throws his right leg out and kicks the big, blue, square handicap button that is on the wall next to the doors. Automatically, the doors slowly swing open, and the four teammates commence entering the Holleder Center.

Before they can enter though, Martin slaps Jimmy on the chest, looks at him, and says, "Come on, man! What'd I tell you about using that button?"

"You're using it too, aren't you?" Jimmy defends himself.

"That's not the point, nut."

"Sure it is. When's the last time you saw a handicapped person use this door. I figure, if it's here, we might as well use it. It's not like we're taking anything away from the handicapped by using these doors."

Frustrated, Martin throws his hands in the air and replies, "Ah, who cares. Let's just get inside and get ready for practice."

Martin ends his and Jimmy's pointless conversation because he knows that he is not going to be able to convince Jimmy to realize his point of view.

Jimmy, in celebration of yet another verbal victory, jumps on Martin's back and shouts, "Come on, Marty Mar. Don't be mad, dawg.

You know I'm right. It's like the old folks say, 'If you don't use God's gifts, baby, he's gonna take 'em away.' And that means this door too."

"You're crazy, nut!" Martin responds as he carries Jimmy into the Holleder Center.

Following Jimmy and Martin, Major and Henry enter the Holleder Center, laughing at another one of Jimmy and Martin's regular tetes.

Waiting for the four firsties in the front lobby is one of their assistant basketball coaches, Coach Chris Townson.

As soon as Coach Townson spots the four firsties, he boasts, "Hey, fellas. Big day today! You guys ready?"

"Hell yes, coach!" Jimmy boasts. "This is the year when we make miracles happen."

Coach Townson shakes his head and smiles. "You guys make me happy to be a coach. Before you go to the back, Coach wants to see you in his office."

"This should be good," Henry states.

Before heading off to Coach O'Hara's office, Henry, Major, and Martin give Coach Townson dap as they pass him by. They then turn right, round a corner, and walk down a hallway.

Jimmy, with all of his crazy ways, slaps Coach Townson in the butt and shouts, "Woo! I hope you're ready for practice, Coach!" Jimmy then runs around the corner and catches up with his teammates.

Coach Townson jumps slightly and responds, "What am I going to do with you, nut?" He laughs to himself and returns to his office to prepare for practice with the other two assistant coaches.

The four firsties stand in front of Coach O'Hara's door and make funny faces through the window slit on the left side of his door. They could easily just walk in, but they have more fun messing with Coach than just acting normal, whatever that is. Coach O'Hara, noticing his team leaders acting a fool outside of his door, waves them in.

As Major, Jimmy, Henry, and Martin enter, Coach O'Hara says, "You knuckleheads can have a seat over there."

Coach points to a couch and two empty chairs. Facing the couch, on the far right side sits the team captain, Derrick Tucker.

"'Sup, fellas? I just got here a few minutes ago," Derrick states.

"Sure you did," Jimmy sarcastically remarks.

He plops himself down beside Derrick, squishing him up against the side of the couch. In response to Jimmy's actions, Derrick turns in his seat, gives Jimmy a big hug, and proclaims, "I love you, nut!"

"The feeling is mutual, brother," Jimmy responds.

Henry and Martin sit on the couch with Jimmy and Derrick, and Major takes the seat that is closest to the couch. Once the firsties are all seated, Coach O'Hara rises from behind his desk and pulls up a chair beside his team leaders. In his hands, Coach O'Hara holds a Nike folder and a ballpoint pin.

"So are we ready to get the season started right?" Coach opens.

Jimmy leans forward and answers, "What kind of question is that, Coach? You know we're ready."

"Yeah, Coach," Derrick chimes in. "As far as we're concerned, if we don't get to the tournament this year, then all of our hard work was for nothing."

"That's good to hear," Coach O'Hara approvingly responds. "I know that that is how all of you feel. I just needed to hear it one more time before we got things under way."

Major turns in his seat and faces Coach O'Hara. Assuredly, he states, "Coach this is your third year as our head coach and for the first time, all you're going to have to worry about is coaching us to victory. If a player gets out of hand or goofs off during practice, be assured that we will handle it on the spot. This season, we're all about business because it's as Jimmy and Derrick said, 'If we don't get to the tournament this year, then we have failed,' and in this case, failure is unacceptable." Major finishes his mini monologue by leaning forward and slapping Coach O'Hara on the knee.

"All right, fellas, I'm going to hold you to that," Coach O'Hara affirms. "You guys are this team's leaders, and I expect nothing less than the best from you five. I know that this season is going to be a success. All you have to do is execute properly, and we can go as far as you lead us. Now get the hell out of here and get ready for practice."

"All right, Coach," the five firsties reply, all with huge grins plastered on their faces.

They leap from their seats and shuffle out of Coach O'Hara's office and head straight for the locker room to join the rest of their teammates for practice.

Russian Training Camp

Killer and Mac stand alone in an open area. Neither man says much to one another. They are merely enjoying the silence and the occasional wisp of air that passes by. Killer stands with his hands in his pocket, Mac with his arms crossed, as he likes to do whenever he is in thought. Not much is on Killer's mind. He likes to use the early morning to clear his head of any interfering thoughts that may cause him to lose focus during a day's work. Mac, he simply likes to watch the sunrise. The artist in him is mesmerized by the color scheme that the sky displays as the sun passes over it during the early morning.

Enjoying their comfortable silence, Colonel Drasneb silently creeps behind them. Mac and Killer are aware of Colonel Drasneb's presence but do not acknowledge him. Colonel Drasneb stands behind Mac and Killer and simply watches them. He too does not say a word. Instead, Colonel Drasneb allows the two mercenaries to carry on as though he were not present, which is how Mac and Killer would act anyway.

Having stood speechless for nearly ten minutes, Colonel Drasneb breaks the silence by saying, "I too like the sunrise."

Without moving to face Colonel Drasneb, Killer replies, "I'm pretty indifferent, myself."

"Then why come out here?" Colonel Drasneb inquires.

"Because this is the quietest time of the day. Nature is still asleep. Only in complete silence can one truly hear God," Killer replies.

Colonel Drasneb is rather intrigued by Killer's response. He was unsure as to how Killer would reply to his question, but he definitely was not expecting the answer that he received.

Colonel Drasneb turns his attention to Mac and asks, "So what brings you out here, Mr. Pollard?"

Mac, still standing stoic with his arms crossed, does not acknowledge Colonel Drasneb's question. Instead, Killer answers for him. "He likes the colors."

"The colors?" Colonel Drasneb replies. Again he is taken aback. "How do you mean?" Colonel Drasneb asks.

"Big Mac's an artist. He's actually pretty good," Killer states for his friend.

Mac does not speak because he makes it a point to only speak to Colonel Drasneb about the job, nothing more.

"Not to take you gentlemen away from your quiet time, I came up here to discuss how the training has gone to date," Colonel Drasneb states.

Mac unfolds his arms and turns around. Now facing Colonel Drasneb, Mac asks, "What in particular do you want to discuss?"

"The progress of my men, of course."

"Well," Killer opens, turning around in mid-speech, "the men are grasping the military tasks very well—a lot faster than I had assumed. Being that Mac and I have never trained with Serb soldiers before, we weren't sure how to assess their progress prior to coming out here."

With a huge smile on his face, Colonel Drasneb replies, "We are a lot more superior than others give us credit for."

"On the cultural side of the house," Killer continues, "some of your guys are hurting. It's understandable though. Very few of them have been exposed to English or American culture, whatever the hell that is. My advice to you, and what I'm going to tell them in our next class, is that they should not speak at all once we get to the US."

"That is all fine and good," Colonel Drasneb comments, "but what are you two doing to remedy the situation?"

"First, sir, there is no situation. Second, we are focusing on short phrases and fragments and body language that will get them by. You need to remember, Colonel, we're not trying to pass them off as US citizens, only tourists. Fluency is not the goal, immersion is."

Colonel Drasneb stands and ponders upon Killer's words. "I guess you are correct once again, Mr. Stewart. That is all I had to speak of this morning. Enjoy the silence." Colonel Drasneb takes two steps back and walks away from the two mercenaries.

As Colonel Drasneb departs, Mac replies, "We will."

1015 Hours: West Point

"Whew!" Jimmy shouts as he enters the locker room. "That had to be the most intense practice ever!"

"You say that every time we do loose ball drills," Martin comments.

"That's true, nut," Henry agrees as he sits down in front of his locker.

The remainder of the team slowly enters the locker room as the three firsties continue with their conversation. None of the players are in much of a rush. They are all extremely tired. The first practice of the year is always a tough one. It also does not help them any that Coach O'Hara does not believe in holding anything back. During practice, the players must go game speed at all times, or else. Discovering what "or else" is is never a good thing.

As the players take their time getting undressed, Theo enters the locker room and says, "You fools need to hurry up. They're asking for you out at the tailgate."

Jimmy jumps up from his seat and shouts, "Ah man! How could I forget!" He then proceeds to rush into the shower.

"The rest of you need to follow suit," Theo says to the team in response to Jimmy's reaction.

The tailgate in which Theo refers to is the Class of 1955's tailgate, the most prominent and featured tailgate during army football games. The reason Theo is rushing the players out to the '55 tailgate is because it is officially the army men's basketball tailgate. Mr. Herbie Lichtenburgh of the Class of '55 sponsors the tailgate. He pays for everything. The men's basketball managers provide the labor; they setup the tailgate while the team practices. Over the years, the women's basketball team as well as both tennis teams and the ice hockey teams have been invited to the Class of '55 tailgate, but as far as the men's basketball team is concerned it is still their tailgate, and they are not afraid to let certain cadets know that.

No one is quite sure as to why the tailgate is so popular. Lieutenant General Holiday makes it a point to bring all of his special guests and VIPs to the Class of '55 tailgate with their appetites still intact. The tailgate's popularity may stem from its location: the front of the Holleder Center across the street from Michie Stadium. Also, the food is incredible. Mr. Lichtenburgh does not play around when selecting his meat for his tailgates. There is nothing the players love more than an all-you-can-eat selection of prime rib, chicken breast, Italian sausage, hamburgers, and hot dogs. For the players, the tailgate is a hearty brunch and a well-deserved reward for a hard day's practice.

Back in the locker room, Major stands in front of his locker, impatiently waiting for Jimmy. Major is not a very patient individual. There are not too many things he hates, but waiting on slow people is definitely one of them.

"You know, if you move any slower, time's going to stop," Major sarcastically says to Jimmy.

"I'm going as fast as I can," Jimmy states, slipping his size 16 feet into his low quarters.

"We go through this every time. I don't know why the hell I wait for you."

"'Cause you love me, brother!"

"If you say so, chump. All I know is you need to hurry the hell up. The rest of the team's almost out there."

"I'm coming. I'm coming."

"I don't understand how you can be the first one in the shower and the last one out."

"Someone's got to look good for the ladies. It may as well be me. Besides, you can't rush perfection."

"Fool, please. I've got your perfection right here." Major waves his left fist in front of his face.

Jimmy jokingly throws his hands in his face and cowers, "Oh! Please don't hurt me."

Major slaps Jimmy's hands, saying, "Man, hurry the hell up!"

Jimmy finishes tying his shoes then shouts, "Ready!"

"It's about friggin' time," Major responds, leading the way out of the locker room.

Major and Jimmy walk down the hallway, passing the training room and the side entrance to Crystal Arena. They exit the hallway through a door that leads them to the Holleder Center front lobby. Approaching the main entrance, Major lightly punches the enlarged silver square that automatically opens the handicap doors. As Jimmy and Major pass through the doors, they laugh, remembering the morning's jovial altercation between Martin and Jimmy.

Stepping outside, Jimmy and Major walk onto the set of the *Army Radio Show*. The host, who just so happens to be the head of sports media at West Point, Eugene Macintosh, waves to Jimmy and Major while he is on the air. Major and Jimmy return the salutation.

The two friends stride past the radio booth and are immediately confronted by a small crowd that is watching the West Point pep band perform and the cheerleaders cheer. Though many of the cheerleaders are friends of Major, he does not care too much for them in their cheerleading capacity. Personally, he feels as though cheerleaders are a waste and are useless. The band, as most cadets would agree, needs much work in terms of song selection and loudness. It never fails that at every Army–Navy basketball game at Crystal, if one closes his eyes, they would swear that they were at Navy because their band greatly overpowers Army's

While on the move through the small crowd, Major and Jimmy acknowledge a few of their friends as well as some of their friends' parents. Out of the crowd, the two friends turn left and pass through the tailgate entrance, which is manned by two plebe managers.

Jimmy and Major say "What's up, fellas?" to the plebes as they move from one small crowd to an even larger one.

"We've got to get some eats. Follow me," Jimmy states as he makes his way through the thick crowd. Major follows close behind as though he was a tailback and Jimmy a fullback.

As Jimmy and Major make their way through the crowd, Major comments, "This joint gets more crowded every year."

"You're telling me," Jimmy agrees. "I feel like I'm going to step on somebody. I'm glad I'm one of the tallest ones out here. It must suck to be you."

"Forget you, punk! You got jokes, huh?"

"Don't I always?"

Major laughs.

Jimmy leads Major to the back of the line where they have to wait for their food. Slowly, the two friends make their way down the line to the front. Jimmy grabs both him and Major a paper plate and hands Major his.

Jimmy fills his plate up with a sausage sandwich, two chicken sandwiches, a prime rib sandwich, and a hot dog. Major follows suit by getting a sausage sandwich, chicken sandwich, prime rib sandwich, and a hamburger. Jimmy and Major are not hungry; they just like to eat. As Major tells some people, "Eating's a hobby for me."

"Man, it's too crowded up in here," Jimmy comments, scanning the area for a somewhat clear spot to eat.

"Let's go over there," Major decides, pointing out an area near the rear of the tailgate entrance.

Major leads Jimmy to the clearing where they are able to eat in relative peace. It is still crowded where they stand, but they can at least swing their arms without hitting anyone. The only people within Jimmy and Major's space are some of the members of the women's basketball team and a couple of their recruits.

While Major and Jimmy enjoy their food, a strong hand presses down on both of their shoulders. The two friends turn around to discover that it is Colonel Wood.

"Hey, sir!" Major and Jimmy exclaim.

"How was practice?" Colonel Wood asks.

Instead of answering, Major sighs and looks up at Colonel Wood, shaking his head.

Colonel Wood laughs at Major's response. "It couldn't have been that bad." Colonel Wood states.

"Sir, we had to do loose-ball drills," Jimmy intercedes.

"Man! Coach isn't playing around this year, huh?"

"You're telling me, sir," Jimmy pouts. "We usually don't do loose-ball drills until after the fourth loss or so. Last time I checked, we haven't even played a game yet!"

"You puss!" Major says.

Colonel Wood laughs again. He then says, "I want you guys to meet someone."

Colonel Wood turns away for a brief moment and returns with a very familiar-looking general.

"Mike," Colonel Wood opens, "these are two of my number 1 guys, Major and Jimmy."

"Major, Jimmy, it's nice to meet you," the general says, extending his hand out. Jimmy and Major take their turn grasping the general's hand.

"It's a pleasure to meet you, sir" Major replies, somewhat shocked that he is meeting his new favorite army leader, Gen. Mike Schultz.

"The pleasure's all mine, Major" General Schultz retorts. "Mike told me how you looked out for him last year."

"Roger, sir. He was getting some unneeded attention, and some of the upperclassmen were messing with him solely because he's a football player. I hate that more than anything."

General Schultz laughs. "I know what you mean." He then turns is attention to Jimmy and says, "So Woody here tells me that you're going to lead this team to the tournament this year."

"That's right, sir. I know you're a football player and all, sir, but it's about time army basketball gets the same recognition as the football team. We're going to do that this season."

"I hope you're right," General Schultz adds.

"There's no hoping about it, sir. It's going to get done."

Major shakes his head in agreement.

As the four gentlemen continue their conversation, Lieutenant General Holiday enters the Class of '55 tailgate, along with his wife and another general that Major and Jimmy are unable to identify. Lieutenant General Holiday spots General Schultz among the crowd, which is not too hard due to his, Colonel Wood's, and Jimmy statures, and makes his way to the group.

Joining the small group, Lieutenant General Holiday says, "General Schultz, sir, how are you today?"

General Schultz shakes Lieutenant General Holiday's hand, saying, "Not too bad, Chris. Great day for a football game. Wouldn't you agree?"

"The only thing that would make the day better is an army victory," Lieutenant General Holiday chimes.

Everyone nods their heads in agreement.

"Jimmy, Major, how're you guys doing?" Lieutenant General Holiday asks, acknowledging the two cadets. "I'm looking forward to the season. This is the year, right?"

Jimmy takes a step toward Lieutenant General Holiday and boasts, "Let me put it to you this way, sir. We're going to make the upcoming season so incredible that when it's all over and you're no longer the supe, you're going to look back at the 1999–2000 basketball season and know that this was the reason why you decided to become superintendent of the military academy."

Major shakes his head at his friend's antics. "You're silly, man," Major softly states.

"I'm going to hold you to that, Jimmy," Lieutenant General Holiday smilingly replies, giving Jimmy a pound.

While the gentlemen converse, Lieutenant General Holiday's aide approaches and politely says, "Sir, it's time for us to get going."

"Thanks, Tom," Lieutenant General Holiday replies. He then says to the group, "I've got to get going. I'll see everyone at the game."

"See you, sir," Jimmy and Major happily state as Lieutenant General Holiday and his small entourage leave the tailgate and heads for Michie Stadium.

1915 Hours

Major has finished his second practice of the day and has returned to his room totally exhausted. Too tired to jump up onto his bunk, Major flops his body on the couch to rest. Realizing the time, Major sits up and changes into a pair of jeans and a casual sweater. Slowly, he slips on his brown Timberland boots, grabs his Chicago Bears baseball cap, and exits his room.

Major steps outside and is hit with a slight chill from the wind. He is not entirely cold, but he sticks his hands in his pockets anyway to warm himself up some. Major crosses Grant Area then walks through Central Area. He quickly passes through the Normandy sally port of Eisenhower Barracks then turns left, passing the mess hall and approaching MacArthur Barracks. Major turns left into the first sally port of Mac and enters the door to his right.

Relieved of the cold and a new sense of warmth streaming through his body, Major removes his hands from his pockets. In full stride, Major heads down the hallway and exits the building, entering yet another sally port. Walking outside for only a brief moment, Major reenters MacArthur Barracks at the other end of the second Mac sally port and strides down toward the near end of the hallway. Major faces right at a door and enters the bedroom.

"You ready yet?" Major asks as he bursts into the room.

"You sure do like to make an entrance, don't you?" JT asks as he stands up from behind his desk.

"You know it!" Major exclaims. "You ready?"

"Yeah. You sure it's cool for us to go over there?"

"How many times do I have to tell you? The Woods are like family to me. I go over there even when they're not home. Plus, I already told Mrs. Wood that I was bringing you guys by, so you have to go now."

"I guess so."

"You guessed right. Now let's get going."

JT and Major leave JT's room and head upstairs to the fifth floor. They turn left and head for the corner of the hallway. Major and JT face the room to their right. JT attempts to knock, but Major simply opens the door.

"You ready to roll, Patty?" Major asks as he bursts into the room.

"Sure am, boy. Let's go," Pat replies.

Pat grabs his jacket from off of his bed and follows Major and JT out of his room.

"Let's take the elevator," JT suggests.

"We can't," Pat answers. "It's not working."

"Again?" JT inquires.

"Yeah," Pat replies.

"That joker's never working," Major adds. "Someone got stuck in that bad boy when I was in STAP two years ago."

Pat leads his two friends down the stairs and out the nearest door. Side by side, the three friends walk across the street from the superintendent and commandant quarters. They have to walk on that side because it is against USCC regulations for cadets to walk alongside the superintendent and commandant quarters. Major has never heard of anyone getting in trouble for doing so, but why take the chance?

Once Major, JT, and Pat pass the commandant's quarters, they turn left then take the immediate right, passing behind the Dean's quarters. They walk past two houses before making their way to the Woods'. Major leads them into the house. Entering into the kitchen, Major, JT, and Pat are bombarded by several people, none of whom Major knows or recognizes.

Standing at the kitchen entrance for a brief moment, Major leads Pat and JT into the dining room. They approach the dining room table, which is covered with food, and take a plate. Major fills his plate full of food. Pat and JT follow Major's lead.

As the three cadets eat in silence, Major does another quick scan of the house. The Woods' home is filled with numerous early-thirties-year-old men and women. Major, Pat, and JT do not know anyone, so they keep to themselves while they continue eating.

With his back turned from the people, a familiar voice sneaks up behind Major and says, "I'm glad to see you made it," Mrs. Wood says to Major as she places a plate of chicken wings onto the dining room table. "So," Mrs. Wood continues, "who are your friends?"

"Ma'am, this is JT Roberts and Patrick Lewis. They're on the football team."

"Oh. I thought your names sounded familiar," Mrs. Wood replies.

"Where's Colonel Wood, ma'am?" Major asks.

"He's out with General Schultz. I'm not really sure when they'll be back. If you wait long enough, you may be able to catch them."

"Maybe," Major replies. "We're going down to the Firstie Club to watch some football a little later."

"Well, if you miss them, I'll let them know that you stopped by."

"I appreciate it, ma'am."

Mrs. Wood squeezes Major's hand in acknowledgment.

JT places his plate down on to the table and says, "Thank you for having us over, ma'am."

"It's not a problem," Mrs. Wood answers. "Any friend of Major's is welcomed here. Make yourselves at home."

"Yes, ma'am," JT and Pat sound off.

Mrs. Wood returns to the kitchen. Pat and Major return to eating. JT, on the other hand, retrieves his plate from off the dining room table and decides to walk off and intermingle among the crowd.

"You've got to love JT," Pat states.

"You're telling me," Major replies.

"You can't take that boy anywhere without him talking to complete strangers."

"That's for sure," Major agrees.

While JT mingles, Pat and Major stick to themselves as they eat their food and discuss the day's hard-earned victory over the University of Southern Mississippi. As Pat and Major eat and converse, four men walk up to them and form a larger group.

One of the gentlemen, who is happily intoxicated, steps between Major and Pat and asks, "Who are you?"

Major looks at the gentleman and says, "Sir, I'm Milton Johnson, and this is my friend Pat Lewis."

"Are you guys Ducks?" the gentleman asks.

"Pat was a Duck his plebe and yuck years. I'm currently the Duck commander."

"Get out of here!" the gentleman shrieks, clearly excited from what he has just heard. He then shouts, "Hey everyone, it's the new Duck-6!"

Everyone in the house turns and faces Major. They then raise their beers in the air in recognition of Major being the commander of Company D-1.

Russian Training Camp

Alex, Killer, Mac, and Colonel Drasneb sit around a table, discussing some of the particulars of training. Every evening, after dinner, the four men meet to brief one another on how training transpired for the day and to impart any information that may make the mission more successful. During the training meetings, Mac rarely, if ever, says a word. He makes it perfectly clear that he is disgruntled over the entire situation.

"Training was okay, today," Killer opens. "No one did anything spectacular, but at the same time, no one did anything stupid either. The men are progressing on schedule."

Colonel Drasneb nods his head in approval of Killer's report.

Alex opens a notebook and flips through a few pages. Gathering his notes, Alex states, "I have finalized the plan on how we are going to ship our weapons."

"I've got to hear this," Killer comments.

Showing somewhat of a sign of interest, Mac sits up in his chair and moves closer to the table.

"As you all know, establishing different forms of credit is quite simple," Alex states.

Mac and Killer nod their heads in recognition of Alex's statement. They know from personal experience—having to create several aliases to execute some of their contracts; this one included.

Alex continues. "I have created three that I have used to purchase the weapons and ammunition that we will need to perform the mission. I went online to three different arms dealers' sites and ordered the weapons. They will be ready for pickup the day the men and I arrive." Alex turns to Mac and says, "The day before mission execution, after we have done our last recon, I want you to come with me to pick up the weapons."

Though Mac is disgruntled, he is not overly difficult. He shakes his head in compliance.

Continuing, Alex informs the group, "All three arms dealers are within a sixty-mile radius from one another, so it should not take us too long to get them."

From out of nowhere, Mac blurts, "Your plan sucks from jump street."

"What do you mean, Mr. Pollard?" Colonel Drasneb quickly asks.

"Alex's plan is doomed to fail as soon as he places that order," Mac explains. "The State of New York will not allow anyone to purchase weapons that expediently. Hold on a second."

Mac leaves the group and jogs off to his and Killer's tent. He quickly returns and, handing Alex a card, says, "Give this guy a call. He'll hook you up. Tell him I sent you and that I'll be with you for the pickup."

Alex takes the card from Mac and studies it closely. "I trust your guidance on this, Mac. Thank you." Alex jots down the information on the card then asks, "Will your contact have everything we want?"

"Yes, and everything we don't want, either," Mac replies. "He may be illegal, but he's as reliable as they come."

19 OCTOBER 1999

1320 Hours: West Point

"**M**ajor, you need to get a handle on the window alignment. The BTO is really pushing this issue," Captain Weiss informs Cadet Johnson.

The BTO requires that the windows in all cadet rooms must be evenly aligned in all of the buildings. To ensure that his compliance is met, the manner in which the cadets must measure how far to open their windows is by opening them a clipboard's width from the bottom, no more, no less. Whether the weather is hot or cold outside, the windows have to remain open a clipboard's width from 0700 hours to 1600 hours every class day. Cadets, as a whole, loathe this policy and feel that it is unimportant to their growth into becoming army officers. Simply put, the cadets feel that the BTO's window policy is stupid.

"Sir, I understand where you're coming from on this, but it doesn't make any sense for everyone to align their windows the same height. I mean, if someone doesn't want any air, they should be able to shut their windows if they want. Take me for instance. I don't like the cold, so when it starts getting cold, I like to shut my windows, but according to the window policy, I can't shut them until 1600 hours."

"That makes sense, Major, but what do you want to do about it?"

"I'm not sure, sir. I would change company policy on this, but this is higher than me. You're the TAC, sir. Can't you do something about it?"

"You'd be surprised at how much more power you cadets have over some of us captains." Major laughs at Captain Weiss's statement. "I'm serious," Captain Weiss says with a grin. "Here's what I'll do.

The TACs have to meet with the BTO tomorrow. I'll bring up your suggestion then. All right?"

"Roger, sir."

Captain Weiss opens a big black notebook then turns to his computer and opens his e-mail inbox. "I don't have too many things for you today. Here you go." He hands Major four sheets of paper.

Major scans over the paperwork quickly then says, "I'll disseminate this stuff out, sir." He then motions to rise from his seat.

Stopping Major in mid-movement, Captain Weiss interjects, "Before you go, we need to discuss one more thing."

"What's that, sir?" Major asks.

"Tim was involved in an alcohol incident."

"What!" Major sits up in his chair, shocked by the news

"Yeah. A plebe lax player was caught drunk in his room Saturday night."

"Ah man."

Captain Weiss instructs Major, saying, "I want you to talk to Tim and see what his side of the story is."

"Roger, sir. I'll talk to Tim and see what's up."

"You do that. Once the investigation is over, I'll have you read it over so you can get a feel as to what actually occurred."

"Yes, sir."

"Also, I want to keep this in house. Since I'm the battalion TAC, we may be able to keep this at our level."

"I agree, sir." Major then looks at his watch and realizes that he is running late. "Hey, sir. I've got to get going."

"All right, Major. I'll see you tomorrow at breakfast formation."

"I'll see you then, sir. I'll get back with you on what Tim says." Major gets up, leaves Captain Weiss's office, and returns to his room to change for practice.

1900 Hours

Major stands on the stoops to enjoy the cool night air. He has finished dinner and has some important company business to attend to, but presently, he waits for Tim to arrive from dinner so he can speak to him about the lacrosse alcohol incident. After waiting for only a couple of minutes, Major spots Tim leaving Central Area and heading for Grant Barracks.

Once Tim reaches the stoops, Major says to him, "Hey, Tim. We need to talk."

"What about?" Tim asks as he walks toward Major.

Major meets Tim halfway.

"It's about a few Saturdays ago," Major answers.

"Oh yeah. I was wondering when you were going to talk to me about that."

"So what happened anyway?"

"I couldn't tell you, Major. All I did was buy the beer. I wasn't even there when they tapped the keg."

Major is a little shocked from what he hears.

"What do you mean you weren't there?"

"My sister was up visiting. The only reason I even went down to South Dock was because it was my turn to buy the beer. When the football game ended, I drove off post and picked the keg up then dropped it off. Once I got it there, I left."

"You left?"

"Yeah. We went to the city. I couldn't tell you who drank that night. All I know is that the entire lacrosse team was down there. We had some recruits there too, but I don't know who the hell they were or if they drank any either."

"Shoot! They probably did."

"You're probably right," Tim agrees. He takes a deep breath then asks the question he has wanted an answer to since the situation occurred. "How much trouble am I in?"

"I can't say yet. I'll tell you this, though. CPT Weiss wants to keep this in house since he's the battalion TAC and all."

"Is that good?"

"It's a lot better than the RTO or BTO finding out. I've got to get going now, got to reeducate a knucklehead yuck. I'll keep you informed as to what happens. All right?"

"Yeah. I appreciate it."

"No prob. You know I've got you."

Major and Tim shake hands. Major then returns to his room and Tim to his.

Major, Sara, Joe, and Dusty sit in Major and Joe's room, waiting for Cdt. Lt. William Gracey and cadet sergeants Brian Hatcher, the platoon sergeant, and Kareem Akbar, the squad leader, for an important meeting/counseling session. Their subordinate Cdt. Cpl. Mike Singer was caught flicking off the TAC during lunch formation by one of his classmates. Fortunately for Cadet Singer, Captain Weiss did not notice his immature action. His chain of command is meeting with Major to speak with him and determine a proper punishment.

Cadet Singer and his chain of command enter the room. Major points to Singer and sternly says, "You wait outside. We'll get you when we're ready for you. Don't go too far."

Cadet Singer bows his head in shame and quickly leaves the room. He waits out in the hall, leaning up against the wall, waiting for his punishment.

Cadet Singer thinks to himself, *That dumb girl! Why'd she have to open her big mouth? I wasn't doing anything to her.*

Major waits for the door to shut behind Singer before he begins the meeting

"All right guys. We all know why we're here. Determining a punishment for Singer is not top priority for me. I want to figure out why he was dumb enough to flick off C-DUBS and then come up with a way to rehabilitate him. His actions were uncalled for and exhibit the highest levels of disrespect. Now I'm not going to tell the TAC. He doesn't need to know about this. We're going to keep this in house. If he were to find out what Singer did, he would kill him. Look at how he treats Meade. That kid didn't really do anything except be a dirtbag. Telling C-DUBS would only make things worse, so whatever punishment we give Singer has to be off the books. So what do you guys recommend?"

"No disrespect, CO," Dusty begins, "but I think we should tell Captain Weiss. What that little puke did was the most disrespectful thing that a soldier can do to an officer!"

"I understand that, Dust, but if we tell C-DUBS what Singer did, he may not get a chance to graduate. Singer may not be the best kid in the world, but I can't believe that he's unredeemable."

"But, sir, he may as well have said 'eff you' to the TAC! That's uncalled for, and we can't tolerate that!" Dustin defends adamantly.

"We aren't going to tolerate his actions, and not telling Captain Weiss isn't toleration, it's policing up after our own. The TAC doesn't need to know everything, especially this."

"Dustin, we all feel you on this," Joe intercedes, "but you need to understand how a situation like this is handled in the army. If a first sergeant were to catch a soldier doing something like Singer did, then he would give him a whole mess load of extra duties on top of locking his butt up and smoking him until he's near death. The first sergeant wouldn't tell the commander because a situation such as that doesn't require his attention. Now if it becomes a continued problem, then yes, he would receive word of the soldier's misconduct. Do you understand where me and the CO are going with this?"

"I don't agree, but I'll support you," Dustin responds.

"Good then. Is everyone in agreement that we do not inform the TAC of Singer's actions?" Major asks everyone present in the room.

Everyone responds with yes.

"All right. Now that we have agreed to not tell the TAC, we have to give Singer a suitable punishment, off the record. Any ideas?"

"I think he should prepare a class on the importance of respecting officers," Sara suggests.

"That sounds pretty good," Cadet Gracey agrees.

"Yeah, I like that. Give him two weeks to prepare it?" Major adds.

"Two weeks is good," Gracey agrees, "but who's he going to teach it to? It can't be a real class 'cause the TAC'll want to know why he's teaching a respect class. You know?"

"Yeah, I hear you. I say he give the first sergeant and me the class," Major responds.

"I want him to give me the class too," Gracey responds.

"That's cool," Major agrees. "He can see you first, make needed corrections, then brief me. Since we're doing it like this, I'll give him an extra week, so he'll see you in two weeks and me no later than three. Cool?"

"Yeah, that'll work."

"Good. Kareem, tell Singer to get in here."

Cadet Akbar opens the door, sticks his head out into the hallway, and tells Cadet Singer to come into the room. Singer humbly walks into the room with his head drooped down and a pitiful look on his face.

"Sir, I would just like to say—"

"Be quiet, Singer. I'll let you know when you can talk," Major sternly interrupts Singer in midsentence. "XO, you have anything to say to him?"

Sara puts her hands on her hips; a stern look grows on her face.

"I am really disappointed in you, Singer," Sara begins. "I thought you were squared away, but now I know better. I'll never see you in the same manner again because now I know how you really are—a disrespectful brat." Sara shakes her head in disappointment.

"Joe, you got anything?" Major asks.

"No. I don't feel like wasting my time with him."

"First Sergeant, you have anything?"

"Yes, sir. I do." Dustin rises from his seat and paces around Cadet Singer, looking him up and down as though he were sizing him up. "You know, you are a disrespect to the corps and the army. If this were the army, we'd be smoking your scrawny butt right now. You better be glad that Major is the type of commander that he is. Most guys would have turned your butt in to the TAC. You can't fathom the heat that you would be in if Captain Weiss knew what you had done. Do you realize the severity of your actions?"

"I didn't—" Cadet Singer tries to interrupt.

"Be quiet!" Dustin barks. "The commander told you not to speak until told to do so. I don't remember telling you to speak. Do you?"

"No."

"Then stay silent! You have a real attitude problem that needs correcting real fast. No one in this room can do that for you. You have to do it yourself. The only problem is I don't think that you have

it in you to fix it. And what's even worse, I don't think you want to."
Dustin turns his back on Cadet Singer and walks back to his seat.
He continues, saying, "Honestly though, I'm probably just wasting my
breath. I know all of this is going in one ear and out the other."

"PL, platoon sergeant, squad leader, you guys have anything to
add?" Major asks Cadet Singer's chain of command.

"No. Everyone's pretty much said what was needed to be said,"
Cadet Gracey replies for the group. "Let's tell him what he has to do."

"Roger that," Major responds. He spins in his chair and faces
Singer. "Singer, your punishment is to do a class on respecting officers
in the army. There is no time limit to the length of the class, but it
needs to be efficiently done. You have two weeks to prepare the class.
At the end of the two weeks, you will report to your PL and give him
the class. You will then make any and all corrections to the class then
report back to me a week later and brief me. Is that understood?"

"Yes."

"Good," Major replies.

"I highly suggest that you use FMs (Field Manuals) and other
resources for your class. Don't just throw something together and
expect us to accept it," Sara intercedes.

"Okay."

"Before you're dismissed, do you have anything to add?" Major asks
Cadet Corporal Singer.

"Yeah, I do," Singer humbly begins. "All of this isn't my fault.
Morgan and Thomas were talking to me in formation. The TAC didn't
see them."

"Are you actually trying to blame your classmates on your mistake?"
Dustin angrily asks. "I don't recall them flicking Captain Weiss off."

"But that's the thing. I didn't."

"What do you mean you didn't?" Major bewilderedly asks.

"This is what I did."

Cadet Singer turns around so that his back is facing Major and
moves to the position of parade rest. Major looks at Singer's hands,
paying close attention to how he places them on top of one another.
Singer's right hand is properly placed over the left, with the thumbs

interlocking. Singer then pulls back all of his fingers, except his middle finger.

"You see, I didn't flick him off." Singer argues.

"You're kidding me, right?" Major sarcastically asks. "Are you trying to tell me that you don't think that you flicked him off? I'm looking at a middle finger right now."

"Yeah, but I didn't stick it out."

"You may not have literally flicked him off, but your actions show that that was your intention. Whether you waved it in his face or did it behind his back, as you did, it's all the same. Whether you like it or not, you said, 'eff you' to the TAC, and we can't tolerate that. I know you don't understand, but someday, you will. Now get out of here before I really get upset with you."

"But—"

"What did I say? Go!"

Cadet Singer drops his head and mopes out of the room.

"I don't think he regrets his actions or will in the future," Joe says.

"Yeah. You're probably right, but I hope he understands someday for his sake," Dustin agrees.

"Oh well," Major sighs as he lowers his head in disappointment. "Grace, I guess you've got yourself a new project."

"Yeah. I guess so," Gracey says, letting out a breath.

"Before we break, we have to make sure that the TAC does not find out about this. He won't mind what we've just done, but he'll friggin' kill Singer and do everything in his power to ensure that his life is miserable."

"We've got you," Gracey answers.

"All right then. I'll see you guys later." Cadets Gracey, Hatcher, and Akbar leave the room as Major, Sara, Joe, and Dustin continue their conversation about the company and other random events throughout the corps.

22 OCTOBER 1999

1400 Hours: West Point

Mid-October is a weird weather period in the Hudson Valley. Predicting the weather is like guessing how much rain will fall on a given day; it is impossible to gauge until the rain stops. There are days when the temperature drops to below freezing and days when the high can reach the low seventies. For the plebe who is the head minute caller in his company, he has to make it a point to call Central Guard Room to ensure that he calls the proper uniform for breakfast and lunch formations so he knows whether to add raincoats to the uniform of the day.

Today is one of those days when the temperature is near freezing. Major is quite acclimated to the cold but definitely does not like it. Getting dressed for his trip up to the Holleder Center, Major dons his corps squad sweats as well as his wool cap, black utility gloves with inserts, and his black parka.

Fully dressed, Major walks out of his room with his hands in his pockets. It is rather quiet in the cadet area during this time of the day. Cadets are either in class or napping in their rooms. Aware of the emptiness around him, Major walks with his head full of thoughts, ambivalent to his surroundings.

As he walks through Grant Area, Major stops in his tracks and turns left because he spots out of the corner of his eye Captain Weiss speed walking down the street. Though he is not totally sure, Major assumes that Captain Weiss wants to speak with him.

"Major, I'm glad I was able to catch you," Captain Weiss states as he approaches Major. "I have some great news!"

"What is it, sir?" Major inquisitively asks: unsure of his TAC's answer.

"Remember your idea for the window policy that you had a few days ago?"

"Yes, sir."

"Well, this morning, the BTO had his regular meeting with the TACs. When the window-policy issue came up, I mentioned your resolution to the BTO and he liked it."

Major raises his head up in amazement. "Sir, you're kidding me, right? You're telling me that the BTO's actually agreed to allow us to align our windows evenly based upon each individual room and not the barracks as a whole?"

"That's right. Starting tomorrow, the barracks windows only have to be aligned by the room, not the entire barrack."

"Get out of here!" Major is still shocked as to what Captain Weiss is telling him. "I didn't think he'd buy it. Thanks for bringing my idea up in the meeting, sir."

"No problem, Major. That's what I'm here for. You should be proud of yourself. You've just done the impossible. You've changed an official West Point reg. Congratulations!"

25 OCTOBER 1999

0555 Hours: West Point

Every Monday morning at 0600 hours, Major holds a training meeting in the study room with his platoon leadership and staff officers and NCOs. Major and Joe wake up with just enough time to slip their clothes on and sloth over to the study room. Fortunately for Major, Sara is the facilitator of the training meeting, so he is able to allow his body to continue resting, though his mind is still racing most of the time, anyway.

Major and Joe enter the study room. Everyone is already present, which is good. It means that the meeting can start on time. Major and Joe make their way to the head of the table, where Sara stands, fully ready to get the meeting underway.

Major takes a seat to Sara's right. Joe, on the other hand, remains standing and runs through the training schedule for the following six weeks. Finished reading, he sits to Sara's left. Sara runs through her own notes and Dusty his.

Sara then states, "Do you have anything, CO?"

Major, who has had his head down throughout the entirety of the training meeting, raises it and says, "Yes, I do. Doobie, you need to get the military training off the ground. It's been two months, and we haven't done any worthwhile training. What's up with the ideas I gave you?"

"Don't worry. I'm handling it," Cdt. Greg Dolby assures Major.

"I'm tired of hearing that, man. Every time I bring this up, you feed me the same line of bull crap. I want to see results. My goal is for this company to be number one in everything by next semester. You're not helping any."

Frustrated, Doobie replies, "I'm dealing with it. Don't worry."

"All right. I'm taking your word this one last time. I want us doing something hoo-ha by Thanksgiving. I have faith in you, Doob. You're the most GI Joe-acting dude up in here."

Everyone in the room laughs.

"Also, so you guys know, we are leading the regiment in room grading. Continue the good work. Let your guys know that if they volunteer their room for grading, I'll give them PMI the next day."

Everyone shakes their heads in agreement.

"That's all I have," Major concludes. "If no one has anything else, I'll see you at formation."

The room quickly empties. Brian follows Major and Joe back to their room. Joe lies on his bed, and Major and Brian plop down on the couch and throw their legs up on the coffee table.

As he lays seemingly back into a complete alpha state of sleep, Joe breaks the long silence, saying, "I think I'm going to do a spirit mission Thursday night. If I do it, you want to come?"

"I know you're not talking to me," Brian is quick to reply.

"Naw, man. I'm not down," Major answers.

"Aw, come on, Major. You've got to come. I've already spoken to the first sergeant. He's in."

"You guys go ahead. You know how I like to get my sleep."

"Whatever."

Major stands up and says, "I'm heading to formation now."

Brian stands up as well.

"I'll see you guys out there," Joe states as Major and Brian leave the room.

1045 Hours: Russian Training Camp

Alex and Colonel Drasneb sit together in Colonel Drasneb's tent, Colonel Drasneb behind his desk and Alex on a metal folding chair in front of the desk. The two men are discussing the flow of training and how much closer the men are to achieving excellence in all of their trained tasks. Today's meeting is different though because Colonel Drasneb unexpectedly called Alex into his tent.

"Thank you for coming on such short notice," Colonel Drasneb opens. "I know you are very busy and were probably in the process of doing something very important to further increase the mission's level of success."

"It is no problem, sir."

"You know, Alex, I have been having some second thoughts about the mission."

"You have, sir?"

"Yes. I have."

"Alex leans forward in his seat and asks, "You're thinking of canceling the mission?"

Colonel Drasneb laughs at the thought. "Of course not." He then picks up a stack of papers and hands them to Alex. "I've been doing some brainstorming and came up with some ideas. Take a look at them and tell me what you think."

Alex flips through the papers and says, "Sir, theses pages have no order."

"I know. I told you that I was brainstorming."

Alex shakes his head. He pulls a cot that is positioned at the far end of the tent and places it in front of him. He then strews the numerous papers onto the cot. As Alex sifts through the pages, Colonel Drasneb remains seated, reading a book. Alex studies each individual paper, placing them in a particular order as his eyes pass over each one.

With the papers in a suitable order, Alex hands them back to Colonel Drasneb. Before taking the papers, Colonel Drasneb marks his page, places his book on the desk, and then takes the papers from Alex's hand. He then quickly reads over the pages, a smile growing on his face after every few pages.

Finished reading the pages, Colonel Drasneb places them beside his book then looks up at Alex, saying, "We're preparing to move into the final phase of training."

"Yes, sir," Alex replies.

"I am glad to see that you were able to make sense of the plans that I had created. Thank you for putting it into a feasible order."

"It was no problem at all, sir."

"Now we need to discuss what you just read."

Alex sits up in his seat, anticipating the words that are soon to spew from his commander's mouth.

Colonel Drasneb begins his explanation, saying, "It would be redundant of me to brief you on the actual mission especially since you are my intelligence officer. What you just read entails my other aspect of the mission that the two mercenaries are unaware of. Understand that it is imperative that you do not inform them of what you have read or anything that we discuss on the matter. I still have your trust, correct?"

"Of course, sir. I owe you my life."

"I know." Colonel Drasneb smiles. He then continues. "Now you're probably wondering why I'm making these last-minute changes to our mission."

"The thought did cross my mind, sir."

"Well, I have decided that our mission must go beyond an attack on West Point. We need to send a message that the entire world will understand without any unneeded interpretation."

"Sir, you don't think that the mess hall is enough?"

"It isn't that it's not enough. It's about the message that we are sending. If we only destroy West Point's mess hall, the world will interpret my plan as solely some unknown grudge that I have against West Point. As you and I both know, I have nothing personal against the school. I simply want to cripple America's army. The destruction of the mess hall is simply a means to an end. What I decided to add—my secret ingredient, you could say—is another action against America that will signal to the world how serious I truly am. The world needs to understand how strong my hatred is."

"You don't think this is a bit much, sir?"

"Not at all. We will make it happen."

"Sir, I trust your military mind and your ability to plan and execute, but how do you plan on training on your side mission without Mac and Killer discovering it?"

"That's simple, my boy. You will train them."

"You still have not answered my question, sir."

"The training sessions that you hold without Mr. Stewart and Mr. Pollard's assistance are when you will train them. All of the training will occur in a classroom environment, of course."

"Of course."

"You will receive all guidance from me. I would head the training myself, but that would look too suspicious. I may not like those two mercenaries, but I didn't hire them because they're stupid. You know?"

"More than you know, sir."

Colonel Drasneb gives Alex a funny look in response to his last statement.

"Before I go, sir, you're plan is all fine and good, but what do we do once Mac and Killer become aware of our actions and attempt to interfere?"

"That's simple. We kill them. I was going to do that anyway. This way, I will have no regrets in doing so."

West Point

Major and Bobby sit in their SE 420, operations management, class. Major is feeling quite anxious. Today, his instructor, Major Word, is returning her class' WPRs to them. Though somewhat nervous, Major feels confident. He is unsure of what he may have scored but is as sure as he is about anything that he did not fail.

Major Word begins handing the WPRs out on the other side of the room, thus increasing Major's anxiety. The closer Major Word gets, the faster his heartbeats.

I know I passed this thing. Think positive. Think positive, Major says to himself. Major even says a silent prayer to relieve his anxiety. *Dear Lord, I studied hard for this PR. I know I knew the material. I pray that I passed the PR. I claim the victory in your name. In your Son's holy name, Amen.*

Major looks up with a new sense of assurance. As he smiles internally, Major Word continues passing the WPRs out. Bobby, who sits to Major's left, receives his WPR. He looks at the front page then looks at Major, nodding his head in a positive manner.

Booby's good grade increases Major's assurance. Major Word hands Major his WPR. Major looks at the front page and is totally flabbergasted. He has just failed his second WPR in SE 420.

"This can't be right," Major says to Bobby.

"Let me see it," Bobby replies.

Major hands Bobby his WPR. While Bobby looks over Major's WPR, Major shakes his head in disgust. He cannot believe that he has failed again. Major is accustomed to failing tests and quizzes, but failing makes him feel as though he wasted his time.

"I may as well've not even have studied," Major says to Bobby as he flips a page.

"You may have failed this, but you really didn't do as bad as you think."

"What do you mean?"

"Look at this," Bobby says, turning to the third page. "You see this." Bobby points to the part of a long equation at the bottom of the page. "You only did half the problem. Look at mine."

Major takes a look at Bobby's work.

"You see. You only answered the first part. You had to take that answer and substitute it into this equation," Bobby says, pointing to the second equation of the problem on his page. "You leaving that part out cost you sixty points."

"No kidding."

"Shake it off, bro. You'll pull out of this. We've got the project coming up. We'll get an A on it. That'll help out a lot."

"Yeah," Major sulks. He then raises his hand and asks, "Ma'am, can I come by for AI tomorrow to go over the PR?"

"Certainly. See me after class so we can find a good time."

28 OCTOBER 1999

0430 Hours: West Point

Major lies sound asleep in his bed. Suddenly his telephone rings, awaking him from his deep slumber.

Waking up, Major softly says, "What the hell?"

Major is not accustomed to his phone ringing so early in the morning. With one ring past, Major sits up and leaps out of his bed, landing hard on the floor.

Major snatches the receiver and says, "This is Cadet Johnson. How may I help you, sir or ma'am?" As Major speaks, he takes a seat in his chair behind his desk.

"Cadet Johnson," a familiar female voice says from the other end, "this is Major Royce. Are you awake?"

"As awake as I can be at four thirty in the morning, ma'am," Major replies.

Major is now somewhat shaken up because he has no idea why Major Royce is calling him so early in the morning. It can only be one thing, and that is not good.

"Good," Major Royce replies. "Your company did a spirit mission last night and tagged every first floor window of all of the barracks as well as the giant glass windows in Washington Hall."

"Thank God!" Major replies, relieved of an unneeded burden.

"Are you all right?" Major Royce asks, confused as to why Major is suddenly so joyful.

"Ma'am, I thought you were calling me because someone's parent died."

"No. That wouldn't be me on that one. Anyway, Colonel Skelton wants it all cleaned up before breakfast formation."

"Yes, ma'am. I'll get right on it."

"All right then. Make it happen. I'll see you. Out." Major Royce hangs up the telephone.

Major returns his receiver to its resting place then says, "Joe, you need to get up."

Slow to move, Joe finally says, "What's going on?"

"What's going on?" Major replies. "You and that stupid spirit mission. That's what!"

"What're you talking about?"

"Major Royce just called. She said that the BTO said that we have to clean up your mess before breakfast formation."

Joe, realizing that Major is becoming angry, replies, "What're you all upset about? The spirit mission was cool."

"Cool? I thought someone's parent died. I could care less about your stupid spirit mission."

"You need to calm down," Joe firmly suggests, annoyed at the fact that Major will not allow himself to appreciate the spirit mission for what it was—a show of D-1's might.

Joe gets out of bed. Since he sleeps in gym A, he only has to slip on his shower shoes. "I'm going to get the first sergeant to go get everyone," Joe says as he leaves the room.

"You do that," Major replies as Joe exits.

With Joe gone, Major rises from his seat and gets dressed, putting on his gym A and his running suit. Major then slips on his outdoor-court basketball shoes then steps out into the hallway. Already there are Joe, Dusty, and Dusty's roommate, Stephen Carlson.

"Hey, sir! How's it going?" Dusty asks with a huge grin on his face.

"Don't talk to me right now," Major grunts. "I'm not in the mood."

While the four cadets stand in the hall, small groups of plebes and yucks and a few cows, begin to congregate down into the hallway, twenty-one in all.

Major shakes his head in disbelief at the number of people who participated in the spirit mission.

As each small group enters, Dusty instructs them to return to their rooms and bring back any form of spray cleaner that they may have under their sink and numerous amounts of paper towels and rags. Having returned and fully loaded, Dusty and Joe lead the rogues outside.

Approaching Bradley Barracks, Major cannot believe what he sees. Every window on the first floor has a picture of a duck painted in artificial snow, the type that is used to spray on Christmas trees.

Joe walks up to Major and says, "Now do you see?"

Major shakes his head and asks, "You guys did this to all the barracks?"

"Yep," Joe replies.

A smirk grows on Major's face.

Seeing that Major's demeanor is changing for the better, Joe follows, asking, "You feel me now?"

"Yeah. I feel you. This is nice. Come on. Let's get this mess cleaned up before we run into the BTO."

Dusty instructs the yearlings as to what they need to accomplish. The yearlings then take a small group of plebes with them and scatter out into several directions.

With the plebes and yearlings executing their mandated orders, Dusty says to the cows, "Let's go."

Dusty leads the cows, with Major and Joe following, to the fourth floor of Washington Hall and into the web, where there are giant windows that face inward, forming a partial circle. Each window is over twenty feet tall and about four feet wide. The shape that the windows make resembles an oversized empty fish tank.

Walking down the hallway, approaching the web, Major is able to see the windows. Again, he is taken aback from what his eyes reveal to him. Written in artificial snow on all of the windows are various phrases praising the Ducks, such as "Go, Ducks," "D-1's #1," and "Bad to the bone," to name a few.

"You guys really had fun, didn't you?" Major says as the group steps in front of the windows.

"We sure did," Steve laughs. Everyone laughs along with him.

Furiously, the group gets to cleaning the windows. They are on the clock. Though Colonel Skelton already knows what they have done, they know that it is better for them to have their mess cleaned up prior to him actually seeing it.

As they clean, Captain Weiss, unbeknown to the group, walks up behind them and asks, "Having fun?"

Joe jumps off of the small windowsill that he is standing on and says with a huge grin, "You bet, sir!"

Captain Weiss laughs at Joe and the scene of his cadets cleaning the Washington Hall windows. The other cadets laugh as well. Though they do not like having to clean up their mess, they are proud of what they accomplished the previous night and so are able to see the humor in their new janitorial role. Captain Weiss stays around for a while to watch his cadets clean. It is the funniest sight that he has seen in a while. To help pass the time, Captain Weiss converses with them as they clean.

As the cadets converse and clean, Colonel Skelton surprises everyone by walking out from behind a corner. Colonel Skelton is known for appearing in places where you least expect him. Word around the corps is that he hides in bushes in order to easily catch cadets in the act of breaking USCC regulations. Others say that when Colonel Skelton runs in the afternoon, it is not for physical-training purposes. It is so he can catch as many cadets as possible. Running allows him to cover more ground in less time.

Major is the first to spot Colonel Skelton in the web.

"Morning, sir," Major states.

"Good morning, Cadet Johnson," Colonel Skelton replies with a devilish smile on his face.

"I can't believe they did this, sir," Major states with a slight smirk.

"Well, Johnson. I guess you're now learning what the burden of leadership is all about. There are times when you have to take responsibility for your unit even if you weren't a part of their misdoings. Have fun."

1200 Hours

During lunch formation, Captain Weiss informed Major that he needs to meet with him immediately after lunch instead of their regular time of 1300 hours. With lunch complete, Major rushes over to his TAC's office to see what is so important to bump their meeting time up.

Major enters Captain Weiss' office.

Before Major can take a seat, Captain Weiss says, "They've completed the investigation. Here it is. I want you to read through it real quick."

Major takes the packet from Captain Weiss's hands and takes a seat in front of his desk. He slowly reads the packet, doubling back on all of the references to Tim. After about five minutes or so, Major lifts his head and says, "Whoa."

"What do you think?" Captain Weiss asks.

Major takes a few moments to organize his thoughts then says, "Sir, I know underage drinking is bad in and of itself, but if this kid's roommate didn't spaz out during the taps check, no one would have been the wiser."

Captain Weiss laughs. "You know? You're right. I didn't even think about that when I read it."

"If the kid's roommate could have just left the door unlocked, the SDO could have just checked the room, seen that both plebes were in there, and went on his way. Instead, this idiot locks the door. For what reason? I don't know. Everyone knows you're not supposed to lock the doors."

"So," Captain Weiss interjects, "what do you think we should do with Tim?"

"Well, sir. His story's solid. The only thing he's guilty of is providing alcohol for underage kids."

"What about the purchase?"

"That was legal, sir."

"How's that?"

"Because he bought it off post. The reg states that cadets may not purchase beer or alcohol on post. It doesn't say anything about off post. Tim knew that. That's why he went into town to get the keg."

"I agree with you. Right now, I'm still not sure whether we can keep this at the battalion level. I should know in a few days."

31 OCTOBER 1999

1830 Hours: West Point

Major has just returned from another night at Hoboken with Ed. Instead of returning to his room, Major decides to stop by the Woods' to see how they are doing. In the house, Major sits at the Woods' dining room table, along with Mike and his friend and teammate, Cdt. Cpl. Steve Whitney, who have been there all day watching football on the television in the basement.

"I'm really upset," Mike says.

"What's wrong, man?" Major asks.

"We came over here so we could hand out candy to the kids. It's almost seven o'clock, and no kids have shown up yet," Mike protests.

Major laughs at Mike's disappointment. "I feel you brother, but think about it. Would you trick-or-treat on this street?"

Steve laughs at Major's rebuttal.

Major continues. "What are there? Like nine houses on this street? A kid's wasting his time if he comes down here for some candy."

"I guess you're right," Mike agrees.

"And then," Major continues, "how many of these colonels have candy ready anyway? Two, three, four tops."

Steve continues laughing. Realizing his blunder, Mike laughs as well.

As the three cadets laugh, Cdt. Jane Denver walks into the dining room. The Woods refer to Jane as Major's sister because she is over at their house as much, if not more, than he is. Jane and Major have been friends since their plebe year. There is one thing that Major does not like about Jane, and that is the fact that she is in Company F-1, the Duck's archnemesis, for the moment anyway.

"What're you fools up to?" Jane asks the three cadets as she enters the dining room.

"I'm chillin'," Major replies. "These two dorks were going to hand out candy to the kids. The only problem is that there are no kids."

"Ha!" Jane laughs. "I could've told you that." Jane raises her head up some and begins to think.

Major notices Jane's change in countenance and asks her, "What's on your mind, girl?"

"I just had a brilliant idea."

"This, I've got to hear."

"You should go put on the Duck suit and trick-or-treat at the supe's house."

"You're crazy!"

"I'm serious. He'd love it!"

Major thinks about it for a few moments. As he ponders, Colonel Wood enters the room.

"What're you guys up to?" Colonel Wood asks while Major still contemplates.

"Major's going trick-or-treating at the supe's house," Steve answers for the group.

Steve's announcement causes Colonel Wood to join in on the laughter.

"Wait," Jane interjects. "You're the commander, Major. You can't wear the suit. You have to represent the company."

"Then you wear the suit," Major suggests.

"Yeah! That'll work," Jane agrees.

"I'll go get the Duck suit," Colonel Wood excitingly states as he rushes upstairs.

A short time later, Colonel Wood returns with the Duck suit and hands it to Jane. Jane puts on the suit. As she does so, Mrs. Wood snaps a photo. Everyone rolls with laughter at the sight of Jane wearing the Duck suit.

Fully dressed and zipped up, Colonel Wood hands Jane the Duck head.

"There you go," Colonel Wood says as he relinquishes the Duck head.

"You ready?" Major asks Jane.

"Let's do this."

Jane follows Major out the front door. She follows mostly because she is having trouble seeing through the eye slots. Major and Jane walk down the steps and turn right toward Cadet Area. To their left is Eisenhower Hall. When they reach the dean's quarters, they cross the street and walk past the commandant's quarters.

Approaching the superintendent's quarters, Major and Jane turn right and walk down the sidewalk and up the steps to the front door. Jane keeps her head down to ensure that she does not trip and fall on a step. The last thing she wants to do is embarrass herself in front of Lieutenant General Holiday and his wife.

Standing on the porch, Major knocks on the front door. After a few seconds, Mrs. Holiday answers the door. Seeing Major and a giant Duck standing before her causes Mrs. Holiday to lean back, cocking her head forward. She is unsure of what to make of the Duck.

"Trick or treat!" Major says with a big smile.

Mrs. Holiday cannot believe what she is seeing and hearing. Here are obviously two cadets out trick-or-treating on her front porch. Mrs. Holiday's face begins to redden due to her near-uncontrollable laughter.

"Hold on a second," Mrs. Holiday responds, still laughing. "Let me get him for you. He's not going to believe this."

Mrs. Holiday steps away for a moment and returns with her husband.

"Trick or treat, sir!" Major and Jane shout.

"Oh my goodness!" Lieutenant General Holiday exclaims. "I don't believe this. Mary, do we have any candy?"

"I think so. Let me see what I can find." Mrs. Holiday steps away again and returns with a handful of assorted candy.

"Who's that under there?" Lieutenant General Holiday asks of the individual wearing the Duck suit.

"It's me, sir. Jane Denver."

"Jane! My goodness, how did you guys come up with this idea?" Lieutenant General Holiday asks.

"We were bored, sir," Jane replies.

The Holidays laugh. Lieutenant General Holiday then asks, "How's the company doing, Major?"

"Man, sir. We're doing great! It's hard being the best sometimes, but we handle it pretty well."

"And the team?" Lieutenant General Holiday follows.

"We're ready to shock the world, sir."

"That's what I like to hear," Lieutenant General Holiday affirms.

"And the volleyball team, Jane?"

"The girls are doing great, sir. We should have a pretty good season this year. We were able to work out some of the kinks during the early-fall season."

"That's good," Lieutenant General Holiday states. He then says, "I don't want to hold you guys up. I'm sure you have a lot of houses to hit."

Everyone laughs.

Lieutenant General Holiday shakes Jane's Duck-outfitted hand. He then shakes Major's hand then, much to Major's surprise, brings him to his chest and hits him on his back, just as Major and his friends do regularly whenever they depart from one another.

As Major and Jane step off of the superintendent's porch, Major thinks to himself, *I knew me and the supe were cool, but I didn't know we were tight like that.*

2 NOVEMBER 1999

0700 Hours: Russian Training Camp

Mac, Killer, and Alex sit together eating breakfast. Mac and Killer eat alone because even though they are giving the Serbs some of the best training that they have ever experienced, the Serbs still do not trust them fully due to their mercenary status Alex eats with Mac and Killer for two reasons. The obvious reason is that he has befriended the two mercenaries. The second is that for as long as Alex can remember, he has always liked to rock the boat. Alex was never one who respected the status quo. That is one of the numerous reasons why he is presently working for Colonel Drasneb.

Mealtime, no matter the food, is one of Mac's favorite times of the day. Killer has never met anyone who can eat as much as Mac. Mac's appetite does waiver though. It is all based upon how interested he is in the food that is before him. If Mac gets bored with a meal, he can no longer eat. You could say that the boredom fills him up. On the other hand, if Mac truly likes what he is eating, he will eat anyone under the table.

Today's breakfast is one of those meals that Mac could eat and enjoy on a regular basis when at home, but because they eat the same thing for breakfast every day, Mac is becoming quite irritable.

"You know," Mac says out of nowhere, "I love oatmeal. I really do, but after eating it every day for nearly two weeks is going to cause me to go postal on someone real soon.

Killer and Alex laugh at Mac's little tirade.

"You know, Mac, it could be worse," Alex states, trying to control his laughter.

"How so?"

"I was training in Afghanistan once, and the only consistent food we had for four straight weeks were potatoes. Anything else, like meat and fruit and vegetables, we had to find on our own."

"Forget that!" Mac says, shaking his head in disbelief.

As the three comrades do their best to eat their breakfast, Colonel Drasneb watches them from the other side of the mess tent. His eyes peer into the back of Alex's head as though they were a laser sighted in on a target.

This does not sit well with me at all, Colonel Drasneb thinks to himself. *I do not like Alex becoming close to those two. They could influence him. Who am I fooling though? Alex has always been loyal and always will be. I should not have to worry, but I still am not comfortable with him making friends with them. Alex is smart though, he may be getting close to them so he can learn how they think. Yes! That is it! He is becoming their friend in order to learn how they operate. That way, he will be able to anticipate when they decide to turn on me and compromise the mission. As always, Alex has surprised me yet again. What a great officer.* Colonel Drasneb smiles internally, having reached the revelation that Alex is playing the roll of double agent.

4 NOVEMBER 1999

0900 Hours: Russian Training Camp

Alex stands alone before one of the Serb teams. Being that he is the only one who has walked the ground at West Point, Alex has been the sole instructor of the layout classes. Alex has in his class teams 1, 2, and 3. Mac and Killer, on the other hand, are currently giving instruction in the proper handling of C4 explosives to teams 4 and 5, nearly twenty kilometers away.

"Good morning, gentlemen," Alex opens. "Today's class will not take the entire two hours, unless you have many questions at the end of the session. The second two hours you will spend together as a team reviewing the information that I am going to hand out in just a moment."

Alex grabs a stack of stapled packets and hands several to the men in the front row. They take the stacks, grab one from the top, and pass them back.

As the packets are being passed back, Alex asks, "Does everyone have one?"

Everyone responds with some form of affirmation.

"Do not open these packets yet. I have more information to give you prior to us reviewing the contents within. Colonel Drasneb and I have finalized your individual team assignments. I am going to hand you a set of packets for each team and their aspect of the mission."

Alex turns again and retrieves another stack of papers from off of his desk. "Stoly, come get your team's packets," Alex instructs.

The team leader for Team 1 steps forward and takes the small stack from Alex.

"You can give them to your team now," Alex says as he hands them to Stoly.

"Thank you," Stoly replies as he returns to his seat area to deliver his packets to his men.

"Greg," Alex says to team leader number 2.

Greg steps forward and retrieves his team's packets from Alex. He then walks away without saying a word.

"Peter, you can come get yours now."

The third team's team leader steps up to Alex, smiling. He takes his packets from Alex, grabs one for himself, then hands them over to another man who commences to passing them out to the remainder of the team.

Now that everyone has two packets, Alex continues with his block of instruction. "Since everyone has a different mission within the mission, this will be the last time that you all have class together for this portion of the training. Team 1, as you can see on page 1, your task involves taking over the MP station. Colonel Drasneb will be with you as you execute, so watch that you do not make too many mistakes. Colonel Drasneb is not a very forgiving man. Teams 2 and 3, your task is to form a perimeter on the Plain in order to halt any interference that may occur once mission execution commences."

Alex takes a couple of steps and moves in front of his desk. He refaces the group then sits on the desk.

"Place those packets down now and open the first packet I handed you," Alex instructs.

The Serbs place their packets down as they were instructed and retrieve the first packet that they had received.

With all of the original packets opened, Alex continues. "What you have in your hands I am classifying as top secret. This aspect of the mission is even more sensitive than what you already know of the mission."

Hearing Alex's words, the men all look at one another, unsure as to what to think. Some of them begin to feed their curiosity by flipping through the packet.

"The reason it is labeled top secret," Alex continues, "is because Mr. Stewart and Mr. Pollard cannot have any semblance of our actions pertaining to this." Alex raises the packet in the air over his head. "If they gain any knowledge of this new part of the mission, then it is very likely that they will do everything in their power to thwart the mission. I don't know about you, but they are two men that I do not want fighting against me."

Though many of the men do not care for the two mercenaries very much, they cannot help but agree with Alex. Mac and Killer are definitely formidable opponents—two men who you do not want to cross or make your enemy.

"What I want you to do now is use the remainder of the time to review your packets as a team," Alex instructs. "I will stay behind to facilitate any questions you may have. So you know, teams 4 and 5 have already received their packets. I will post the new class schedule at dinner. As always, be punctual.

1836 Hours: West Point

Major steps off of the sports shuttle with a numerous assortment of athletes—basketball, tennis, lacrosse, and ice hockey players. When Major stepped onto the sports shuttle up at the Holleder Center, he saw Tim and told him to meet him once they got off down the hill.

Waiting at the sports shuttle door, Tim finally walks off with a group of his teammates.

"Hey, Major," Tim says as he and Major shake hands. "You need to talk to me?"

"Yeah," Major confirms. "Let's walk to the mess hall as we talk."

Major and Tim head for the mess hall behind the pack of athletes, but far enough behind so that no one can hear what they are saying.

Tim continues the conversation, saying, "It's about the situation, huh?"

"Yeah," Major states.

"How's it look for me?"

"Not too bad, actually. Don't ask me how, but it seems as though C-DUBS is really going to be able to keep your punishment down at the battalion level."

"But I thought you said you were going to keep it in house?"

"Fool! Who's the battalion TAC?"

"Captain Weiss."

"Exactly."

"Oh. I got you. My bad."

"Yeah. No kidding. Anyway, we need you to come by the office tomorrow at twelve fifteen. Are you free then?"

"Yeah. I'll be there."

"Good deal. I'll see you then."

Russian Training Camp

Mac and Killer stand in the chow line for dinner. Mac has taken a few moments to psyche himself up for yet another original meal—beef stroganoff. Unlike breakfast, they only have beef stroganoff every fourth day, so that is not too bad.

"Yeah. Beef stroganoff," Mac cynically comments as he and Killer make their way through the chow line.

Killer laughs at his friend's sarcasm.

As they sidestep forward, Killer spots Alex and shouts, "Hey, Alex! You eating?"

"Yeah," Alex responds. "I'll be right there."

Alex turns away and heads for the information board, which is located to the rear center of the mess tent.

Killer and Mac watch Alex place a sheet of paper on the information board in a location where all of the Serbs cannot help but see it.

"I wonder what he's putting up there?" Killer asks.

"Beats me," Mac replies. "He may be your boy and all, but he's still Colonel Drasneb's lackey, so you never know."

"I'll ask him when he sits."

Mac and Killer make their way to the front of the chow line. Mac, who is in front of Killer, sticks his tray out to receive his food. A big, burly man who looks more like a grizzly bear than a man slops a large spoonful of beef stroganoff onto Mac's aluminum tray.

"Thanks," Mac cynically replies.

The burly man, aware that Mac is being rude, simply growls at him. In return, Mac laughs at him as he moves further down the line.

Alex receives his food and says, "Thanks, man."

The burly man nods his head in recognition.

Mac waits at the end of the chow line for Killer.

When Killer reaches Mac, he asks, "Why do you have to be so rude all of the time? The man's just doing his job."

"Because a brother feels like it. Happy?" Mac retorts.

Killer simply shakes his head. Killer assumed that his friend's attitude would have changed for the better by now. Instead, Mac has been rude and cold toward everyone since jump street. *Oh well,* Killer thinks to himself as he walks with Mac to their table. *At least his attitude hasn't gotten worst. God knows they're not ready for that*

Seated, Mac and Killer eat their meal.

"This isn't too bad," Killer says after having eaten a few bites.

"Sure it is," Mac replies without lifting his face from his tray.

"You wouldn't know you didn't like the food by looking at you."

"The food may suck, but I can't deprive the body of its nourishment. My body's my temple. Know what I'm saying?"

"I hear you, brother."

As Killer and Mac continue eating, Alex finally sits down and joins them.

With Alex seated, Killer asks him, "What was that you were putting up on the board?"

"Just the new class schedule," Alex answers.

"New schedule?" Mac asks.

"Don't worry. It does not interfere with any of your classes or training events," Alex affirms.

"Well, that's good," Killer states.

"It is," Alex agrees. "It just means that me and the men will be pulling some late nights until we fly out of here."

"Sucks to be you," Mac laughs.

"What's the new class schedule for?" Killer asks.

"Oh, it's just added time for the teams to work unhindered on their particular parts of the mission"

"I hear you," Killer replies.

"For instance," Alex continues, "after your classes with Team 5, instead of taking their hour break, they will move to another location and continue training on their own. They will then meet up after dinner and continue training for another two hours."

"Whose brilliant idea was this?" Killer asks. "Don't tell me it was yours."

"No, this was not my idea," Alex replies. "It was Colonel Drasneb's."

"Go figure," Mac chimes.

"Colonel Drasneb takes this mission very seriously," Alex defends.

"No kidding," Mac blurts. "The man treats this thing like he's on a mission from God. Who's he think he is? The Blues Brothers or something?"

"The Blues Brothers?" Alex asks, bewildered.

"Don't worry about it," Mac replies. "It would take too long to explain."

5 NOVEMBER 1999

1200 Hours: West Point

Major sits with Captain Weiss in his office, discussing Tim's punishment prior to his arrival.

"I can't believe you were able to keep this at our level, sir," Major proclaims.

"It took some doing, but with the circumstances behind Tim's involvement, it was worth fighting," Captain Weiss replies. He then continues, "So what should we give him?"

"What can we give him?"

"The max for a battalion board is forty hours and four weeks restriction."

Major leans forward in his seat and places his elbows on his knees. Major ponders Tim's punishment for a few minutes, ensuring that he properly weighs the act with the punishment.

Major sits up and says, "Sir, I think we should go with the full forty hours, but give him two-weeks restriction. For the hours though, I think we should split the punishment in half, twenty hours of walking tours and the other twenty, details."

"Okay," Captain Weiss affirms. "I'll go with that."

Tim steps out of the mess hall much slower than usual. He has never been in any trouble before. Though he knows he is not facing separation from the academy, Tim is still unsure as to what his fate is. Major and Captain Weiss hold his livelihood in their hands.

Tim reaches Grant Barracks and drags himself up the steps to Captain Weiss's office. As he walks into Grant Barracks, Tim hears

Captain Weiss and Major speaking to one another. Instead of walking into the office and interrupting his TAC and company commander, Tim makes the right decision by staying out in the hallway and waiting to be called. He patiently stands outside of Captain Weiss's office at the position of parade rest.

While in the middle of a conversation with Major, Captain Weiss spots Tim standing out in the hall.

"Come on in, Tim," Captain Weiss says, waiving Tim into the office.

Major rises from his seat and slides his chair back and out of the way.

Tim marches in front of Captain Weiss's desk, executes a left face, and says, saluting, "Sir, Cadet Thomas reports as ordered."

Captain Weiss stands to his feet, returns the salute, and replies, "Relax, Tim."

Tim goes to at ease, while Major walks from behind and stands beside him.

"Tim," Captain Weiss opens, "you know why you are here. You supplied an alcoholic beverage to a party where underage cadets were present. Due to your actions, several underage cadets drank against the laws of the State of New York. For your punishment, you will receive two weeks of restriction and forty hours. Twenty of them will be walking tours, the others, work details. During your restriction, you must remain in your room at all times. When you leave, you must sign in and out at the CQ desk. Ensure that you read the reg so you don't break your restriction. Do you understand?"

"Yes, sir," Tim replies.

"Good. Do you have any questions?" Captain Weiss asks.

"No, sir."

"Okay then. Your restriction begins today and your tours tomorrow. Do you want to walk or do the details first?"

"I'll walk first, sir."

"Okay. Walk it is. Do you have any questions of me?"

"No, sir."

"You're dismissed then."

Tim salutes Captain Weiss then exits the office. Major gives a signal to Captain Weiss then follows Tim out into the hallway, waiting for Major near the exit out to Grant Area.

"Thanks a lot, man. I really appreciate it," Tim says to Major as he approaches.

"It's no problem, Timmy," Major replies, slapping Tim on the back. "That's what I'm here for. I'm always looking out."

8 NOVEMBER 1999

2130 Hours: Russian Training Camp

Mac and Killer have been high in the trees for several hours. The Serb teams have completed their additional training in the area and have now moved further north toward the Volga River.

The area clear, Mac and Killer descend from their perch and return to base camp. Instead of going to their tent, Killer and Mac head for Alex's. Entering, Mac and Killer discover that Alex's tent is empty and that he is nowhere around.

Upset, Mac flips Alex's cot over. More in control, Killer sits down in a chair.

"You know where that punk is, right?" Mac asks.

"More than likely he's down at the river," Killer replies.

"This extra training mess is really pissing me off!"

"Yeah. Me too. Drasneb's up to something."

"Yeah. The problem is we don't have a friggin' clue."

"We're going to have to keep our eyes open."

"Killer! If we keep our eyes open anymore, them jokers'll fall out if we cough!"

"Yeah. I feel you. It's not like we're not doing our jobs."

"I haven't slacked any. Have you?"

"Not a bit."

"That means Drasneb's a lot smarter than we gave him credit for."

"Or more twisted."

"True. But either way, we need to stay extra alert when we get stateside."

"Alex may become a problem."

"Your little buddy? Maybe, but I don't think he'd turn on us."

"I thought you were the one who's supposed to not like Alex?"

"It has nothing to do with like or dislike. Loyalty is one of Alex's strongest characteristics. He's grown attached to us. He'll keep us in the dark for as long as he needs to, but he won't betray our trust. Not even for Drasneb."

"Yeah. I guess you're right, but enough about that. We're not going to sit here and wait for him all night. We'll confront him again sometime tomorrow."

"Works for me. You know how I like my sleep anyway."

Mac picks the cot up that he kicked over. He and Killer leave Alex's tent without a trace of their presence having been there.

11 NOVEMBER 1999

0500 Hours: Russian Training Camp

Team 2 is receiving training from Mac and Killer on how to properly set and establish a perimeter. The men stand in the middle of an immense overgrowth of trees, shrubbery, and other foliage. Killer stands among Team 2 as the primary instructor. Mac stands off to the side in observation.

"All right, guys," Killer begins. "We've been through this one before. This'll be the last time that we train on establishing perimeters. If the mission goes according to plan, then as you guys know, you will be the only ones actually lying in some form of a perimeter once we move into the execution phase."

While Killer instructs the team, he notices several of the team members yawning. He even spots a few standing with their eyes closed. *This is ridiculous,* Killer thinks. *Drasneb is wearing them out with all of the extra training that these guys are doing.*

Taking himself out of internal thought, Killer continues his class saying, "Form up and move into position."

The men take their weapons off of their shoulders and move away from Killer with their weapons at the ready. They spread out and move further away from one another, careful not to step on any dry leaves or sticks. It is very imperative that the team makes no sound as they move.

Team 2 moves closer to Mac's position. The closer they come, the further out Mac moves. Mac makes it a point not to be seen or heard. Killer, on the other hand, stands in the center of the forming perimeter to ensure that Team 2 properly performs the exercise.

As the team members move into their respective positions, they slowly take their bodies down on the ground and lie in the prone, their weapons aimed outward. In the prone, each man is a minimum of five meters apart from one another. They are positioned in such a manner to alleviate the threat of an exploded grenade killing more than one man.

Mac, afar off in the wood line, recognizes that Team 2 is in position. Killer throws Mac a sign, signaling that he can begin the infiltration phase of the training. Stealthily, Mac moves around the perimeter, searching for any and all weak spots that may exist. Mac's assessment is that the perimeter looks very good. Now it is time for him to check and see if the Serbs are alert and prepared to defend against an infiltration.

Moving ever so cautiously, Mac moves closer and closer to the Serb perimeter. He has his weapon at the ready—buttstock deep in his shoulder, prepared to kill at will. The speed at which Mac moves is such that if one were to keenly watch him, it would appear as though he is not moving. If one were to look away periodically, it would appear as though Mac was jumping from one location to another. Some would say that Mac's movements are so smooth and mechanical that it appears as though the luminance from the sky were an oversized strobe light.

Mac reaches ten meters from the Serb perimeter. At this point, the soldier in position, if he can see the enemy, is supposed to fire a warning shoot at his feet. As realistic as the training is, none of the soldiers carry live ammunition. Everyone trains with blanks and blank adapters over the muzzles of their weapons.

No shot is fired. Mac does not think too much of it. He knows that he is good at what he does, so he concludes that the soldiers simply did not see him. Shrugging the no fire off, Mac continues forward.

About three minutes later, Mac is seven meters from the perimeter. The reason it takes Mac an extended length of time to move forward is that he does not move in a straight line. During his entire movement toward the Serb position, Mac has been moving in a counter clockwise motion around the perimeter. In an actual mission, Mac would not move in such a manner, but for training purposes, he feels that it is pertinent that every soldier's eyes are trained to track the enemy, thus is moving technique.

Again no shot is fired. This time, Mac is somewhat worried. *Something's wrong*, Mac begins to ponder. *Someone would have spotted me earlier, but now there's no excuse. I'm not wearing any special camo. These guys are better than this. I've got to see what's up.*

Upset, Mac slowly drops to the ground and low crawls forward. His movement now is straight. Mac is curious as to why he was not spotted and is determined to discover the cause as swiftly as possible. While in motion, Mac decides to split two Serbs. This way he can check on more than one soldier at a time.

Two meters from the perimeter, Mac spies a Serb preparing to fire upon him. Quickly, Mac turns and aims his weapon at the Serb, which is the signal he uses with them not to fire. Recognizing the signal, the Serb does not fire.

Mac continues his forward motion. Slowly, he creeps forward. Passing the one-meter mark, Mac is now full of rage. *These bastards!* Mac shouts internally. *I know they're asleep! I know it!*

Frustrated, Mac leaps to his feet and charges forward. He leaps on the soldier to his left, rolling over and then leaping on the soldier to his right. The soldiers shriek in terror, totally caught off guard because they were not expecting anyone to jump on them, especially a man of Mac's stature. He returns to his feet, huffing and puffing. It is evident that he is not very happy.

Mac stands over the two bruised Serbs and glares at them as though he were looking into their souls, saying, "I will kick the living Jesus out of you if I find you asleep again! Understand this." Mac then slings his weapon over his shoulder and walks off.

12 NOVEMBER 1999

1300 Hours: Russian Training Camp

"You're taxing your men, sir." Killer says to Colonel Drasneb. "A little adversity never hurt anyone, Mr. Stewart," Colonel Drasneb replies.

"That may be true, sir, but Mac caught two men sleeping while on perimeter training."

"It happens."

"I understand, sir, but they hadn't been on the ground for a full hour."

Colonel Drasneb leans back in his chair, his hands folded in front of him. "You gentlemen need to understand that the men are training very hard, and that a little sleep deprivation is going to set in from time to time."

"No one knows better than us about how hard these men are training, but this sleeping thing is a new problem that's only been occurring for the past week or so. And it's not just that, sir. The men are dozing off during their classroom sessions as well."

"The bottom line, sir," Mac interjects, "is that if your men keep up this new pace that you've set for them, they're going to get themselves killed."

"I believe I know my men a little better than you, Mr. Pollard," Colonel Drasneb informs. "Allow me to be the judge of their abilities."

"All right, sir," Killer states. "Their lives are in your hands. If they fail due to lack of proper rest, then the blame lies with you."

"So it does," Colonel Drasneb agrees. "You gentlemen have anything else for me?"

"Yes, we do," Killer answers. "What is all of this extra training for anyway? We can't get a straight answer out of Alex."

"It is of no concern of yours," Colonel Drasneb snides.

"Yes, it is," Mac states. "When we signed on, it was with the clear understanding that we were in control of all aspects of training."

"And so you are," Colonel Drasneb retorts. "All they are doing is extended training with their individual teams."

"We understand that, sir," Killer says, "but when Mac and I designed the training program, we did so to ensure that the teams were receiving the adequate amount of training needed to achieve mission success."

"I agree, Mr. Stewart," Colonel Drasneb affirms. "I just feel that they need this little extra bit."

"Whatever you say, sir," Mac interjects. "They're your men, and it's your mission."

Colonel Drasneb sits up in his seat and says, "Mr. Pollard, that is the most exact thing you have said since I have met your acquaintance."

15 NOVEMBER 1999

2130 Hours: Russian Training Camp

Armed with only a pair of binoculars, Mac and Killer sit high in a couple of trees. Their training for the night is complete, but they decided to stay out a little longer than usual. Mac and Killer's intent is to feed their curiosity by discovering what the teams are doing during their additional training sessions. The teams' recent post-training activities have Mac and Killer quite concerned. They do not know what to make of the situation. Colonel Drasneb threw up a road block during their inquiry, and Alex is no help because he is Colonel Drasneb's number 1 guy.

Mac and Killer are watching teams 4 and 5 operate. The two teams are not moving very much. On the contrary, in terms of military training, they are not doing anything. Everyone is gathered around what appears to be a map of some sort. Mac and Killer are unable to make out exactly what the teams are studying.

One of the team members shifts his body, allowing Killer to get a better look at the map. *That's a map of the Hudson Valley*, Killer says to himself. *What are they looking at that for? We've gone over that several times already.*

While Killer thinks, he spots a Serb, using a long stick, point from the West Point side of the Hudson River to the other.

I wonder what that motion's for? Killer asks himself.

1830 Hours: West Point

The locker room is quite busy. Tonight, Army plays Yale. Yale is not a basketball powerhouse by any means, but neither is Army. Whenever the two teams meet on the court, the game is always a tough battle. Unfortunately though, Yale usually ends up on top. As far as the firsties on the team are concerned, that was then. This is now.

Major sits in front of his locker with his headphones on over his ears, full blast. Before every game, Major listens to a mix CD that he created his yearling year, which he uses to prepare himself mentally for the game. The songs are not soft by any means. Other than two James Brown songs, Major listens to solely hard-core hip-hop before a game. The last thing he needs in his system before he steps out on the court is Mr. Nice Guy. Major's music prepares him for the toughness of the upcoming game.

For nearly fifteen minutes, Major sits near motionless. Other than the slight rocking from side to side and some head bobs, Major does not move at all. Though he is aware of his surroundings, Major does not acknowledge any of the activity around him. Major sits in his game shorts, game shoes, and his signature white knee-high socks. He used to catch a lot a flack for the socks his plebe year, but once he was able to prove his worth on the team, he was left alone. Now several players wear their socks up to their knees, including Jimmy.

As Major mentally prepares for the game, Theo approaches him and says, "Here you go, Major."

Theo hands Major his game jersey. Major's number is thirteen. People used to always ask him why he has the unluckiest number in the world as his number. Major's response to them is, "Because I am bad luck for the other team." Everyone tends to agree.

Major takes his jersey from Theo and nods his head in thanks. He then places it on his lap and continues listening to his music.

———————————————————

Time progresses, and it is near time for the team to exit the locker room and head out to the gym. The team begins to slowly congregate into the center of the locker room. Major turns his discman off and takes his head phones from off of his head then places them in the top shelf of his locker. He rises from his seat and stands on the edge of the pack.

The team all grabs onto one another's shoulders, forming a huge tight circle. Major makes his way into the center of the circle and, along with the firsties on the team, form their own circle within the larger one. Back and forth, the two circles rock. When one circle sways right, the other sways left.

As the firsties rock, they begin to chant "Army" over and over again.

After a few chants of "Army," the underclassmen begin to jump up and down together and chant "Victory!" as they rock from side to side.

Jimmy then steps out of his huddle into the center of the circles. Bouncing a few inches off of the ground and turning in all directions, he shouts, "Tonight, we do this thing! Yale is nothing! They're nobody! They're nothing but a bump in the road to the true goal! Understand this! Know this! Victory is the only outcome tonight!"

Jimmy returns to the huddle and is followed by Derrick, who says to his team, "Jimmy's right, fellas! Tonight, we defeat Yale, but don't allow over confidence to blind you. Yale is tough, but we're tougher!" Derrick states, clinching his left fist. He continues, "We have only one goal in sight, and that's going to the big dance. Nothing else is acceptable. Every victory is one step closer. Tonight, Yale will get stepped on."

Finished speaking, Derrick returns to the huddle and is followed by Major. When he enters the huddle, everyone grows silent. Major raises his right fist over his head and says, "Bring it in."

The team huddle collapses around Major, their hands all touching in the air.

Major raises his head skyward and prays. "Lord, tonight we play a very formidable Yale team. We have practiced long and hard for this game and pray that you grant us the ability to achieve victory. Lord, you know our hearts, and we ask you to guide us toward our one true goal—going to the NCAA Tournament. We claim the victory, Lord. In your Son Jesus's name, Amen."

With the prayer complete, everyone shouts, "Amen!"

Major then shouts, "One! Two! Three!"

"Victory!" the team replies.

The men's varsity basketball team, full of adrenaline and totally psyched for the game, rush out of the locker room for Crystal Arena on a quest for yet another victory.

2130 Hours

As the Black Knights had anticipated, they defeated Yale. Whenever Army and Yale meet, the game is always very close. The score was relatively close throughout the course of the game. Several times, the lead switched from one team to the other. Not until the final stretch was Army able to truly pull away mostly due to Yale's constant fouling during the last two minutes. Jimmy shot several key free throws to lock the victory for the Black Knights.

The crowd tonight was not very packed, which, unfortunately, is the norm. No Army home basketball games are ever filled to capacity, except when they play Navy and Major's yearling year when they played Duke. Rarely is Crystal Arena filled with cheering fans. The lack of a crowd used to bother Major greatly, but he has grown accustomed to the small crowds that are infinitely smaller and quieter than the ones at his high school. In fact, Major kind of likes the small crowds. At least he knows who the real fans are—friends and families of the team, the women's basketball team, several football players, and some of the West Point staff and faculty.

With the game over, Major stands in the locker room, waiting for Jimmy as usual.

"You ready to go? I want to get some pizza before the plebes eat it all," Major says in an attempt to rush Jimmy.

"I'm moving," Jimmy replies as he tosses his dirty uniform into the dirty clothes bin.

He and Major walk out of the locker room together. Entering Crystal Arena, the two teammates are bombarded by a mob of little kids begging for autographs. The little kids hold up game programs, and the team media guides for Major and Jimmy to sign. Fervently, Major and Jimmy take the articles from the kids and sign their autographs while talking to them about the game.

After signing a multiple of autographs, the crowd finally subsides and Jimmy and Major are able to make their way to the end court bleachers where the managers have the pizzas and drinks laid out. Jimmy and Major each grab a large sausage pizza. Jimmy takes a Coke and Major grabs a Gatorade. They then sit down on the bleachers and eat.

While Jimmy and Major eat, Coach O'Hara's two teenage daughters, Jennifer and Leslie, and assistant coach Bob Christmas's daughter, Carrie, walk over to them. Jennifer is a year older than her sister. Leslie and Carrie are the same age and are like best friends. Major and Jimmy treat the girls like they are their little sisters.

"Great game, guys!" Jennifer congratulates as the three girls approach.

"Thanks," Jimmy replies with a mouthful of pizza.

"I don't think you missed a shot tonight," Carrie suggests.

"I missed three," Jimmy answers with a straight face. Jimmy may be the biggest joker one will ever meet, but he is dead serious about his sport.

"I didn't miss a shot," Major jokes, giving a five to each of the girls.

"That shot you blocked was incredible!" Leslie states. "Mom jumped out of her seat!"

"I bet she did," Major replies with a slight chuckle.

"What about my dunks?" Jimmy asks.

"God!" Jennifer begins. "She went nuts, like always."

"There's nothing T loves more than a good dunk," Major adds, nudging Jimmy in the side with his elbow.

Jimmy returns the nudge with a punch to Major's shoulder. The group laughs at Jimmy and Major's exchange.

As Major and Jimmy continue eating and conversing with the girls, Mrs. Wood joins the group and says to Major and Jimmy, "You guys need a ride down?"

"Yes, ma'am!" Jimmy quickly answers. He closes his pizza box and leaps to his feet.

"The Big Guy's bringing the car around now. You ready?"

"Yes, ma'am," Major replies, slowly moving himself from the bleachers.

Already wearing his winter attire, Jimmy stands beside Mrs. Wood with his arm around her shoulder. While Major puts his parka on, the girls give Jimmy a hug. They then give Major a hug once he is zipped up.

"We'll see you guys," Major says to the girls as he and Jimmy follow Mrs. Wood out of Crystal Arena.

"Bye, Major. Bye, Jimmy," the girls reply.

Mrs. Wood, Jimmy, and Major turn left and exit the Holleder Center. Fortunately, they walk beneath the handicap ramp overhang because it is raining out. The temperature has dropped considerably since Major and Jimmy arrived at the Holleder Center earlier in the afternoon.

"I hope the roads don't freeze over," Mrs. Wood wishes as the three of them walk down the side ramp.

"Shoot!" Major exclaims. "I just hope it doesn't get too cold tomorrow. I hate standing in formation when it's freezing out."

"I hear you, brother," Jimmy agrees.

Mrs. Wood laughs at her surrogate sons' complaining.

"You know? It's not like we're going to be driving anywhere tomorrow," Major comments.

"Yeah. As long as I don't fall on my butt in front of anyone, it's all good," Jimmy adds.

At the bottom of the ramp, a Lexus sedan idles on the side of the road. Mrs. Wood, Jimmy, and Major rush to the car to escape the freezing rain. Jimmy throws the rear passenger's side door open, while Major opens the front passenger side door for Mrs. Wood. Jimmy leaps in, leaving the door open for Major. Mrs. Wood scurries into her seat, the door quickly closing as she enters. Major then steps back and throws himself into the backseat.

"Way to play tonight, guys," Colonel Wood congratulates as he pulls away from the Holleder Center and heads down to Cadet Area.

"Thanks, sir," Major and Jimmy reply.

"Where do you guys want me to drop you off?" Colonel Wood asks as they pass alongside Lusk Reservoir.

"Can you drop me off in front of Scott?" Jimmy asks.

"Scott it is," Colonel Wood replies as they all drive past the Cadet Chapel.

Between MacArthur Barracks and Arvin Gym and the front of Scott Barracks, Colonel Wood stops the car.

"Thanks, sir," Jimmy says as he leaps out of the car, moving in haste for his room in Scott Barracks.

Major begins to slide to the side and exit the car when Colonel Wood says, "You don't want me to take you over to Grant?"

"You can do that, sir?" Major asks.

"Of course, I can," Colonel Wood boasts.

"Let's do it then, sir," Major happily says as he shuts the car door.

The last thing Major wanted to do was walk in the rain. After most basketball games, the players and the managers have to walk back to the barracks unless Theo decides to have one of his managers drive them down to Cadet Area. The drive down is a privilege due to its rarity because the managers have to stay later than everyone and clean up. Theo does make it a point though to drive the team up and down the hill whenever possible. He remembers the walking days and hates the wet and cold just like everyone else.

Colonel Wood drives through the outskirts of Cadet Area, stopping in front of Grant Barracks.

"Here you are, man," Colonel Wood announces as the Lexus comes to a stop. "Nothing like curb-side service."

"You're right about that, sir," Major agrees.

Major jumps out of the Lexus and speed walks to the nearest set of steps to the stoops. Protection from the elements, as well as keeping his pizza dry, is all that matters to him. The least amount of time Major has to spend being wet and cold, the better.

16 NOVEMBER 1999

0830 Hours: Russian Training Camp

Mac and Killer have finished their training session early. They now stand in front of the tent where Alex is giving instruction. Mac and Killer patiently wait. The conversation they intend on having with Alex has been rehearsed in their heads several times. Alex does not owe them his loyalty or even friendship, but trust and integrity is one that none of them can forfeit, especially in the world in which Mac and Killer live.

After waiting just under an hour, several Serbs begin exiting the tent. As usual, Mac and Killer receive mixed emotions from the men. A few of the Serbs smile, many scowl, and some how no expression at all. Mac thinks that the lack of facial emotion is a cultural thing. Personally, he does not want to visit Serbia a second time to test his hypothesis.

With all of the Serbs clear of the tent, Killer enters and coldly says to Alex, "Step outside. We need to talk."

Alex looks up from his desk and replies, "I'll be right there." He quickly organizes a stack of folders then meets Mac and Killer outside of the tent.

As Alex steps out of the tent, Mac says, "Come with us."

With a humorous tone in his voice, Alex replies, "If I didn't know you guys better, I would think that you wanted to kill me."

"It has crossed my mind," Mac quickly informs.

Alex is unsure of what to think about Mac and Killer's unusual behavior. He knows that he is not in any danger, but at the same time, he knows that whatever is about to occur is not going to be pleasant.

Mac and Killer lead Alex out to an open field. The view is clear of any trees or large brush. Mac and Killer chose the location more for security purposes than privacy.

"We need to talk," Killer says, turning around and looking at Alex.

"About what?" Alex asks.

"You know what," Mac interjects.

Killer puts his hand in the air, signaling Mac to calm down.

"The extra training that your guys have been doing the past couple of weeks or so," Killer continues.

"What is wrong with a little extra training?" Alex responds.

"When it's interfering with the assigned training, that's when we have a problem with it."

"Gentlemen, we've already discussed this once, and we all know that I know that you've discussed this subject once with Colonel Drasneb. Nothing has changed since your previous conversations."

"Damn it, Alex! Stop messing around!" Mac jumps in. "We know something's going on. Drasneb's not paying us all this money 'cause we're stupid."

Alex puts his head down and begins pacing in a small circle. His breathing increases somewhat, and his heart beats just a little faster. Mac and Killer can tell that Alex is nervous, but nerves are not really his problem as they see it. Alex is torn between his new friends and his mentor and leader.

After a few minutes in deep thought, Alex stops in place and looks up at Mac and Killer. "I have been ordered not to divulge what the additional training is for or what it entails. I will tell you this though. At the end of the mission, Colonel Drasneb is going to kill you."

Mac laughs uncontrollably at the last part of Alex's statement. Confused, Alex looks at Mac in a peculiar manner.

"Mac's laughing," Killer explains, "because we already knew that. Shoot! We knew he wanted to kill us the first day we got to Belgrade. We're not too worried about it."

"Oh," Alex replies, a bit stunned, "I guess you're not too worried then?"

Still laughing, Mac shakes his head no.

Killer waits for Mac to calm down some before he continues with the conversation. "Alex, do you ever ponder the morality of this mission?"

"Not at all," Alex is quick to answer.

"How can you not?"

"The cadets are future officers. As far as I am concerned, they are soldiers. They may not have any experience, but they have already sworn to fight and die for their country."

"But, Alex, they're just kids. They're still wet behind the ears. Are you telling me that you have no compassion whatsoever?"

"I will say that I do not agree with our mission execution."

"What do you mean?"

"The way the cadets are going to die, there's no honor in that. It's one thing to shoot someone face-to-face, but when you are not able to see your killer—no pun intended—face-to-face, that is not right."

"I agree with you on that one," Mac adds to the two-way conversation.

Killer continues, saying, "But you've been there. You saw those kids. Are you telling me that you felt so threatened that your only recourse was to join Colonel Drasneb in his unholy campaign?"

"That's not it at all."

"Then what is it?"

"I cannot say. I owe Colonel Drasneb my life. I am indebted to him. I have no love for the Americans, so working for him directly on this mission does not cause me to lose any sleep."

Mac, tired of the continuous back and forth nature of Killer and Alex's conversation, places his hand on Killers chest and steps forward.

"Alex," Mac begins, "let's say that a platoon of US Army soldiers or Marines are on patrol one day and come across an enemy village where the population is 50 percent young adults, 15 percent between the ages of forty to sixty-five, and the remainder percentage is a combination of the remaining ages. Being that the US is at war, the platoon leader assumes that everyone in the young adult 50 percent range is a clear and present threat to his country's operations. Why? Because at any time, they can pick up a weapon and fight for their country against the US. To thwart this threat, the platoon leader decides to take it upon himself and kill the young adults in the village. Mind you now, they are not carrying any weapons, and any military knowledge they may have has mostly come through verbal lesson. While killing the young adults in the village, others are killed as well, but the platoon leader doesn't care. Why? Because they're a possible threat as well."

"That platoon leader has no honor," Alex comments.

"Well, neither do we," Mac states, "because we're doing the same friggin' thing. Those cadets aren't even getting a chance to defend themselves. They're going to die for one reason— they chose the wrong school to go to."

"I never thought of it like that."

"Of course, you didn't. You did like us. We thought the money would ease our consciences. I never knew mine was so strong until now. We thought that thinking of this mission as only a job would make it easier on us. We were wrong."

"I can't turn on Colonel Drasneb."

"We don't expect you to," Killer includes, "but you should do something. What? I don't know."

"I'm going to put it to you this way," Mac adds. "When this is all over, the Killer and I will more than likely be the last men standing. I'll put you down if I have to, but I'd rather have you leave with us. It's a thought."

"You have thought all of this out already?" Alex asks.

"We're not getting paid five mil a piece for our good looks. We always have an escape route. Shoot! We could leave now and be back in Paris for breakfast right now if we really wanted to, but that'd be a breach of contract."

"And your deaths."

"Since you put it so bluntly," Mac states, "yes, we would be hunted down if we were to not see this mission to the end."

"That's not going to happen though," Killer adds. "We're professionals, but understand that Drasneb will get his in the end."

West Point

"How's the team looking this year, Major?"

"We're friggin' getting it done, brother. You saw what we did to Yale last night. We've got a great crop of freshman this year, and the rest of the guys are looking pretty good."

"We going to the tournament this year?"

"Hell yes!" Major exclaims. "Didn't I say that we'd get there by our firstie year?"

"Yeah, you did."

"Well then. You know I'm never wrong," Major boasts with a smirk on his face. "Hey, Chris, I'll check you later. I've got to get to class."

"No problem. I'll holler at you later."

"All right then," Major answers. "Stop by my room later tonight so I can give you those notes. A little after eight, all right?"

"Yeah. That'll work."

Major has been hanging out with his good friend, Cdt. Chris York. They have been friends since their plebe years when Major was in E-3 and Chris was in I-1. Chris is nearly twice Major's size and is the starting left guard on the football team. He is also one of the biggest supporters of army basketball, which seems to take up the majority of he and Major's conversations.

Major gets up from his seat and grabs his SE 485: Combat Modeling notebook. Chris walks out of his room with Major. He gives Chris a pound then strolls down the hallway of Pershing Barracks as they part ways.

Major walks through the hallway with a sway and an attitude that he knows that he is the best. He is not the greatest basketball player or scholar, but when it comes to overall success and will power, he is in a class all his own. His attitude is homegrown, something his father passed on to him over the years. He does not see it as an attitude problem or having a chip on his shoulder.

On the contrary, Major sees his great feeling of self-worth as a badge of honor. One of his favorite mottoes is "If everyone on this planet had the mind-set that they were truly great, then the world would be a much better place because everyone would show equal respect for one another." Unfortunately, everyone is not built in such a manner.

Down the hall from several directions, cadets greet Major. He'd rather be left alone at times, but his upbringing and manners will not allow him to ignore everyone. Major politely returns their greetings, gives dap to a few, and even slaps some guys on the back and the chest.

It is twenty-three degrees out. Yesterday afternoon, it had rained then snowed before the freezing temperatures moved in. The roads, though they have been cleared and sanded, are not totally without ice. It is still a little slick out on some parts of the road.

Every morning, trucks drive in and out of Central Area to make deliveries and pick up and drop off laundry. One such truck making a delivery today is a six-wheeled Mitsubishi mini tractor-trailer. The driver, a middle-aged man in his late forties, has been on the road for the past nine hours and is exhausted from the trip. His route is routine for him, so he figures on finishing it up instead of resting for a while.

━━━━━━━━━━━━━━━━━━━

"Goddawg, it's cold out here!" Major shouts as he steps out of Pershing Barracks.

"You aren't kidding, dawg," shouts one of Major's friends who just happens to hear Major from a few yards away.

"God did not make man to live in weather like this. Why do you think the Garden of Eden was in the Middle East?" Major proclaims as he throws the Omega Psi Phi sign in the air.

Major's friend and fraternity brother throws it up as well, walking off to the left toward Lincoln Hall.

Major steps out of the sally port facing Thayer Road. As the frigid wind smacks Major in the face, he stiffens so as to keep from freezing to death, or so he would like to think. Major dislikes the cold more than anything. Though his hate for the cold is quite strong, all he wears is his gray letter jacket and a pair of black gloves. Having spent four years experiencing the worst of Northeast winters, Major has come quite acclimated to the cold, but as far as he is concerned, that does not mean that he has to like it.

Carefully, Major walks toward Mahan Hall. Realizing that someone did a lousy job of sanding the sidewalks, Major steps out onto the street to ease his monotonous trip to yet another class. All around him, cadets scurry to and from class like rats in a cage. Major does not move out of anyone's way. He allows them to get out of his.

About a hundred yards or so down the road, he eyes a white truck. By the shape of the hood, Major is able to make out that it is Japanese in origin, probably a Mitsubishi. For some reason, cadets are not afraid of cars. Sure, pedestrians have the right of way, but who is going to live if the two collide?

As Major continues toward Mahan Hall, suddenly from out of nowhere, the truck driver loses control of his vehicle. The cadets in the road spring out of the truck's ensuing path, unable to scream from the sheer shock of a near-death experience.

One cadet stands in the middle of the road, staring at the oncoming truck as though she was a deer staring into headlights. The cadet is unable to move. No thoughts flow through her head, only an immense sense of fear. What is only a couple of seconds seems to last an eternity.

Seeing the girl in trouble and realizing that the truck is going to hit her, Major's instincts suddenly take over and force him to react. Major drops his books and, with all of his will, sprints toward the girl. A couple of yards from where the frozen girl stands, Major leaps into the air and spears her with his shoulder as he would have done an opponent back in his high school football-playing days.

As Major's shoulder hits the girl's torso, he grabs her with his left arm, ensuring that his momentum caries her with him out of harm's way. The force of Major's impact lifts the girl up off of the ground and forward in the air. Together, the two cadets hit the ground hard, with the truck sliding past them, only inches from where they land.

Skidding and sliding out of control, the truck hits a light post dead-on. The brutal crash instantly stops the truck in its tracks. The driver, who was not wearing a seat belt, is thrown out of his seat and crashes through the windshield. The MPs in the area rush to the truck driver's body, only to discover that he is already dead due to a crushed vertebrate and skull.

Some twenty or so yards away from the demolished truck, Major lies in the middle of the road on top of the female cadet, whom he does not know. His head somewhat clear, Major slowly raises up from on top of her. The pain that courses through his body is excruciating. Both of his knees and his right elbow are cut up and bleeding profusely. Ignoring his pain, Major squats down to check on the cadet whose life he had just saved.

"Hey, are you all right?" Major asks, lightly rubbing the cadet on her back.

The cadet moans then slowly rolls over, saying, "Yeah. I think so. What just happened? Last thing I remember is some truck coming straight at me."

"Well," Major begins, "that's about the gist of it."

While the two cadets converse on the ground, the paramedics finally arrive at the scene. Major informs the cadet all that had occurred from his perspective.

Realizing that he does not know who he has just saved, Major asks the cadet, "So what's your name, anyway?"

"Cheryl. Cheryl Lewis."

Major throws his hand out and says, "Hello, Cheryl. I'm Major. Maybe I'll see you around sometime. Under better circumstances, I hope."

"Yeah. Me too," Cheryl smilingly replies as the paramedics lift her onto a stretcher and into an ambulance.

19 NOVEMBER 1999

1830 Hours: West Point

Major sits in the sports shuttle on his way back from practice, his thoughts on his saving Cheryl's life the other day and the ceremony in his honor that will take place next Tuesday. Personally, Major does not know why he is receiving an award, the Army Commendation Medal. Yes, he understands the technicalities as to why, but Major feels as though anyone would have done what he did under the same set of circumstances.

Turning around and facing several other athletes in the sports shuttle, Major asks, "Who's going to the mess hall?"

Over half of the bus replies with some form of yes.

"Cool," Major responds.

The sports shuttle stops at the corner of Bartlett Hall, and everyone steps off. The plebes, who are still unrecognized, huddle around the corps squad upperclassmen so they do not have to greet any other upperclassmen.

"Come on, kiddies! Let's go!" Major shouts as he leads the way to the mess hall.

Unbeknown to Major, one of his friends sneaks up from behind, grabs him, and picks him up, saying, "Brother! I haven't seen you in a while. Where've you been hiding?"

"It's been rough, bro," Major replies once Chris places him gently back onto the ground.

Major continues. "I've been busy as hell. You know? And with me and my death-defying feats, I've had to meet with the supe, the com, the BTO, my RTO, and my TAC more times in the past three days than I can count. It hasn't made for much free time."

"So you're the reason we're having that mandatory thing at Ike after lunch next Tuesday."

"Yep. It's all my fault." Major clowns.

"You chump," Chris playfully replies.

Chris and Major put their arms around one another and b.s. as they head for the mess hall. As they walk, Jimmy catches up with them from the rear of the group and joins in on the conversation.

The mix of basketball, ice hockey, lacrosse, and football players finally makes its way to the mess hall. Major and his small basketball contingent grab themselves a table, where Major nonchalantly sits at the table com's position.

Slouching in his seat, Major turns to Jimmy and says, "I think I'm going to go see Cheryl tonight."

"Who?" Jimmy asks.

"Cheryl Lewis. The girl I saved the other day."

"Oh yeah. How is she anyway?"

"I don't know, dummy. That's why I'm going to go see her. I haven't spoken to her since that morning. I meant to visit her in the hospital, but I was too busy, meetings and what not."

"Yeah. I hear you."

The waitress, a Hispanic immigrant, brings Major's table their food. Major knows that the waitress is an immigrant because she cannot speak any English. Some cadets joke that the mess hall staff is filled with illegal immigrants, but that is not possible because they all work for a government contractor.

"Dang it!" Major shouts "This isn't enough food! Let me go find Miss C."

Miss C is a part of modern West Point lore. She has worked in the mess hall since the 1960s, or at least that is what every cadet is led to believe. What the cadets do know is that Miss C was a waitress at West Point when the Great Food Fight of 1965 occurred. Smart cadets know to be friendly with Miss C and give her a hug whenever they see her because her position on the West Point mess hall staff allows her to give them more food when asked. Being the man that Major is, he is one such individual.

"Hey, Miss C!" Major shouts as he approaches. "How're you doing, ma'am?"

"Not too bad," Miss C replies. "Can't wait to get home though. I need to soak my feet."

"I feel you on that, ma'am. Mine are killing me from practice." Major places his arm around Miss C's shoulder while they laugh. He then asks her, "Can I get some more food for my table?"

"Sure, baby. Where're you sitting?"

Major points to his table where a hungry group of basketball players anxiously wait.

Recognizing the table, Miss C says, "Okay. I'll get it there in a second."

"Thank you, ma'am," Major graciously states as he waves good-bye.

Major returns to his table and takes a seat. Micah, one of the cows and centers on the basketball team, asks, "Hey, Major. Were you able to get more food?"

"Come on, Big Chief. You disappoint me. When have I ever let you down?" Major sarcastically asks.

"Never."

"Well then. The food'll be here in a sec."

Upon Major's last word, James, one of the few black waiters who works in the mess hall, comes slipping between the tables with a large tray full of food.

Stopping at Major's table, James says to him, "Hey, little man. How's it going?"

"Not too bad, sir," Major replies as he and Jimmy take the food from the tray. Major then continues. "We have a game in five days. You want tickets?"

"Yeah," James boastfully replies. "Put me down for two."

"Good deal. You know where to pick them up at."

"All right then, little brother. I'll see you tomorrow then," James states as he gives Major a pound. He then leaves to continue waiting on his other tables.

With the food in front of them, Major and Jimmy take a hearty helping of veal parmigiana and spaghetti. They then pass the food down to the other guys at the table.

Finished eating, Major quickly rises from his seat and says to Jimmy, "I'm a go see Cheryl now. I'll holler at you later."

The two friends shake hands before Major takes off. As Major prepares to leave the mess hall, he puts his skull cap and gloves back on then sprints across North Area over to Scott Barracks.

Reaching Cheryl's company, H-4, Major enters the CQ room and says to the CQ, "Hey, man. You know where Cheryl Lewis's room is?"

"Yeah," the CQ replies as he checks the room list. "It's 4623."

"Thanks, man," Major states as he bolts out of the CQ room and over to the forty-sixth division and up to the second floor. He strides to Cheryl's door and lightly knocks.

"Enter," a female voice says from the other side of the door.

Major opens the door and enters the room. He places a garbage can between the door and the entranceway to keep the door from closing fully. West Point regulations requires that the bedroom door must remain open at all times when a male and female cadet are alone in a room.

"Hey, girl! How're you doing?" Major asks.

Somewhat surprised by seeing Major, Cheryl replies, "Wow! I didn't think I'd see you again. At least not for awhile, anyway."

"Yeah. I know. I'm sorry for not seeing you over at Keller. They had me at all of these meetings and whatnot. I barely had time to breathe."

"I know what you mean. I've been doing nothing but homework, trying to catch up with all of the assignments I missed."

"Man! That sucks!" Major exclaims, pulling up a seat beside Cheryl, who is sitting on her bed.

The two cadets sit and just talk about life and the things that only those who share a common bond can understand. Cheryl and Major are now eternally linked.

23 NOVEMBER 1999

1235 Hours: West Point

Making their way down to Eisenhower Hall, three first class cadets converse on the events that had recently occurred over the past week.

"Can you believe Major's getting a medal today?"

"Naw, man. Sure can't. It's unbelievable."

"Forget the fact he's getting a friggin' medal. I can't believe my man jumped in front of a moving truck to save that girl."

"What's her name, anyway?"

"Lewis. I couldn't tell you what her first name is."

"She better be glad Major was there."

"Yeah. No kidding."

The three firsties, two males and a female, cross the street and head in the direction of the hostess's house. As they walk, they pass several small mobs of cadets, some they know and some they do not know. The three firsties greet the cadets who they recognize.

"I wonder how many of these guys really want to be here?"

"Probably not too many. They'd rather be sleeping."

"Most of the corps has at least heard of who Major is though."

"So. They're not his friends. They could care less. It's like those people who go to tap vigils because it's tradition or because it's expected of them. They don't go because their friend died."

"True."

"You think his parents'll be here?"

"They should be. I mean, I would be if my son was getting something like this."

"Yeah. Me too."

The three firsties pass the hostess's house and walk down the first flight of stairs at Eisenhower Hall then turn left into the fourth-floor entrance. Passing the Broadway theater posters, the three firsties enter through the second set of double doors on the left, and into the theater.

Walking down the aisleway and past the first section of seats, the three firsties spot some of their friends from among the immense crowd. They walk toward their friends' direction and take a seat. The group of friends, a combination of firsties and a handful of cows, sit and talk as they wait for the first captain to call the room to attention.

After about ten minutes, the first captain walks out from behind the left curtain on the stage and heads for the main floor.

Standing before the entire corps, the first captain calls, "On your feet! The superintendent."

Lieutenant General Holiday steps out onto the stage and faces the Corps of Cadets. "Take your seats," he kindly orders. "Today, we are here to honor a great American—a young man who was willing to sacrifice his own personal safety for that of a fellow cadet's. Cdt. Capt. Milton Johnson embodies the edict Duty, Honor, Country. Cadet Johnson exemplifies all that we here at West Point instill in each of you every day. Instead of thinking of himself, Cadet Johnson reacted properly by going to the aid of another. Would anyone fault him if he had not done so? Of course not, but knowing Cadet Johnson as I do, I know that he would not have been able to face himself had he not done what he did. Cadet Johnson's quick decision and reaction to aid a fellow classmate proves that the leadership attributes that you all acquire throughout your years here are embodied within each and everyone of you. The army is a much better place for it. I am proud to know Cadet Johnson, Major, personally as the great young man that he is, company commander, and basketball player. It is my honor to present Cadet Johnson with the Army Commendation Medal.

With the completion of his speech, Lieutenant General Holiday gives the command, "On your feet!"

Everyone in the theater hurriedly rise to their feet and move to the position of attention. The superintendent walks to the center of the stage, moves to the position of attention, then gives the command, "Cadet Johnson, post!"

Upon the command, Major marches to the center of the stage from the right side. He faces Lieutenant General Holiday, renders a salute, then reports. Lieutenant General Holiday returns the salute and orders Major to execute an about-face.

With the full attention of all present, Lieutenant General Holiday commands his adjutant, Major Fleming, to publish the orders.

Holding the award in his hand, Major Fleming, in a clear and concise voice, announces, "Attention to orders. The president of the United States presents the Army Commendation Medal to Cdt. Milton Aynes Johnson for his actions by saving the life of a fellow cadet without the thought of his own life. Cadet Johnson's quick thinking and ability to react properly to a dangerous situation exemplifies the seven army values. His heralded actions serve as an example for all cadets to emulate and reflect distinct credit upon himself, the United States Military Academy, and the United States Army."

Lieutenant General Holiday, upon completion of the orders, gives the command, "Colonel Johnson, post to present the award."

Much to Major's surprise, his father steps from behind the left curtain and out onto stage. Colonel Johnson marches out and stands beside Lieutenant General Holiday, who then hands him Major's Army Commendation Medal. Colonel Johnson walks over to his son, removes the medal from its box, and, to everyone's amazement, hands the medal over to his son. Major willingly takes the medal from his father with his right hand and pins it onto his dress gray uniform, himself.

With Major's napoleonic-style pinning ceremony complete, Lieutenant General Holiday asks, "Major, do you wish to address the corps?"

"Yes, sir. I would," Major replies as he steps forward to the center front of the stage.

Lieutenant General Holiday and Colonel Johnson move a few paces back, so not to crowd Major too much. Major gazes out into the crowd and is able to find a few familiar faces throughout the plethora of cadets, staff, and faculty. Some smile huge grins of happiness, others give a slight, inconspicuous wave. Major notices them and nods his head in acknowledgment, smiling as well.

Seeing his mother in the front row to his right and seated beside Mrs. Holiday, Major begins his speech with "Hey, Mom. I didn't expect you guys to come up here for this."

Major's mother smiles. With a feeling of immense pride, she straightens up in her seat then leans to her left and whispers to Mrs. Holiday, "This should be good."

"What do you mean?" Mrs. Holiday inquires. "Is Major a good public speaker?"

"Well," Mrs. Johnson replies, "let's just say it'll be interesting. My son has a way with words like no one I know. He can talk himself into and out of any situation he's in. Knowing him, he probably already knows what he's going to say."

"Having known Major for a couple of years now," Mrs. Holiday replies, "I understand fully."

On stage, Major gives the proper military courtesies then begins his speech. First, Major decides to open with a joke.

"You know? I always told myself that if I were to ever get hit by a car, I would want it to be a nice, hot, sunny day out. Why? So when I'm lying on the ground in extreme anxiety, at least I won't die from the elements. That just goes to show that you have to be careful of what you wish for. I never said anything to Jesus about a truck."

The crowd roars with laughter from Major's sarcasm. He waits for the jubilation to subside before continuing.

"No one wakes up in the morning and says to himself, 'I think I'm going to jump in front of a truck and save someone today.' God knows I didn't. I just thank him that I was where I was when I needed to be." Major touches his Army Commendation Medal, stating, "I look at this medal and know in my heart of hearts that I am not the only one here who would have done what I did. All I did was my duty. Please, do not look at me as a hero. Instead, look at me as a man who saw a problem and fixed it. Each and every one of you is capable of doing what I did. God just so happened to place me at the scene.

"People have asked me, 'Major, what was going on in your head?' My reply to them is, 'Nothing.' All I did was execute. There are times when there is no time for thought, only action. Too much thinking can cause one to miss a lay up or, more applicable to us as future leaders in the army, get our soldiers killed. If I would have stood on the corner and thought out my actions, Cheryl may not be here with us today. As bad as that may sound, that is reality. It is scary to think of what the world would be like if people did not have the ability to make personal sacrifices for others even at the expense of their own lives."

"Our country would not exist if it were not for those individuals who laid down their lives so that we, their progeny would live in relative peace and freedom. If we as a country are unable to emulate those great heroes, then our country is lost. Without self-sacrifice, there is no freedom because there would be no one willing to die for it. In closing, I would like to thank God for creating me and making me the man that I am and to my parents for instilling strong values in me. Much respect to my brothers, my friends, my army basketball family, and the greatest company in the corps. Go Ducks!"

1 DECEMBER 1999

1400 Hours: West Point

Major strolls through Central Area on his way back to his room from a meeting that he had with Lieutenant Colonel Turner. As he passes Bradley Barracks, Major's good friend, Cdt. Capt. Ben Irons, comes within Major's view from the far side of Eisenhower Barracks.

Ben is the starting middle linebacker of the football team and is the defensives team captain. He and Major have been friends since the second semester of their yearling year when they had a systems-engineering class together.

Seeing one another, the two friends trot to meet at the French Monument.

"What's the word, Major?" Ben asks as he slows to a stop.

"Not much, cousin. Just got out of a meeting with my RTO," Major answers as he extends his hand.

Major and Ben shake hands and embrace.

"That's cool," Ben replies. "You're girl's coming up Friday, right?"

"Yeah," Major says, shaking his head, "but I wouldn't call her my girl yet. Hopefully she will be once the weekend's over though."

"I hear that."

"What time you guys leave for Philly on Friday? I always forget."

"Eleven, but we only have to go to our first class."

"Must be nice."

Grinning, Ben shakes his head several times. Ben is happy because the football team is preparing to play Navy in the annual Army–Navy football game, which this year is scheduled for Saturday, December 4. When the football team departs at eleven in the morning, they will leave to the cheers of the corps. The cadets line up along Thayer Road to wish the team well and send them off.

Later that day, a large majority of the corps will take pass and head for Philadelphia. The remainder of the corps will leave early Saturday morning to join those who left before them, everyone except for the men's and women's basketball teams. They remain behind because they are still in season and either have a game that day or have to practice.

The last time Major saw an Army–Navy football game live was his plebe year when he was still on the junior varsity team. All of the other times, Major watched the Army–Navy game on television either before or after a game or practice. This year is no different.

Continuing their conversation, Ben asks, "Who are you guys playing Saturday?"

"Columbia," Major replies.

"Win or lose?"

"Win, of course."

"Of course. Hey! I just thought. Come by my room Wednesday. I'm going to take some pictures over the weekend. I should have them developed by then."

"Bet. You guys have early lunch still next week?"

"Yeah."

"Cool then. I'll just stop by your room after I march my company in."

"That'll work."

"All right then. If I don't see you before Friday, hurt a squid for me."

"I'll do that."

Major and Ben give each other a pound then part ways.

2100 Hours

Major sits on his couch with his feet propped up on his coffee table with his cell phone in his hand. Tomorrow is a very big day for Major. Tomorrow, Terry flies in to spend the weekend with him. Somehow, she was able to find a free weekend in her very hectic public-speaking schedule. One of the happiest days of Major's life was the day that Terry said she was able to come to West Point for a visit.

Major scrolls through his address book and stops on Terry's name. He then pushes the call button and waits for a response.

After a couple of seconds of waiting, Terry answers and says, "Hello?"

"Hey, Terry. It's Milton."

"Hey, Milton. How are you?"

"I can't be doing any better than I am right now."

Terry laughs. "You're silly," she replies.

"If you only knew."

After a few moments of mutual laughter, Major says, "So you ready for tomorrow?"

"Sure am. I've never been to New York before."

"Well, it's just your luck that you'll be with me. I promise you. You're going to have the time of your life."

"I better," Terry sarcastically answers.

"Your plane still lands at eight thirty?"

"Yeah."

"Good deal. I'll be at the gate waiting."

"I can't wait to see you."

"You too."

There is a short pause that seems to last an eternity. Major then breaks the silence, saying, "I don't want to let you go, but I have to get to some work. We'll have all kinds of time to talk when you get here."

"It's okay. I need to take care of some stuff myself. We definitely will talk when I get there. I'll see you tomorrow."

"See you."

"Bye."

2 DECEMBER 1999

0430 Hours: Russian Training Camp

It is a very luminescent early morning. The stars are out and shining as though they were multiple flashlights in the sky. The brightness is such that one can read outdoors without the aid of artificial light.

Mac stands outside on the tarmac, staring up at the bright night sky. Two things are on his mind—leaving Russia once and for all and flying. Oh, how Mac loves to fly. On the other hand, Mac loathes Russia and everything to do with the place, especially now.

Killer meets with Colonel Drasneb in his tent prior to their departure. Mac does not accompany Killer because he wants as little to do with Colonel Drasneb as possible.

Seeing Killer step into the tent, Colonel Drasneb says, "Are we prepared for departure?"

"Yes, sir," Killer replies. "We're all ready to go. Mac's at the airfield squaring things away."

"Very good. Your diligence is most exemplary."

"We aim to please," Killer jokes as he and Colonel Drasneb exit the tent and head for the airstrip.

While Colonel Drasneb and Killer walk, Colonel Drasneb, asks, "Do you have the itinerary?"

"Right here, sir," Killer replies, handing Colonel Drasneb a blue folder.

Colonel Drasneb opens the folder and reads its contents. While reading, he makes a few facial gestures and nods his head.

"You're covering our tracks very well," Colonel Drasneb approvingly states.

"That we are," Killer replies. "As you can see, you have two different passports other than your own. It is safe for you to use your passport from Belgrade to London, but from London to Boston and then Boston to Newark, it is imperative that you use one of the fakes. Each passport matches your tickets, so just ensure that you use the correct one. We've come too far to get stopped at customs."

"That we have," Colonel Drasneb laughs.

3 DECEMBER 1999

1815 Hours: West Point

Basketball practice was short today due to the team having a game against Columbia tomorrow. Instead of the usual intense practice, practices just before games are very light. The team shoots around, walks through their plays as well as their opponent's plays, and then watches game film of their upcoming opponent.

Practice began at three and ended at five. Major, having plenty of spare time on his hands, shot around some more with Coach O'Hara then watched some additional game film. Since Major plans on leaving for Newark airport a little after six thirty, he did not want to waste time going down to his room then having to go back up to the lots to get his 4Runner. Instead, Major hangs out with his plebe teammates who remain in the team lounge watching television and eating pizza.

Through relaxing, Major leaves the lounge to take a quick shower. Clean, Major goes to the locker room and puts on some civilian clothes. Wanting to impress Terry but not overdo it, Major wears a simple pair of blue slacks and a gray cotton sweater with a white-collared dress shirt underneath.

As Major gets dressed, one of the plebes steps into the locker room, saying, "Getting ready to get your girl, huh?"

"Something like that," Major replies while he slips on his gray Lugz.

"I heard she's pretty hot."

"Yeah, she's cute."

"How'd you ever hook up with her anyway? Wasn't she in the Miss America Pageant or something?"

"Yeah, she was, but it's a long story. I'll have to tell it to you someday, but right now, I've got to get going. You'll see her tomorrow at the game."

"Have fun then."

With a huge grin on his face, Major says, "Trust me, Tuck. I will," as he strides out the locker room.

1825 Hours: Newark International Airport, Newark, New Jersey

Major is running a little late. He ran into a little unanticipated traffic on the Palisades Parkway. The last thing he wants is to be late meeting Terry at her gate. Major zooms into the Newark airport short-term parking area and takes the first empty space that he finds. He jumps out of his 4Runner and sprints into C terminal because Terry is flying Continental.

Major reaches the escalator and darts up it. He skirts past people, doing his best not to run into anyone. Major moves as though he were back on the football field after intercepting a pass. On the second floor, Major speeds his way to the next escalator and runs up it as well.

Now on the third floor, Major slows to a trot. As he slows down, Major begins to empty his pockets of his wallet, pen, and keys because he is nearing security. His turn through the metal detector, Major puts his belongings, along with his watch and class ring, into a plastic bowl and places it onto the conveyor belt. When signaled by the TSA agent, Major walks through the metal detector. Fortunately, the green light appears, so security waves Major through. Quickly, Major grabs his belongings from the plastic bowl and places them back into his pockets as he continues his quick pace.

Terminal C is separated into three hallways. To ensure that he does not head down the wrong hallway, Major rushes to the arrival board and checks to see at which gate Terry's plane is landing. Major's eyes quickly search for Indianapolis, Indiana. Finding the proper gate, Major leaps away from the arrival board and heads down the hallway where gate C-5 is located.

■────────────■

Mac, Killer, and Colonel Drasneb's plane lands smoothly on the tarmac. Colonel Drasneb has had a very extensive and tiring trip. Mac and Killer, on the other hand, enjoyed themselves quite well. Since they fly all of the time, Mac and Killer know how to entertain themselves on long flights and, most importantly, help pass the time.

Finally on US soil, in Newark, New Jersey, Mac, Killer, and Colonel Drasneb depart the plane. Because they are riding first class, they step off of the plane first. Mac and Killer, followed by Colonel Drasneb, step out from the gate and enter the terminal.

Walking out into the terminal, Mac looks up and notices that they are at gate C-17.

Terminal C, Mac says to himself, *how familiar.*

■————————————————————————————————————■

Major speeds through the terminal. There is only one thought on his mind: *I cannot miss Terry's flight.* First impressions are everything and the last thing that Major wants is for Terry to have an ill initial opinion of him.

Major darts through the immense airport crowd. Every time Major is at Newark airport, it is crowded. Of course, he understands that Newark airport is one of the busiest and most important airports in the world. The majority of the people whose destination is New York City lands at Newark International Airport.

As Major moves, he avoids running into the numerous people who are congesting the terminal. As he jogs around a small group of women, Major looks up and is suddenly knocked back a few feet by a seemingly immense and unmovable force. Major looks straight ahead at the force that knocked him back and is shell-shocked by what stands before him. Staring Major square at his face is the largest chest that he has ever seen.

"Excuse me, sir," Major says as he looks up and steps to the side out of the way of the extremely huge gentleman.

"No problem, little man," the extremely large gentleman replies as he and the two gentlemen who accompany him continue on their way as though nothing has occurred.

"Goddawg!" Major softly says aloud as he walks backward a few paces. "That brother is friggin' huge!"

As Major gawks at the size of the man he had just ran into, the man suddenly snaps his head around and looks at Major. The gaze only lasts for a split second, but Major feels as though the man just stared into his soul.

———————————————————

"You didn't hurt that kid, did you?" Killer jokingly asks.

"Naw, man. The kid actually had a little bit of strength in him," Mac replies with a soft smile on his face. He then says, "You know, I think I know that kid from somewhere."

"What do you mean?" Killer asks.

"Can't say. I just have this weird feeling that I know him, but I know I don't. You know what I'm saying?"

"Deja vu's a killer, bro. No pun intended, of course."

"Of course."

Colonel Drasneb interrupts Mac and Killer's conversation, saying, "Gentlemen, you need to get serious."

"Colonel," Killer says without turning around, "you need to relax. If you don't, you're going to find yourself stressing out over stupid stuff."

"I just want you two to stay focused," Colonel Drasneb replies.

"Don't worry, sir. We're always focused."

———————————————————

Major reaches gate C-5 just as the plane pulls into the gate.

Thank God! Major internally praises.

While he eagerly waits for the plane to de-board, Major becomes somewhat nervous. He makes every attempt to clear his mind and not allow any negative thoughts to enter. Self-doubt is the last thing Major needs filling his head before he finally meets Terry.

The gate door opens, and the passengers begin to flow out slowly at first, but after the first ten passengers or so, a steady stream of people exit the gate.

Major keeps his cool. He does not allow himself to become overly anxious or excited, though if one were to ask Major now, he would say that his meeting Terry is the most exciting moment of his life, at least for right now—even more so than rappelling out of a Black Hawk helicopter nine hundred feet in the air. To relax, Major sticks to his routine—softly singing a James Brown song to himself. For the current occasion, Major sings, "I've Got the Feeling."

While Major watches the flow of people exit the gate, he notices a familiar face from among the crowd. 'That's got to be her,' Major says to himself. The only time Major has ever seen Terry in person was at the Miss America pageant.

Closer and closer, the familiar vision of beauty casually approaches. Now twenty feet away from Major, he realizes internally with a huge boyish smile on his face, *It's her!*

Major slowly walks toward Terry's direction. Major becomes ambivalent to his surroundings. His only focus is on Terry. The people in front of Major seem to move out of his way as though an invisible force were pushing them to the sides. Finally, after three months of excruciating anticipation, Major and Terry finally meet.

4 DECEMBER 1999

1000 Hours: Highland Falls, New York

The West Point Motel is a frequent venue for the academy's thousands of visitors who tour its grounds year after year. The motel is only half a mile outside of Thayer gate in the tranquil town of Highland Falls. Three of the West Point Motel's newest guests are Mac, Killer, and Colonel Drasneb.

Alex chose the West Point Motel as their staging area because of its close proximity to the military academy. The men can walk to and from West Point without the hint of suspicion. It is very common for foreign travelers to tour West Point on a regular basis, no matter the time of year or the weather.

Mac, Killer, and Colonel Drasneb kneel around a bed that has a layout of West Point strewn across it.

Mac points to the layout and says, "That appears to be the highest accessible point."

"The chapel? Are you sure?" Colonel Drasneb asks.

"Yes. The chapel," Mac coldly replies. He does not take well to someone questioning his judgment, especially an individual who is not experienced in his line of work. Mac continues. "If you look here, you'll notice that the chapel has a steeple. More than likely, we should be able to climb to the top of it."

"I agree," Killer affirms.

"How do you propose we reach this steeple?" Colonel Drasneb asks.

"That's simple," Mac answers. "We go to church."

1700 Hours: Harlem, New York

Major and Terry have arrived at Columbia University for the army basketball game. Coach O'Hara allowed Major to meet the team at Columbia instead of driving back to West Point and riding with the team. Coach has full faith and trust in Major and knows that he is a very responsible young man. Major proves his level of responsibility yet again by showing up at Columbia's athletic center on time.

The couple enters the athletic center, escaping the cold weather. Major escorts Terry into the gym, finding T and Mrs. Wood sitting on the bleachers behind Army's bench. Seeing the two lovely ladies, Major takes Terry by the hand and walks her over to his two surrogate aunts.

"Ladies," Major opens as he approaches, "this is my friend Terry Boyd. Terry, this is Mrs. Wood and Mrs. O'Hara. You can call her T though."

The ladies exchange pleasantries then T says to Major, "You can go now. We'll take care of her."

"I bet you will," Major replies. He kisses Terry on the cheek and says, "Anything they say about me is true, but watch out for them. These ladies are slick."

Everyone laughs as Major trots off to the visitors' locker room. As he exits the gym, Terry takes a seat in the bleachers beside T.

While sitting, Mrs. Wood leans over to T and opens the conversation, saying, "Major has told me so much about you, Terry."

"Really?" Terry asks.

"Oh yes!" Mrs. Wood exclaims. "When he came back from the pageant, just the sight of you alone had him smiling more than I've ever seen him. Usually, Major walks around with this cool tough-guy look, but whenever he mentions you, he's all smiles."

"He must be controlling his smile then," Terry adds.

"He's probably trying to play tough for you. You know how guys can be," T interjects.

"That's probably what it is," Mrs. Wood agrees She then asks, "So what's it like being Miss Indiana?"

"Busy," Terry quickly answers. "I've never been this busy before in my life. The speaking engagements are like a full-time job. I have hardly any time for myself."

"It's a wonder you were able to make it down here for the weekend," T states.

"It was tough, but surprisingly, there was a hole in my calendar," Terry answers.

"Well, we're happy you were able to make it and finally meet you," Mrs. Wood expresses with a smile.

Terry decides to change the subject from herself and shift it over to Major. "So," she begins, "how good is Major, anyway?"

"At basketball?" T inquirers. "Not too bad. He's one of the toughest and best all-around players we've had on the team."

"Oh yes!" Mrs. Wood asserts. "Major's the type of player who's always where the action is. If there's a loose ball on the floor, he's right there on the floor with it. If there's a mismatch on the court, he's the smaller guy, but don't think he's being overplayed. Oh no! Major's the one causing the trouble for the bigger guy."

"That's good to know," Terry states, "because I asked him how good he was and he said he was just okay."

"That's Major for you," T replies. "Always the modest one."

While the three women speak, Jennifer, Leslie, and Carrie enter the gym and sit among them. Seeing Terry, the three girls' faces light up with giant grins. Carrie and Leslie blush and giggle like the little schoolgirls they are.

Seated, Leslie faces Terry and, instead of beating around the bush, gets straight to the point and asks, "So are you and Major dating yet?"

Jennifer hits her little sister in the arm, saying, "Dummy! Don't ask her that!"

Terry laughs and says, "No, we're not."

"Well, you should be," Leslie declares. "Major's the best guy we know. He's like our big brother."

"Yeah?" Terry asks.

"He really is," Carrie adds. "He's always giving us advice and stuff."

"What kind of advice?" Terry inquirers.

"Basketball, boys, and life," Leslie boldly states.

"What's he say about boys?" Terry pushes.

"That they can't be trusted, unless you realize that you're in control," Leslie explains.

Terry is somewhat puzzled by Leslie's statement. "In control?"

"Yeah," Jennifer jumps in. "Major says that when it comes to real men, all women are in control of the relationship."

"Hmm," Terry ponders. "That's interesting. Where'd he come up with that interesting philosophy?"

"Beats us," Carrie says. "Major said he'd explain it to us some other time."

"Yeah," Leslie interjects. "Major said that *Maxim* would help explain a lot, but he won't let us read it until we're in college."

Terry laughs at Leslie and Carrie's statements. "*Maxim*. That's funny."

"Here comes the team!" Jennifer says, interrupting the conversation.

The Army men's basketball team comes running out onto the gym floor for their warm-up. As Major steps out onto the court floor, he looks in Terry's direction and gives her a slight head nod. Terry returns the gesture with a discrete wave. Major smiles.

5 DECEMBER 1999

0730 Hours: West Point

Major drives down the all-so-familiar Palisades Parkway. In the passenger's seat, Terry sits, sleeping. Major glances over at her and smiles. As far as Major is concerned, this has been the best weekend of his life. He won a tough game against Columbia the other night—another notch in army basketball's rope and one step closer to their dream of making it to the NCAA tournament. Major also had an amazing time with the most beautiful and intelligent woman he has ever met, besides his mother, grandmothers, aunties, and older cousins, of course.

Major drives down the edge of Bear Mountain and comes to a traffic circle, which is the northern end of the Palisades Parkway.

Wanting Terry to see everything from here on, Major softly shakes her and says, "Hey, babe. We're here."

Terry is slow to open her eyes. She stretches then pushes herself up in her seat. "That didn't take so long," Terry says as she fully reaches consciousness.

"Everything's fast when you're asleep," Major jokes.

"All right, funny man," Terry responds, lightly punching Major in the shoulder.

Major drives around the traffic circle and takes the last right into Fort Montgomery. As he and Terry pass through the tranquil village, Major points the sites out to her. After about a three-minute drive, Major veers right up a ramp, entering Highland Falls. At the end of town, Major enters West Point through Thayer Gate. He passes through the gate unhindered and turns left at the first stop sign. Major drives up what is unofficially known as Buffalo Soldier Hill. The road is entitled as such because it ends at Buffalo Soldier Field, where the women's softball stadium is and several community softball fields are located.

As Major slowly drives up Buffalo Soldier Hill, he begins to reminisce of his cadet basic training (CBT) days. During CBT, or what is more noticeably referred to as Beast Barracks or Beast, the new cadets are separated into running ability groups during PT. Major was in the green group, which was the fastest group, of course. They were known as the Big Dogs. Major never fell out of any runs and usually ran in the front if he could help it. The only time he ever fell out of a run was the two times the Big Dogs ran up Buffalo Soldier Hill, which was a pariah on his body and his soul. Running up Buffalo Soldier Hill was like running through mud waist deep. Once he reached the top though, he would sprint with all of his might and link back up with green group. Understand that Major was not the only new cadet who fell out of formation at Buffalo Soldier Hill. Out of the Big Dogs, not even half of them were able to make it all of the way up Buffalo Soldier Hill without falling out—that included the upperclassmen.

As Major passes the AOG (Association of Graduates) building to his right, Major softly says, "God! I hate this hill," and laughs.

"What was that?" Terry asks.

"Oh, nothing. I used to have to run up this hill back in Beast. This joker sucked!"

"It doesn't look too steep to me," Terry comments.

"Trust me. Looks can be deceiving."

"I guess so. Maybe you just couldn't hang."

"Ah. Now you have jokes."

Major and Terry share a laugh.

Atop Buffalo Soldier Hill, they come upon Lusk Reservoir. Continuing his tour, Major says, "That's Lusk Reservoir."

Terry looks to her right.

Before she has a chance to say anything, Major states, "To your left's Michie Stadium."

The couple drives around Lusk Reservoir then down another hill, passing the Cadet Chapel. As they pass the Cadet Chapel, Major says, "After breakfast, I'll take you there. You'll like it."

"Okay," Terry simply replies.

Major drives to the end of the hill and comes to a complete stop. He turns right and heads down the street along what is known as Colonel's Row. Colonel's Row is where West Point's most senior colonels reside, Colonel Wood being one such individual.

As Terry and Major approach the Woods' home, Major points and says, "That's where the Woods live, and that over there is Ike Hall and the Hudson River. You'll see it better once we get out."

Major drives past Trophy Point then turns right into a parking lot. Finding the first spot he can pull all the way through, Major parks. He jumps out of his 4Runner and trots over to Terry's side to let her out. Major politely opens the door for Terry.

Stepping out of the 4Runner, Terry replies, "Thank you."

"Always," Major smilingly retorts.

1000 Hours

After an extensive, personalized West Point tour, Major and Terry head for the Woods' home for breakfast. They enter the house through the kitchen to find Colonel and Mrs. Wood busy preparing the meal.

Seeing the couple enter, Mrs. Wood says to them, "Good morning, you two. Relax your feet, Terry. I know Major had you all over the place this morning."

As Terry takes a seat, she replies, "Yes, ma'am. He did. It's so beautiful here. I never thought a military school would look anything like this."

"I know what you mean," Mrs. Wood agrees. "It blew me away too the first time I visited oh so long ago. I don't think I'll ever get over how gorgeous it is here, especially during this time of the year." After a slight pause, Mrs. Wood asks Terry, "What time do you leave today?"

"Six thirty," Terry replies.

"That's not too bad. Are you going to watch the team practice then?"

"Yes, ma'am."

"That will definitely be an interesting experience."

"What do you mean?"

"Well, if you think Coach O'Hara was interesting last night, wait until you see him when he doesn't think one of the players isn't practicing hard."

While the two ladies converse about Terry's West Point tour, Major simply stands out of the way beside the kitchen door.

Noticing that Major is doing absolutely nothing, Mrs. Wood orders, "Major, get over here and help me."

"Yes, ma'am," Major replies as he runs over to the stove where Mrs. Wood stands. Major relieves Mrs. Wood of her pancake-making duties.

"Off shooting night, man," Colonel Wood states as he opens the refrigerator, grabbing a carton of orange juice.

"Yeah, sir. I don't know what it was," Major replies, shaking his head.

"I think he was distracted," Mrs. Wood interjects.

Terry blushes. Major bows his head, shaking it again.

"I think you may have something there," Colonel Wood agrees.

"My defense was on, sir," Major defends himself.

"Yes, it was. Those two blocked shocks were impressive," Colonel Wood states.

"That's right! And that steal and cross-court pass to Jimmy for the jam was money too!" Major continues to defend as he flips a pancake.

"Yes, Major," Mrs. Wood states, "you played pretty well, considering your distraction."

Everyone laughs.

"Pretty nice distraction though, if you ask me," Colonel Wood adds as he takes a plate of sausage links into the dining room.

Finished cooking the pancakes, Major takes the dish that he placed them on and takes them to the dining room as well.

"You can take these, Terry," Mrs. Wood says, handing Terry a stack of four plates.

"Yes, ma'am," Terry smilingly replies. She takes the plates from Mrs. Woods' hands and follows Colonel Wood and Major into the dining room.

Mrs. Wood follows everyone into the dining room with a dish of scrambled eggs in her hands. As Mrs. Wood enters the dining room, Major darts out of her way and returns to the kitchen to retrieve the silverware and napkins. Colonel Wood follows suit and returns to the dining room with four small glasses. With all of the food on the dining room table, everyone takes a seat.

As Colonel Wood sits, he shouts, "Man! We forgot the butter and syrup!" Colonel Wood pushes himself back from his seat and returns to the kitchen to retrieve the missing butter and syrup.

Colonel Wood quickly returns with the butter and syrup in hand, saying, "Now we can eat." Colonel Wood takes his seat then says, "Major, you can say grace this time."

"Yes, sir," Major somberly replies.

Everyone grasps each other's hands.

Major bows his head and says, "Dear Lord. Thank you for this day. Thank you for what you've given us. Lord, bless this meal and the hands that've prepared it. Help it to nourish and strengthen our bodies. In Jesus's name, I pray. Amen."

1100 Hours

Mac and Killer sit in the Cadet Chapel for the Protestant service. They do not consider themselves religious, but they do believe in God. Today's visit to church is not for worshipping purposes though. Mac decided that the best way to reach the top of the steeple is to go right after the church service ends. Since Mac and Killer were unable to determine exactly when the service ends, the only way to ensure that they do not miss their window of opportunity is to sit through the entire service.

As the service moves through its schedule, it finally reaches time for the sermon.

The minister steps up to the podium and says, "Good morning, church."

The church rings with "Good morning."

The minister places his Bible on the lectern and sifts through some papers. He lifts his head and opens, "The sermon that I'm rendering today I usually save for the period leading up to Easter, but as I always say, 'There's nothing wrong with stepping away from tradition every once and a while.' Tuesday, I was watching the news and saw that a man was getting ready to get executed that night. The state and the man's names are not important, and no, the state was not Texas."

The congregation lets out a slight chuckle at the minister's reference to Texas and an execution.

After a slight pause for the congregation to settle back down, the minister continues, saying, "Prior to the man's execution, someone asked him if he had any last words. Instead of saying anything, the man simply shook his head no. After the execution, a reporter announced that though the man did not have a last statement, he did leave behind a note that he wished to be read after he was pronounced dead. The note read:

To the families, friends, and loved ones of the victims,

I know that anything that I say or do cannot repair the damage that I have caused to each of you. I do not ask for your forgiveness because I understand that many of you may not want to give it. I do want you to know that I have made peace with God and that he has forgiven me of my sins. I pray that God takes the burden away from your heart and that you all are able to live happy and fulfilling lives.

"After the reporter read the note, the network aired the reactions of the victims' family and friends. Not one of them had a positive reaction to the man's letter. None of them could fathom the possibility that a murderer could receive forgiveness from God. Most of them thought that the man was lying and was trying to fool everyone—an attempt to get some post-death attention. As far as they were concerned, the letter was a ruse. To these people, a murderer is unable to atone for his sins. I sat their in my den, flabbergasted at the numerous negative reactions. Do I know if the man was genuine? No. Of course, I don't, but I do know that it's a lot more possible than people allow themselves to believe.

"Please, turn with me to Luke chapter 23, verses 39–43." The minister waits a few moments before continuing. "The scripture reads, 'And one of the malefactors which were hanged railed on him, saying, If though be Christ, save thyself and us. But the other answering rebuked him, saying, Dost not thou fear God, seeing thou art in the same condemnation? And we indeed justly; for we receive the due reward of our deeds: but this man hath done nothing amiss. And he said unto Jesus, Lord, remember me when thou comest into thy kingdom. And Jesus said unto him, Verily I say unto thee, Today shalt thou be with me in paradise.'"

Lifting his head from his Bible, the minister continues, "Here we have two criminals: one who only cares about one thing—himself and another who is sincere in his speech. When the one criminal attempts to con Jesus into helping them escape, the other criminal shuts him up. He tells him to show some respect and recognize the fact that they are in the presence of God. He further goes on to tell the other criminal that their fate is due to their criminal acts of which they are truly guilty, whereas Christ has done nothing wrong. Here we have, not a remorseful criminal, but a man who knows that he did wrong and is willing to accept whatever fate society has placed on him, in this case, death on a cross. Once he verbalizes this to the smart-mouth criminal, he then goes on to ask Christ to remember him once he gets to heaven. We all know Christ's response. Now understand that Christ did not answer the criminal the way he did just because he asked. If asking to get into heaven was one of the ways in, everyone would be there. No, Christ responded as he did because the criminal approached him with a sincere heart."

Mac rocks slightly in the pew, listening intently to the sermon. The minister's words are touching Mac in places that he did not want touched. While Mac takes in the sermon, a very tiny smile grows on his face. If anyone were to look at him, they would not notice the hint of a smile or a dimple whatsoever, but the smile is there.

"Christ knew that the criminal truly was apologetic for what he had done," the minister continues. "When the criminal told his compatriot that their execution was due to their guilt, he had remised of his sin. After the remission of his sin, the criminal then acknowledges Christ for who he truly is. It is not important if others believe us or agree with us or accept what we say or do. All that matters is that our relationship with Christ is true. Other than blaspheming the Holy Spirit, all sins are forgivable. God does not look at sin as we do. To God, a lie is equal to murder. It is hard for us as a society to swallow that concept, but that's just how it is with God." The minister closes his Bible, gathers his notes, then returns to his seat.

With the church service complete, the congregation begins to mingle among themselves. Mac and Killer rise to their feet and step out into the aisle. Mac though, instead of following Killer to the side, walks down the aisle to the front of the church. The minister stands in front of the altar, surrounded by several people, conversing.

Mac steps in front of the minister, extends his hand, and says, "Sir, I just want to let you know that your sermon really touched me today."

"Why, thank you, young man. I'm glad that I was able to say something that helped you in some way," the minister replies, shaking Mac's swallowing hand.

"You helped me more than you know," Mac smilingly states. He then quickly turns around and returns to Killer's position.

Killer stands at the top of the aisle with his arms folded. He does not look too happy, but he is able to conceal his disdain from the general public. As Mac, approaches, he notices his friend's poor demeanor.

"What's wrong with you?" Mac asks.

"With me? What's with you talking to the minister?" Killer inquirers.

"Just wanted to say hey. That's all. What? You have a problem with church and stuff?"

"No. It's just, you're the one who's all about work and whatnot. It's not like you to get distracted like this."

"I didn't get distracted. Actually, I had a moment of clarity."

"A moment of clarity?"

"Yeah. We'll talk about it some other time."

Killer unfolds his arms and says, "All right then. No harm, no foul. I guess."

Mac pats Killer on the back, stating, "Come on. Let's get to work."

Mac and Killer walk around the church, as many of the other morning service members do. Their purpose in doing so is to blend in with the crowd as much as possible. Though people go to the Protestant Chapel for church services, it is still one of West Point's most popular tourist attractions. Knowing this fact, Mac and Killer act like tourists.

As the crowd begins to make its way out of the chapel, Mac and Killer intermix among it. Instead of exiting the chapel, Mac and Killer head to their right and enter a door that leads them to a room that is no larger than a broom closet. The room is very dark, musty, and somewhat damp. The room though is not really a room at all, but a miniature foyer with a set of stairs that wind up to where is unknown because the way is not lit.

Killer and Mac stealthily dash up the stairs until they reach another door, which they open to enter another room that is similar from the one from where they came, except that this room is much larger in size. The room resembles a medieval torture chamber. None of the tools of the trade are present, but that is the first thought that comes to Mac and Killer's minds as they stand there.

In front of Mac and Killer, at the far side of the room, is a window. They head for the window but do so in manner that does not allow anyone from the outside to detect their presence. Mac goes to the right and Killer to the left. From the angle in which they crouch, Killer and Mac are able to view the skyline. They then stand to their feet, peering out the window, in order to get a look at the ground below. The view from where Killer and Mac look is incredible. They are able to see everything from the front steps of the Cadet Chapel all the way to the other side of the Hudson River.

"I see another possible escape route," Mac states.

"I see it too," Killer affirms.

■────────────────────────────■

"Why do we have to walk up all of these steps?" Terry asks Major with a loss of breath. "There has to be an easier way up here."

"There is," Major replies, "but that requires driving, which we can't do right now."

"Why not?"

"Because church is just letting out. Between the people leaving and the tour buses coming in and out, we'd never make it in there."

"Tour buses?"

"Yeah. The museum has a tour stop at the Cadet Chapel."

"Maybe we should have taken that."

"I guess we could have, but then you wouldn't get the full experience. I have to walk this on the regular. Lucky for you I didn't take you up Ho Chi Minh Trail."

"Ho Chi Minh Trail?"

"It's another way up to the chapel. I wouldn't say it's dangerous, but it isn't the best way to go. I'll put it like that."

The steps that Major is leading Terry up lead directly to the front of the Cadet Chapel. At the bottom, the steps lead to the side of Boodler's, West Point's answer to 7-Eleven. It looks similar to your typical convenient store. The cadets are able to purchase a large variety of drinks and snacks as well as pizza and calzones. For plebes and yucks who are unable to leave West Point, Boodlers is a godsend.

The steps are very steep and, during the winter when it is wet out, are very slippery. Falling down the steps would not be pleasant at all. Every time Major walks up to the Holleder Center, he dreads the experience because he has to climb the steps. No matter what shape one's body is in, once at the top, all energy is expended, and the body knows that it has been through a physical ordeal.

Terry and Major finally make it to the top of the steps and are immediately faced by a mob of tourists. Major is very relieved that he is not presently wearing his uniform. He cannot count how many times people have stopped him on his way to practice so they could take a picture with him.

Hand in hand, Major leads Terry around a corner to a gray stone wall that overlooks Cadet Area. The wall is very congested. The tourists stand at its edge snapping pictures of the spectacular view. Instead of pushing his way through the crowd, Major simply waits for the crowd to dissipate because he knows that the tourists will leave soon.

After a few moments of reconnaissance, Mac and Killer slide to the side of the window then quickly step to the door. Mac heads down the stairwell first, ensuring that he and Killer's presence is still unknown to the regular population. Seeing that the area below is clear, Mac signals for Killer to follow. He then casually walks outside and joins the crowd. From his pocket, Mac pulls out his digital camera and begins taking several photographs. Mac attempts to make his way to the edge of the gray stone wall, but the crowd in front of him is very thick, and he does not feel the need to trample through them.

Mac clears his head and takes in the sounds and smells surrounding him. He hears people talking about how beautiful West Point is. He hears people discuss their plans for lunch. He hears a group of people discuss their timetable for the day and that they need to hurry and move on to the next site. Mac notices the numerous ethnic backgrounds and nationalities of the tourists who are present. Among the tourists, there are Japanese, Egyptians, Italian-Americans, Hasidic Jews, and even an Amish family.

The crowd finally begins to die down as the tourists return to the idling tour buses. Mac makes his way to the gray stone wall and takes several more pictures in numerous directions. He then sits on the wall's edge, waiting for Killer.

●————————————●

Major and Terry stand in the rear of the crowd. Major's affinity for tourists keeps him at arm's length. Besides what he goes through with taking photographs with tourists, Major also does not like them due to his growing up in the Washington, DC, metropolitan area. Being harassed by out-of-towners on how to get to a museum or a monument gets old real fast. That is why whenever Major visits a city where he has never been, he either studies the map prior to hitting the street or he ensures that he is with someone who knows their way around.

After waiting about ten minutes, the crowd finally begins to walk away from the wall and returns to their West Point tour buses. With the crowd out of the way, Major leads Terry to the wall's edge. Holding her from behind, Major points out all of the buildings where he had taken Terry earlier.

●————————————●

Having received the signal from Mac, Killer waits a moment then silently walks down the stairs and reenters the chapel lobby. Killer walks outside, and much to his surprise, there is hardly anyone in front of the chapel. He looks to his left and notices the tourists stepping onto their buses. With no one in his way, Killer turns right and walks to the gray stone wall where Mac sits and waits.

"Been waiting long?" Killer asks Mac as he approaches his friend.

"Not really. Had to wait for the crowd to die down some though," Mac responds.

"I bet. Got any good shots?"

"Yeah. We'll be good. My stuff's better than Alex's."

"Not bad."

"I didn't do anything special. The layout is right there. The next best things to this are satellite pictures."

"Modest, like always."

Killer looks to his left and notices a young couple standing a little more than ten feet away from he and Mac. Killer nudges Mac and points the young couple out to his friend.

Mac rolls his eyes at Killer then says, "Come on, man. Let's go."

"Young love. Got to love it," Killer jests as he and Mac walk away.

1900 Hours: Russian training camp

Alex stands before the experts who sit according to their respective teams. Tonight is the final brief they will receive in Russia.

"Good evening, gentlemen," Alex opens. "Tomorrow morning, we leave for America." Alex hands a set of packets to each of the team leaders, who then passes them out among their team members. Seeing that everyone has a packet in hand, Alex continues with his brief. "Flip through the packet as I speak. We all will fly out from Moscow. Team 1 will fly to Amsterdam then to Newark International Airport. Team 2 will fly into London and then into Albany, New York. Team 3, you are flying into Paris and connecting to JFK International Airport. Team 4 is flying from Frankfurt to Philadelphia, Pennsylvania. Team 5, you too are flying out of London, but will fly into Newark as Team 1 is doing. Teams 1 and 5, your flights do not land at the same time. Teams 2 and 5, your flights do not depart from London at the same time. If you look in your packets, you will find several road maps. Study them. The American highway system is not very difficult, but if you happen to go the wrong way, you may find it difficult to get back on track.

"Also, in each team leader's packet, there is a credit card. Each of your credit cards has been used to rent a minivan. You all know how to use credit cards and rent vehicles, so I will not go into to the particulars on that. The card is only good for the van rental. As soon as you receive the minivan, discretely discard of the credit card. We will only use cash during this mission. We cannot chance the American authorities tracking our activities. Once you reach the West Point vicinity, go to the West Point Motel. Directions are in your packets. We will go over those at the end of the brief. Check in at the front desk. Ensure that only two of you go in. No more. No less. Once in your rooms, relax and wait for me to contact you. Do not leave the room for any reason. Keep the curtains closed. We cannot chance anyone knowing how many of us there are. We must be as discrete as possible. No one knows that we will be there, so if the phone rings, answer it. It will either be me or housekeeping."

6 DECEMBER 1999

1130 Hours: West Point

Mac, Killer, and Colonel Drasneb stand behind Pershing Barracks watching the Corps of Cadets during their lunch formation. They are not alone. The three conspirators are immersed among a mob of tourists. During the winter months, the tourists usually do not watch lunch formations because of the inclement weather, but for some unknown reason, they always know when the weather is decent. Today, it is cold yet bearable. The temperature is in the high thirties, and the wind is not blowing, much to the delight of the cadets who have to stand in formation, especially those in Third Regiment, who face the Plain.

The reason the tourists stand on the other side of Pershing Barracks and not in Central Area where the cadets are is that non-academy personnel are not admitted entrance. There are chain links that separate the cadets from the camera-armed tourists. Non-academy personnel have to be escorted by either a cadet or a member of the faculty or staff to enter Cadet Area. The tourists curiously peer at the cadets like they are animals in a zoo, except that you can feed these animals.

The purpose of Mac, Killer, and Colonel Drasneb viewing the lunch formation is to monitor the cadets' actions during the lunch period. It is important for them to become extremely familiar with how and where the cadets move throughout their day in order to make the proper adjustments to their mission execution. All of the intelligence in the world is good, but nothing is better than one's own eyes. As Mac and Killer have learned from past jobs, nothing beats viewing your target in his natural environment.

Major stands before a plebe and asks him, "Miko, what's for lunch?"

"Sir, for lunch we are having meatball sandwiches, Italian-style vegetables, cake, and punch."

"What kind of cake?"

"Sir, I do not know."

"Why not?"

"No excuse, sir."

"Come on, Miko. I know 'no excuse' is the proper response, but you're talking to your commander here. I want you to really tell me why."

"Sir, because the menu did not say."

"Really?"

"Yes, sir."

"Dang it! I believe you, man. I just hate being surprised with these meals. You know what I'm saying?"

"Yes, sir."

"Tell me about my Chicago Bears."

"Sir, today in the *Washington Post*, it was reported that the mighty Chicago Bears, the greatest team ever formed in the history of the National Football League, defeated the Green Bay Packers 23–14 at Soldier Field."

"Yes!" Major shouts, throwing a clinched right fist in the air.

Major's favorite professional football team is the Chicago Bears. They have been so since 1985, when Major was in the third grade. Whenever a plebe recites Chicago Bear knowledge to Major, that plebe has to refer to them as "the greatest team ever formed in the history of the National Football League." Major does not have as many particulars for the plebes to know that are specific for him, but the Chicago Bears is definitely one of them.

Calmed down somewhat to the wonderful news of yet another Bear victory, Major looks to the back of formation and receives a signal from Sara. Answering, Major heads for the rear of formation so the first sergeant can fall the Ducks in. With the report rendered, Dusty does an about-face. Major marches to the front of the formation, splitting it down the middle, and faces his first sergeant.

Dusty turns the company over to Major, saying, "Sir, everyone is all accounted for."

"Thanks, Dust," Major silently replies to his first sergeant. He then turns his head to the right and shouts, "Post!"

The first sergeant steps off, while the platoon sergeants and platoon leaders exchange positions among their respective platoons. Now the platoon leaders stand in front of their platoons as Major stands before his company.

■————————————————————■

Mac stands a little to the front of Killer and Colonel Drasneb. A small part of Mac misses the pomp and circumstance of the military. He has not seen an actual formation in several years.

As he stands, Mac hears a voice from the other side of Pershing Barracks shout, "Parade rest!"

"Man, that voice sounds familiar," Mac whispers aloud. He shakes the thought off as a coincidence.

A few moments later, Mac hears several voices simultaneously shout, "Company! Attention!"

With only seconds passing, Mac hears the same familiar voice shout, "The mighty, dirty Ducks are all accounted for!"

Come on, Mac, Mac says to himself. *You don't believe in coincidence. That voice sounds too familiar, like I know or used to know the person who's speaking, but I can't know who it is. I don't know any cadets.* Mac shakes his head in disbelief then continues thinking, *It's probably nothing, just my mind playing tricks on me. I swear to God though, I've heard that voice somewhere!*

2200 Hours: Highland Falls, New York

All of the Serbs have arrived at the West Point Motel without any incident. As instructed by Alex, they sit and wait in their rooms until called upon. At approximately ten o'clock in the evening, each room receives a telephone call from Alex, instructing the team members to report to room 215 at ten thirty. They are instructed not to bring anything to write on or with. All they will need is a clear mind. They cannot chance leaving any evidence behind after they have completed the mission.

In room 215, Alex stands alongside Colonel Drasneb, Mac, and Killer in front of the bathroom sink, which faces the room. Before them assembled are all five teams. The team members are anywhere where they are able to find a seat—on the two beds, the two chairs, the dresser, and the floor.

The teams fully assembled, Colonel Drasneb opens, saying, "I am very pleased that you all made it here safe and without detection. I need you all to sleep well tonight. We begin work tomorrow morning—recon. Mr. Stewart and Mr. Pollard accompanied me today on our own recon of the post. After some thought and analyzation, our plan will stand as is. Tomorrow, we will all recon West Point, arriving on site one hour prior to their lunch formation, and we will stay until they are dismissed from their mess hall. It is important that you all pay close attention to the cadets' actions. Their routine is the same every weekday, which is why we only need the one day of reconnaissance. Now in the early afternoon, sometime after we have lunch—Alex will fill you in on the times—we will take an official West Point tour. This will give us a clearer view and professional understanding of the post. At the end of the day, we will have our final briefs, gentlemen. You all have done exceptionally thus far. Stay alert and aware tomorrow, but relax, as Mr. Stewart always says. If we appear too stressed out, some people may get the wrong idea. I am going to retire for the evening. Alex, Mr. Stewart, and Mr. Pollard will take over now. Have a good evening."

Colonel Drasneb nods his head to his men. They all jump to their feet and lock their bodies at the position of attention. Once Colonel Drasneb exits the room, the men quickly return to their original comfortable positions.

With Colonel Drasneb out of the room, Killer steps forward to continue the brief where Colonel Drasneb left off.

"Colonel Drasneb gave you guys a pretty good overview of tomorrow's activities. Here's the plan."

Killer turns around and faces the sink. Sitting on the sink are a stack of papers and documents, the stack containing several maps. Mac grabs one of the maps and hands it to Killer, who then turns back around and walks to the closest bed.

"Excuse me there, fellas," Killer says to the team members who are sitting on the bed that he is standing beside.

The Serbs rise from their seats. The bed now clear, Killer opens the map up and lays it out for everyone to see. Those team members who are unable to see the map from their positions get up and gather around the bed.

Everyone gathered around Killer, he continues his brief, saying, "West Point has three accessible gates in which we can enter the post. The one closest to our current location is Thayer gate. Teams 1 and 2 will use this gate tomorrow. Departure time from here is 1000 hours. Team 2, leave five minutes after Team 1. This will alleviate any possible suspicion." Killer points to a position on the map and says, "This is North Gate. Teams 3 and 4, you will utilize this gate. Departure times are the same."

Killer points to another position on the map, saying, "This is Washington Gate. Team 5, this is your gate. We will all meet at a location known as Trophy Point. It is a giant monument made out of granite. You can't miss it. Here's where it is." Killer points Trophy Point out to the Serbs on the map. "You all have a copy of this map in your rooms. Ensure that you study it tonight. You can take it with you tomorrow as well. Remember, we're tourists. And what do tourists always carry with them? Maps. Now like I said, we will meet at Trophy Point at 1030 hours. This will give us more than enough time to enter the instillation, find parking, and get to the link-up point. Make sure you guys park where there are other cars. Not that a ticket would really mean anything to us, but we still want to keep as low a profile as possible. Mac is going to ride with Team 5. Alex will be with teams 3 and 4. Colonel Drasneb and I will ride with 1 and 2. Oh! I almost forgot. Do not bring any weapons whatsoever. No guns and no knives. Army bases have a tendency to do random car searches. We can't chance them checking us and finding something. Understood?"

The Serbs all nod their heads in compliance.

"That's all I have for you guys. If you don't have any questions, I will see you gentlemen bright and early at breakfast."

"McDonald's?" one Serb blurts.

Killer laughs, replying, "Yeah. There's a Mickey D's down the street on the right-hand side right before you get to Thayer gate. You can eat there if you want. Me personally? I'm going to try to find me a bowl of grits."

The Serbs laugh at Killer's comment. They are all excited to have a chance to go to a real American McDonald's and not a Europeanized McDonald's that they would frequent back home.

Killer shakes his head in partial disbelief and a huge grin on his face. He then says, "If you guys don't have anymore important questions, I'll see you at departure time because I sure as hell am not going to McDonald's for breakfast."

7 DECEMBER 1999

1030 Hours: West Point

Will walks back to his room from his Calculus I class in Thayer Hall. He is rather elated because there are not too many upperclassmen out at this time, which means that he does not have to go around greeting anyone. Will hates greeting upperclassmen. It makes him feel like a second-class citizen. There are hundreds of tourists out though, but they are all flocked around the several statues and monuments that are sprawled across West Point. Fortunately for Will, the tourists are not bothering him with photograph requests.

Passing the majestic statue of Gen. George S. Patton that overlooks the library, Will begins to veer to the right toward the front of Eisenhower Barracks overlooking the Plain. Turning though, Will's eyes are averted to the left. Much to his surprise, he spots his brother walking in his general direction past Grant Hall. Will quickly turns around, and seeing that there are not any upperclassmen in the vicinity, other than those who are with Major, he jogs to his brother's position.

Seeing Will heading his way, Major shouts, "What's up, little bro?"

Reaching Major, Will replies, "Not much, fool. I saw you over here, so I thought I'd say what's up."

"Walk with us," Major tells Will as he continues his path to Grant Barracks.

Approaching Grant, one of Major's friends says, "All right, Major. I'll see you around, man."

"All right. Cool. I'll holler at you later," Major replies.

"See you, Major," the remainder of his friends state as they all head off in separate directions.

Major and Will walk into Grant Area and head for Major's room.

"So what's up, man?" Major asks Will.

"Not much, really. Same old nonsense," Will answers.

"Everything going all right over there in Eagle Land?"

"Yeah. They're not messing with me anymore."

"Good deal. I figured as much."

As the two brothers walk up onto the stoops, Will asks, "Can I take a nap in your room tomorrow during lunch?"

"What's wrong with your room?"

"Nothing really. I just don't feel like being bothered with someone coming in and asking me why I'm not at lunch."

"I understand. Yeah. You can come by the room if you want. I have early lunch too tomorrow, but I'll be chillin' with Ben, so I won't be in my room."

"Man! I appreciate it, Major."

"It's no problem. You are my little brother and all. It's my job to look out for you."

"Bet!" Will happily responds as he and Major shake hands. "I'm a go drop my books off in my room so I can get to the mess hall early."

"All right then. I'll check you later, bro," Major states as Will walks back down the steps onto Grant Area, heading back to his room in Eisenhower Barracks.

Major heads to his room with a slight smile on his face.

That boy is a trip, Major thinks to himself as he opens the door to his room.

Major drops his books on his desk then plops himself down on his couch. He reaches under the coffee table and grabs his basketball that has been lying there all morning. With his ball in hand and in front of his face, Major fervently tosses the basketball from one hand to the other. As he does so, Major takes his mind into very deep thought, a near-trance-like state.

Tomorrow's a big day—a very big day. Tomorrow we play Indiana. Tomorrow we beat Indiana. Bobby Knight may have coached here thirty some odd years ago, but he's going to wish he didn't come back to the Point for this reunion game. I'm going to score every four minutes. I'm going to apply defensive pressure to the ball and force at least seven turnovers. I will block a shot. I will steal the ball. I will set hard picks that will knock the defender down on his butt. I will win.

While in thought, Joe enters the room, saying, "Hey, Major. What's up?"

"Not much, man," Major responds, taking himself out of his trance. "Just thinking about tomorrow's game."

"You guys are playing Indiana, right?"

"Yep."

"Man! That's going to be tough."

"It will be, but we can get it done, if we stay focused."

"You think so?"

"I know so. Indiana's good, but they're not all that good this year."

"Well, I'll be there for this one."

"Good deal. Tell all your friends to come. They're going to see one of the best games of their lives."

"I hope you're right."

"Am I ever wrong?"

"Actually, yeah. You are quite a bit."

"All right. All right. You are partial to everything I do, but I'm telling you, this game is going to be friggin' amazing."

"I'll take your word on that. If you guys do get blown out, you owe me a pizza, but not one of those ones you get from the team. I want mine specially made."

"You know I don't make bets, but I'll take you up on that one. Not that we're going to get blown out, let alone lose, but if I do for some strange reason have to buy that pizza, I want a slice. Fair?"

"Yeah. That'll work."

Major rises from his place on the couch then steps over the coffee table. He and Joe shake hands to solidify their bet.

Releasing their grip, Major says, "Oh! I almost forgot. Will's going to take a nap in here tomorrow during lunch."

"Huh?" Joe asks. He is silent for a brief moment then says, "Oh! Never mind. I forgot that he eats early lunch every day. That must be nice."

"It is. Trust me. I have early lunch too tomorrow, but I'll be back in time to march the company in."

"All right. I'll let Sara know, just in case you forget to tell her."

"'Preciate it."

———————————————

The air is brisk and clean. Though it is rather cold out, the wind hardly moves a single leaf from a tree, making the weather rather bearable for those who are acclimated. The sky is partly cloudy, which makes for a more-interesting view. No clouds in the sky is rather boring at times. The sun shines bright, illuminating off of the Hudson River.

Today is rather ideal for tourists to visit the academy. With the sun shining so bright, West Point looks as picturesque as it possibly can. The statues and monuments beam outward with a slight glisten of sunshine.

The Serb teams have all assembled at Trophy Point with no difficulties. The men stand in awe at what their eyes behold. Their military academy is not nearly as majestic as West Point. None of them utter this feeling aloud, but they know it to be true. Every man carries a disposable camera on their person, which they immediately begin using, snapping away in all directions. For a moment, the Serbs forget that they are executing a mission and truly begin acting like tourists. Killer watches the Serbs' reaction to being at West Point and smiles.

After watching the Serbs' elation for a while, Killer says to them, "Gather around for a second, guys. You all are free to do what you want as long as you stick to our itinerary. Teams 2 and 3, you will watch lunch formation from the Plain. Ensure that you stay on what West Point refers to as Diagonal Walk. It's the long sidewalk that stretches across the Plain. The rest of you will come with us behind Pershing Barracks. Enjoy yourselves, gentlemen. I'll see you at 1120 hours.

1120 Hours

Major and Joe step out of their room on their way to lunch formation. In the hallway, they bump into Sara, who says while running up the stairs, "I'll meet you guys out there."

"We'll see you there," Joe and Major reply as they walk out onto the stoops.

———————————————

As Major and Joe walk across the street toward Central Area, they notice an unusually large number of tourists standing in front of Pershing Barracks and near the library.

"They sure are out today?" Joe comments, referring to the large number of tourists.

"You ain't kidding," Major agrees.

Not thinking anymore of the tourists, Major and Joe head for their formation area. Joe stands with the few upperclassmen who are present, while Major walks over to third platoon to converse with the plebes.

"How's it going there, Slim?" Major asks a third platoon plebe.

Major named Cdt. Pvt. Adam Slidell "Slim" many months ago because of his physical stature. Slim is tall and scrawny. He is a great kid but lacks a single athletic bone in his body. Whenever Major sees Slim, he always thinks to himself, *What a waste of height.*

Slim answers Major, saying, "I'm fine, sir."

"That's great, Slim. Let me hear 'The Corps.'"

"Sir, 'The Corps'!"

The Corps! The Corps! The Corps!
The Corps bareheaded salute it,
*   With eyes up thanking our God*
That we of the Corps are treading
*   Where they of the Corps have trod*
They are here in ghostly assemblage.
*   The men of the Corps long dead.*
And our hearts are standing attention
*   While we wait for your passing tread.*
We sons of to-day, we salute you
*   You, sons of an earlier day;*
We follow close order behind you,
*   Where you have pointed the way;*
The long gray line of us stretches
*   Thro' the years of a century told*
And the last man feels to his marrow
*   The grip of your far off hold.*
Grip hands with us now though we see not.

Grip hands with us, strengthen our hearts
As the long line stiffens and straightens
With the thrill that your presence imparts.
Grip hands though it be from the shadows.
While we swear as you did of yore.
Or living or dying to honor
The Corps, and The Corps, and The Corps!"

"Good job, Slim," Major replies, shaking his head in satisfaction. He then continues talking to Slim, saying, "That's what it's all about, Slim. We are all preparing to join something that is greater than ourselves. Think of all of the great leaders West Point has produced. It just goes to show that you have the potential to do great things for our nation. West Point is all about training leaders of character for the nation, whether they're in the army or out in the civilian world. I want you to think about that, Slim. Use it as motivation."

"Yes, sir. I will," Slim states with his small chest puffing out with pride.

"You like reciting 'The Corps,' don't you?" Major asks, lightly slapping Slim on his chest.

With a huge grin on his face, Slim answers, "Yes, sir, I do. I love West Point!"

"So do I, Slim. So do I."

———————————————————————

Killer and Colonel Drasneb stand in front of Pershing Barracks, along with Teams one, four, and five. Alex is positioned with teams 2 and 3 along Diagonal Walk. Both groups are surrounded by numerous tourists seemingly from all over the world. Killer was not anticipating the number of legitimate tourists who would be present the day prior to mission execution. The plethora of tourists makes him sit much easier though because it helps the Serbs blend in that much more.

Killer looks down at his watch to check the time then looks up and to his right. On time, as always, is Mac. Mac was with Alex and teams 2 and 3 to ensure that they were properly in position. Mac carefully makes his way through the loose group of tourists who stand in anticipation of watching the Corps of Cadets' lunch formation. The majority of the tourists stand on Diagonal Walk because that is where the army band stands poised to play the marching music.

Now standing beside Killer, Mac says, "They're in position."

"Good," Killer responds.

1130 Hours

Major still converses with the plebes in third platoon, asking them army knowledge and how their personal lives are going. While in the middle of speaking with a plebe, Major looks over his left shoulder and notices Dusty walking to the front of formation, thus signaling Major that it is time to fall in. Major turns and heads for the rear of formation, standing between Sara and Captain Weiss.

Standing in front of the Duck formation, Dusty shouts, "Fall in!" The Ducks all snap to the position of attention. Dusty then follows by shouting, "Receive the report!"

The platoon sergeants execute an about-face to receive the accountability report from their squad leaders. As each platoon sergeant receives their accountability reports from their squad leaders, they execute another about-face, their backs once again to their platoons.

With all of the platoon sergeants facing him, Dusty shouts, "Report!"

The platoon sergeants, in order of headquarters, first, second, and third platoons, salutes the first sergeant and renders the accountability report.

"Headquarters has thirty-three assigned, thirty-one present. Two are conducting security checks."

"First platoon is all present!"

"Second platoon! Thirty-four assigned, thirty-two present, two at football."

"Third platoon! Thirty-one assigned, twenty nine present, two at football."

Having received all of the reports from his platoon sergeants, Dusty executes an about-face so his commander may take over the company.

Mac leans over to Killer and says, "After all these years, I still love this stuff."

"You like formations?" Killer inquires.

"Yeah, but it's not the actual formation that I like. It's the whole pomp and circumstance behind it—the tradition and all."

"I guess so. I never cared too much for formations, myself."

As Mac and Killer converse on their likes and dislikes concerning formations, Mac hears the same familiar voice from the other day shout "Post!"

"There it is again," Mac says to Killer.

"What?" Killer asks.

"That voice. The one I told you about yesterday. I swear on my mother's grave that I've heard that voice somewhere before."

"I think your mind's playing tricks on you."

"Brother. This isn't some Ghetto Boys song I'm talking about here."

Killer chuckles at Mac's musical reference then says, "All right. Let's assume you know the voice. Whoever is speaking doesn't know that you're here. Besides, you don't know any cadets, so as far as you're concerned, you need to chalk the voice similarity up as nothing more than a coincidence."

Colonel Drasneb hears Mac and Killer conversing. He is unable to discern what they are discussing, so he steps forward and says, "Are you gentlemen discussing anything of any importance?"

Killer turns his head and quickly replies, "In fact, sir, we were discussing the cadets' mannerisms and demeanor while in their formation."

"Yes, it is impressive. Is it not?" Colonel Drasneb states. "They truly are professionals. Their deaths will surely be a great blow to their army." Colonel Drasneb pats both Mac and Killer on the shoulder then returns to his original position alongside teams one, four, and five.

"That bastard!" Mac blurts as Colonel Drasneb walks away.

"Yeah. I can't wait to be rid of that man after tomorrow," Killer comments.

"You and me both, brother. You and me both."

2000 Hours: Highland Falls, New York

Alex sits in a chair in Mac and Killer's room. As far as Alex is aware, this will be the last time he will probably ever spend with his two new friends.

"Tomorrow's it, Alex," Killer states. "You ready for this?"

"Of course," Alex replies. "Tomorrow is what we have been training for all these months."

"That's not what he means, Alex," Mac interjects.

"What is Killer saying then?" Alex asks.

"The question is, are you ready to kill four thousand kids?" Mac states.

"They are not kids, Mac," Alex answers.

"Were you not paying attention today?" Mac replies. "Obviously you and I were looking at two totally different groups of people today because the cadets I saw today look like a bunch of kids who're still wet behind the ear."

"Whether they are kids or not is of no consequence to me," Alex responds. "We have a mission to execute. That is all that matters."

Killer leans forward in his seat and says, "Have you ever killed anyone before?"

"No, I have not," Alex states.

"Then you truly don't know the burden your soul carries when you do," Killer comments.

Mac interjects, stating, "Alex, we're not telling you not to go through with the mission. All we're saying is that you need to weigh the consequences of tomorrow's actions. You need to understand that once we kill those kids tomorrow, there's no turning back. Once you go down that road, you're on it forever. Take it from a couple of guys who've traveled that road for many years."

"You've killed children before?" Alex asks.

"No. We haven't," Killer answers. "This is the first and will definitely be the last."

"So what it comes down to for you is money," Alex suggests.

"It's not like that," Mac answers. "We got caught in, how do you say, a contractual loophole? The money is a motivator, but only because it's the only thing that allows me to keep whatever ounce of sanity I have left. Do I like what we're getting ready to do? Hell no! But the money allows me to sleep at night."

"This is it for us," Killer informs Alex. "After tomorrow, we're out of the business forever."

"Why?" Alex asks.

"After a job like this," Mac replies, "we know that whatever pleasure we get out of our work will no longer exist. I know that if I were to ever do another job, I'd think of what we're getting ready to do tomorrow. I couldn't live with that. We have to get out for sanity's sake."

"Mac's right, Alex," Killer affirms. "The morality of what we're getting ready to do is as wrong as wrong can be. The money helps, but honestly, it barely keeps me from losing myself. Nonetheless, we have to go through with this. The world in which we live does not allow us to just up and quit our profession when we want. This job is our ticket out."

"We're going to do the job, as wrong as it may be," Mac adds. "You and Colonel Drasneb can rest assured of that, but as soon as it's over, we're ghost."

"That's right," Killer states. "You know, you can come with us if you like."

"I appreciate the offer. I truly do," Alex thanks Killer, "but I cannot leave the colonel, no matter the circumstance."

"Understood," Killer responds. He sticks his hand out and says, "It was nice knowing you Alex."

8 DECEMBER 1999

0300 Hours: West Point

Mac jumps into the van with Team 4. Killer rides with Team 5. All of the men are dressed in black pants, a white shirt, a maroon vest, and don black baseball caps on their heads—the mess hall employee uniform. Killer and Alex planned the entrance for 0300 Hours because that is approximately one hour prior to the actual mess hall employees reporting for duty. Killer and Alex assessed that the MPs would not think twice about allowing them access onto post if they looked like the mess hall employees. The MPs do not track the mess hall schedule or calendar, so as far as they are concerned, a packed van of people arriving at West Point at the crack of dawn are there to work, nothing more, nothing less.

The two teams pull out of the West Point Motel and head for West Point, entering through Washington Gate. Unlike the reconnaissance aspect of the mission, the two teams both enter through Washington Gate because it is the closest one to Newburgh, which is where all of the mess hall employees live.

Teams 4 and 5 drive through Washington Gate with ease. Obeying the 25 mph speed limit, the two vans slowly drive down the road, passing the hospital to their left. Further down the road, they pass the Post Exchange to their left, cross an intersection, then pass the West Point cemetery, also to the their left. Still moving, the two teams pass the fire station to their right then come to another intersection, halting in place. They turn right, immediately driving up a steep hill. To their right, they pass the Catholic chapel and to their left, Arvin Gymnasium. Finally, arriving at their destination, the two vans turn left and head for the Cadet Chapel. Winding down the road, they veer to the right and take the road approximately a hundred meters until it ends.

Parked, teams 4 and 5 exit their respective vans. Team 4 exits with AK-47s in hand, Team 5 with a medium-sized knapsack, each containing a pound of C4 explosives, detonators, and a roll of duct tape. Mac and Killer lead teams 4 and 5 to the perimeter of the Cadet Chapel then down the winding steps into Cadet Area. The men enter the mess hall from an unlocked side entrance, ensuring that they are neither seen nor heard.

In the mess hall, the members of Team 5 move to their designated pillar and commence climbing to the ceiling. Team 4 pulls security, while Mac and Killer supervise Team 5's actions. With their knapsacks secured on their backs, Team 5 climbs to the ceiling. At the top, they open up their knapsacks and pull out a roll of duct tape. Ripping a piece from the roll, they place it on their respective pillar so that it dangles in the air. Next, they carefully extract the C4 and place it onto the pillars. They then take the pre-ripped duct tape and secure the C4 to the pillars.

With the C4 properly placed on the pillars, the men all look down at Killer. Killer, noticing that the Serbs are ready for the next phase, gives them a signal. Receiving the signal, the men take the detonators from out of their knapsacks and place them onto the C4 then look back at Killer. Killer throws his right hand in the air and begins counting down, lowering each finger for its respective number, "Five, four, three, two, one." When Killer clinches his fist, the Serbs push a black button on the detonator, thus setting the timer for the explosives.

Now that the timers are set, Team 5 slides down their pillars and exit the mess hall as covert as they had entered. Mac and Killer lead Team 5 back up to where they had parked the vans, and Team 4 runs to Bradley Barracks.

Team 4 stealthily enters Bradley Barracks. They move in such a manner as to not disturb the slumber of the sleeping cadets. With map in hand, Team 4's team leader leads his team to the sixth floor of Bradley Barracks and navigates them to the roof entrance. On the roof, Team 4 executes a tactical sweep of the area. Though Team 4 knows that it is very unlikely that anyone is on the roof, they do not want to deviate from any of their training. Doing so would show a lack of discipline. Positive that the area is clear, Team 4 takes their designated positions, ensuring that no one from the ground below or from the neighboring barracks will detect their presence.

At the vans, Team 5 splits themselves evenly between the two vans. They then leave West Point and return to the motel, exiting through Thayer Gate. The next phase of the mission for them is to prepare everyone for departure.

To the west side of the Cadet Chapel, there is a wood line that stretches for thousands of yards. It is very isolated and people rarely ever walk through it due to the fact that it does not lead to anywhere of any significance.

When Mac and Killer went to church the other Sunday, they noticed the wood line and recognized its potential as an excellent lookout post for the mission. They had walked down the portion of road that runs alongside the wood line and noticed that the foliage was relatively undisturbed, meaning that no one travels through it on a regular basis.

Mac and Killer had determined that the risk was low enough to position themselves in the wood line rather than in the Cadet Chapel steeple. As ideal as the steeple is as a lookout post, the wood line provides them an easy escape route.

In the wood line, Mac and Killer set up their positions, utilizing the dead foliage that lies on the ground as their camouflage. The ground is somewhat wet due to the melted snow. Anticipating this fact, Mac and Killer wear, as they always do, the proper gear to sustain themselves for an extended period of time.

With their rifles and binoculars in hand, Mac and Killer lie and wait for the Serbs to execute the mission. They have several hours to wait, and as tired as they may be, Mac and Killer know that it is of the utmost importance that they keep one another awake.

1045 Hours

Major and three of his SE 401 project partners, cadets Brian Christopher, Kenney Thurston, and Shawn Danbury, exit Mahan Hall en route to their individual rooms. The four cadets had just completed a portion of their semester-long project brief to their instructor, Maj. Jack Murphy. Their project is designing components for the army's super-soldier system. As system engineers, the cadets' job is not to build the system but create four possible options for their client. In this case, the client is Major Murphy. The focus of systems engineering, as taught at West Point, covers two areas: problem solving and minimizing cost while maximizing utility. The system with the largest utility theoretically is the most ideal.

Major, Brian, Ken, and Shawn have just completed the third of four briefs. Once they complete their fourth brief in two weeks, they will have completed the class with an A, and more importantly, they do not have to take a term-end exam for the course.

As the project partners leave Mahan Hall and step out onto Thayer Road, Major says, "It's not too bad out today."

"Man, what are you talking about?" Brian exclaims. "It's freezing out here!"

"It is cold, but it really is a pretty nice day out," Shawn agrees with Major.

"I don't care how nice it looks outside," Brian states. "If it's cold out, the day sucks."

"What a puss," Ken jokes.

"Forget ya'll," Brian says as Major, Ken, and Shawn laugh at him.

■———————————————————■

The members of Team 1 jump into their fifteen-passenger van. Beneath their seats is one AK-47 per man and plenty of ammunition to fight a small army. They are dressed in civilian clothes, though they originally had wanted to wear their military fatigues. Killer had explained to them back in Russia that there was no way the military police were going to allow them access onto the post wearing any form of a foreign military uniform. The easiest way, as Killer explained, is to dress like regular people. That way, there is no suspicion of their true motives.

Team 1 enters West Point via North Gate. Down the road, they drive, passing the commissary to their left. Further down the hill to their right is an incredible view of the Hudson River Valley. As the hill comes to an end, Team 1 drives between the Holleder Center and Michie Stadium. At the end of the road, with Lusk Reservoir facing them, the van stops then turns right, passing the AOG headquarters to their left. At the next intersection, Team 1 turns right then takes the immediate right, driving into an oversized parking lot for Buffalo Soldier Field. Around the parking lot, Team 1 drives, passing the post office, the bowling alley, and several administrative offices.

In front of the MP station, the driver of the van parks as close to the building as is legally possible. Colonel Drasneb, who sits in the front seat, turns around and faces his men, saying, "This is the moment that we have all trained so hard for, gentlemen. Remember, we do this for the sanctity of Serbia."

The men of Team 1 all nod their heads in agreement. They would cheer, but they do not want to attract any unneeded attention.

Colonel Drasneb then states, "Your signal to exit the van is when I reach the other side of the street."

Colonel Drasneb exits the van and casually walks across the street. When his foot touches the sidewalk, his men burst out of the van, weapons in hand, and sprint across the parking lot. Colonel Drasneb had timed their execution quite well. He approaches the main entrance to the MP station, and as soon he opens the door, without a pause, his men rush in and bombard the MP station.

Team 1 races through the doors of the MP station. Their sudden and unexpected action catches the unsuspecting MPs off guard. The MPs are unable to react properly due to the suprise attack. Before the MPs are able to draw their .45mm handguns, the Serbs have contained the entire station. The Serbs do not have to fire a single shot to detain and control the station, but they do so anyway, killing every MP inside.

As Team 1 secures the MP station, Colonel Drasneb approaches the desk sergeant and puts the barrel of his .45 to the sergeant's head, saying "In case you did not know, Sergeant, I am taking over your station."

1100 Hours

Teams 2 and 3 leave the West Point Motel simultaneously. Entering through Thayer Gate, the two teams drive their vans to the parking lot that is situated behind Doubleday baseball field and beside the outdoor tennis courts. It is surprising that they are able to find a parking space at all. As usual, there is an immense crowd present for lunch formation, much to the team leaders' satisfaction. Being among the crowd puts their nerves at ease.

The two teams wear heavy winter coats. Though it is cold outside, the true reason for the bulkiness of the coats is to conceal the AK-47s that they carry underneath, which hang on a sling on their arm. Relaxed, the men step out of their vans and join a group of tourists who are heading toward Diagonal Walk to watch Third Regiment's lunch formation.

Major and Brian turn left into Grant Area, leaving Ken and Shawn who head right toward Central Area.

"You know," Brian says, "with the season you guys are having, I wish to God I wouldn't have hurt my knee yuck year."

"Yeah, me too," Major agrees. "We sure had a great time down in JV though, didn't we?"

"Yeah, we did," Brian states, he and Major reminiscing about their junior varsity basketball days.

"We sucked, but we had fun. You know?"

Brian begins to laugh uncontrollably. "Yeah, we did. I don't think we won a single game our plebe year."

"I don't think we did either," Major laughingly replies

The two friends laugh as they reminisce of their JV glory days, though there was not too much glory on the basketball court.

Walking up the steps onto the stoops, Major says to Brian, "I'll check you later, bro. I've got to get to early lunch."

"All right man," Brian says, shaking Major's hand. "Tell the fellas I said good luck. I'll be up there tonight."

"Most definitely. I'll see you at formation."

"All right."

Major enters his division and goes to his room. He places his notebook on his desk then grabs the small stack of pictures of he and Terry's weekend that are lying beside his computer monitor. Sticking the pictures in his parka pocket, Major immediately exits his room and heads for the mess hall.

Entering the mess hall, it is very empty at this time. Not too many people are in the mess hall prior to lunch. The football team, a corps squad team that has a home game, and the mess hall employees are all who are inside. Major walks through the mess hall and heads for the corps squad section where the basketball and football teams are assembling.

Major takes his seat at his table. The food is already present, so when he sits, he passes his plate down so one of the plebes can pile on the food. With the breaded chicken and baked ziti piled high on Major's plate, the plebes pass it back down to him. They also hand him a glass of fruit punch with no ice.

While Major eats, he and Jimmy converse about the game and their personal strategy on how they believe they can defeat Indiana tonight.

"You know," Jimmy states, "win or lose, it's going to be cool as hell meeting Bobby Knight."

"I hear you, man. You know, Colonel Wood's friggin' excited about tonight," Major replies.

"Yeah, I know," Jimmy agrees. "He was going on and on about Coach Knight last night. He's more excited than we are."

"He ought to be. He did play for him back when he was a cadet."

"Man! That sure was a long time ago."

"Yeah it was."

Major looks up at his watch and realizes that it is time for him to head out to his formation. "Hey, Jimmy. I've got to roll. I'll see you up top."

"All right, Major. I'll see you," Jimmy replies. He and Major give each other a pound as Major gets up from the table.

Before leaving the mess hall, Major trots over to the football section and goes to one of the linebacker tables where Ben sits.

"Hey, Ben," Major blurts as he approaches his friend. "I'm going to go march my company in for lunch. I'll meet you in your room."

"All right, Major," Ben shouts. "I'll see you up there."

Major then faces Will's direction, who is at the far end of the wing with the defensive backs, and shouts, "You still going to my room after this?"

"Yeah!" Will shouts back in return.

"All right! Don't oversleep."

"I won't."

"Cool. I'll holler at you later." Major begins backing up then quickly heads for the nearest exit.

Central Area during lunch formation is a giant mob scene. Thousands of cadets move in all directions, going to their rooms and going to their formation areas. Realizing that he no longer has to rush, Major slows his pace down some. As he moves, Major attempts to not run into as many cadets as he can possibly avoid. Major makes his way through Second Regiment's area, saying hello to his friends and acquaintances who he passes.

After walking between A-1 and B-1's formation areas, Major finally makes it to his company. Sara spots Major walking to the formation, so she meets him as he arrives.

"I wasn't sure if you were going to make it or not," Sara says.

"I figured I'd march us in," Major replies. "I'm going to leave as soon as I do though."

1130 Hours

Taylor Hall, standing at over 160 feet high, is the tallest all-stone masonry building in the world. It houses the offices of USMA Headquarters, the Thayer Award Room, and the West Point Federal Credit Union. Situated in Taylor Hall are the offices of the superintendent of the military academy, Lieutenant General Holiday.

Lieutenant General Holiday sits behind his desk, finishing up some paperwork before he heads home for lunch. Unless there is a special guest or a VIP visiting West Point, Lieutenant General Holiday goes home to have lunch with his wife every day. Looking up at the clock that hangs on the far end of his office, Lieutenant General Holiday realizes that it is time for him to head home.

Lieutenant General Holiday stacks his papers neatly then rises from behind his desk. He walks over to his coat rack that is positioned near the door and grabs his black trench coat, slipping it on.

Walking out of his office and into the receptionist area, Lieutenant General Holiday tells his secretary, "I'll be back at one, Jamie."

"Enjoy your lunch, sir," Jamie smilingly replies as Lieutenant General Holiday walks off.

Lieutenant General Holiday exits Taylor Hall and steps out onto Thayer Road. Other than the numerous tourists who are present, the street is rather empty, but that is due to the fact that all of the cadets are currently in lunch formation. Lieutenant General Holiday walks across Diagonal Walk without very little hindrance.

After an easy five-minute walk, Lieutenant General Holiday is home. He enters the house and shouts, "Hey, honey! What's for lunch?"

1135 Hours

Team 5, which returned to their hotel room around four in the morning, awoke from their restful slumber an hour ago and now pile back into their van. One of the team members carries a large black duffel bag that is filled to capacity. The driver backs out and heads for West Point, entering through Thayer Gate. The team enters West Point unhindered. They drive past Michie Stadium and around Lusk Reservoir. Passing the Cadet Chapel then Arvin Gymnasium, Team 5 turns right just before the road ends. They drive along the side of Arvin Gymnasium then park the van and wait.

■————————————————————————■

Major marches the Ducks to lunch, taking his least favorite path, which leads them between Bradley Barracks and the cliff where Boodler's sits. He takes this path because Second Regiment has not yet finished giving their report. Major prefers marching the Ducks through Cadet Area because he takes pride in showing his company off to the entire corps, which he does every chance he gets.

Leading the Ducks to the mess hall, Major steps out of their way so they can enter. Because he has already eaten, Major, technically, is not authorized to eat again. Even if he were, though, he probably would not eat a second lunch. It is not that Major does not like eating. In fact, eating is one of Major's favorite activities. It is the fact the mess hall food is not the best in the world. It is adequate at best. The cadets blame the lack of food quality on the numerous defense-budget cuts that have occurred over the past ten years.

Now that his company is assembled in the mess hall, Major turns and walks the short distance to the sally port that separates Bradley Short and Bradley Long Barracks. He turns right and enters Bradley Long, heading for the elevator. Ben lives on the sixth floor, and Major does not feel like walking up all those stairs. Major pushes the up button and waits impatiently for the elevator to arrive at the first floor. Waiting, Major becomes extremely anxious.

Major thinks, *I'd be up there by now if I had taken the stairs.*

As his thought ends, the elevator arrives. The doors creak open and with the smallest possible opening available, Major leaps into the elevator. He pushes the button for the sixth floor then fervently taps the close door button. Much to Major's relief, the door finally closes. For a brief moment, or at least during the course of the ride up to the sixth floor, Major is able to relax. So far, so good.

The elevator stops at the sixth floor, and Major jumps out as soon as he is physically able. In the hallway, Major plays it off as though he was not in the elevator. Since no one caught him riding the elevator, Major is now truly able to relax. He strides down to the far end of the hall and enters the third-to-the-last room which is on his right, the men's restroom to his left.

Entering the room, Ben says, "About time you made it. You bring your pictures?"

"Got 'em right here," Major replies as he walks toward Ben, who is sitting on a chair behind his desk.

Major takes his parka off and tosses it onto Ben's bed. As he takes a seat on the bed, Major then says, "Check 'em out."

Major tosses his pictures to Ben. Ben catches the pictures then tosses Major his stack of pictures that he had taken during the pre- and post-Army-Navy-game festivities.

———————————————————

Team 4's team leader's watch beeps four times. In response to the alarm, the team leader slaps his chest four times, signaling his men to place their earplugs into their ears and put on their goggles. The team leader then takes a knee and overlooks the roof, the view of the mess hall directly in front of him. His men follow suit.

The watches of the two team leaders for Teams 2 and 3 also go off, beeping four times. Team 3 place skullcaps over their heads, which contain hearing protection. Team 2, on the other hand, walks down Diagonal Walk and casually head for the Officers Club. Alongside the Officers Club, there is a long, steep metal staircase that Team 2 uses to go down to South Dock. Team 3 remains in place and waits.

1144 Hours

Killer looks to his left at Mac. There is one more minute until detonation. Mac, with a calm, yet focused look on his face, in recognition, subtly nods his head at Killer.

There's no going back now, Killer thinks.

Mac and Killer's watches softly beep. An instant later, Killer jerks his head up and leans forward on his elbows. What Killer does not see—what has not occurred—causes his mind to begin processing contingency plans at a rapid pace.

Before Killer can react any further, Mac somberly says, "I couldn't do it. I just couldn't do it..."

Going against the plan, the timers on the columns in the mess hall did not detonate as planned and executed. Though the bombs were set to a timer, Mac had a kill-switch, just in case the mission went array. The kill-switch was not meant to be used to check one's conscience; obviously, Mac disagreed.

Realizing what has been weighing on Mac's heart and the severity of his action, Killer says to his friend, "What's done is done, brother. We'll simply have to deal with the repercussions as they come."

———————————————

Major and Ben look over one another's pictures that they had taken the previous weekend. Both friends are rather excited at what they see.

"This picture of you and Pete Dawkins is money!" Major boasts.

"Yeah," Ben agrees. "It was pretty cool getting to meet him and all."

"You know? Pete Dawkins is like the perfect American," Major comments.

"What do you mean?" Ben asks.

"Think about it. The guy's a grad, was the brigade captain, valedictorian, captain of the football team, a Rhodes Scholar, a college football All-American, a Heisman Trophy winner, a retired general, and a CEO of a company. It doesn't get much better than that. The only thing the man hasn't done is be president of the United States."

"I never thought of that. But you know? You're right," Ben replies.

Ben flips through a couple of Major's pictures and says, "Terry's beautiful, man."

"Thanks, bro, 'preciate it," Major replies.

"I'm just calling it like I see it," Ben remarks. Slapping Major hard on his back, Ben continues, saying, "I can't believe you were able to pull this off. Good for you."

"You're telling me. Sometimes I can't believe it myself."

"What'd you guys get into?"

"I took her to the ESPN Zone in Times Square to watch the game. Thank God we won 'cause I dropped some loot for that bad boy. My game against Columbia was that night—"

"Ah man! I forgot! How'd you do?"

"We won. My shot was off, but it's all good."

Suddenly, Ben and Major leap to their feet—their bodies reacting to the unexpected sounds of automatic gunfire out in the hall. They are further startled by the eerie shouts and agonizing screams of cadets from throughout Bradley Barracks.

Ben shouts, "What the hell's going on?!"

"I don't know, but we can't stay here," Major answers, doing his best to remain composed.

"All right then. Let's get out of here and see what's going on."

The two friends give each other a pound and exchange a blazing glance—like it may be the last time they see one another alive.

━━━━━━━━━━━━━━━━━━

"That's gunfire," Mac states.

"That's not good," Killer replies.

"Team 5's supposed to be on their way up here, which wouldn't be good either, considering..."

"Something's not right."

"The plan's changed. Drasneb's changed the mission."

"All bets are off now. We've got to get down there and fix this."

Killer and Mac spring to their feet from their prone positions and race down the hill with their weapons at the ready. Instead of taking the stairs, they approach the small cliff and slide down it, landing in Cadet Area on the backside of Bradley Barracks.

"I hear more gunfire," Killer calmly states. "This way."

Mac follows Killer into Bradley Barracks. Hearing the continuous rifle fire, they chase after the sharp reverberating sounds, racing up the nearest set of Bradley Barracks staircases.

━━━━━━━━━━━━━━━━━━

Major slowly opens the bedroom door and peers out to inspect the hallway. "I see three guys about three rooms down. They've got their backs to us," Major whispers to Ben. "If we move fast enough, I think we can take 'em."

"Let's do this. We can't just sit here and wait to die," Ben silently states. "I'll lead. You follow."

Major opens the door all the way. Ben then leaps out into the hallway and, without hesitating, sprints with all his might down the hallway. Mentally, Ben goes into linebacker mode. Ben has only one thought on his mind, and that is knocking out the man who is directly in front of him.

Major races close behind Ben, using him as a blocker. Ben spear-tackles the first man in his path. The sudden impact of the collision causes the man to yelp like a hurt puppy. Ben hits the man with such ferocity that he knocks the rifle out of his hands. When it crashes to the floor, Major instantly dives down and scoops the rifle up into his hands. Major then slides to his right and sporadically fires a volley of rounds down the other end of the hallway, taking out the other two rifle-holding men.

As Major fires his weapon, Ben jumps from off of the man he had just spear-tackled and commences to stomping on his head and chest until he stops moving. At the same time, Major races to the end of the hallway and retrieves one of the rifles and slides it back down the hall to Ben, who picks it up from off of the ground when it reaches his feet.

"God! That was intense!" Ben shouts.

Major runs over to where Ben stands and rhetorically asks, "What the hell is going on here!?"

Before Ben can respond, the two friends hear more gunfire coming from downstairs.

"Come on," Ben says. "I know where to go."

Major follows Ben down the hall, moving as fast as their feet will allow. They race down the stairs to the fifth floor then head down another hallway. Hearing more gunfire and the shrill of someone's voice, Ben stops in his tracks and throws his back up against the wall, causing Major to do the same. The two friends creep forward with extreme caution, doing their best to veil their presence from their unknown enemy.

Ben and Major reach the other end of the hallway and stop at the corner.

Ben turns to Major and whispers, "I'm going to see what's up. Follow me in about five seconds."

Major nods his head in compliance.

With his rifle stretched out in front at the ready, Ben carefully maneuvers around the corner with his back to the wall and is immediately met with a barrage of gunfire. Ben groans in agony from the rounds cutting through his flesh. Major, out of pure instinct, drops to the ground and high crawls around the corner, praying that his friend is still alive. By the grace of God, Major finds Ben alive and sort-of-well, sprawled out on the ground. Major grabs the back of

Ben's shirt collar and attempts to drag him to safety, but gunfire begins to ring over his head, ceasing his actions.

"Jesus!" Major shouts as he tries to keep himself from being shot and Ben from being shot again.

———————————————————

Mac and Killer race up the stairs to put an end to the senseless violence they know the Serbs are reigning down on the unsuspecting cadets. Hearing gunfire on the fifth floor, Killer and Mac jump out of the staircase and race down the hallway toward the ensuing action. As the two mercenaries move down the hallway, Killer spots a Serb firing upon a helpless cadet, who immediately shrieks in extreme agony. The cadet hits the ground like a limp rag. Without a thought, Killer raises his rifle and fires on the Serb, killing him instantly.

Fifty meters behind Killer, Mac takes a knee and provides Killer with cover fire. As Killer moves, the other Serbs in the hallway turn their attention from the bleeding cadet and another cadet who is attempting to drag him away and focus their sights on their two former instructors. Mac and Killer effortlessly pick off the remainder of the Serbs, killing them without a thought.

———————————————————

With the enemies' attention averted, Major grabs Ben from underneath his shoulders and drags him around the corner to safety. Out of harm's way, Major sits Ben up against the wall. As Major assists Ben, they both hear two unfamiliar voices from the other end of the hall where Ben was shot.

"Who the hell is that?" Major asks.

In extreme agony, Ben replies, "How the hell should I know!?"

"My bad. My bad. Are you all right?" Major asks.

Breathing heavily, Ben replies, "I think so. They got me in the leg. It feels like it's on fire!" Ben bangs his head up against the wall and shouts, "God this hurts! I didn't think it would hurt like this!"

Ben's left leg is bleeding profusely. The bullet wound is above the knee, in the thigh region. Looking at the wound, it appears as though the bullet went straight through. Major takes his tie off and uses it to tie a tourniquet around Ben's left leg, above the bullet wound, to cut off the circulation.

———————————————————

All of the members of Team 5 lay strung out across the hall—dead. The cause of death is very obvious: multiple gun shot wounds to the head and torso. A few of the Serbs have wounds in various parts of their bodies, but they all have an entrance and exit point in their skulls.

Killer turns around and says to Mac, "Come on, man. We need to check on those kids."

"I'm with you," Mac replies, rising to his feet and joining Killer down the hall. As they pass the lifeless Serbs, Mac and Killer collect all of their personal weapons—knives, rifles, and pistols. One Serb has a cigar in his cargo pocket. Mac takes it and places it in his mouth.

Their hands full of weapons, Mac and Killer turn the corner and find two cadets on the floor, one sitting up against the wall bleeding and the other kneeling and tending to his friend's wound.

Mac looks at the cadets and realizes that the one who is not wounded looks very familiar. Studying the uninjured cadet's face, a wave of memories of long ago flood Mac's mind.

Mac says to himself, *This kid looks just like my last company commander, Captain Johnson. Wait a second. No. It can't be. I know this kid. He's got to be his son. You've got to be kidding me. I met this kid back when I was in LeJeun.*

———————————————————

Mac's mind wonders off to July of 1988, when he was stationed in Camp LeJeun, North Carolina. That summer, his battalion was deploying to the Mediterranean Sea for their regular six-month rotation. Mac's company commander, then-Capt. Sydney Johnson, was a squared-away officer—a PT stud. The day the battalion was scheduled to leave camp and head to Norfolk, Virginia, to board their ships, all of the families came to wish the Marines off. Mac, who was with a group of marines whose families were not able to attend the send-off, stand to the side as to not get in the way of the festivities.

As Mac and his friends converse, Captain Johnson joins their group. In his arms, Captain Johnson carries his seven-year-old son, and following on the edge of his boots is his eleven-year-old son. Mac remembers Captain Johnson telling the guys to watch out for his son Major, the eleven-year-old.

"He can make any of you eat his dust in a race," Mac remembers Captain Johnson boasting to his Marines.

Obviously, their commander was trying to hype his son up. The Marines all laugh at their commander's ridiculous claim. Mac then bends down and hands the eleven-year-old his M60 machine gun. The kid places the M60 on his hip. He struggles to carry the M60 but manages to hold onto it for a little while. The Marines laugh at the kid's valiant effort.

Mac takes the machine gun away from the kid and pats him on the head saying, "You were born to be a Marine, kid."

The kid replies, "Ooh raah!"

Motivated by the kid's Marine Corps pride, all of the Marines in the group join the kid in a loud and thunderous, "Ooh raah!"

Captain Johnson then says to his Marines, "All right guys. I'll see you on the buses."

"Aye, aye, sir!" the Marines reply as Captain Johnson walks off with his sons.

While Mac stands there basking in a happy thought as he guards the area, Killer squats down and says to the uninjured cadet, "We need to get your friend into a room."

"Roger," Major replies, not caring who the men are, only that they are obviously on their side.

Killer helps Major lift Ben from off of the ground and takes him to the nearest room. Gently, they place Ben on the nearest bed. Killer rushes to a bookshelf and grabs several books. He takes them back to the bed and elevates the wounded cadet's leg onto them.

"Grab some alcohol, kid, and pour it on your friend's wound," Killer instructs Major.

Major rushes to the medicine cabinet and grabs a bottle of alcohol, immediately pouring its contents onto Ben's wound. Ben moans in agonizing pain, doing his best to stay strong.

"You should be all right," Killer says to Ben. "Your buddy tied on a pretty good tourniquet." Killer hands Ben an AK-47 and a .45mm then says, "Take these just in case there are any stray Serbs running around."

"Serbs?" Ben and Major echo, looking at one another in a confused manner.

"Yeah," Killer replies, "but don't worry about it. We don't have time to explain." Walking out the room, Killer says to Major, "You. Come with us."

"Yes, sir," Major responds, following Killer out the door. Before exiting the room though, Major turns to Ben and says, "Call Colonel Wood at home. His number's 446-5049. Let him know what's happening."

"All right," Ben answers.

"I almost forgot," Major states. He runs to a dresser and rummages through it until he finds an athletic sweater. He grabs it and puts it on as he steps out into the hallway.

When Major steps out of the room, Killer begins to stride down the hallway. He asks Major, "So, kid, what's your name?"

Following close behind the two men, Major responds, "Milton Johnson, sir. My friends call me Major."

"I knew it," Mac, in calm excitement, says to Killer.

As they race down the staircase, Killer introduces himself, saying, "I'm Killer. The big guy's Mac."

Reaching the first floor, Killer states, "We're going to need your help, kid. There's only the two of us, maybe a third. I can't tell you what's happening, but if someone shoots at you, shoot back."

"Got you," Major quickly replies, swallowing a hard lump in his throat.

The three men rush out of Bradley barracks and turn right, heading for Thayer Road. As they pass Grant Barracks, Major finds Will standing on the stoops with a small group of extremely confused and perplexed cadets. Will sees his brother as well and immediately runs out to meet him.

Running, Will shouts, "Major, what's going on!? We heard a fire-fight going on in Bradley!"

In full stride, Major says to Will without directly answering his question, "Get my cell from off my desk and call Dad. Tell him there're Serbs on the ground attacking us."

Will stops in his tracks before reaching his brother. "Huh?"

Major turns around and runs backward so Will can still see his face. "You heard me! Call Dad! And tell him what I just told you!"

"Here kid. Take these, just in case." Mac hands Will two AK-47s and a large hunting knife.

Still not fully comprehending the transpiring events, Will dutifully takes the weapons that are offered him. Major, Mac, and Killer then run off in the direction they were headed, leaving Will and a small contingent of cadets standing in the middle of the street with their mouths wide open. After a moment of astonishment, Will runs back to Grant Barracks to call his dad.

Mac, Killer, and Major run past Mahan Hall and building 606. Leaving Cadet Area, they approach a Ford Explorer parked alongside the road. Mac bashes the driver's side window with the butt stock of his AK-47. He reaches his arm into the Explorer and unlocks the door. When Killer jumps into the Explorer, he bends down underneath the steering column and messes with a few wires until, after only a couple of seconds of work, the Explorer's engine turns over.

Killer jumps into the driver's seat and, with Mac and Major seated, rips out of the parking spot and speeds down the road.

"We're going to the MP station. That's where Drasneb is," Killer informs Major.

"Let's do it," Mac replies.

Speeding down Thayer Road, Mac instructs Major; "When we stop, you get out and tell the MPs at the gate what's going on. Say whatever you have to convince them of what the hell's going on."

Major takes a deep breath and exhales, nodding in compliance.

Killer drives the Explorer to Thayer Gate. Slowing down to a crawl but not stopping. Major jumps out of the Explorer as it zooms off to the MP station.

With his AK-47 still in hand, Major runs up to the MPs who are manning Thayer Gate, shouting, "Hey guys! I need your help!"

Hearing a shout, one of the MPs turns around to find a cadet running toward him with an assault rifle in his hands. The MP immediately draws his .09mm pistol from out of his holster and shouts as he aims it at the seemingly crazy person, "Drop the weapon now!"

The rifle-wielding cadet freezes in his tracks and slowly places the weapon on the ground. He then calmly states, "I need you to listen to me."

"Shut up and put your hands on your head!" the other MP shouts, he too now with his weapon drawn.

The cadet places his hands on his head. Unfazed by what is occurring, he states, "I am Cdt. Milton Johnson. I'm the D-1 company commander. I'm on the basketball team."

"Go to your knees!" an MP loudly commands.

Cadet Johnson slowly drops to his knees, saying, "I need you to listen to me. There's an army of Serbs attacking West Point."

One of the two MPs, who is actually listening to what Cadet Johnson is saying, replies, "What did you just say?"

Thank God one of them's listening! Cadet Johnson prays silently.

He then says to the MPs, "I just fought a group of Serbs in Bradley Barracks. Call Central Guard Room, if you don't believe me. They'll confirm they heard a fire fight."

"Go call Central Guard Room," the E-6 MP orders the E-5 MP.

The E-5 MP immediately runs to the gate to call Central Guard Room.

After a few moments, the E-5 MP steps out of the gate and shouts, "Hey, Sergeant, Central Guard Room confirmed the cadet's story."

"What the hell's going on?" the E-6 asks.

Still on his knees with his hands behind his back, Cadet Johnson replies, "It's like I said, a bunch of Serbs have attacked us. I'm here to help, but I can't help like this."

Shaking his head in disbelief, the E-6 says, "Oh, yeah. Sorry. You can get up."

Cadet Johnson rises to his feet and retrieves his rifle from off of the ground. The E-6 then says, "So what do we do?"

"Call all the other MPs and get them calling everyone they can think of with some authority around here. Then call the National Guard and the police, state and local. If they laugh, forget them. Make them believe what you know is true," Cadet Johnson answers.

"What are you going to do?" the E-6 asks.

"I've got to go help some friends," Cadet Johnson responds as he runs away from Thayer Gate toward the MP station.

With Major safely on the ground and heading for Thayer Gate, Killer screeches off to the MP station, which is approximately one hundred meters away. Pulling in front of the MP station, Killer quickly applies the breaks and brings the Explorer to a screeching halt. Because the windows of the MP station are tinted from the outside, Killer and Mac are unable to tell where the members of Team 1 are positioned.

"This'll be fun," Mac comments as he and Killer jump out of the Explorer.

Mac and Killer position themselves on the side of the Explorer, it standing between them and the MP station. Utilizing the Explorer as a shield, Mac and Killer take one shot a piece at the door and the front windows. As Killer and Mac anticipated, the doors and windows are bullet proof.

"This is good and bad," Killer states as he stands to his feet.

"At least there aren't any snipers on the roof," Mac responds, looking up at the roof. "They'd have shot us by now."

Mac and Killer gingerly walk over to the front door. Mac pulls some C4 out of one of his cargo pockets. Killer positions himself with his back to the door to cover Mac as he shapes the C4. Mac places the shaped charge onto the MP station door. He and Killer then immediately race back to the Explorer, where Killer fires a round at the C4. The applied force of the bullet impacting with the C4 causes the charge to ignite, creating a massive explosion. Mac and Killer duck to the ground behind the Explorer to protect themselves from the flying debris.

The door and all of the windows shatter from the explosion's force. Once the debris settles, Killer and Mac rush into the MP station, rifles on full automatic-fire mode. Two Serbs sit crouched behind the desk sergeant's station. They leap to their feet. Killer easily takes them out. Mac immediately hurdles over the desk and busts through the door that leads into a hallway.

Mac finds a lone Serb in the hallway, who he instantly shoots down, then jumps over and behind the desk sergeant's station.

Mac informs Killer, who is now standing next to him, "There are two more. Drasneb must be in one of the back offices."

"Roger. I wonder where the hell the rest of the MPs are?" Killer responds.

"I guess we'll find out soon enough," Mac answers.

Before stepping out into the hallway, Killer takes the low position and Mac high. The two mercenaries step out into the hallway and stealthily move alongside the wall, doing their best to avoid detection and, more importantly, death.

Suddenly Killer and Mac hear gunfire from one of the back offices. They immediately sprint down the hallway to investigate the source of the gunfire. When they reach the source of the gunfire, Mac does not hesitate. He kicks open the office door, and Killer stealthily slips into the room, who, upon entering, cannot believe what he sees. Standing over two dead Serbs is Alex holding a smoking AK-47.

■———————————————————■

Running at full speed, Major reaches the MP station. The sight of the shattered glass scattered all over the asphalt causes him to say only one thing: "Whoa."

Unsure of what to do, Major takes cover on the side of the Explorer that faces away from the MP station. The last thing he wants to do is die.

I've made it this far, Major thinks, his heart beating heavily. *I can't die now.*

Protected by the Explorer, Major shouts, "Killer! Mac! You guys in there!?" Major waits a moment then shouts, "It's me! Major! Is it safe to go in?"

■———————————————————■

Mac smoothly walks up to Alex, his weapon pointed at his head, and asks, "In or out?"

"I'm in," Alex replies.

Killer hears a faint sound coming from outside. He gives Mac a look then steps out into the hallway to hear better.

Recognizing what he hears, Killer tells Mac, "It's the kid. Deal with Alex then meet me outside."

"Got you," Mac states as Killer runs out of the MP station.

Stepping outside, Killer says to Major, "Hey, kid. It's safe for you to get up."

"Thank God," Major replies, rising to his feet. "What happened in there?"

"Just another day at the office," Killer answers with a slight smirk on his face.

"If you say so," Major replies, not really knowing what he ought to say.

■———————————————————■

Mac presses the barrel of his AK-47 up against Alex's forehead, saying, "You know, I could kill you right now and the Killer would say nothing of it."

"I know," Alex somberly replies.

"You seem to know a lot. So tell me this. Where's Drasneb?"

"He's at General Holiday's house."

"Who?"

"The superintendent of the academy."

"Why are you down here?"

"Colonel Drasneb ordered me to. He knew that this would be the first place you would go after everything happened."

"You're damn right!" Mac states. "I wish I had time to ask you what the hell's going on, but I believe all questions are answered in the end. And by the way, where the hell are the MPs?"

"They're in the storage room at the end of the hall,"

"They're dead, aren't they?"

Alex simply shakes his head in relative shame. Mac does not react to the news. The MPs are combatants. Though they died for unjust reasons, Mac will not lose any sleep over their deaths.

Mac removes his rifle barrel from Alex's forehead and says, "Come on. It's time we finished this."

Mac turns around and runs out of the office and returns to the Explorer, with Alex following close behind him. Outside, Mac and Alex find Killer and Major sitting in the front seats. Without hesitation, Mac and Alex jump into the back.

As Mac shuts the door, he says, "Drasneb's at General Holiday's house. You know where that is, kid?"

"Yeah," Major quickly replies. "Go back the way we came."

With Major's words spoken, Killer screeches off back down Thayer Road. Speeding down the street, Major asks, "Do you guys want to go through the front or the back?"

"We want the front," Mac answers.

Reentering Cadet Area and passing Mahan Hall to their right, Major replies, "All right. Keep straight."

The Explorer reaches the corner of Eisenhower Barracks and Bartlett Hall. Mac looks to his right and spots a lone bulldozer.

"Hold on a sec!" Mac shouts.

Killer brings the Explorer to a grinding halt.

Mac jumps out, shouting, "Wait for me. I have an idea."

Mac runs up to the bulldozer and jumps into the driver's seat. Much to Mac's delight, the keys are still in the ignition. It appears that the bulldozer operator left his machinery for lunch with the keys still in the ignition, assuming that no one would steal his bulldozer. If this were only a regular day.

Mac starts the bulldozer engine and drives it alongside the Explorer. He shouts to Major, "Where's the house?"

"That first one right there," Major loudly answers, pointing to the house situated next to Mac Arthur Barracks.

"Follow me!" Mac says to Killer, pulling off ahead of the Explorer.

The bulldozer leads the Explorer across Diagonal Walk. Passing a majestic statue of Gen. George Washington riding his gallant steed, the Explorer follows the bulldozer to the right and onto the Plain. Mac raises the bulldozer's arm in order to shield himself from any possible gunfire. Once the vehicles pass MacArthur statue, they turn left and race across the street. Mac jumps the curb and drives the bulldozer up the front porch of the superintendent's house.

Killer stops before crossing the street and says to Major, "You can get out now if you want, kid. You've helped enough already."

"I'm in it to the end," Major replies with no emotion.

"All right then," Killer states. "Take us to the back of the house."

Killer and Alex step out of the Explorer, following Major to the back of Lieutenant General Holiday's house.

With the initial crack made to Lieutenant General Holiday's house, all hell breaks loose. Mac quickly looks to his rear to check on Killer's status. He spots Major leading Killer and Alex around back. Mac knows what Killer is planning to do. The Serbs fire their weapons with very little control. They are unsure as to what is causing this new round of chaos. All they know is that someone is breaching their perimeter with a very large machine. Mac takes two smoke canisters from one of his cargo pockets, pops them, and then tosses them inside. Mac drives the bulldozer further into the house, letting off a few choice rounds aimed toward the floor.

Major leads Killer and Alex to the side of the house where there is a large eight-foot brick wall that wraps around the entire backyard. Positioned next to the house is a door that leads to the other side of the wall.

"Hold up, kid," Killer orders Major. "Get to the side."

Killer steps in front of Major and slightly moves him to the side and out of his way, moving to the side of the wall. Killer grabs the door handle and swings it open. Suddenly multiple gunshots are fired in his direction. Killer waits for the gunfire to cease then leaps across the doorway to get a look inside.

"There are five guys back there," Killer informs. "From the door, two are at its eleven o'clock, one's at its one o'clock, and two are at its eight o'clock. Hold this for me for a second," Killer says to Major.

Handing Major his AK-47, Killer retrieves three grenades from his pocket. He tosses one to Alex and says, "Toss this to me when my hands are empty."

Alex nods his head in compliance.

Holding the two grenades, Killer pulls their pins. Killer leaps in front of the entranceway and hurls the two grenades into the backyard, one to his eight o'clock position and the other to the eleven.

Now on the other side of the doorway, Alex tosses Killer the other grenade. Killer catches it and immediately pulls its pin. Without having to leap to the other side, Killer hurls the grenade at the one o'clock position. He then leaps across the entranceway to sneak another peak into the back yard.

"All right," Killer states. "The area's clear. Follow me."

Killer runs into Lieutenant General Holiday's backyard, Major and Alex following close behind. As they move, the three men scan the area to ensure that no other Serbs are lurking. Reaching the patio, Killer, Major, and Alex crouch down and shoot the French doors off of their hinges. The doors falling, the three men rush into the house, where a thick cloud of purple smoke suddenly meets them.

Within the smoke, they hear a myriad of voices yelling and shouting at one another. Major is unsure what the voices are saying, but it is clear that the men whose voices he hears are very confused as to what is currently unfolding. Major can almost sense their fear.

"Shoot anything that moves!" Killer commands as they all run in.

Major spots a moving object to his right and fires three rounds from his rifle. The man Major shoots screams in excruciating agony and drops to the ground. Killer rushes into the smoke, letting off several shots as he moves. Alex stays in the rear, picking off every man that comes within his sight

The purple smoke finally begins to dissipate. As the smoke lingers out of the house, Major is able to see the bulldozer in the front living room with dead bodies surrounding it.

"Hold your fire!" Mac barks, jumping off of the bulldozer. "I think we got everyone." Mac walks over to Major and asks, "You all right, kid?"

Major's nerves are on edge. He has never had to kill anyone before today. His hands begin to tremble just a bit as the reality of the battle which he had just participated in finally sinks in. Major always knew that he would have to defend his nation against all enemies, foreign and domestic, but never did he think he would have to do so on US soil, let alone before he graduated.

Calming down some, Major replies, "Considering? Yeah. I'm all right."

Killer turns and faces Alex stating, "Where's Drasneb?"

"The basement," Alex answers.

"I know where it is. Follow me," Major replies.

Killer, Mac, and Alex follow Major through the house to the basement entrance.

Mac then steps in front of Major and says, "Get in the back, kid. I can't have you dying on my watch."

Major does as he is instructed and steps to the side, moving behind Alex. Mac opens the basement door and leads the men slowly down the stairs.

As they walk down the stairs, Mac, Killer, and Alex hear a voice shout, "What is going on up there? Alex, is that you?"

Major is unable to discern what the person is shouting because he cannot speak the language that he hears. Major assumes that the person shouting is speaking Serbo-Croatian since he has been fighting Serbs all afternoon.

Mac, Killer, and Alex do not answer Colonel Drasneb. The three men reach the bottom of the stairs, with Major close behind, and turn right around a corner. Much to Major's surprise, he finds some short old man wearing a foreign military uniform standing over General and Mrs. Holiday, who are tied and gagged.

"You traitor!" Colonel Drasneb curses at the top of his lungs upon seeing Alex standing alongside Mac and Killer. "I trusted you!"

"We were wrong, sir," Alex pleads with a somber look on his face.

"You fool! Do you really think you three can stop my plan?"

"What the hell are you talking about, Drasneb?" Killer barks. "What plan?"

"Ah. I see Alex has not told you everything. Good," Colonel Drasneb states with a grimacing evil smile running across his face. He pulls a two-way radio out of one of his pockets and speaks into it, saying, "It's your commander. Go."

Without warning, Colonel Drasneb quickly raises his .45mm pistol and shoots Alex several times in the abdomen.

"No!" Major shouts at the sight of his newfound comrade being shot.

Without thought—and out of sheer reflex caused by the day's events—Major raises his AK-47 and sporadically shoots Colonel Drasneb until he falls to the ground, dead.

Major drops his weapon and immediately rushes over to where Lieutenant General Holiday and his wife sit back to back, tied, and gagged. He rips the duck tape from off of their mouths then pulls a knife out from his belt and cuts the ropes off from around their wrists and ankles.

His mouth free, Lieutenant General Holiday frantically asks, "Major, what's going on?"

"I'll explain later, sir," Major replies.

As Major frees the Holidays of their bonds, Mac drops to his knees and pulls Alex into his arms. "Don't die on me, Alex," Mac states. "Fight!"

Alex lies in Mac's arms, his entire torso bleeding profusely in such a manner that one cannot tell by looking where the bullet wounds actually entered his body. Alex's entire abdomen looks like nothing but a giant mess of red mush. Alex struggles to speak as blood dribbles out of his mouth.

Alex looks up at Mac with his last bit of energy and whispers, "He knew you couldn't do it…You…you must go."

"What? Where?" Mac asks.

Alex profusely coughs up blood then forces out a few fragments. "Train…Across Hudson…Bomb."

"Where?" Mac asks again.

"Team 2. Grand..." Alex coughs up even more blood than before. He then struggles with his words, saying, "Grand...Central...Station."

With his last words, Alex closes his eyes and falls into an eternal sleep. Mac carefully lays Alex onto the floor and stands to his feet.

"Killer, we've got to get going. Team 2's putting a bomb on a train heading for Grand Central Station," Mac informs, his face turning ominously serious.

"I can get you there," Major adds.

"No, kid," Mac interjects. "You've had enough excitement for one day. We'll take it from here. You're on clean up detail."

Somewhat disappointed yet understanding that his action for the day must end, Major simply replies, "Okay."

Though Major wants to run off and continue fighting with Mac and Killer, he understands the importance of his staying behind. One, someone has to stay to report the truth of what had just occurred. Second, there is no need to rush death. It will come in time. God willing, Major survived the day's events. He has made it this far with his life. There is no need to push the envelope any further.

Killer walks over to Major and says, extending his right hand, "Major, it was an honor serving with you." Major and Killer firmly shake hands.

Mac steps up to Major and says, "You did well, Major. You're going to be all right." Mac and Major shake hands as well.

Finished with the farewells, Mac and Killer race up the stairs. Halfway up, Mac turns around and stares at Major, saying, "Tell your dad Big Mac Pollard said hey."

Major stands there, unsure of what Mac means by his off-the-wall statement, so he simply replies, "I will."

Mac continues his path up the stairs, while Killer waits for him at the top. Meeting Killer on the main floor, Mac and Killer race out of the superintendent's house and head directly for South Dock.

Still in the basement, Major assists Lieutenant General and Mrs. Holiday out of their ropes and onto their feet. Mrs. Holiday is a little shaken up. Lieutenant General Holiday, on the other hand, is calm as though nothing has hardly occurred. He is a Vietnam combat veteran after all.

Free from bondage, Lieutenant General Holiday asks Major, "Who were those men, Major?"

"Honestly, sir. I have no idea," Major replies. "Ben and I ran into them in Bradley."

"Ben Irons?"

"Yes, sir."

"Where's he now?"

"We took him to a room after he got shot in the leg." Major pauses for a moment then asks, "Sir, you don't know what's been going on, do you?"

"No, Major, I don't. I believe I heard some gunshots just before sitting down for lunch, but that's when that Drasneb character came storming in here with his men."

"We fought the Serbs in Bradley, and then at the MP station, before heading over here, once Alex told us that Drasneb was holding you and your wife prisoner."

Lieutenant General Holiday and Major's attention is averted off to the side by Mrs. Holiday saying, "Honey, I'm not feeling too good."

"You want to lie down, dear?" Lieutenant General Holiday compassionately asks his wife as he makes his way over to her.

"Yes. I think that would be best," Mrs. Holiday agrees.

Lieutenant General Holiday takes his wife by the hand and places the other around her waist. He assists her to one of the rooms at the far end of the basement. In the room, Lieutenant General Holiday walks Mrs. Holiday to a bed. She slowly lowers herself onto the bed then lies down.

"Rest now, dear," Lieutenant General Holiday solemnly states. "I'll be back for you as soon as I can."

"Take your time," Mrs. Holiday replies. "You have a job to do."

The couple softly kisses one another. Lieutenant General Holiday then stands to his feet and returns to where Major waits for him at the other end of the basement, near the stairs.

"Let's go assess the battle damage, Major," Lieutenant General Holiday states.

"Yes, sir," Major responds.

Lieutenant General Holiday follows Major up the basement stairs and onto the main floor. The state of Lieutenant General Holiday's home causes him to take a mental step back. Though he heard the commotion during the firefight earlier, he was not prepared to witness his home torn asunder.

"You guys had a little war up here, huh?" Lieutenant General Holiday sarcastically asks.

"Roger, sir," Major says with a slight chuckle.

Lieutenant General Holiday softly pats Major on the back. They walk carefully over the debris and the strewn-out dead Serbs. Instead of using the front door, Lieutenant General Holiday and Major walk around the bulldozer and step through the giant hole that Mac had created at the onset of the assault. Lieutenant General Holiday looks up at the bulldozer and shakes his head, still not able to fully believe the chaos that has recently occurred in his home.

Stepping outside, Major and Lieutenant General Holiday walk off of the front porch. Before them stand several parked MP and state-trooper vehicles that had just arrived on the scene. The MPs and state troopers rush toward Lieutenant General Holiday and Major, but Lieutenant General Holiday waves them off. Four Blackhawk helicopters fly in the air over Cadet Area. Standing on the apron is a company's worth of soldiers; more than likely, they are the garrison assigned and off-duty personnel.

"Take me to Bradley, Major, and tell me of your harrowing experience," says Lieutenant General Holiday.

"Yes, sir," Major replies as he and the superintendent step off of the porch and head towards Central Area.

Major begins recanting to Lieutenant General Holiday his version of the day's events with Mac and Killer and the Serbs, as they walk with a trail of soldiers and state troopers following close behind.

While speaking, Major looks out across the horizon for one final hopeful glimpse of Mac and Killer; yet to his dismay, they are gone.

'I guess I'll never see them again,' Major says to himself as he and Lieutenant General Holiday pass MacArthure statue.

■————————————————————————————■

Mac and Killer have made their way out of the superintendent's house and across the Plain. Running, Mac and Killer notice several MP and police cars racing down Thayer Road. Above them, they spot helicopters in the horizon speeding from the north over the Hudson River—obviously heading for West Point.

Mac and Killer reach the Officer's Club and head for the metal stairwell that runs alongside it and down to South Dock. They race down the stairs, careful not to slip and fall. The last thing Killer and Mac need is to hurt themselves before they can stop the next major catastrophe from occurring.

The metal stairwell that Mac and Killer take to South Dock winds in three different directions, zigzagging down. During the winter months and when it is moist out, the stairs become quite slippery. The view from the stairs is spectacular because it lies alongside a cliff that overlooks the Hudson River. The metal stairs are also another route to Flirtation Walk, but that is presently of little importance.

As Mac and Killer race down the stairs, they spot a medium-sized boat carrying a group of men skimming across the river. At the dock where the boat was tied lay two bodies.

"Thank God for prior planning," Mac comments.

Once Mac and Killer reach the ground below, instead of running to the dock, they race to a concrete building and go inside, reemerging with a Zodiac held high over their heads. Mac and Killer sprint to the dock where the bodies lay.

Approaching the dock, the two mercenaries realize that the two men lying on the dock are dead. In full stride, Mac and Killer toss the Zodiac into the water then quickly step into it. Killer starts the engine, and the two friends zoom off across the river after the renegade boat.

■————————————————————————————■

The boat is piloted by the Serbs of Team 2. They reach the opposite shore as the two mercenaries begin their chase. Team 2 docks in the town of Garrison, which is located directly across the Hudson River from West Point. Garrison is very popular with cadets for one reason; it has the most accessible train station that heads to New York City.

Team 2 jumps out of the boat and race to the train station, which sits alongside the dock. As they wait for the train to arrive, Team 2 nervously watch Mac and Killer get closer and closer to their position.

───────────────────

Racing across the river, Killer looks to his left and eyes a train speeding south down the track. He nudges Mac in the side and points to the incoming train. Mac nods his head, recognizing what is on Killer's mind. Calculating the speed of the Zodiac and the speed of the train, Killer realizes that he and Mac will not make it to the Garrison train station in time to board.

Instead of making a useless effort of trying to make it to the Garrison train station in time to board, Killer steers the Zodiac south down the river.

Killer shouts to Mac, "There has to be another station further south!" Mac nods his head in compliance.

───────────────────

Team 2 watch the two mercenaries change their direction and head down the Hudson River. They all look at one another in bewilderment, unsure as to why Mac and Killer are not still racing to their position.

Hearing the sound of a horn, Team 2 turns its attention from the river and looks down the train tracks. Closer and closer, the train comes. The men become very anxious. Finally, in what seems like an eternity, the train pulls into the Garrison train station and comes to a halt. The doors open, and the men quickly board the train. They sit among themselves near the doors in order to make a quick exit.

Killer and Mac speed across the ice-cold river. Chunks of ice float by as they cut through the Hudson. Moving as fast as the Zodiac will allow, Mac and Killer pass underneath the Bear Mountain Bridge. A few hundred meters past the bridge, Mac and Killer are able to spot the city of Peekskill, New York.

Killer turns the rudder, steering the Zodiac toward Peekskill. Mac looks behind him and is able to see the train coming. It does not appear as though it will catch them, but it is within eyesight. Mac sits at ease with the current situation, but he knows that time is of the essence.

Mac signals Killer and makes him aware of the approaching train. Killer acknowledges Mac's observation then attempts to take a more direct route to Peekskill. Killer attempts to gain as much time as he can for him and Mac.

———————■■———————

Riding in the train, some of the Serbs look out the window that faces the Hudson River, keeping a close eye on the forward-moving Zodiac.

"This is not good," one of the Serbs complains.

"We will be fine," Team 2's team leader states. "You must believe in Colonel Drasneb's plan. He has not failed us yet." The men agree with their leader. He then says, "Stay alert though. If those mercenaries get on this train, we have a serious fight on our hands."

———————■■———————

Faster than they had anticipated, Killer and Mac arrive in Peekskill way ahead of the train. Like the Garrison train station, Peekskill's train station sits on the banks of the Hudson River. Killer slows the Zodiac down and steers it over to the train station. Pulling the Zodiac up onto shore, Mac and Killer jump out and run up to the side of the train station.

The people waiting for the next train stand in awe at the two rifle-carrying men. No one moves or screams. They simply stand there, some in shock and others just clueless as to what they are witnessing.

As Killer steps onto the train platform he shouts, "You people cannot board the next train! There's a bomb on board!"

Hearing the word *bomb*, the people finally react, screaming and running frantically in all directions. After a brief period of extreme chaos, the platform is finally clear of people, all except for Mac and Killer.

With the people free from danger, Mac suggests to Killer, "You take the front. I'll take the back. We'll meet wherever those bastards are."

"Works for me," Killer agrees.

From off in the distance, Mac and Killer watch the train slowly approach. The two friends split up, heading to the two far ends of the station platform.

As the Serbs sit and wait in anticipation of their two adversaries to board the train, their team leader states, "Everyone drop to the ground and lay up against the wall so they can't see where we are."

Upon command, the members of Team 2 act as their leader commands. Now on the ground, Team 2 is unable to gauge how close they are to the next station. Preparing for a fight, they all clinch their rifles, their fingers on the trigger, ready to fire.

"Here it comes," Killer says to Mac as the train begins to pull into the Peekskill station.

Mac and Killer peer into the windows as the train slowly passes them, coming to a screeching halt. They are unable to see any of the Serbs on board. Killer and Mac give one another a curious look.

Once the train doors open, they step inside, their minds totally focused on one thing: meet and close with the enemy. Slowly and cautiously, Mac and Killer walk through the cars. As they enter each car, Mac and Killer force all of the people out of their seats and into the cars behind them. Many people scream and holler, not knowing why a man carrying a machine gun is running through the train.

Mac walks closer to the middle of the train. From a distance, he looks forward into the next car and says to himself, *That car's empty. Something's not right.*

Mac crouches down and continues moving forward. He presses his left side against the door and peers up through the window. As Mac pops his head up, a bullet flies past his right ear. Mac immediately drops back to the ground.

There they are, Mac says to himself with a small smile on his face.

Killer walks through his set of cars, moving forward. He is becoming frustrated because Team 2 is nowhere to be found. Suddenly he hears a shot fired ahead of him. Reacting, Killer races forward, sprinting through the cars. The passengers who Killer runs past shriek in fright from seeing a gun-wielding man on their train.

"Stay down!" Killer shouts to the passengers as he races through each car.

As Killer moves forward, he hears more shots ring out. Finally, approaching the car where the action is, Killer crouches down to keep Team 2 from detecting his presence, though they should be aware that he is near their position.

Mac pushes the "door open" button and moves into the open space that connects his car and the one that Team 2 is occupying. Moving forward, he leaps up and smashes the window with the buttstock of his AK-47. Shots begin to ring and ricochet off of the door. A couple of bullets make it through the window. Mac leaps up and bashes the window again with the buttstock of his weapon. This time, the window shatters from Mac's force. He ducks further down to protect himself from the falling glass.

When Mac smashed the window, he was able to get a good look as to where each of the five members of Team 2 is positioned within their car. There are three to the right and two on the left. Four of the Serbs face Mac's direction. One faces the other way, obviously awaiting Killer's arrival.

Crouched behind the door, Mac counts in his head, *One. Two. Three.* On three, he leaps to his feet and lets out a volley of shots. Mac drops back down. A few rounds are fired in retaliation. Listening carefully, Mac determines that rounds are fired from both directions, meaning that Killer has fired as well.

Killer, who is also crouched against the door, hears gunshots fired ahead of him. On instinct, he pushes the "door open" button and rushes forward into the area between the two cars. Instead of crouching back down, Killer fires three shots through the window, mortally wounding one man. He then drops to the ground. Pushing the button again, he lets out another volley into the car, spraying the entire area. No shots are returned.

After hearing the volleys fired within the car in front of him, Mac moves to the side and presses the "door open" button. Much to his relief, no shots are fired when the door opens. While the door begins to shut, Mac peeks in to investigate the scene. Mac identifies a few bodies lying on the floor and crouched over the seats. Blood is splattered in all directions—on the windows, on the floor, and on the seats. The door closes, and immediately, Mac presses the "door open" button again, this time standing to his feet.

Aware that there is no longer any danger, Mac enters the car and shouts, "The area's clear!"

At the other end of the car, the door slides open and in walks Killer. He walks to where his friend stands and gives him a pound then says, "Let's find this bomb."

"Yeah," Mac states. "I almost forgot."

Mac and Killer inspect each seat, searching for a possible explosive device. With only a few seconds passing, Mac bends down in the fourth row and says, "I've got it."

In front of Mac, beside one of the fallen Serbs, lies a blue gym bag. The reason Mac knows that he has found the explosive device is because it is the only bag in the car. He picks the bag up from off of the ground and places it onto the seat. Opening the bag, Mac proves to be correct. Inside the bag is an explosive device that has been preset to detonate at 1400 hours.

As Mac studies the bomb, Killer asks him, "Can you defuse it?"

Mac turns his head and looks at Killer, giving him a funny look. "What kind of question is that?"

"My bad, brother," Killer remarks, laughing. "Dumb question." Mac feels each of the many multicolored wires with his fingers to see where each one is connected. He then pulls a knife out of his left side pocket and pulls the blade out, saying, "You ready?"

"When am I not?" Killer sarcastically replies.

Mac and Killer cut the red and green wires simultaneously and disable the timer.

"That should do it," Mac states as he rises to his feet. "Let's get out of here."

Mac zips the bag back up and throws it over his shoulder. He and Killer then drop their weapons on the ground. They do not wipe them off because they have been wearing gloves throughout the entire day. Mac and Killer then walk out of the car and through several others until they reach a car that is beside one that is populated. They take a seat with their backs to the populated car to ensure that no one gets a better look at them.

Once the train stops at the Haverstraw station, Mac and Killer exit the train. As they step out onto the station platform, several of the people who exit the train look at the two mercenaries in awe. Killer and Mac pay the people no mind. Once the platform is clear and Mac notices that there are no witnesses present, he heaves the bomb with all of his might out into the Hudson River.

"Just in case I was wrong on which wires to cut," Mac simply states as the bomb sinks to the bottom of the river.

Killer smiles and shakes his head at Mac's statement. The two friends walk off of the train platform in a calm manner and hail a cab. When the cab pulls alongside the curb, Mac and Killer quickly get in.

As Mac shuts the door, he says to the cab driver, "Take us to the nearest hotel."

"You care which one?" the cab driver asks.

"The nearest one," Mac bluntly states.

"Got you," the cab driver states as he pulls off.

Mac and Killer ride for only a couple of minutes. The cab driver pulls in front of a generic motel. As soon as the cab comes to a stop, Mac and Killer get out.

Killer says to the cab driver, "Be back here in an hour."

"Will do," the cab driver replies.

Killer pays the cab driver, while Mac heads into the motel to check-in. As the cab pulls away from the curb, Killer walks down the street in search of a clothing store.

Mac checks-in to the motel and calls Killer, saying, "Room 227."

"Got you. I found what we need. I'll be about thirty minutes," Killer responds as he walks into a male clothing boutique.

Killer finds a pair of black slacks for himself and dark blue for Mac. He then selects a light-blue long-sleeved shirt for himself and a long-sleeved white shirt for Mac. Killer does not buy shoes because he and Mac will clean their boots back in the room. Killer then selects two black belts, a package of undershirts and underwear, and a small tote bag. Killer pays for the items and expeditiously exits the boutique.

At the motel, Mac waits for Killer to arrive. He has already cleaned his boots and has cleaned the mess that he had created from his boot cleaning. Mac cracks the motel room door open so that Killer may enter then goes to the bathroom to take a shower. As Mac showers, he hears Killer enter the room.

"I'm in the shower!" Mac shouts.

"Your clothes are on the bed," Killer states as he places his and Mac's newly bought clothes on the bed.

Mac steps out of the shower and dries off as he walks out of the bathroom. Killer immediately walks into the bathroom to take a quick shower and to clean his boots. It is imperative that Killer and Mac wash away all evidence of their day's activities.

As Killer showers, Mac gets dressed. He places the towels that he used and the clothes he was wearing into the bag that Killer had bought. Killer steps out of the shower and rinses the tub out. He then dries off and walks out of the bathroom to get dressed.

Dressed and his towels and clothes in the bag, Killer says to Mac, "Ready?"

"Yeah. Let's get out of here," Mac replies.

Mac and Killer leave their motel room, with Killer carrying the bag that contains their towels and old clothes. He spots a dumpster to the side of the motel and tosses the bag into it. The two mercenaries walk to the front of the motel to find their cab idling. Without pausing, Killer and Mac step into the cab.

"Where to now?" the cab driver asks.

"Newark airport," Killer answers.

9 DECEMBER 1999

0700 Hours: Paris, France

Mac and Killer arrived in Paris last night. Instead of meeting with J right away, as they generally would, Mac and Killer thought it best to take long showers, eat a good meal, and enjoy a good night's sleep. After yesterday's events, a good night's sleep was definitely in order.

Now fully rested, Mac and Killer sit in J's office.

"I'm glad to see you two made it back alive, and honestly, I'm pleased that you didn't fully execute the mission," J happily comments.

"I couldn't do it, J," says Mac. "A man gets to a point where he can only justify doing so much evil. Destroying the mess hall and killing all those kids would've put me over the edge. When I slept last night, I felt a pleasant calm that I haven't had in a really long time."

Softly squeezing Mac's shoulder, Killer simply states, "Thank you."

After a slight pause, J asks, "Have you gentlemen seen the reports from yesterday?"

"No, we haven't," Killer answers. "We haven't seen a newspaper or watched any TV since we got here."

"Well, let me just say that the Serbian government has a great deal of explaining to do," J states. "They're tap dancing like crazy trying to convince the US that Drasneb was a rogue acting on his own accord."

"Not to be disrespectful or anything, J," Mac interrupts, "but we really don't care."

"Big Mac Pollard. You'll never change, will you? Always so straight and to the point, so we'll get to the point. You guys still want out?"

"That's right," Mac quickly answers.

"I am a man of my word. That is what I promised you, and that is what you will have," J states. "Are you sure you still want out?"

"Yes, we are," Killer replies.

"Well, if you ever want back in, let me know. You two are my best. There's always room for you here at Black Jack. Oh, and by the way, I'll have the remainder of your salary wired to your accounts by COB today," J remarks.

"We appreciate that," Mac thanks, "but as for returning, I don't think we'll be coming back."

A small silence fills the office for a brief moment, the three colleagues unsure of what to say to one another other than good-bye.

J breaks the ice by asking, "So, Killer, are you going to inform Sharon of your now-past profession?"

"God knows I don't have to," Killer answers, "but telling her's the right thing to do."

"What about your kids?"

"They don't need to know. Maybe when they're older."

Mac jumps into the conversation, saying, "Before you ask me. No. I'm not telling my dad anything. He doesn't need to know."

Ready to leave, Mac and Killer rise to their feet. J does the same. The two friends, with huge smiles on their faces, firmly shake J's hand.

"Thanks for all the years, J. It's been fun," Killer states.

"Yeah, J. We may have bumped heads at times, but you always took care of us. I'm going to miss you, man," Mac thanks.

"It was my pleasure, gentlemen. I will miss you as well."

Mac and Killer walk out of J's office for the last time and do not look back. Their lives as mercenaries are now over, the weight of the world now finally lifted from off of their shoulders. Never shall Mac and Killer return to the life and profession from whence they came. Though they had to fulfill their contract, they still pray that when their days end on this earth, their final actions will allow them to leave with their honor in hand.

EPILOGUE

24 DECEMBER 1999

1200 Hours: Washington, DC

The White House, home to the president of the United States, is not simply a home but also serves as an office building, a place used to hold meetings, press conferences, balls, and, with respect to today's event, special ceremonies. More often than not, when a special ceremony takes place in the White House grounds, it is held in the Rose Garden.

Several of Major's family and friends, including Terry and Ben, sit before a lectern, waiting for the ceremony to begin. It is cold out, but everyone is dressed appropriately, so the weather is bearable. Plus, the impending ceremony has everyone's blood flowing.

Not having to wait long, the Marine Corps band, the President's Own, begins playing "The President's March." As the music plays, everyone rises to their feet. Those among the crowd who are in the military stand at the position of attention.

The president, along with Lieutenant General Holiday and Major, steps out of the White House and into the Rose Garden. Approaching the small crowd, the president steps to the lectern. Lieutenant General Holiday stands at the president's left and Major at his right. With the president in place, everyone remains standing.

The president opens, "The day of December 8 was a tragic one, but I can find no better way to spend this Christmas Eve than performing this hallowed, time-honored ceremony. It is a president's esteemed honor to bestow a nation's hero with the Medal of Honor. It is even more of an honor when one can do so when that hero is still with us to share in the moment.

"Standing beside me is a young man who you all know and love. From West Point's tragedy, he emerged a hero, showing that through the most impossible of adversities, all things are possible. He and his friend, Ben Irons, who by the way was awarded the Distinguished Service Cross, could easily have stayed in their rooms during the melee, and nothing negative would ever have been thought of them, but they did not.

"Major proved to us all that fateful day that true heroes are those who—when faced with the most impossible adversity—rise to the occasion and risk it all to overcome that adversity. If it were not for Major's actions, I am afraid to even imagine what further events would have transpired that day at West Point."

The president, finished with his speech, signals a colonel on his staff to publish the orders.

"Attention to orders. For his valiant actions and without sake of his own life in defeating an overwhelming Serb force from occupying The United States Military Academy at West Point and preventing the deaths of thousands of his fellow cadets, the president of the United States awards the Medal of Honor to Cdt. Milton Aynes Johnson this day of our Lord, twenty-fourth of December 1999."

EPILOGUE II

27 MAY 2000

0900 Hours: West Point, New York

It is a beautiful day out. The sun shines bright, it's rays sparkling like twilight off of Lusk Reservoir. There is a lot of commotion and excitement in the air. People move in all directions. Graduation day is always exciting—a day the firsties look forward to more than any other day at West Point. Today's graduation is especially symbolic because of the events of December 8, 1999. The largest crowd to ever fill the stands of Michie Stadium is present to observe the Class of 2000's graduation ceremony.

In the front row sit the honor graduates—a position of prestige held for those graduating cadets who have set themselves apart from amongst their peers in academics and athletics. For their selfless heroics of December 8th, Major and Ben—who is now able to walk without his crutches—are honor graduates, along with Jimmy, who is the Army Male Athlete of the Year, for leading the men's basketball team to the Patriot League Championship and a berth in the NCAA tournament. Also seated in the front row is Cdt. Heather Thomas, the valedictorian and Rhodes Scholarship recipient.

The graduation ceremony begins. The cadets rise to their feet and proceed up the ramp to receive their diplomas as their names are called. Standing on the platform is the president of the United States.

As each cadet receives his diploma, the president firmly shakes his hand with both of his.

When Major receives his diploma, he walks down a ramp from the back of the platform. Back on the football field, his TAC, Major Weiss, is there to greet and congratulate him. Major Weiss was promoted to said rank on 1 December 1999, along with several other of his classmates.

"Great job this year, Major!" Major Weiss exclaims. "You were an excellent commander."

As Major Weiss speaks, Major becomes overwhelmed with emotion. He knows that if he does not move soon, he will begin crying in front of his TAC.

Quickly, Major replies, "Sir, thank you for giving me the chance to command. It's the only job I wanted in the corps."

Major Weiss and Major shake hands then Major moves on to his seat. As he sits down, unexpectedly, tears rush down the sides of Major's cheeks. Overwhelmed with joy—and crying at the same time—Major lets out a big whoop. As his friends Ben, Jimmy, JT, and a host of others return to their seats, Major jumps to his feet to give them all big hugs.

With all of the cadets having returned to their seats, the president steps to the lectern on the platform and begins his graduation address.

"Today is one of the most beautiful days I have ever experienced. Today, I have participated in one of the most elite, the most sacred of ceremonies: the graduation exercise at the United States Military Academy at West Point. Standing before us today are America's leaders— not her future leaders. I say this because they have demonstrated to the world that they have already borne that yoke of responsibility. Through the events of December 8, these fine young women and men seated before you showed the world how tough our country's young people truly are. From the ashes, these soon-to-be officers rose like a phoenix, brighter and stronger than ever.

"You have all faced an adversity that will now truly make you ready to face and fight the evils of the world. Having conquered one evil, you now know that you each have it within you to face and overcome any and all obstacles. There may come a time when you come across a situation that resembles that of December 8, but you can always look back and comfort yourselves with the fact that since you overcame one adversity, you can overcome another.

"You, the Class of 2000, are the living reminders and torch bearers of your fallen brothers and sisters. Their spirits live within each of you. Keep their spirits alive through your honorable actions and your leadership. Know that they are always with you. We have taken the time to mourn, and now, it is time for us to respect their lives through selfless service to the nation.

"We are Americans, and we are fighters. As you all the Class of 2000 have demonstrated, we do not go down very easy, yet on those rare occasions when we are knocked down, we immediately jump back up, fighting, because the fight for Duty, Honor, and Country is one that we must continue fighting until our last breath.

"To the Class of 2000, I wish you all of God's blessings, and I pray for your continued success. Continue to serve our nation with distinction and lead it into the future. Our faith and trust as a nation is in your hands."